A Cord of Three Strands

A football novel

by Tom Van Heest

To Doctor Bill,
I Hope you enjoy!
Jo V. Hot

*This is a work of fiction. Characters, places, and incidents are either the product of the author's imagination or are used fictitiously. Any resemblance to actual persons, places, or events is entirely coincidental.

For Barb,

the love of my life

And to the One who makes

all things possible...

2 Cor. 4:7

Chapter One

"We're going all the way, baby!" boasted the ever-so-cocky, extremely naïve Roger Collins. He possessed all the confidence a quarterback would ever need, but he had not yet proven whether or not he commanded the poise and skill to lead this year's team to a another state championship.

To repeat as state champions would be a nearly impossible task as there were only a handful of players returning from last year's state championship team. The primary ingredients required for such a feat are senior leadership, a talented backfield and secondary, and an aggressive, experienced line; unfortunately, the Juddville Jaguars came up empty in at least two of the three areas.

Scattered about the room that first meeting was a fairly equal balance of juniors and seniors. In addition to the seven returning seniors, there were five new seniors, 14 juniors, and one sophomore moved up from the jayvees. One of the few and proud returning seniors was Pete O'Connor.

Pete had taken a beating his junior year. With over twenty returning seniors playing Juddville Football the previous season, he had had very little chance of starting—even on special teams. Yet while many of his junior classmates opted to sit the season out, he had calculated that if he could endure the season, he would have an advantage in earning a starting position his senior season. And since last year's state championship team was so loaded with talent, there were numerous opportunities for second team players to get into the game in the second half during "garbage" time. The ecstasy of playing almost the entire fourth quarter was almost worth the beatings he would encounter during the week of practice. Because of the dues he paid his junior year and his superior strength and quickness, Pete believed he was the "heir apparent" to assume one of the running back positions this season as a senior.

Judging from the voluntary running and conditioning sessions during the summer, Pete knew there were a handful of juniors and one sophomore who were pretty decent athletes, but it wouldn't be until the pads went on—the fourth official practice on Thursday—that he would clearly separate himself from the rest of the pack.

At exactly 8:00 a.m., clad in an ash colored tee-shirt, royal blue polyester shorts, white athletic socks, and black Nike coaching shoes, the head coach officially commenced the new season.

"I know most of you already know who I am. My name—if you don't know by now—is Coach Abraham. I want you all to know that I am glad that each of you has decided to become a part of our football team this year. First off, I want to encourage you to keep a positive attitude, abide by the school athletic code of conduct, and make a genuine commitment to this team. If you can do this, I am certain that the next thirteen weeks will be a very rewarding experience for us all. Furthermore, if things go our way—like they did last season—we will earn the privilege of advancing to post-season play. This is my 25th year coaching football at Juddville, and I am looking forward to the challenge ahead of us. As you know, we are a pretty inexperienced team this year, so we will be looking to fill a lot of vacant positions. We are looking for players who have an intense desire to succeed and who will commit themselves wholeheartedly to being leaders on and off the field."

Coach Abraham was one of the most knowledgeable defensive coaches in the state of Michigan. He spent countless hours during the off-season picking the minds of defensive coaches from the most successful high school and college coaching staffs across the entire country. Even though he was a few years past his physical prime, his 6'2'' frame was still a formidable sight to behold. While many of his peers in the high school coaching ranks possessed a waistline that resembled a fully-inflated beach ball, Coach Abraham maintained a relatively slim midsection and was in excellent physical health. His bodyweight was a modest 215 pounds, the result of his disciplined adherence to running four miles, four to five times a week. Although his upper body strength was declining, he was still able to bench press 225 pounds for reps—though the tendonitis in his shoulders would require him to apply ice to his shoulders immediately after his workout and to consume Advil for the next two to three days.

After roll call, Coach began to discuss the philosophy and various responsibilities of the base 5-2 defense. By 9:15, nine of the juniors were fast asleep, and two of the new seniors were also in Alice's Wonderland. At 9:25 Coach Abraham—suddenly aware of the time—introduced Coach Allen, the offensive coordinator. Coach Allen hurriedly introduced the basic tenets of Juddville's offense, including the base T-formation, the positions, the hole numbering system, and the first play: the inside trap.

When the meeting finally concluded, the temperature on this August morning had already reached 80 degrees. The players exited the meeting room and jogged out to the practice field. At exactly 10:00 a.m., 27 players huddled around Coach Abraham as he blew his whistle, signaling the official beginning of their first practice.

4

"To start out, you're going to run around the big oak tree and all the way around the practice field. When you get back to me, you will divide into six even lines for stretching."

Pete O'Connor immediately assumed the lead in the warm-up lap until Mike Owens—arguably the biggest, quickest sophomore on this side of the state—sped effortlessly ahead of Pete to a distance of ten yards, and they weren't even to the oak tree yet. Pete decided that was enough of that, and he quickly closed the distance to a couple of yards. As they rounded the tree, Pete recaptured the lead while behind him he could hear the pounding feet of an out-of-shape herd of buffalo trying to keep up with the pace.

As Pete completed the warm-up run, he assumed the front position in the first line and immediately bent over his knees, gasping desperately for oxygen. Lifting his head a half a minute later, he looked over at Mike, occupying the next position in the front line. A minute later, they were joined by the rest of the team, who were spread out evenly in four rows of six lines, plus three players in the last row. Coach Abraham, who had been conferring with Coach Allen, called out, "Pete... Mike, I want you two to lead in stretching today. Everyone else fill in the empty spots in their lines."

Coach Abraham barked out the instructions the first time through the stretching routine, calling out the cadence while Mike and Pete demonstrated each exercise technique.

Fifteen minutes later, the team was divided into five lines— each on a sideline—for form-running. First, 20 yards down and back, lifting knees high to the chest, followed by striders, backward run, ¾ sprints, and finally all-out sprints.

At the conclusion of form-running, Coach Abraham blew his whistle shrewdly, "Get some water now. We do not want anyone dehydrating the first day of practice."

Helmets immediately unsnapped as the twenty-seven bodies collapsed to the soft green blades of grass. Two hundred and thirty-five pound Gary Osborn could be heard puking his corn flakes before he was able to remove his helmet.

When Pete reached the water fountain, he stuck his sweltering head under the cool stream of water, relaxing for several seconds while trying to regain his breath. Seconds later, he was slurping down huge gulps of water.

"I could be lying down in my bed right now," whined an anonymous junior.

5

"What's up with these coaches, any way? Are they mad at their wives or something? They're trying to kill us on the first day," added another sulky junior who happened to be coming out for football for the first time.

Pete thought about breaking the news to his uninformed teammates that they hadn't seen anything yet, but he was too winded to speak.

Suddenly, Coach Abraham's whistle blew. "Anyone trying out for a position in the offensive backfield, go with Coach Allen. Everyone else is with me."

Pete hustled over to Coach Allen with the rest of the backs. There were fifteen running backs ranging from over six feet tall and 220 pounds all the way down to barely five feet tall and 125 pounds soaking wet. The most distressing fact was that not one of the running back candidates had started a single game on the varsity the prior season.

Coach Allen divided the backs into four lines and gave detailed instructions on the proper stance for nearly five minutes. Next, the boys ran agility drills, practiced proper handoffs and ball carrying techniques, and ended with several running drills through the ropes. Finally, Coach Allen directed the young men to take a knee as he began lecturing about the philosophy of Juddville's offense.

"In our offense, we rely on a few critical principles. Number one is unselfishness. At no time is it acceptable for a member of this team to be more concerned about his own stats and his own glory than the success of this team. If you want to earn a spot in this backfield, you must understand that the needs of the team outweigh your need for personal stardom. As a running back, you will be expected to block and to fake until the whistle blows. You will run without turning over the football and catch passes when the ball is thrown to you. Each time Juddville gains possession of the ball, our goal is to score; our goal is not to get you the minimum amount of carries you and your agent have negotiated with the team's general manager. This isn't the United Football League. If you are out here to get your name in the Juddville Gazette headlines, you're out for the wrong team. The only headline we're concerned with around here is the final score. Furthermore, let me remind me your best friend is the offensive line, and I better never hear you griping about their blocking. If they're not doing their job, they'll be getting an earful from Coach Abraham and me. Unfortunately, you'll be receiving most of the credit for all of their hard work, so you better treat them with the utmost honor and respect. They're the ones who make things happen out here; don't you ever forget that!"

Looking around at each prospective running back, he added, "In addition, I want you to realize that some of you are invariably going to be asked to move to a position on the line. There are only four backfield positions in our offense, and at this moment there are 15 of you. We're going to have to ask some of you to put the team ahead of your own agenda and try out for a position on the line."

After his brief pep talk, Coach Allen set up one group of backs into the T-formation:

HB FB HB
QB
0

Then he walked through the assignments for the quarterback and three running backs for the inside trap from the "T". Next, he divided the backs into three units and each group ran the inside trap three times to the right side of the formation and three times to the left side of the formation.

Coach Abraham's whistle sounded, and the team was given a brief water break before beginning the next session of practice: team offense.

For team offense, players were assigned to play on either the red or white offensive team. Pete was called out for red offense, along with sophomore Mike Owens, Roger Collins, and a junior running back named Bast. Collins was the starting quarterback the past two seasons on the jayvee team, and everyone expected that he would automatically inherit the starting position at quarterback. A handful of second-team linemen from last year's varsity filled in the positions on the red unit; naturally, the white unit didn't have a clue about what they were supposed to do.

Gathering together in the first official huddle, Collins called out the first play.

"34 inside trap on two. Ready, BREAK!"

Clap-clap-clap.

The red unit had not even taken a step towards the line of scrimmage before Coach Allen's whistle shrieked through the muggy air.

"What kind of break was that? Get back in the huddle. When a quarterback says BREAK, you better break together, as one team."

One more time, Collins called the play and the count, and on the second try, the break went much better. Coach Abraham

7

checked the alignment of the line, making sure each lineman was as close to the line of scrimmage as possible without breaking the neutral zone. Then Collins took three practice snaps with the center, and the offense was ready to run the first play.

"Blue 38, blue 38… Set, Go… Go!" From his fullback position, Mike took a lead step with his right foot, planted with his left, and cut toward the line of scrimmage. He lifted his inside elbow, making a large pocket for the quarterback to place the ball, but the tip of the football brushed against Mike's hip and fell to the ground at Collins's feet.

"Fumble! Get on the ball," screamed Coach Abraham. Collins looked at the coach dumbfoundedly. Owens dove back on the ball.

Coach Allen interjected, "Collins? Are you a quarterback or what? Whenever that football is loose, you dive on it. You hear? Especially when you are the one responsible for it being loose in the first place."

"But it wasn't my fault, Coach. Owens missed the handoff, I put it right…"

"I don't want to hear any excuses. Take a lap around the tree, Collins." Then turning to the reserves standing behind the offense, he commanded, "Get me another quarterback in there. Riley, get in there and run the play correctly."

On the second attempt, with senior David Riley as quarterback, the red offense was able to execute a successful snap and handoff. Pete came around next and received the fake handoff, ran a few yards, and looked back to see how far Owens got up the field with the ball.

"Pete O'Connor, do you call that a fake?" Coach Allen's tenor-pitched voice was already beginning to break. "You couldn't convince my grandma that you had the ball. Take a lap around the tree, and in the future I expect to see you carry out your fakes no less than 25 yards upfield."

Pete turned and quickly created as much distance between him and the team. Much to his embarrassment, he felt a tear just about begin to form in the corner of his right eye socket.

The first day and I'm already running around the tree.

By the time he got back to the red huddle, the white offense had finally broke from its huddle successfully. Then they required three attempts to run the play correctly. Both the red and the white units ran the 34 inside trap three more times, followed by the mirror play to the opposite side of the formation—the 36 inside trap. After each play, a whistle blew, followed by Coach Abraham and Coach Allen critiquing each individual error.

"Right tackle, you're lined up offsides."

"Collins, you are moving your right foot before the ball is snapped!"

"Bast, is that all the harder you can run? We're putting pads on in two more days. If you run like that we'll have to call 911."

"Owens, cover that ball with both hands. We do not accept fumbles at Juddville… period."

"Left guard, put less weight on your hand when you're going to pull, or you'll never get to your trap block."

By the time the offensive segment of practice concluded, only one running play had been introduced, and the execution of that play had been woeful. By comparison, on the first day of practice the previous year, four offensive plays had been introduced.

After water break, the team divided into defensive groups. Pete went with the defensive line and linebackers. He had always dreamed of playing inside linebacker like his all-time favorite professional football player, Kent Karchinski of the New Jersey Dragons.

Coach Abraham ran his players through various agility drills for what seemed like an eternity. They sprinted, shuffled, and hopped over and around five full-length dummies lying on the ground, lifting their knees up to the chest, trying to move their feet as quickly as possible over each bag without stumbling.

Pete's lungs burned like dry pine needles on a hot summer campfire, and his head was beginning to feel like he had just spun himself in circles for sixty seconds. At the conclusion of the drills, he leaned down on one knee, expecting a well-deserved break, but Coach yelled, "Okay, now we're going to see who can move on all fours."

For the next five minutes they bear-crawled around four cones placed in the shape of a square, about 10 yards apart. Pete's fingers were numb from being bent backwards, and his legs felt about as agile as a pair of bulky blocks of concrete. When Coach Abraham finally blew his whistle, each player collapsed to the ground, exhausted to their utmost limit. After a quick minute, the defensive linemen and linebackers were joined by Coach Allen and the defensive backs.

"Anyone who thinks he can long snap or punt come with me," said Coach Abraham. "Everyone else divide into our white and red huddles from team offense."

9

While Coach Allen organized the two huddles, Coach Abraham gave the two snappers and three punters a few fundamental coaching points. Finally, the snappers and punters joined their respective huddles, and the first punter called out the play.

"Punt, on snap. Punt, on snap. Ready... Break!"

Clap-clap-clap.

"What the heck was that?" yelled Coach Allen. "That was horrible. Haven't you learned anything today? Push up position, punt team."

The red punt unit spread out and hit the ground, lifting themselves up into the up-position of a pushup. After allowing nearly a half a minute to transpire, Coach Allen finally began the pushup command.

"Down."

Eleven punt team players' bodies descended to the ground, and then rebounded jerkily to an upright position.

"One" counted the fatigued players, in unison.

And so on, until 15 pushups were completed. Coach Allen paused for 30 seconds between the 14th and 15th pushup, enabling the players to experience a burn in their triceps like they had never ever felt in their lives.

"Huddle up, and try it again. You can do this," encouraged Coach Abraham.

The red unit broke from their huddle a second time, lining up in two-point stances, hands on their knees.

Coach Allen interjected, "It is crucial that everyone is set for a full count. You must remain absolutely still until the ball is snapped. When everyone is still for a count, the punter will yell, SET. Center, when you are ready, you will snap the ball back to the punter. He'll be exactly 13 yards from the ball. The three upbacks will line up exactly five yards behind the line of scrimmage. Upbacks, let me give you a most important warning: never, ever, back up. If you get driven backwards, upbacks, you'll end up either getting a football or the punter's foot jammed right up your rectum. And I assure you, we will at that point have to call an ambulance because neither Coach Abraham nor I will be willing to reach up and retrieve the football."

Instantly, Coach Abraham erupted in laughter, followed by the team. After a minute or two of frivolity, the business of practice resumed.

The first punt attempt was successful: the snap reached the punter without bouncing, and Bryan Cox, a second year end, kicked the ball upfield about 25 to 30 yards from the line of scrimmage. The white unit had no such luck. A junior back, weighing no more than 145 pounds, snapped the ball six yards over the punter's head. The next attempt bounced twice. His final snap didn't even make it to the next punter, Roger Collins; it came to a dead stop two yards short. A new snapper was enlisted. He snapped it perfectly on the first try. The next several snaps weren't nearly as lucky. After five more punts by the white and red units, Coach Abraham blew his whistle.

"We've got a lot of work to do, fellas. Snappers and punters, you have to put in the extra time before and after practice, to perfect your crucial contributions to this game. We can not afford to be weak in specialty. I'm telling you, a lot of games in the course of a season are decided by special team play."

Silence. The handful of returning varsity players were dreading what would inevitably follow; the remainder of the team was foolishly hoping for a much anticipated official pronouncement of the end of practice number one.

"All right, line up on the goal line and spread out. Give yourself plenty of room. We have got to get into shape. Do you know we have only three weeks until our first game? And to be perfectly honest, most of you did not do enough running this summer. But the past is the past. What we can affect right now is the present and ultimately the future. And that is what we intend to do right now."

Twenty seven Jaguars spread out for wind sprints. As Coach Abraham looked over his team, he wondered how many of his players would return the next day. They could not afford to lose anyone. At this point the prospect for the season was bleak, but it was only the first day. And they certainly hadn't lost a game yet.

"All right, put your hands on the line. The first sprint is on two," yelled Coach Allen, "Blue 36, Blue 36, Set… Go… Go!"

At least five of the players jumped on the first "Go", so everyone had to back up five yards and try it again. On the second try, only one player jumped, and in a rare act of mercy, the coaches pretended not to see it. It must have taken twenty minutes to complete ten 30 yard sprints and ten 20 yard sprints. On just about every sprint, someone jumped offsides. Finally, it was time for the last sprint.

"Okay, I want you to imagine that it's fourth down," exhorted Coach Allen, "We need to score on this play to win the game. Concentrate. We're going into the end zone on three. Red 34… Red 34… Set… Go!"

Eight players jumped. Two counts too early.

"Back it up 5 yards. On three. Red 34... Red 34... Set... Go... Go!"

Three players jumped this time.

"Come on, you idiot," shouted a frustrated teammate.

"We'll be here forever. Use your brain!" screamed another.

Coach Abraham walked off another 5 yards; now they were running 30 yards instead of the original 20.

"Discipline," shouted Coach Allen, "we must learn to be more disciplined. You jump in a game, and we move back five yards. And if we can't go on different counts, the defense usurps our advantage and will surely tee off on us. The end result will be that we will have zero success moving the ball on the ground or through the air. One more time now. On three. Red 34... Red 34... Set... Go... Go... Go!"

At that precise moment 27 dilapidated football players fired out from their stances, running as hard as their worn-down bodies would allow. Crossing the goal line, helmets flew off, bodies dropped to the ground as lungs gasped for air.

After a few minutes, Coach Abraham blew his whistle. "Gather around me in a circle and take a knee... That was a great effort on the last sprint. I saw many players pushing themselves. We need more of that from every player on this team. There is so much work to be done. You have to realize that if we are going to be competitive this season, it will demand an extraordinary amount of commitment and effort.

"Also, it is vitally important that when you leave this practice field each day, you immediately begin to replace the fluids you burned off by drinking lots of water, and continue to do so throughout the rest of the day. And tomorrow, make sure you eat a light, nutritious breakfast before reporting to practice at 8:00 a.m. sharp. Some of you ran out of gas early in our practice. Eat some cereal and fruit. Coach Allen, do you have a few things to add?"

Coach Allen raised himself up from his kneeling position. "We only put in one offensive play today." He gazed around the huddle of beleaguered young men, trying to hide the discouragement on his face.

"Tomorrow, we'll be reviewing the 34 and 36 inside trap, and we'll be putting in the 22 and 48 power. You have to understand we can only play one quarterback and three halfbacks at one time. At this moment there are 15 of you trying out for those 4 positions.

"Our goal here at Juddville is to develop the strongest possible team and in the process have fun. It's a heck of a lot more fun

12

walking off the game field knowing that your team just outscored the opposing team. For this purpose alone, we are going to be asking some of you to move to another position for the sake of the team. It is crucial that we make these position changes now, so the players can learn the assignments and techniques during the preseason where most of the teaching takes place.

"We've also got a long way to go with specialty. I want all our punters and snappers to stay a few minutes after practice to get some more work. We have a lot of work to do, men, but if you pay attention, if you learn from your mistakes, and if you give us everything you've got in practice, I guarantee that we will begin to see positive results. But it's going to take a total team effort. Our motto this season is T.E.A.M. Together... Everyone... Achieves... More."

"Bring it in," yelled Coach Abraham, sweat now streaming down the sides of his face as he held out his right fist into the middle of the circle. Twenty-seven players gathered round, reaching a hand into the inner circle or placing a hand on a shoulder if they were on the outskirts of the ring.

"Good first practice today. It might not have felt like fun this morning, but you need to remember that football is the greatest game on earth. There is no game more physical. There is no game even close to as exciting. But it takes a huge investment to play the game well. Tomorrow, we're going to work harder and build on what we learned today. TEAM, on three. One... two... three..."

"Team!" shouted twenty-seven players in unison.

The sun—from its position directly above—was blazing down on Pete's overheating body. He staggered to the water fountain and let the cool streams of water saturate his hair, rinsing out the warm, salty perspiration. In spite of the extreme heat and hard work, Pete thought the three hours of torture had gone rather quickly. He looked around at his teammates: some were lying on the ground, groaning in agony while others were frantically fleeing the practice field, fearing that Coach Abraham might blow his whistle one more time, lining the team up for one more set of sprints. A few players were already in their cars evacuating the premises as if there was a bomb scare. A handful of punters and snappers were returning from the water hose to get their extra practice.

Coach Abraham and Allen were talking among themselves; the expression on Coach Allen's face was one of despair. They were accustomed to winning. Today's practice had been a shock to their systems. In the last two seasons they had lost only one regular season game.

On more than one occasion, Pete had detected desperation in Coach Allen's voice. In contrast, Coach Abraham had maintained his usual optimistic spirit. If the coaches still had hopes for this team, then so would Pete.

Pete ran up along side sophomore Mike Owens. "Hey, Mike. Welcome to varsity football. I bet you miss the jayvee practices now, don't you?"

"You aren't kidding. I've never been through anything like that before. Is it always that intense?"

"You ain't seen nothing yet," promised Pete. "You did a great job running that inside trap today. You're going to be getting a lot of yards with that play this year. And when teams starting plugging up the middle to stop you, I'll take it off-tackle all the way to the end zone. Then when they try to shut me down outside, back to you up the gut."

"Sounds like a winning strategy to me. I just hope I don't screw up. I get so nervous that I'm going to fumble or go the wrong way or something. Does Coach Allen always yell like that?"

"Only on Mondays through Fridays. But I've heard he can be human on the weekends," joked Pete. "You've just got to learn to not take it personally, Mike. It gets pretty hot out here on the battlefield... in more ways than one."

"Yeah, I guess. Hey, would you like to come over this afternoon for a swim? I'm planning on soaking my aching body for a minimum of three hours in the shallow end of my pool this afternoon."

"I can't think of a better way to recuperate from practice. I'll be over as soon as I'm done eating lunch."

Chapter Two

Anguish.

Agony.

Going into the season, Coach Allen had expected great challenges. The team was inexperienced; they had no running backs returning with any significant playing time at the varsity level.

But walking off the practice field that first day, Coach was overwhelmed by disappointment and dismay. He had never seen a group of players so unprepared for varsity football. Part of the blame, he put on his own shoulders. Maybe they should have spent more practice time last year, developing their second teamers. Perhaps, he should have been more aggressive in recruiting Juddville athletes for summer conditioning. Coach Allen privately wondered if they should be paying more attention to the quality of teaching and coaching taking place down on the jayvee and junior high programs. The reality of their situation, however, was that the past was now history.

Only the present mattered, now. He had to make do with the cards that were now dealt to him. His confidence level as a coach would now face its ultimate test. At this point, he still felt capable of building an offense that could be counted on to score two to three touchdowns a game. But his ego had become accustomed to scores of 40 points a game or more. During the past two seasons, there was a learned expectation that a 35 point advantage over an opponent— initiating the mercy rule in high school football or "the running clock"—meant a job well-done. At this point, Jim could not foresee mercying anyone on this year's schedule, not even perennial basement dweller Hartville.

Surveying the practice field one last time, Coach Allen removed his hat, wiped his sweaty brow and called out to Coach Abraham, "Keith, I'll meet you inside. I've got to get a break from this sun."

"Give me fifteen minutes, Jim. I've got to get equipment for a couple players, and then we can get started with our meeting."

An inestimable amount of questions were racing like bumper cars through Coach Allen's sun-scorched brain as he staggered off the field.

Who's my quarterback? What did I forget to cover today? Where are the leaders? Is this the year our rivals get their revenge? All those lopsided victories the past two seasons? Is it our turn to take the beating?

The first item on the agenda was to build a stronger commitment; attendance had been sparse at weightlifting and conditioning during June and July. In fact, the jayvee team had more kids working out than the varsity. Coach Allen was a seventh grade math teacher in the middle school, so he had prior exposure to this group of kids.

Although three to four years had elapsed since he had taught these juniors and seniors in the middle school, Jim remembered well the abysmal lack of parent support that many of these kids had to overcome. Attendance at parent teacher conferences? Less than 25%. Returning phone calls to a teacher concerned about their child's declining performance in school? Don't hold your breath waiting. Not surprisingly, a majority of this year's team came from broken homes. When their parents had vowed to stay faithful to one another till death do us part, surely it wasn't meant to be taken literally.

Bottom line? A coach better define and then model what *commitment* means to a group of boys who have had minimal exposure to that concept at home. Otherwise, all the preaching in the world would have very little sticking power.

Coach Allen's post-practice ritual was to immediately quench his thirst with a 12 ounce can of diet Coke, fresh out of the vending machine. After purchasing two cans of his favorite soft drink—one for himself and one for Keith—he sat down and looked over the team roster. Somehow they had to find a way to rearrange the 27 pieces of this puzzle into a winning football team. Surely, a .500 or better season would be a considerable achievement. But there were so many unknowns. Too many positions destined to be filled by the inexperienced and unproven.

As Jim sipped on his diet Coke, he began to physically and mentally cool down. He realized how quickly he had allowed his mind to be taken captive by pessimism. Was he going to give up so quickly? He decided to refocus his thoughts on a few of the strengths they had going for them.

Mike Owens, for one, looked like the real deal. He definitely showed promise to become the next great Juddville running back. Having provided the majority of offense on last year's jayvee team, he looked outstanding on his first day. His quickness was immediately apparent, separating himself from the rest of the backs by a wide margin. But who would fill the remaining backfield positions?

The door abruptly opened, jolting Jim out of his reverie. Coach Abraham surfaced into the meeting room.

"What do you think, Coach? Can we bring back another championship with these boys?" joked Keith, then shifting to a serious tone. "I know these kids are raw, but they have lots of enthusiasm. We've got a lot to teach them in so little time, so we've got to be as efficient in our practice time as possible."

Coach Abraham sat down and opened his manila file folder labeled *Week One Practice Plans.*

"We better talk about personnel, first," Jim suggested. "I've got to give you some of my backs to help you out on the line. There must be one or two of my guys that could make the transition to the line. Who do have penciled in on the line so far?"

Lifting himself up from his seat, Coach Abraham walked over to the white board and vigorously started scribbling names with a blue dry erase marker. "I've got Daniels at center. Wilcox at right guard. Osborn at right tackle. Hardings at right end. Eventually, I think Miller can fit in at left tackle, but I've got no one at left guard or left end. On the bright side, three of these guys played for us last year, so they know our system and developed a few fundamentals along the way. Who do you see in the backfield right now?"

"I definitely like Owens at fullback. He's the fastest guy on the team, and he's got above-average size. He should be pretty tough to bring down, but I don't know about his durability. Collins has the edge at quarterback because of his jayvee experience and competitive spirit. O'Connor is our next back; he's got good speed and plenty of power and muscle; he'll be a formidable lead blocker. We don't know anything about Bast, but he seems to be a cut more aggressive than the rest of the backs. He wouldn't have had a chance in the backfield last year though—that's for sure. Overall, I don't think we've ever had such a timid group. We'll just have to see what happens when the pads come on."

"What about moving O'Connor to guard?" asked Coach Abraham.

Coach Allen's eyes nearly popped out of their sockets.

"What? He's my only back with varsity experience." Jim paused, forcing his mind to reconsider. After a few moments of tense silence, "I have to admit, he's the only back we've got that I would put money on to handle himself in the trenches. He's the only back who did anything in the weight room this summer. I know he's tough enough. Remember all those shots he took last year playing scout offense?"

"The harder my defense hit Pete, the more determined he became to not show any signs of pain or defeat. You remember that time Eddie pulverized him, lifting Pete up off his feet and pile driving him into the mud. I thought for sure he wouldn't get up. But he popped up on his feet and trotted back to the huddle like nothing ever happened."

"Keith, as much as I hate to give up my hardest working running back, I know he's the man. But do you think we can get him to agree to it?"

"Let me handle it, Coach. I think I can get him to see things our way. If he likes to hit, he'll get a lot of opportunities playing guard in our offense."

"Where do we go from here? There's no sense in looking at last year's practice plans. We're already way behind that pace. It's almost like we're coaching jayvee."

"It's not all that bad, Jim. Yes, we've certainly got our work cut out for us, but have a little faith. The kids got the first play down today, and I feel pretty good about what we accomplished defensively and in specialty."

"I'll just have to adjust to the slower pace, I guess. But just remember, Coach, our offense this year is going to have to be much simpler—nothing too fancy. If O'Connor moves up to the line, that should open up a lot of possibilities. I can see him becoming an all-area, possibly all-state lineman, depending on how far the team goes."

"On defense, I think we're a little more experienced. I think we have a few hard-nosed kids that can hold their own at the line of scrimmage. And we've got one stud linebacker in Pete. We'll stunt our backers like crazy to keep other teams off balance. How do our prospects look in the secondary?"

"Weak. Very weak," responded Coach Allen. "We have one or two athletes at best, and no one with any aggressiveness. I don't know if I can fill four secondary positions. Maybe we'll have to take another look at the jayvee roster and see if they have anyone else that could play for us. Either that or maybe we might want to go back to a 6-2 with only three defensive backs."

"No, Jim, we have to stick to our system. We'll teach the 5-2, and a little 6-2 for goal line, but we aren't going to abandon what's been successful for us in the past."

"You're right, Coach, but you have to admit this may be our biggest coaching challenge ever."

"That's what we love about coaching isn't it, Jim? Let's stick with the same classroom schedule for tomorrow, and then we'll just have to spend as much time out on the field as it takes. Is there anything else we need to cover?"

"That's all I can think of at the moment. We're just going to have to coach them up."

"I agree. By the way, Jim, you remember Gary Oliver? I got a note in my mailbox that he's going to be doing his student teaching in the high school this semester, and he's interested in coaching. Gary was one of my best linemen ever. I know it's kind of a late notice, but he could really help us out, especially on defense. The defensive line could be his specialty. I'd take linebackers, and then you could concentrate on the secondary. What do you think?"

18

"We've always wanted a third coach on staff. Maybe after this season, we'd be able to convince the school board to give us one more paid varsity position. I know how intense he was as a player, but is he dependable? Is he organized enough to fit into our tight schedule? Can we count on him to be here every day? You know how guys slip into lazy habits in college sometimes."

"I have confidence in him, and if anyone's got Juddville blood, it's Gary."

"Let's do it. If I remember correctly, he was a pretty good leader on and off the field. I'm sure he'll make a great teacher. If ever we had a need for an extra coach it would be right now."

"I'll call him then this afternoon. He'll work with me on offense with the linemen, and then we'll split up during defense."

"Let me know if anything else comes up, Coach."

"See you tomorrow, Jim."

Chapter Three

As Jim stepped out of the classroom, a sense of relief passed over his weary body; he realized he had made it through the first practice and follow-up meeting in one piece and his sanity still intact.

The driver seat of his navy blue Chrysler minivan was burning hot when he plopped his rear end upon it. He scooted forward until the back of his bare thighs was not touching the seat. The engine started right up, and hot air blasted through the air conditioning vents. He turned the air down to low for the moment, and set his sights for home.

As he drove through the town of Juddville, he visualized himself floating on a raft in his cool, sparkling clean swimming pool, with a marguerite in his hand. Reality squelched his fantasy as he reminded himself that the moment he completed his 20 minute drive home and set one foot out of his car, he would be viciously attacked by his three bouncing kids.

If only there were a few more weeks left of summer.

There were actually two more weeks of summer before school began, but not for athletes and coaches participating in a fall sport. Consequently, Jim set off for practice at exactly 7:00 a.m. and usually returned home anytime between 2:30 and 4:00 p.m. That did not include the time spent at home completing practice plans and studying film.

19

But when school started, Jim's time away from home would generally expand to a twelve hour day—7:00 a.m. to 7:00 p.m.—Mondays through Wednesdays. Those were the *light* days. Thursdays, immediately after practice Keith and Jim would hurry over to the jayvee game which would conclude sometime around 9:00 p.m. Naturally, Friday nights often extended past midnight depending how far they had to travel for away games.

On Saturday mornings, the staff met at 8:00 a.m. to review the prior evening's game and to break down their next week's opponent by viewing the scout's game film and scouting report. Usually the meeting would conclude four to five hours later. By this time Jim would have drained all of his energy reserve. By the time he reached the comforts of home, he would be ready to collapse on the nearest available couch for the next two to three hours. Meanwhile, Mary, his wife of 12 years, would take up the challenge of caring for their three high-octane, high-maintenance children.

As the cool air finally began to stream out of the air conditioning vents, Jim's overcharged brain began to gradually unwind. So many thoughts were ricocheting about; he gave up trying to gain mastery over them.

Who could play right halfback? Did we cover the automatic "ICE" call on an errant punt snap? Should we add two plays tomorrow or three? How does Keith always keep so optimistic? Will Mary ask about going back to work again tonight?

In nearly no time at all, Jim was pulling into his driveway where he was greeted by his seven year old Luke who was running around in circles wearing turquoise swimming trunks, arms whipping around in huge circles, legs jumping up and down like a crazed kangaroo.

"Dad's let go swimming. Can we? Can we?"

"Sure, Luke. Just let me get a bite to eat, then we'll go right out to the pool," promised Jim. Opening the door leading from the garage to the kitchen, he was greeted by a refreshing gust of cool air. Mary was no where to be seen.

"Is the paper here yet?" called out Jim sidestepping Luke like he was a blitzing linebacker before withdrawing to the living room.

Mary emerged from the kitchen, immediately identifying that faraway, preoccupied look in the eyes of her husband, an immediate confirmation that her annual sentence of football "widow-hood" had officially commenced. Some time in November she would hope to get her husband back. She tossed him the newspaper and returned to the kitchen.

After loading the dishwasher, Mary cautiously reentered the living room. "How was practice, Jim? Was it as bad as you predicted?"

Jim tersely replied, "Worse." Flinging the newspaper aside before asking, "Where are Kevin and Katie?"

"They're upstairs in Katie's room playing."

"Shouldn't they be taking their naps? It's already 3:00."

"They said you promised to go swimming with them today because you were too tired to play *Candyland* last night."

"Well, I'm famished, and I've got an awful headache, just let me get a bite to eat…"

"Never mind, Jim. I'm sure they'll understand."

"What do you mean by that? I didn't say I wouldn't play with them. Give me a break. It's the first day of football. Just let me get my wind."

"Hey, I didn't mean anything by it," said Mary, her voice calm and soothing, as she walked gingerly up to her husband, wrapping her arms around his neck. "Football is important to you. It's alright, honey. You make up for it during the rest of the year. You're a great dad. It will just take them a little time to get used to your being gone all the time. Once Friday nights come around, it will all be worth it when we can look down from the bleachers and see you coaching the Jaguars to another victory!"

Mary couldn't help but notice the sad expression in Jim's eyes.

What's hiding behind those eyes?

Realizing that her husband needed his "alone" time, she said, "I've got to go get the groceries, Jim. I'll put Katie and Kevin down for their naps, but can you keep an eye on Luke?"

"Sure, no problem. We can hang out in the pool together."

"I'm sure he'll love that. I'll be back in a couple of hours. I fixed you a sandwich. It's in the fridge."

"Thanks, Mary."

Part of Jim wanted to take his wife in his arms and carry her up to bed and fall asleep, safely nestled in her arms. Yet his finely-tuned defense system was calling for him to back off… to avert this sneaky attempt by his soft side to take over his edgy, always-prepared-for-battle side that had faithfully provided him with that competitive edge necessary for being successful each autumn season.

Jim thought to himself: *this isn't really fair, is it, you creep? Mary didn't sign up for this seasonal abandonment, did she? But she's got no choice, does she? I hope not anyways..*

21

As soon as Mary left, Jim exchanged his sweaty coaching shorts and shirt for a pair of loose-fitting swimming trunks. Stopping in the kitchen, he gobbled down the turkey and Swiss cheese sandwich on pumpernickel bread while his son paced the floor in his swimming fins. He topped the sandwich off with a not-quite-ripe nectarine and a cold glass of 2% milk.

As Jim looked down into the eyes of his oldest child, he saw innocence, he saw expectation, and perhaps, already a slight hint of resentment. Maybe he could squeeze in a half hour of one-on-one time with Luke before crashing on the couch for a much-needed nap. With a last ditch surge of energy, Coach Allen finally asked, "You ready to go swimming, Luke?"

"Dad, I've been waiting my whole life."

With a grin on his face, Jim responded, "Well, then what are we waiting for?"

Luke and his dad spent an hour in the pool together splashing each other, racing across the length of the pool, doing cannon balls off the diving board, and tossing a rubber football back and forth.

Finally, Jim lifted himself out of the pool, toweled off, and retired to a poolside lounge chair where the Juddville Gazette was waiting for him. Meanwhile, Luke splashed around in the shallow end, entertaining himself with a toy dolphin and alligator.

Chapter Four

Pete's alarm clock shrilled through the darkness of his bedroom; he quickly sat up and checked the time. 6:30 a.m. He had slept soundly for a good eight hours. He had not slept that well all month. Ever since the end of July, the anticipation of football season had him tossing and turning, and now that football was here, Pete finally felt the peace which only came when one was in the midst of a worthy challenge.

His purpose in life was now clearly defined. In about three hours, he would be sprinting across that immaculate sea of green, grunting, perspiring, in hot pursuit of a brown leather football, his heart pounding to the beat of the Juddville Jaguar Football Team. Pete couldn't wait to get started.

Hopping out of bed, he felt stiffness in his thighs and calf muscles. Even with all the time he had invested in preseason weight training and conditioning, he still wasn't able to escape the annoying cramping and soreness that was the inevitable byproduct of the first official football practice. Nevertheless, the pain wasn't anything that a five minute shower couldn't alleviate.

Pete's mother was still asleep as usual. Her second shift factory job kept her up until nearly 1:00 a.m. every evening during the week. Occasionally, she would get up for breakfast with Pete— maybe once or twice a week—but judging from the silence coming from her room this morning, he knew his mother wouldn't be going anywhere soon.

Stumbling across the bedroom, down the short hallway, and into the bathroom, Pete cautiously flicked on the light switch. Staring into the mirror, he analyzed his chest and arm muscles with a discontented, critical eye. Although Pete had added about 15 pounds of muscle to his frame over the last six months, he was always hungry for more muscle mass, more sheer power, especially in his chest and upper body.

As soon as he jumped into the shower, the steamy hot water began to loosen the tightness in his legs, and as he began to visualize the day's practice, his energy level began to soar. After drying off, Pete slipped into a pair of loose fitting shorts and pulled on one of his most prized possessions: the elite Juddville 300 lb. Bench Press Shirt he had earned in June.

Quietly, he made his way into the kitchen where he prepared a mammoth-sized bowl of Cheerios with a sliced banana—bananas, according to Coach Abraham, were great for preventing leg cramps and for providing extended energy.

Ten minutes later, Pete descended the steps of his trailer and was cheerfully on his way to practice—headphones on, mind and body in tune to the thrashing beat of his favorite Metallica CD. The sun was beginning to emit its powerful heat, and the air was already thick with August humidity.

As he walked down Strawberry Lane, he began to visualize himself carrying the football, running with as much speed, power, and agility, as humanly possible. Pete imagined his first big hit playing linebacker: he sheds a want-to-be blocker, accelerates towards a panicky running back, dips with his hips, thrusts his shoulder pads into the back's solar plexus, wraps his brutal arms around him, lifts him off the ground, and drives him onto his back with megaton power. He could actually hear the "Uugh…" of his fallen opponent, and the inevitable wincing that comes from having the wind knocked out of you.

Just then, Pete heard a sudden rumbling coming from behind him. Then a Yamaha motorcycle came whizzing by him. The rider was some punk with a black leather jacket, greasy black hair, and blue jeans. Before turning out onto Henry Street, he tilted his head back towards Pete, offering him a You-Better-Stay-Out-Of-My-Way look.

That's right, punk. You better keep going. You don't want any of this, thought Pete.

His mind returned once again to the football field where all of his teammates were jumping up and down screaming their approval of his monstrous hit on the disabled running back. It wouldn't be long now before his dreams came into fruition. The name of Pete O'Connor would be well-known throughout this great football town of Juddville, and privately, Pete had one wish that he knew would never happen, but if there was anyway in the world, nothing could possibly make him happier. Maybe—just maybe—his father might be able to one day see him perform on the football field.

As Pete approached the high school parking lot, he noticed the coaches' cars parked in front of the meeting room. There was an unfamiliar car, however; a small-sized red Ford pickup that—judging by the rust covering it—must be going on 200,000 miles. Several players were huddled outside of the building, either too nervous to go inside or too undisciplined to cleanup their language so they might be able to continue their conversations inside within earshot of the coaching staff.

"Hey guys. What's up?"

"Hi, Pete. We figured *you* would be the first one here this morning," said Roger Collins, with the usual arrogance in his voice, typical of most quarterbacks Pete had ever known.

"I guess you beat me here today, Roger. You know what your prize is? You get to be the first one I hit today."

"Ooh, tough guy. You wouldn't dare. If you take out the star quarterback, how is Juddville ever going to win a game this season?"

"You misunderstood me, Roger. Who said anything about hitting David Riley? I was talking about hitting you."

Pete's taunting of Roger was met with much laughter by the other Juddville players congregating around them.

Feeling a bit humiliated, Roger chirped back, "Very funny. But you should have been at the party down at the Pit last night, Pete. It's seems your old sweetheart Melanie has decided to move on… to bigger and better things. She was hanging all over our sophomore prince, Mikey Owens."

In an instant, Pete's hands found himself grabbing hold of Roger's shirt, tightening his shirt around his neck like a noose before slamming him into the side of the building.

24

Looking straight into his teammate's eyes, "Don't you ever mention her name in front of me again. And don't let me ever hear that you have been out partying the night before a practice or a game. Happens again, and I'll kick your butt so bad, you'll wish you never came out for football. You understand me?"

A small drop of condensation began to form in the corner of Roger's left eye as his skin tone transformed from pale to crimson.

"I said, 'Do you understand me?'" grinding Roger's back into the rough brick exterior of the building.

"Yep," whimpered Roger.

"Good," answered Pete, slowly releasing his grip from the "star" quarterback. Regaining control of himself, Pete noticed the smiles on his teammates's faces had been replaced by looks of worry and fear.

Whoa, what just happened? I've got to calm down. I didn't need to go that far, did I?

Feeling self-conscious and somewhat embarrassed, Pete excused himself and entered the meeting room. After a brief visit to the restroom, he sat down in a seat in the front row of the classroom. Several players were now seated behind him, and he could hear the muffled murmuring about the brief altercation that had just transpired between him and Roger. Even still, the atmosphere was uncharacteristically quiet for a meeting that wasn't scheduled to begin for another 10 minutes.

Coach Allen walked up to the desk where Coach Abraham was sitting and whispered something into his ear. Coach Abraham looked straight at Pete and then nodded back to Coach Allen.

"O'Connor, can we speak with you a moment?"

Pete turned red in the face as he heard a chorus of "Uh, oh's" coming from behind him.

"Yes, sir."

A wave of uneasiness swept across the room as Pete followed the coaches into the office in the back of the classroom. Coach Abraham sat behind the desk and offered Pete a seat. Coach Allen firmly closed the door.

"Peter," Coach Abraham began, "Let me be straight with you. We are going to ask you to make a tremendous sacrifice for the good of this team. As you know, we are young and inexperienced. We have a lot of players trying out for a spot in the backfield right now; at the same time, we are extremely weak on the line. Now we realize that you busted your butt in the weight room all winter and summer—more than any other player on this team—and we realize that you are without a doubt, one of our best backs right now. But we feel that we can become a much better team—a stronger team—if you'd consider moving to offensive guard."

Pete's fingernails dug into the arms of the chair. He couldn't believe what he was hearing. He was one of the few returning seniors on the team, yet here he was being asked to relinquish his dreams of carrying the football for the unglamorous, thankless role of offensive lineman.

Why me? Why not one of the other backs?

Clearing his throat, lifting his chin, and then looking Coach Abraham square in the eye, Pete responded, "Coach, I'll play where ever you want me to play if it's for the good of the team…"

The two coaches exchanged enthusiastic nods of approval, and then Coach Allen stretched out his hand, giving Pete a firm hand shake, saying, "I am proud of you, Peter. You are making a huge sacrifice for this team, and you're also demonstrating what true leadership is all about. We're lucky to have you on this team, young man."

Wow, was that Coach Allen? I've never heard him speak like that before.

"We'll start you out today at left guard," said Coach Abraham. "That's the side that traditionally does the most pulling and trapping in our offense."

As Pete exited the coaches' office, he immediately felt the stares of his teammates. Reclaiming his seat in the front of the classroom, he abruptly turned around to stare back at his teammates, but their eyes shot down to the floor like a jury that has voted to send a murderer off to the electric chair. By now, most of the players were present, and a few new players were standing by the entrance door looking nervously around at the rest of the team. Coach Abraham walked over to the door, introduced himself, and coarsely ushered them to the empty seats in the back of the classroom.

"What did the coaches want?" whispered Mike Owens. "Did they hear about your little run in with Collins this morning?"

"No, they wanted to know if I knew anything about you going to a party out at the Pit last night."

"Are you serious?" asked Mike, turning white in the face.

"No, just joking. Actually, they just want me to make a position change."

"What do you mean? They're not thinking about moving you out of the backfield, are they?"

Before Pete could respond, however, Coach Abraham decisively called the second official football meeting to order.

Meanwhile, Pete began to worry about how difficult the challenge was going to be making the transition from offensive back to offensive lineman. His dreams had always been of 80 yard touchdown runs, of diving catches in the end zone with arms-fully-extended.

Am I big enough? Am I strong enough to play on the line? Is there enough time for me to learn all the complicated blocking schemes?

Peter realized that the coaches must have moved him out of desperation. There was simply no one else able to do the job. He wasn't quite sure, however, why they had waited until the second practice to make the change. Nevertheless, it didn't take very long for Pete's competitive instincts to emerge. Instead of viewing the change as a demotion—as most of his peers would have reacted—Pete faced his new assignment as just another challenge, and as he looked around the room, he was fully aware that he could crush each and every one of his teammates, on or off the playing field.

From the podium at the front of the meeting room, Coach Abraham's boisterous bass voice began, "Welcome back, players. I am very pleased to see that all 27 players from yesterday are here and on time. First, I want to introduce to you two new players coming out for football today. I think many of you already know Tommy Schultz; he's decided to give football a try. And new to our district is Adam Foster. He comes from Billington and played jayvee ball last season on their pretty successful team, as most of you underclassmen can surely remember."

A number of heads turned in Adam's direction. His head hung low, his eyes buried beneath a sea of ruffled brown hair, extending all the way down to his shoulders; a few juniors who had faced him last year on the jayvees muttered phrases of disdain. The mere mention of "Billington" was enough to precipitate an upset stomach for most Juddville Jaguars. Unbeknownst to his teammates, however, Pete had once lived in Billington, so he inconspicuously gave his new teammate a brief once over, half-expecting to recognize him, yet having to remind himself that that had been a very long time ago.

Pete pitied his new comrade.

They must wear their hair a little differently in Billington these days. By the end of today's practice, he'll be looking up the nearest barber in the yellow pages. Billington Boy's going to burn up out there.

Coach Abraham continued, "In addition, I am delighted to report that we are adding a volunteer coach to our staff. He is a graduate of Juddville and former player for us. Over the years, there haven't been too many linemen who could dominate the line of scrimmage like Coach Oliver. Coach Oliver is going to be doing his student teaching at the high school this fall, and he will be assisting me in coaching the offensive and defensive line.

"Men, there's one more thing I want speak to before Coach Allen starts diagramming Xs and Os. You know, I've been coaching for a lot of years, and I've always worked my tail off year round to make this football program as successful as possible, but I want you to know that football is *not* the most important thing in my life. My first priority is my relationship with the Lord. And the second most important thing in my life is my family: my wife and my two daughters."

Roger Collins, sitting in the back row of seats, whispered to Dan Hardings, "Man, would I ever like to have a night alone with his daughter Julia. She is a major babe."

"Yeah, I'd walk away from football and take up soccer if I could spend a night with her," responded Dan.

"Well, go for it, Dan. Why don't you do the team a favor?"

"No can do, Roger. I'm the only one on this team that can catch your wobbly passes."

Suddenly Coach Abraham's voice increased to full strength.

"You boys, got some thing you want to say back there?"

Roger and Dan turned burgundy in the face.

"I didn't think so. Where was I? Oh yeah, whenever I have to choose between football and family, family wins every time, hands down," Coach Abraham boldly proclaimed. "After God and family, comes teaching and coaching football. This doesn't mean I neglect football. No, it means that I make sure that I budget my time, so that after taking care of my most important responsibilities, I can approach this great game of football with all the intensity and energy it takes to be a winner.

"Let's go to offense, Coach Allen."

It took Jim a moment to gather his thoughts. He had been pondering his own priorities, ever mindful that his list was probably in the reverse order of Keith's. That was what he secretly despised about football. It was like a jealous monster that usurped his mind, heart, and soul each autumn. Worse yet, was the way this monster forced him to relate to people: to players, parents, opponents, and much to his own dismay, to his own family.

As Coach Allen took the floor, he cleared his throat, scanning across the room, making eye contact with each player before beginning. "Right now, we're in a unique situation. With school not beginning for another two weeks, we have a most crucial opportunity. This is our training camp. Our minds right now are on football. After a great night's sleep, our energy level should be high. As a result, what we can accomplish during these two weeks is far greater than what we can accomplish once we return to school. It is imperative that you give us everything you've got out on that practice field, and as difficult as it may be for some of you, you must give us your complete attention during our meetings so you can learn all that you can about our offense, defense, and special teams. You might think you're some super stud athlete, but if you don't have a clue about what you're supposed to be doing, you'll never hit the field. That would embarrass you, embarrass this team, and embarrass your girlfriend, as well...

"Oh, that's right, I forgot. You boys are too butt-ugly to have girlfriends."

A much-welcomed wave of laughter spread throughout the meeting room. Once the hooting and finger pointing subsided, Coach Allen reviewed the inside trap from Monday and then introduced the off-tackle halfback power. Pete's heart sunk as he fully-realized that this would have been his play, his opportunity to gain a ton of yardage this season. But as Coach Allen described the responsibility of the backside guard—pull three steps, lead up the hole, and annihilate the first opposite color jersey—a surge of adrenaline bolted through Pete's veins. He was going to love this play!

After Coach Allen diagrammed the mirror play to the left side of the formation, Coach Abraham reclaimed control of the floor and reviewed the base 5-2 defense and introduced the Mike stunts. On a Mike Left stunt, instead of playing the center head up using a read technique, the nose guard instead rushed through the center/guard gap to his left while the left inside linebacker scraped behind the nose to the gap on the other side of the center. If the linebacker got a good jump off the snap of the ball and stayed low, he could penetrate the line of scrimmage and make a ferocious hit on the running back for negative yardage.

Pete had a made a couple of good hits on this stunt last season during garbage time—late in the game when because of a blowout, all the scrubs were playing. One time he happened to bust through the line of scrimmage at the same time the fullback was receiving the handoff, and the impact of his shoulder pads meeting the fullback's shoulder pads jarred the ball loose, bouncing right out of the back's hands into his own. Pete ran with the ball for 30 yards until he was dragged down at about the 10 yard line by the quarterback and halfback. It had been Pete's most memorable play of the season—of his life, actually. Coach Abraham had even given him a high five when he got to the sideline.

After defense came a brief description of the kickoff formation and coverage responsibilities. Finally, the team was dismissed to the practice field. The meeting had lasted nearly an hour and a half, and most of the players were itching to put on their helmets and go to work.

Chapter Five

As Pete tightened the white laces of his new pair of black Nike cleats, he listened to the enthusiastic, high-pitched voices of the junior varsity team who had already taken the field; they were counting out jumping jacks, spelling in unison, "J-U-D-D-V-I-L-L-E".

Beads of sweat trickled down Pete's cheeks, soaking his chin strap while he surveyed the sweltering, olive-colored battlefield. The weather forecast for the first part of the week had called for temperatures in the low 90s with excessive humidity. Pete questioned whether a sane person would voluntarily rise out of bed at 7:00 a.m., surrender the most precious moments of what remained of summer vacation, and trade them all in for three to four hours of extreme torture.

The fact that no less than 12,000 other boys across the state were putting themselves through the same agony for the goal of one day playing for a state championship did very little to comfort any of the Juddville boys on this particularly blistering morning.

"Hey Pete, what do you say we sneak out of here and head back to my house for a swim?" joked Mike Owens.

"Go right ahead, Mike," snapped Pete, "but why don't you invite Melanie instead. And while you're enjoying yourself, I'm sure we can find someone else to take your place at fullback."

Pete paused a moment, allowing his young teammate an opportunity to try and interpret the motivation behind his off-handed comment.

Not finished, Pete threw one more dart, "I figured it wouldn't take long for Melanie to find a new pet to lead around by the collar, but I never imagined she'd stoop all the way down to the sophomore class to find her latest victim."

"Hey Pete, I swear I didn't lay a hand on her. She had a couple beers and was hanging all over every guy at the party. I never touched her, though. As soon as I could, I bolted that party and rode my bike home as quick as I could. Honest, Pete."

"Listen, Mike," said the senior captain, putting his arm around the young running back's shoulder. "I really don't give a rip about Melanie anymore. It is football season, you know. There's no time for that. But if you get your butt busted for drinking, moron, my moving from the backfield up to the line will all be for nothing. And more than that, our team will suffer. Don't you dare let this team down. In addition, if you know what's good for you, you'll stay as far away from Roger Collins as possible. He's going to get his due one of these days, and you don't want to be around when that happens. You'll be letting down the whole team, and you'll be sitting up in the stands on Friday nights feeling sick to your stomach because you thought it would be more fun to party with the boys than to score touchdowns for the next Juddville Jaguar State Championship Team."

"I won't let it happen again, Pete. I got cornered into going, in the first place. After you left my house yesterday, I rode down to Piggly Wiggly to buy some Doritos, and all of a sudden I bump into Roger. Well, he talked me into going to the party. I didn't really want to go, but he said there would be tons of babes, and he said everyone on the team would be there. Obviously, he was lying. Roger and Dan were the only players there."

"Like I said. Stay away from Roger. He's bad news. From now on, kid, just stick with me. I know how to keep Roger in his place. Come on. Let's get our minds back on football. I'm sure Billington's not sitting around talking about their girlfriends right now."

Calisthenics and form running went much more smoothly than the day before. After water break, the team divided into offensive groups. Pete followed Coach Abraham and Coach Oliver and the rest of the linemen to their drill station.

With renewed purpose, Pete made up his mind that he would be the best player on the field where ever he was asked to play, period. Eagerly, he knelt on one knee in front of Coach Abraham.

Coach Abraham removed his hat and ran his fingers through his dark, thinning brown hair as he introduced the first offensive line drill of the day. "The first thing we're going to review today is stance. To start the drill, I want you to come up to the line and get in your 3-point stance. After I check each player's stance, I will give the command to step. Remember to move your left foot

31

forward as quickly as possible, but no more than six inches. When everyone has gone through the drill twice, we'll do the same thing only stepping with the right foot. Okay, then? Break into four lines."

The drill seemed rather elementary to Pete, but watching the other players through his peripheral vision, Pete quickly realized that this simple drill was a major challenge for many of his peers. Many of his teammates could not maintain their balance after taking their step; some players struggled to understand the concept of a "short" step, moving their foot 18 to 24 inches instead of the six inch maximum.

The next drill was to walk through the basic blocking progression from start to finish. Then they worked on pulling technique, and finally they ran through the blocking schemes for the fullback trap and halfback power. There was a lot to remember, but Pete was familiar enough with the offense to absorb most of it the first time through.

Coach Abraham was true to his word: he inserted Pete immediately into the left guard position with the red team. Considering that he had never played on the line before, Pete felt that he must have done a pretty decent job in group offense, for he didn't hear his name yelled once during the entire group offense session—which was not true for most of his fellow linemen. Even still, Pete hadn't hit anyone yet, and he wouldn't get a chance for the rest of this practice and the next.

While Coach Abraham was wrapping up his closing remarks before breaking into team offense, all of a sudden Coach Allen exploded into a tirade. Though more than 60 yards down the practice field, the linemen could plainly see the crimson shade of Coach Allen's face. Furthermore, anyone within a mile radius could easily make out each and every word proceeding from his mouth. You didn't have to be a genius to be able to identify the target of his indignation, for Coach Allen's chin was within an inch of Roger Collins's face mask.

"You're supposed to be a leader…if you can't take a little constructive criticism, there's the gate…you don't deserve to wear a Juddville uniform! The next time you turn your back to me when I'm coaching you, you'll be running the rest of the week…I don't give a damn what you accomplished as a jayvee player. I don't care if there are scouts from every major college lining up outside the fence to recruit you. I'm going to keep on doing my job: making you a better football player. And you *will* listen to your coaches, and you *will* give us the respect we deserve. Now start running around this field. I will tell you when you can stop as soon as I get tired."

By this time, the entire junior varsity team had ceased practicing, completely entranced by the Oscar-winning performance of the infamous Coach Allen. Surely, he had a voice, and he knew how to use it. Pete was relieved to be with the linemen at that moment, yet having a season of varsity football under his belt, he knew that the entire team would inevitably reap some of the after shocks of Coach Allen's blowup, and he was quite certain that the rest of the practice had the makings of a nightmare.

Perfect time for a water break.

Roger just happened to be circling the same corner of the practice field where the water trough was located at the same time his teammates were drenching their sweating, throbbing heads with cool, refreshing water.

"Way to go Collins," shouted Steve Wilcox. "Now we all can expect a practice from Hell."

Roger ignored the chiding of his teammate and continued his marathon around the grisly gridiron.

The water trough—so aptly named—was crudely designed by Coach Abraham. It was simply a water hose connected to a thin PCV tube with holes drilled every six inches, as to shoot water in alternating directions. The tube rested on two saw horses that were painted Jaguar blue.

Pete couldn't help but snicker. Watching Roger circle the field reminded him of a dog just having gotten the snot beat out it for peeing on brand new carpet. It wasn't even 10:30 a.m., and Roger had already been humiliated twice in front of his teammates.

Coach Allen grabbed one of the newest-looking footballs and set it on the fading white line marking where the 20 yard line would be located.

What a piece of work that Roger Collins. How am I supposed to build an offense around a punk like that? thought Coach Allen.

"Hey Jim, what happened with Collins?" asked Coach Abraham.

"I hate to blow a gasket so early, Coach. All I tried to do was correct him on his ball carrying technique, and do you know what he did? He had the audacity to toss the ball at my face, turn his back to me, and walk to the end of the line. And you should have seen the cocky smirk on his face. I wanted to…"

"Well, I think it's a good idea for him to spend a little time circling the field, contemplating whether he wants to play football."

"Coach, I really feel bad about losing it so soon in the season, especially with this young team. I probably had a hundred witnesses that heard every word that spewed out of my mouth." Jim's irate expression suddenly turned somber as he asked, "Do you think I overreacted, Keith?"

"Did you handle it the way I would have handled it? No. But Jim you and I have different coaching styles. Something had to be said. We certainly can't let that kind of attitude breed around here. The ball's in Roger's court now. This will be a great opportunity to see how he reacts when the heat is on."

Coach Allen's eyes scanned the field, finally locating Roger in the south east corner of the field. "I'll let him run about five more minutes, and then I give him a second chance with the white unit."

"It's 10:40, Coach. Let's get team offense going."

The red and white units huddled hastily. "Riley, you take the helm at quarterback with the red unit, and Don Jacobs, you're quarterback with the white unit. Riley, 34 inside trap. Be a leader."

Riley stammered out the first play, and his ten teammates broke sharply out of the huddle as one highly-focused unit.

"Red...38, Red...38, Set...Go...Go...!" Daniels snapped the ball crisply. Riley received the ball, reverse pivoted into the backfield, carefully handing the ball to Owens who charged from his stance toward the line of scrimmage, cutting right behind a perfectly-executed trap block by left guard Pete O'Connor. Riley carried out his fake to the left halfback and continued his deception all the way to the sideline with his hands on his back hip, faking the quarterback keep. When Owens had carried the ball 30 yards up field, Coach Allen blew his whistle.

"Great job, red offense," shouted Coach Allen. "That's the way the trap is supposed to be run. Okay, white offense, now you do the same. Call the play, Jacobs."

The sudden increase in the intensity of the team was amazing. The red offense seemed to be performing better without Collins at quarterback; Riley—who played scout team quarterback on the varsity the previous season—was certainly taking full advantage of his big opportunity. Coach Allen began to ponder whether Collins's insubordination had actually done the team a huge favor. The red and white offense both managed to run the 34 and 36 trap successfully and were now ready to run the play of the day: the halfback power. Meanwhile, Collins's extracurricular conditioning time had finally expired.

"Collins, get a quick drink and switch off with Jacobs at quarterback with the white group." Roger stared contemptuously at Coach Allen before trotting off for water.

In the mean time, the red offense had fumbled on their first attempt at the 22 halfback power. When the white offense ran the play, both the left and the right guard pulled, colliding into one another behind the center's rear end.

The team's enthusiasm was now beginning to wear thin.

"All right offense, let's get it right this time," shouted Coach Abraham.

Riley barked out the cadence and pulled out from behind the center a count before the ball was snapped, and the ball trickled to the ground. David wisely dove on it.

"Come on, Riley. Get your head in the game. Concentrate on what you're doing. Run the play again, on one," yelled Coach Allen.

Once again, Riley walked back up to the center, wiping his hands off on his shorts before beginning the cadence. "Blue...28, Blue...28, Set...Go!" The ball snapped crisply into Riley's hands. Then he pivoted in the wrong direction, missing the fake to the fullback, and running into the back that was supposed to be receiving the handoff.

An unexpected, semi-muffled snicker emerged from the white huddle. Coach Allen turned his head 180 degrees behind him, eyes like lasers, determined to identify the perpetrator. Immediately, the white team's huddle parted like the Red Sea, leaving Roger Collins standing all alone, a guilty-as-charged look on his face, his eyes staring down at his top-of-the-line Nike cleats.

This time it was Coach Abraham, in a calm yet commanding voice, "Collins, you're done for the day. Hit the showers."

"What?" Collins retorted, "I didn't say nothing. This is a bunch of crap. Why does everyone have it out for me?"

"Close your mouth and get off this field before you get yourself in even more trouble," warned Coach Abraham, showing an uncommon degree of self-control towards the mutinous behavior of his junior quarterback.

Collins turned his back, ripping his helmet off, slamming it to the ground, and then stomping off the field.

Coach Allen was about to run after him and really lay into him for throwing his most expensive piece of equipment to the ground. His mission was aborted, however, when Coach Abraham blew his whistle.

"Run the play again," commanded Coach Abraham to the red offensive team, who were still dumbstruck by their teammate's performance.

"Come on, Jaguars. Let's get it right this time," shouted Pete, trying to recapture the attention of his teammates.

After several failed attempts at running the 22 and 48 halfback power, the offensive segment of practice finally came to a slow and painful death, and the team went directly to defense with no water break.

Coach Allen was still fuming over Roger.

If that's the way this kid's going to act, we better collect his equipment today. Who does he think he is challenging my authority—and then—having the audacity to laugh at another player's mistake. He's history...

Switching gears to defense allowed Coach Allen to regain his focus and to some degree, his composure. He put his defensive backs—minus Roger, of course—through a series of speed, agility, and reaction drills. Wanting to see who could hold up the longest, he ran the drills at a quick, no-nonsense pace. Under these hot, adverse conditions, he believed he would be able to quickly identify his toughest three or four kids.

Surprisingly, the new kid from Billington, Adam Foster, made the first positive impression. He went full-speed on every drill. In addition, the kid had a scowl on his face often preferred by coaches who were always happy to find a strong safety that liked to punish people. Foster had the look of a dog defending his property, and even though he might not have the quickness of some of the more elite athletes in their conference, Coach Allen had a hunch that this kid might be hitter—perhaps, even an assassin.

Another pleasant surprise was the other new face—Tommy Schultz—who hadn't come out for football his freshman or sophomore year, but he did play basketball, and he was one of their top scorers and rebounders. Tommy seemed to have a natural instinct for jumping and extending his arms at just the right moment, catching the ball at the peak of his leap with ultra-soft hands. Coach Allen envisioned Schultz as the type of defensive back who might lead the team in interceptions and knockdowns. All Tommy was lacking was experience and confidence.

After 15 minutes of drills involving backpedaling, changing directions, and leaping for lofted footballs, Coach Allen sympathetically sent the young men over for a brief, unscheduled water break. Once they returned, he quickly reviewed the alignment, responsibilities, and keys for cornerbacks and safeties. Then they walked through the basic Cover 2 Zone.

At exactly 12:00 noon, Coach Abraham blew his whistle for specialty. "Kickers, get a tee and a football and line up in the middle of the field on the 35 yard line. Everyone else divide into ten equal lines: five lines to the kicker's left and five lines to the kicker's right."

Next Coach Abraham reviewed the responsibilities for each of the ten lines: four of the lines were assigned a lane to defend downfield; four of the lines were designated as headhunters and were charged with responsibility of sprinting directly to the ball; and finally, the contain lines on the far left and far right were responsible for squeezing the return into the middle of the field, never letting a return get to the sideline. Once the ball was kicked, the kicker assumed the responsibility of safety, mirroring the ball without crossing the 50 yard line, posturing as a last defense should the opponent break a long return.

"Let's see some hustle now," piped in Coach Oliver.

Coach Abraham added, "This is a sprint, and did I fail to mention that one of the greatest honors is earning a spot on the kickoff team? Some of the best hits occur on kickoffs. We need eleven players who love contact, eleven men who aren't afraid to collide full-speed with the ball carrier."

Meanwhile Coach Allen's focus began to wander. His eyes scanned the practice field, noting that the junior varsity team was still practicing—a welcomed sight for the program, that was for sure.

I wish they would have spent more time on the field with last year's team.

He turned and look behind him, beyond the outer fence separating the field from the high school parking lot. Roger Collins and his mother were standing next to their silver BMW. Not wanting to communicate to them the impression that he was available for a conference, he turned his back to them, and rejoined the practice with a renewed enthusiasm, now giving his full attention to the kickoff drill. Nevertheless, Coach Allen could not completely divorce his mind from the imminent showdown that would be taking place immediately after practice.

After about ten kicks, ranging from mediocre to horrible, Coach Abraham blew his whistle, gathering the team together. Only the handful of returning seniors knew what was coming next; meanwhile, the juniors and other first year players naively crossed their fingers, praying that the end of practice was near, entirely ignorant of the impending torture awaiting them.

"Everybody take a knee." Twenty-eight sweaty, dirty, worn-out teenagers looked up towards Coach Abraham, anticipating his next words. "I've got some good news and some bad news. First, the good news. You can all take off your helmets. Next, the bad news. To finish up today, we're going to do some distance running." The players' hearts sank like one gigantic boulder, toppling off the edge of a two hundred foot cliff.

The voice of Coach Abraham rose above the muffled groans of displeasure, "Here's what you're going to do. You're going to run all the way down the west fence of the practice field, through the gate, out to the softball diamond, around the entire softball field, around the tennis courts, and then back to me. Ready? Take off."

Desperate to be done with practice, the varsity Jaguars trampled across the field like a frantic herd of buffalo. After no more than 20 yards, the players who reported to football camp in decent shape had clearly distinguished themselves from the rest of the pack who had obviously limited their football preparation to watching day-time talk shows and playing videogames while gorging upon massive quantities of potato chips, Oreos, and two liter bottles of Coke.

When all the players were out of hearing, Coach Allen spoke up. "Do you see who is waiting in the parking lot in that shiny BMW, Keith?"

"What a surprise! Roger and his mommy. That didn't take long."

"Probably already had a visit with the superintendent, too," unable to disguise a tone of worry in his voice.

"Hey Gary, are you ready to take over the offense after Jim loses his job?"

"That's not even funny, Keith. She's probably got a brother on the school board," responded Jim.

"Is that the brother she married or the brother she had Roger with?" joked Gary.

"I'm impressed with you, Gary," said Coach Allen, "You've already got a handle on how things are run around here."

"Don't listen to Jim, Coach Oliver. He's got over a decade of cynicism accumulating around his midsection. On a serious side, though. The day were reprimanded for administering discipline to a discipline-deprived teenager, I know at least one coach who'll be turning in his resignation," confided Coach Abraham.

Over a span of five to ten minutes, a diverse collection of shapes, sizes, and speeds completed their grueling ¾ mile cross country run.

The coaches were ready to greet them upon arrival.

"Great effort, Mike," said Coach Abraham to the sophomore running back who was the first to complete the course.

Next, was Tommy Schultz, the basketball player; followed by David Riley, newly enthroned quarterback. Pete O'Connor was fourth.

"Hey look, Coach Oliver. I finally got a lineman in the top five! Way to push yourself, Pete," shouted Coach Abraham.

Within the next few minutes, the rest of the players completed the cross country run with the exception of Larry Moore, the biggest player on the team by at least 50 pounds. Larry weighed in at 285; he even had trouble with the form running at the beginning of practice. At least 25 pounds would have to go before he would ever have any hope of completing the course without walking. Finally, Larry's oversized frame emerged from behind the tennis courts. The earth began to rumble at the approach of the last buffalo.

"Come on, big Larry, you can make it," cheered O'Connor, running out to meet his teammate 50 yards shy of the finish line. "We're almost there. You can make it. Don't quit. Do it for the team."

Several other players chimed in, and eventually, the entire team was standing on their feet chanting, "Larry, Larry, Larry..." As if on cue, the XXXL player responded by picking up his size 16 feet, giving his best attempt at sprinting across the finish line. Young men who hadn't even known that a Larry Moore existed were now patting him on the back as if he had just hit a bases-loaded, grand slam homerun, in the bottom of the ninth inning.

Enjoying one of the first satisfying moments of practice, Coach Abraham deliberately waited until the applause died to down to next to nothing before bringing the squad to attention. "Listen up, men. Outstanding example of unity and enthusiasm. If we can develop more of that kind of spirit around here, we'll be able to accomplish any goal we set our minds to.

"We had some adversity out here today. All I want to say about that is that the team is much more important than one individual's ego. If you want to be part of the Juddville tradition, you will show respect to your coaches at all times. Your job is to give us your complete attention when we're coaching you, and at no time will you ever make fun of another player or laugh at their mistakes. Do you understand me?"

"Yes, sir," responded the team in unison.

"If you can't live within those rules, you know where the gate is," pointing in the direction of the practice field's primary exit. "We've got a lot of work ahead of us. Tomorrow is our last day without pads, and then on Thursday, the hitting begins. Get yourselves plenty of rest and fluids, and we'll see you tomorrow at 8:00 a.m. sharp. Why don't you send them off today in Juddville fashion, Coach Oliver?"

Surprised, yet duly appreciative of the honor, Gary called out in a commanding voice, "Bring it in here."

Twenty-eight players reached a hand into the circle of unity.

"One more day until pads, fellas. You don't how lucky you are to be able to hit and play this great game of football. Study your plays tonight and get yourself ready for tomorrow's practice. TEAM on three. One... two... three."

"TEAM," resounded from the mouths of twenty-eight Jaguars, surely making its way half-way into town.

One by one the players departed from the torn up practice field onto the sizzling black top of the adjacent parking lot. Pete O'Connor slowly tugged his Juddville helmet from his throbbing forehead as he made his way toward the water. Mike quickly caught up to him, punching him solidly on his unprotected shoulder.

"You better watch that, rookie. You might break your tender knuckles."

"Ha, you're the one who better be on the look out. Do you see Roger sitting over in that car with his mommy? You better put your helmet back on before she tries to bite your head off for laying hands on her boy this morning."

"I bet she's more vicious than a pit bull. But I'm sure she's got bigger fish to fry. I'm sure she is here for Coach Allen's head for picking on her baby this morning. You don't know how badly I wanted to be over with you guys so I could have a front row seat as Coach Allen ripped him a new one. Just tell me one thing. Did Roger start crying?"

"I think I saw a few tears. Do you think he'll get booted from the team, Pete?"

"He might as well. The coaches here are pretty big on quarterbacks being leaders. Since he's only a junior, they might be a little more patient with him. But if he sticks it out, I'm sure he'll just be riding the pine. That's for sure. Remember what I said about him earlier, Mike. Stay away from him. He's bad news."

"What do you say we go to the beach this afternoon? Maybe we can hook up with some babes, maybe even talk them into giving us "star" football players some back massages while we fall asleep on the beach? I heard about this girl named Melanie who..."

"Very funny," interrupted Pete, smacking the rookie running back on the shoulder.

"Ouch," groaned Mike, "Take it easy, I was only kidding."

"I know. Sorry, but I've got things to do this afternoon. I'll have to pass."

"Like what?" pried Mike.

"I've gotta lift, for one."

"Lift? Are you nuts?"

"Yeah, someone's got to provide some muscle around here you know. Maybe another day though, okay?"

"Suit yourself. I'll have all the ladies to myself then."

"Keep dreaming," responded Pete turning abruptly for the water trough to soak his head one last time before leaving the practice field. When he exited the field, he glared at Roger who was sitting slumped down in the passenger's seat of his mother's car, trying to remain inconspicuous, but failing miserably.

How embarrassing. Why doesn't he just carry his mother around in his backpack so she can always be there for him whenever he needs her?

Pete walked into the meeting room to retrieve his Walkman and playbook. Now that he was playing a new offensive position, he had a lot more to study. With only one more day without pads, he wanted to be fully prepared.

The coaches were still huddled in the middle of the field watching Larry Moore squeeze his way through the gate. Coach Abraham broke the silence, "Jim, why don't you go wait inside until I take care of handing out equipment to the new players. Roger's mother will have to wait. It will only take about 15 minutes. I'll speak to her on my way into the locker room."

Coach Allen uttered, "That's fine with me, Coach. In the mean time, Gary and I will go over a few of the blocking schemes for tomorrow's practice. Don't be too long, though. I would like to get this over with as soon as possible."

"Fifteen minutes, maximum. I promise," assured Coach Abraham, checking his watch.

Chapter Six

Kate Perkins pounced through the door at exactly 1:15 with her son Roger walking sheepishly behind. She was wearing a flashy blue dress, beige nylons, and black high-heels. A stylish Gucci purse was tucked under her right arm. Her wavy brown hair extended half way down her back, and her Once-Upon-A-Time Homecoming Queen complexion could not be replicated at this stage in her life, despite the multi-layer application of pricey mascara and overdone blush.

Coach Abraham met her several strides into the room, cavalierly extending his right hand. "Hello, I'm Keith Abraham, and these are my assistants, Jim Allen and Gary Oliver."

"I'm sure you can guess, I'm Roger's mother."

"Why don't you have a seat at one of these desks," offered Coach Abraham, "and Roger, why don't you have a seat, too, if that's okay with you, Mrs. Collins?"

"It's Perkins, Mrs. Kate Perkins," snapped Roger's mother, sitting down in the nearest desk, Roger assuming the desk shielded directly behind her. "No, Roger, up here next to me, pointing to the desk on her left. "Well, I'm a very busy woman, but when I got a phone call from Roger, I came straight from work."

Pausing for a moment, and then looking each coach in the eye before proceeding.

"What exactly happened out on the practice field this morning? Roger says he's getting on picked on and that he doesn't think he wants to play football anymore—which would certainly be fine with me—and he said that Coach Allen is always getting on his case."

Coach Abraham interjected, "Mrs. Perkins, would it be alright if I asked Roger a question."

Mrs. Perkins was taken off-guard by Coach Abraham's request. "Who? Roger? Well, I guess it would be okay. Go right ahead."

"Roger, would you mind telling us what made you feel like you were getting picked on?"

Throughout the entire exchange of informalities, Coach Allen's eyes darted back and forth between Roger, Coach Abraham, and Mrs. Perkins. He wondered how long he could endure this educator-to-parent protocol before they would get around to the God's honest truth.

Roger's mom shifted nervously in her seat, her hands clutching the sides of the desk as she waited for her son's response.

"Well, I guess," began Roger, his eyes glued to the desk top in front of him, "it's just that Coach Allen only points out what I'm doing wrong. He has never once given me a compliment, only put downs. Then he made me run laps in the middle of practice for no good reason."

Coach Allen nearly fell out of his seat, as he was forced to draw upon every ounce of self-control to suppress his desire to speak.

What a little baby, thought Jim. *Is this kid in junior high or high school?*

"Well, is this true, Coach Allen?" asked Mrs. Perkins with a snarl on her face.

Wary of how his assistant might respond, Coach Abraham interjected, "Roger, is there anything else you want to add before Coach Allen speaks?"

"No," he paused, "that's all."

"Jim, why don't you go ahead and tell Mrs. Perkins your version of what happened," advised Coach Abraham.

"Mrs. Perkins," began Coach Allen, trying to be as polite as possible under the circumstances, "let me add a few of the missing details. Roger had just run a play at quarterback. I was attempting to instruct him on what he had done wrong when all of a sudden, he whips the ball at my face, waltzes right by me—with his back turned to me—completely ignoring everything I was trying to communicate to him.

"Maintaining discipline is essential to the success of any team or organization, so I felt it necessary to raise my voice in reprimanding Roger. In all my years of coaching, I have never had a kid throw a ball at my face. My first thought was to kick him off the practice field immediately, but since today is only the second practice of the season, I decided to go light on him and have him run laps instead. Generally, I try to exercise self-discipline and keep from raising my voice on the football field—and in my own home, as well—but I guess getting the ball thrown in my face caused me to lose my temper. So I will apologize for the tone of my voice, Roger, but I will stand behind my comment about your coachability. And let me remind you of something else: you weren't the first Juddville player to ever run laps around the practice field, and I'm quite sure you won't be the last."

Coach Abraham spoke, "I want to add, Mrs. Perkins, that I was the one who kicked Roger off the practice field. Roger was snickering after one of our other quarterbacks fumbled the football."

"That's not what I was laughing at," interrupted Roger.

"Excuse me, Roger. This is my turn to speak. Because we can not take time out of our practices for player-to-coach conferences, I sent him in for the day."

The face of Mrs. Perkins was now beet red. Unable to hold back a torrent of emotions, "Well, I can see clearly why Roger's so upset. It is obvious to me what's going on here. Two, maybe three, grown men ganging up on one player. He is just a boy, you know. And I am having a hard time believing that Roger would throw a ball at anyone's face. He's never acted disrespectful in my house. I would perfectly understand, right now, if you want to quit this team, Roger. You know I don't condone quitting, but under the circumstances, you certainly have my support. But Roger, you're old enough to make your own decisions. I'll let you decide, even though I could never imagine why you might want to play for a hot-headed coach like that one," pointing directly at Jim, who was sitting with his arms folded tightly across his chest. He looked like a volcano ready to erupt at any moment.

Having said the last word, Mrs. Perkins grabbed Roger's hand, yanking him out of his desk before abruptly exiting the room. A couple awkward moments passed, allowing the coaches to try to process the brief conversation that had just ensued. The silence was finally interrupted by Coach Abraham.

"Well, Coach Hot-Head, can I get you a diet Coke? I guess we now know a little more about where Roger's coming from, anyways. Seriously, Jim, don't second-guess yourself over this one. I think most people would have reacted the same way you did. It's pretty obvious that we're going to have to go with David Riley at quarterback whether or not Roger decides to come back tomorrow."

"Wow, I've never seen a high school boy so babied. I couldn't think of anything more embarrassing for a boy than to have his mom come in like that and make a complete fool of him. There's no way in the world we could have a kid like that leading our offense."

The Juddville Jaguar Coaching Staff quickly put the episode with Roger and his mom behind them, and immediately shifted their attention to planning Wednesday's practice. The only personnel adjustment was moving David Riley into Roger Collin's position as first team quarterback.

The meeting lasted until 3:30 before Coach Allen excused himself for a bathroom break. When he returned, Coach Abraham and Gary were discussing defensive terminology.

"Coach, I've got to get going. My kids are going to have Mary half-way in the loony bin if I don't get home soon."

"I think we've covered everything, Coach. See you tomorrow, Jim."

Disillusionment reigning supreme, Coach Allen pulled out of the Juddville High School parking lot. He had never felt this way so early in the season. Even though he had experienced numerous run-ins with disgruntled parents over the years, he still took each conflict personally; consequently, he was absolutely certain he would spending the rest of the day and most of the night trying to rid his mind of Mrs. Perkins's ruthless appraisal of his coaching ability and character.

Parents had no clue just how much heart and soul coaches poured into their work. Jim was already feeling overwhelmed by the pressures of football. His mind was perpetually sabotaged by thoughts of new plays, old plays, personnel changes, and practice plan details.

Where do we need the most improvement?
What kind of drill could develop that skill best?
At what position are we weakest?
Who could we move?
What if _____ got hurt?
Who's our backup?

In the background, foreground, background, then again foreground, was the meeting with Roger's mom. She had called him "hot-headed" in front of her son and the other coaches. Didn't she hear a word that was said about Roger? And, excuse me, but was an apology from Roger missing somewhere in their discussion? What bothered Jim the most, however, was that once again, a parent had completely overlooked the fact that there was more than one kid on the team. In other words, it wasn't all about *their* son. There were, in fact, 28 other sons on the team, and they mattered, too.

At least Coach Abraham had stood by him. Jim had always been able to count on Keith's loyalty, especially during times like these. Whenever Jim felt like he was at the end of the rope, he imagined how painfully difficult it would be to break the news to his long time friend, Coach Abraham. They had forged an impenetrable bond through thirteen seasons of thrills and heartbreaks. Last year's state championship season had been the pot of gold at the end of the rainbow, only the rainbow wasn't composed of sparkling blues, purples, and pinks; no, their rainbow was instead made up of the stains of blood, sweat, mud, and yes, tears. Jim had entertained the notion of going out on top, but now with another season upon them, it was too late.

All of a sudden he remembered he hadn't given Keith an answer about Saturday. Keith had invited him to a men's breakfast being held at his church. The speaker was going to be Jimmy Harrison, a former professional football player.

Jim had already spoken with Mary about the possibility of attending the breakfast. Surprisingly, Mary was all for his attending. He had expected her to take offense to his even thinking about spending more time away from home during an already hectic football season.

What was becoming increasingly apparent to Jim, however, was that Mary was deeply concerned about him. She had communicated this to him on more than one occasion. It was impossible to deny; Jim was becoming increasingly distant to her. They barely even spoke to each other even on those rare occasions when they were alone. If the kids were sleeping, he would invariably disappear to the basement and immerse himself in whatever sport happened to be playing that night. To be sure, Mary never complained about his fulfilling the role of father to their three kids. For most of June and July, he faithfully entertained the children, utilizing his experience as an educator in teaching and disciplining Luke, Katie, and Kevin.

In addition, Jim had made significant sacrifices for the family; he had given up participating in all those bowling, softball, basketball, and touch-football leagues that he had been so preoccupied with in the early years of their marriage. Furthermore, Friday nights at the bar with the boys had become a thing of the past.

Yet somehow Jim was feeling like he was running out of steam. His sense of adventure and excitement for life was dissipating. Winning the state championship last season was a monumental milestone in his coaching career; unfortunately, however, it was now a goal achieved, and Jim feared he would now be less motivated, less driven to duplicate the feat.

Deep down, Jim realized that what he was yearning for was a new challenge, a new goal in his life. He had always been a goal setter—whether academically or athletically. Once he had set his aim on something, he pursued it with full force, never wavering and never quitting until he ultimately fulfilled that goal. What if he couldn't find a new goal, a new purpose? Perhaps, his finest hour had now passed, and he would now be forced to live out some meaningless, mundane existence, struggling to accept the finality of his former glory days.

As Jim pulled into his driveway, he opened the garage door with the remote and slowly rolled his minivan into park. He figured he would grab a quick bite to eat, take a quick glance at the newspaper, and catch a quick nap. Once school started, he wouldn't have the luxury of afternoon naps anymore.

As he opened the door from the garage to the kitchen, his eyes shot down to the floor. Spread out in front of him was a pile of Winnie Pooh books, a half-dozen Hot Wheels, a dirty sock, a beach sandal, and a couple handfuls of half-crushed Cheerios.

"Mary," he called out, unsure whether to take another step, "Mary, is anybody home?"

Jim paced through the kitchen and into the living room. Pajamas were lying on the couch; the Juddville Gazette and crumpled issue of *Sports News* were scattered across the floor.

"Not my new UFL Preview Edition," screamed Jim. "Mary, where are you?"

After searching both upstairs and in the basement, he opened the French doors and walked out onto the deck. No one in the backyard either. Jim returned to the kitchen and opened the fridge. On the second shelf was a sandwich wrapped in cellophane with a brief note attached:

> Jim,
> Sorry about the mess. I took the kids with me to Mom's for the afternoon. Be back for supper.
> Love,
> Mary
>
> P.S. I made you a sandwich.

"Yee Haw!" exclaimed Jim as stood up on his tippy-toes, opening the cabinet above the refrigerator and grabbing the bottle of gin. He grabbed an extra-large tumbler from the cupboard and filled it halfway with ice, adding about 3 to 4 ounces of spirits. He opened a bottle of tonic from the pantry, filling the rest of the glass, and then topped it off with a twist of lime juice.

Proceeding outside to the deck, Jim moved his favorite lounge chair into a shady corner where he methodically gobbled down the ham and Swiss sandwich, followed by the miniature bag of Fritos, and then the small bowl of fresh blueberries. Finally, he washed it all down with his ice-cold gin and tonic, still somewhat in shock that he was fortunate enough to have an afternoon of solitude.

47

After skimming through the sports section, Jim lay back on his chair, closing his eyes and drifting back 15 years to his days at Warren College where he had been the starting fullback his junior and senior years.

In the privacy of his own mind, Jim relived the last game he had ever played; it was the eighth game of his senior year versus undefeated Brighton College. The conference title was on the line. During the first half, Jim had scored four touchdowns—a school record.

Running the ball in the red zone had been Jim's specialty. Whenever the offense drove the ball inside their opponent's 20 yard line, it became "Allen Time". If Jim was unable to find a seam into the end zone on a quick dive or trap, on the next play he would sneak out into the flats wide open for a short, but highly-efficient, play action pass.

Jim's partner in the backfield was a powerful, but slightly faster, running back by the name of Jarid Hendrickson. On this particular date in history, the Brighton Bulldogs were having difficulty shutting down Hendrickson on the off-tackle power and the toss sweep, so by the time the Warren Wildcats had driven the ball all the way down the field to the red zone, the fullback trap and dive up the gut were wide open. Three of Jim's touchdowns were inside traps behind the punishing trap blocks of Jason Monroe.

Unfortunately for Jim, the second half of this legendary game hadn't gone so well. His collegiate career came to a painfully abrupt conclusion when he was knocked out of the game by knee-wrenching tackle on the very first drive of the second half. The play was intended to hit off-tackle, but Jim thought he saw daylight to the outside so he opted to bounce it outside for a big one. What he didn't foresee was the corner coming up to contain, nor did Jim see the ornery linebacker trailing him in hot pursuit from the inside.

As Jim slammed to the ground—sandwiched between the two defenders—he heard his knee snap. His stomach grew nauseous as he had fully realized that his season was over.

His dream shifted from his college glory days to coaching high school football. There he was out on the Juddville practice field, trying in vain to hold his players' attention. But it was like Jim was there, yet wasn't. Nobody made eye contact with him. He was being completely ignored.

Desperate, Coach Allen grabbed a football from one of the players and blew his whistle fiercely. Next, came a string of profanity. But that had no effect on his players either. They just went on fooling around, pinching each other, and kicking at one another, trying out their latest professional wrestling moves—basically acting as if they were ten year olds at a sleepover.

Jim whipped the ball to the ground, his face bright red, his breathing frantically irregular. All of a sudden Jim was awakened by a door slamming, followed by footsteps running toward him.

"Daddy, Daddy, look what I got!" shouted Luke, holding a king-size Snickers bar less than an inch from Jim's face.

Rubbing his eyes, Coach Allen lifted his stiff body into a sitting position. Slowly he regathered his senses and glanced at his ever-present watch. Already 5:30. He could hear Mary in kitchen getting supper ready.

Mrs. Perkins dropped off her son at home before returning to her job at the local women's clothing store. Roger quickly exited the car without turning to say a word to his mother. He jogged up the sidewalk to the porch, unlocking the front door with his house key, doggedly-determined to avoid offering even a casual glance back towards his mother. Never in his life had he ever felt so humiliated.

How could he ever face his teammates again? If he returned to practice the next day, he'd get made fun of nonstop. Roger could already hear them jeering, "Hey, don't hit Roger. He'll sic his mommy on you."

Just why had he called his mom in the first place? What had he been thinking? Now matters were worse. Not only were the coaches on his back, but the players would now target him, too. Given the option between coaches or players, Roger would prefer taking the heat from the coaches. He knew how ruthless players could be. He was one of the worst. Now, it was his turn to be on the receiving end.

The only other choice Roger had was quitting. But then he'd be labeled a loser. And quitting football was something he just couldn't do. His dad used to always preach, "Winners never quit, and quitters never win." It didn't matter if they'd been playing a game of Memory, one-on-one basketball, or table top hockey. His dad never let him quit, period. "If you start a game, you finish" was another of his favorite sayings.

Too bad he never followed his own advice, though.

April 18th. Roger was in the sixth grade. His dad just packed a suitcase and left. No goodbyes, no explanations, nothing. His mom cried for two weeks straight. She had to take a leave of absence from work for two months. After twelve months of weekly counseling appointments and daily dosages of anti-depressants, she finally began to get her life back together.

Several times his mother had set up an appointment for Roger with her psychiatrist, but he had always been so resistant to the idea, and she had been forced to cancel his appointment.

For some odd reason, Roger felt somewhat responsible for his father leaving. But he kept those feelings hidden, especially from his mother, thinking that if he remained cool and under control, maybe she would get off his case. Instead, Roger focused all his energy on football, basketball, and baseball. He secretly hoped that if he became a star athlete in high school—like his dad had once been—then surely, his dad would want to come back and see him play. Maybe then Roger could even convince him to move back to Juddville.

His step-father, Bill Perkins, was another story. If you looked up the definition of geek in the dictionary, you would see a picture of his step-dad—or a close facsimile, at least. Plain and simple, Roger couldn't stand him. They had only *one* thing in common: they both used public restrooms marked MEN, and even then, Bill could probably just as easily pass for the alternative option.

What Roger found most appalling about Bill was that he had absolutely zero interest in sports. Whenever Roger had a game, his mom would always be there, by herself, cheering him on while Bill would be home reading a stupid investment magazine or working on the computer.

The first time Roger met Bill was a Kodak moment if there ever was one. It had been nearly two years since his father had deserted them, and the divorce had been finalized only a few short months. His mom had invited a very "special" guest over for dinner. When Roger was first introduced to Bill, they shook hands, and for Roger, it was like shaking hands with the insides of a slimy clam. And he would forever remember the high-pitched voice saying, "How you doing, Kiddo?"

For an icebreaker, his mother had suggested that they go in the backyard and play catch with the football while she finished preparing dinner. Less than five minutes later, Bill was cursing loud enough for the entire neighborhood to hear. His hands were covering his nose as he tried in vain to keep the blood from spurting all over his neatly-pressed dress shirt.

When Roger's mother came running out of the house, she saw Bill bent over with blood seeping through his fingers. He stood up shakily. His face looked so pale, like he was going to topple over at any moment.

With enough volume for the whole neighborhood to hear, Kate screamed, "Call an ambulance, Roger."

She caught him just in time, escorting him carefully up the steps of deck, through the sliding door, and into the kitchen. Sitting him down at the table, she grabbed a towel, and quickly made an ice pack.

After the bleeding had slowed down to a mere trickle, Bill had assured her that he was going to be okay. Meanwhile, Roger had disappeared into the basement; he had to shove an over-stuffed pillow into his mouth in order to stifle the laughter that had been waiting to erupt like a volcano that had been lying dormant for hundreds of years.

He had missed his mother's explanation to the emergency medical respondents. She had delicately informed them that her "special" friend was going to be all right now, and that it had just been an unfortunate "accident" with a football. Nevertheless, the medics insisted upon giving Bill a quick analysis to make sure his nose wasn't broken.

As Roger had found out later, the diagnosis was favorable: a simple nosebleed. What was even more humorous was that before Bill went home for the evening, he was escorted down to the basement by his mother so he could apologize to her son for losing his temper and for using vulgar language. For Roger, the experience had inspired him to become a quarterback, but the downside, however, was that it somehow had drawn Bill and his mom closer.

A few days later, Roger had to choke down his own vomit when he overheard his mother saying to his grandmother on the phone, "And you should see how good he is with Roger. So patient and self-controlled. Nothing like his hot-headed father used to be."

Three years had gone by. His mother now went by the name of Mrs. Kate Perkins, wife of Bill Perkins, Super-Geek. They had celebrated their first anniversary in April.

So now what was Roger going to do? He loved football. Wasn't it every boy's dream to play quarterback for the Juddville Jaguars? Deep down inside, Roger knew there was no possible way he could quit football. It was his whole life, and the dream of his dad's return hinged upon it. He would just have to force himself to put up with Coach Allen, just as he had learned to tolerate Bill. No hot-headed coach could prevent him from playing the game he loved. For the time being, Roger resolved to bite his tongue and march in step to the commands of the coaching staff, even to the commands of his position coach Jim Allen.

Chapter Seven

The dawn of a new day brought renewed excitement and energy to Pete O'Connor, especially since this day would be the last day of practicing without pads. Wednesday, or "Hump Day", was the official half-way point in the traditional week, but for thousands of football players across the state, this Wednesday was the last day of masquerading as a football gladiator while wearing the equipment of a soccer player, plus a helmet.

Overall, Pete had been satisfied with his performance at guard the day before, but he fully realized that the true test would not begin until Thursday when pad met pad. Be a victor in the trenches, and the starting position was yours. Fail to win your share of battles on the line of scrimmage, and find your reserved seat on the pine.

Trench warfare was not exactly unchartered territory for Pete as he had engaged in many turf battles from the other side of the ball from his defensive position of linebacker—a position he had played the last two seasons. Linebackers fight most of their battles in the front lines when they aren't chasing the ball from sideline to sideline or dropping back to their hook zones in pass coverage. When it is fourth down and inches, and the ball is close enough to the end zone to stick out its tongue for a score, this is the venue where a linebacker earns his honor or shame.

The fundamental requirements of a linebacker are as follows:

- **Guts**, the feint-hearted would never line up nose-to-nose with an offensive guard or be willing to meet a fullback's lead block head-on.
- **Determination**, possessing a stubbornness to not concede even an inch of your team's real estate is essential.
- **Speed**, pursuing the ball requires quickness, not necessarily "track" speed, but the-shortest-distance-between-two-points speed—if there isn't an open lane to the ball carrier, you'd better make a lane of your own.
- Last but not least **Intelligence**, exhibiting a vast knowledge of football and fully committing to extensive weekly game planning is crucial. A linebacker is literally an on-the-field coach who must recognize offensive formations and be able to recall from memory what the opponent's tendencies are by formation, specific down-and-

distances, and field position. Basically, he must commit the essentials of each week's scouting reports to memory. Paying attention in practice and studying hours of film on the opponent go hand in hand with the job of linebacker.

As a result, Pete now had the best of both worlds: opening huge holes on offense and plugging them on defense. He would always be at the fiercest point of battle; consequently, he would have to work even harder in the weight room, for all that hitting would surely take a toll on him physically over the course of the next two to three months.

On this particular Wednesday morning, Pete was so hungry for a bone crushing collision that he was tempted to tackle the nearest telephone pole. As a matter of fact, he had even set his alarm clock 30 minutes earlier so he could get to the locker room early enough to make sure all of his pads were in order for Thursday.

Pete entered the high school and walked unassumingly down the quiet corridor. The lights were not turned on yet, but he knew the way to the locker room. He grasped the door handle firmly and stepped into the relatively-clean smelling locker room; he headed straight to Locker #18, the same locker he had used the year before—Pete was one of only a handful of returning lettermen that could make that boast. He spun the combination dial two full revolutions to the right, then left to 16, right to 18, and finally, left to 6. Bingo, the lock opened on the first try.

As he opened the door, he noticed a nauseating smell emanating from the bottom of his locker.

"What the…" exclaimed Pete, grabbing a hold of his practice pants. His sparkling-white, brand new practice pants were damp. Lifting them up to his nose, he immediately identified the putrid scent of urine. He flung them to floor, and with all his might, punched the locker to his right.

All of a sudden, Coach Allen entered the locker room, cradling five brand new leather Wilson footballs in his arms. Pete quickly picked up his pants from the floor and tossed them back into his locker.

"Hey, Pete. Bet you can't wait for tomorrow, can you?"

"That's for sure, Coach," sitting down on the bench in front of his locker, feeling an odd sense of guilt over the fate of his new practice pants. Unable to extinguish his fury, Pete added, "Tomorrow can't come soon enough."

Pleasantly surprised by the extreme intensity—at such an early hour in the day—of one of Juddville's premier captains, Coach Allen replied, "I know there are quite a few running backs that will be glad they won't have to pair up with you in our hitting drills tomorrow. They'll be thanking their lucky stars you'll be over banging heads with the rest of the linemen."

Pete's face turned blush and his rigid jaw relaxed momentarily as the corners of his mouth gave way to an artificial smile. He cleared his throat, uncertain of the correct way to respond. After a few moments of uncomfortable silence, Pete stammered, "I'm just making sure my equipment's good to go for tomorrow."

"Good idea. Have a good practice, Pete," then he proceeded to the storage room in the back of the locker room.

After taking a deep breath, Pete hurriedly picked up his pants, stuffing them into his duffle bag. Then he scurried over to the sink, grabbed a handful of paper towels from the dispenser, saturated them with soapy water, and returned to his locker where he scrubbed out the atrocity before any of his teammates arrived for practice. Before exiting the locker room, he vigorously washed his hands under scalding water with twice the regular amount of anti-bacterial soap. After he turned off the water and dried his hands with several sheets of paper towel, he smelled his fingers, and much to his relief, the awful smell was gone.

Yet his rage remained. Pete feared he might blow a gasket at any moment. Instead of going ballistic on the spot though, he opted to store away his ire in a remote corner of his mind. When he found out who the perpetrator was, there would be hell to pay. As he considered possible suspects, the name of one of his teammates immediately came to mind.

Chaos prevailed throughout Wednesday's practice, especially during team offense. Linemen jumped on the wrong count, running backs fumbled handoffs and ran half-heartedly, and quarterbacks failed to execute their handoffs and fakes without even the smallest hint of pride. Even Pete jumped on the wrong count, and then on the very next play, he pulled to the right instead of his left, creating quite a pile up behind the center. Unfortunately, Pete's last mental error was the straw that broke the coach's back.

First, Coach Allen pitched his hat to the ground, followed by his whistle, and finally, his clipboard. He picked up his whistle, tried to blow in it, but it failed to produce a sound.

Then his voice broke the sound barrier. "Enough! Enough! I have never seen such a pitiful performance. I have only seen one decent play in 20 minutes of team offense. I can't take any more of this today," wiping his sweaty brow before continuing. "We're so pathetic; we couldn't even move the ball against the jayvees. Coach Abraham, let's go to defense. We'll use the rest of the offense time at the end for extra conditioning."

Jim's comment about the jayvees drew a look of displeasure from Coach Abraham. Providing constructive criticism is a major component of a coach's job responsibilities, but to refer to the jayvees was an insult not only to the varsity, but more importantly, to the jayvee program. Keith made a mental note to speak with Jim privately on this issue after practice.

Fortunately, group defense went much better. Coach Abraham refused to allow the team's early misfires during offense to deter him from his responsibility of coaching defense. Of course, kids need discipline and appropriate correction, but what they needed even more was encouragement and praise when deserved.

In a deep growling voice, Coach Abraham barked out the commands for each drill, generating intensity from even the most timid of players. Coach Oliver watched his mentor closely as he drove this group of untested athletes from one drill to the next, pausing every once in a while to demonstrate a specific technique, making use of every opportunity to pour out positive praise upon each exemplary performance.

After about 20 minutes, Keith gave his defensive players an unscheduled water break, and then split them into two groups: defensive linemen with Coach Oliver, and the outside and inside linebackers with himself.

Meanwhile, Coach Allen was running the defensive backs into the ground. To describe his treatment of the defensive backs as "torture" would be putting it mildly. After their routine sets of backpedaling, cutting, turning and pursuing, they immediately went to ladders—10 yards and back, 20 yards and back, 30 yards and back, and finally, 40 yards and back—only instead of running them in the traditional way, they had to run them backpedaling, which produces an extraordinary burn in the quadriceps muscles. They ran not one, not two, but three sets of backpedaling ladders.

A bit of a surprise was Roger Collins who had seen very little action at quarterback during team offense but had unexpectedly finished first in all three sets of ladders. Coach Allen had never even considered Roger as a potential starter in the secondary before yesterday's act of insubordination. Both Jim and Keith had assumed Roger would be this year's quarterback, and they generally preferred to keep their quarterback on the sideline, out of harm's way, while the defense was on the field.

Yet on this sweltering day, drill after drill, Roger was leading the pack. During a man-to-man coverage drill, Coach Allen badly overthrew both the receiver and Roger who was covering him, and it was Roger who retrieved the ball, running it all the way back, before respectfully handing the ball over to him.

At this point in practice, Jim had to admit, Roger had been the one bright spot. One lesson Coach Allen relearned year after year was that you could never fully predict the behavior or the performance of teenagers. Just when you thought your kids were doomed to defeat, some unexpected hero would step forward and make a big play, shifting the momentum back to your side. Or the opposite might occur: when the sweet taste of victory was only a few ticks away, then one of the most dependable, most consistent players would suddenly commit a stupid penalty or turn the ball over, and then BOOM, the entire team's confidence would be shaken. This phenomenon sometimes occurred during the off season, as well. Last season's sensational sophomore might become the next season's underachieving, waste-of-talent, bench warming junior. You just could never tell what a teenager was going to do.

Finally, Coach Allen topped off Wednesday's barbaric session with his defensive backs with 15 down ups. Jogging in place, the players would listen for the command "Down", signaling them to drop to the ground into a push up position from where they would immediately thrust themselves back up to a standing position, only to resume jogging until the next "Down" command. At the completion of 15 repetitions, the players collapsed back to the ground with the exception of one: Roger Collins.

What's got into him? wondered Jim, as he blew his whistle and yelled, "Water break!"

During specialty, two punt teams alternated reps, each unit punting the ball five times. Roger was the punter for the first group, and in the huddle, he called out the play with a no-nonsense, commanding voice.

"Everyone hustles. Punt, on snap. Punt, on snap. Ready... Break."

All eleven players clapped and yelled "Break" in unison. They hurried to the line of scrimmage, crouched into a two-point stance with their hands on their knees, ready to step to their inside gap on the snap.

56

Roger scanned both sides of the formation. When every player had been set for a count, he barked out the command, "Set."

The center paused a few seconds and snapped the ball back on a line. Roger caught the ball in his hands, took two steps, and punted the ball in a high, spiraling arc sailing in excess of forty yards down field.

"Middle, middle," yelled Roger, as the punt team sprinted down the field, spreading out into their assigned coverage lanes.

The ball descended into the returnman's hands, and three punt team members grabbed hold of him as he was about to take his first step with the ball.

"Great job, punt team. Great job. That's exactly what a punt should look like every time," shouted an enthusiastic Coach Abraham.

The punt team sprinted back to the huddle beaming with confidence. The second team broke out of their huddle determined to duplicate the first unit's performance. Although the majority of the second unit's players were inexperienced, they executed a half-way decent punt, as well. During the next eight punts there was only one bad snap, and most of the punts sailed down the field in the range of 30 to 40 yards.

As the special team's portion of practice came to an end, Coach Abraham blew his whistle and 29 rejuvenated players clustered around him.

"Excellent job on specialty, Jaguars. Today, we're going to run gassers. Spread out along the sideline, linemen to my left, backs and receivers to my right. On my command, sprint across the field, touch the sideline with your foot, run back to me; then run there-and-back a second time. Once the linemen finish, the backs and ends will run while the linemen catch their breath. Since there are four quarters in a football game—and possibly, sudden death overtime—each group will run five.

"Spread out linemen, and get your hand on the line. First quarter. The count is on one. Blue, 38... Blue, 38... Set... GO."

One by one, the linemen sprinted out from their stances, their pace was somewhere between a jog and a sprint; the goal was to keep as close as possible to the rest of the pack. Falling too far behind, definitely made you stick out, in a less than admirable way. On the other hand, leading your position group, especially by considerable margin, was usually a surefire way to attract the attention of the coaches. At the moment, Pete O'Connor—as expected—led the rest of the linemen by more than 10 yards, and he hadn't even reached the first sideline yet. By the time he had reached the halfway point, he had extended his lead to 30 yards.

Stepping on the line and turning to cross the field again, Pete eyed a couple of heavier linemen just touching the first sideline. If he ran as fast as possible, maybe he could catch them. Pete pursued them with vengeance. In no time at all, he was across the field, pushing off the line with his right foot, determined to pass the last two linemen—thus, completing his first gasser by the time they were only halfway through. As he crossed midfield, his targets were about 15 yards from the next sideline. Pete felt his stomach tightening and his legs burning. He broke out into an all-out sprint, stepping over the sideline a half second before his teammates. Falling to a knee, Pete regained his breath after about 20 seconds of rest, and then he began to bark out encouragement to his teammates.

"Come on, fellas. Push yourselves. Do you want to be the stronger team at the end of the game, or the weaker?"

Coach Abraham glanced over at Pete in silent admiration. He was the kind of kid every coach loved to have on his team. He was a pure joy to coach. A genuine blue chipper. Always giving his best effort. Doing everything asked of him and then some. Ultra-dependable. Even as a second team player last year, Pete showed the same work ethic and enthusiasm. Now, as a definite two-way starter, his attitude was more noticeable and much more crucial.

Larry Moore was the last lineman to complete the first gasser, and the backs and ends were anxious to begin their first gasser.

"Okay, backs, on one. White, 18... White, 18... Set... Go!" commanded Coach Abraham.

The backs and ends appeared to be running in fast forward in comparison to the pace set by the linemen; Mike Owens, Tommy Schultz, and Roger Collins quickly pulled ahead of the others, fighting amongst one another to gain control of the lead. As they reached the first sideline and turned to head back across the field, they were neck-and-neck. By midfield, Tommy and Roger were pulling slightly ahead, with Mike struggling to keep up. Halfway through the first gasser, their lead had increased to about 10 yards.

Coach Allen called out to his sophomore running back, "Come on, Mike, you're not getting tired already are you? It's only the first quarter."

Mike doubled his effort to catch up, but there was too much ground to make up; Tommy and Roger were already touching the next sideline, and he was only at the hash mark.

By this time, the linemen were getting back on their feet—not to ready themselves for their next gasser, but to see who would win between Tommy and Roger. Having extensive conditioning from his participation in summer basketball certainly gave Tommy the edge. He seemed like he was in his groove, but all of a sudden, Roger pulled a couple of inches ahead. As they crossed the finish line, Roger had beaten Tommy by a foot and a half. Mike was in third place, about 15 yards behind. The recently promoted starting quarterback, David Riley, finished in a distant fourth place.

"Way to set the pace, Roger and Tommy. That type of effort and leadership can only make this team better!" yelled Coach Abraham, with Coach Allen and Coach Oliver nodding their heads in approval.

As promised, Coach Abraham was good to his word, and both units ran five gassers. No one was shocked to see Pete O'Connor finish in first place with the linemen for all five gassers. Roger won the first three and then fifth gassers. Mike Owens coasted at half-speed for the second and third gasser, and then outran Tommy and Roger in the fourth one, but the coaches were not fooled.

"If you go half-speed during the 2nd and 3rd quarters of a real game, Michael, I guarantee your butt won't be on the field for the 4th quarter," jeered Coach Allen. "You can't just go all out some of the time. It's got to be all of the time."

At the conclusion of conditioning, Coach Allen was the first to speak.

"Today, I think we learned a little about ourselves and about how far we have to go; I know I sure did, anyways. We had a pretty dismal offensive session. The worst in my coaching experience, as a matter of fact. We had way too many mental breakdowns for the third practice of the season. What this team is lacking right now is leadership. I realize we don't have many returning players from last season, but we need more of you to accept greater responsibility for this team by taking charge out here. We need more of you to set the tone by going all out in drills and in scrimmage. And we need leaders who are focused, whose minds are on football, not somewhere else.

"As offensive coordinator for this team, I'll take responsibility for today's catastrophe. I promise you, things will go much different tomorrow. Tonight, be sure to review all the plays we've put in the last three days. I think you can expect tomorrow's practice to be more fun since you will get your first opportunity to hit. It's the one day of the season when we coaches would surely love to be in your shoes, to be able to put on the pads one more time, especially for the Oklahoma hitting drill."

Coach Abraham added one more comment, "Players, make sure you have all your pads in place and that all your gear is ready to go, so you won't be late for the start of practice. Bring it in."

The players rose to their feet and formed a huddle around Coach Abraham.

"Today's word is unity. Now put your hands in here."

All different sizes and shapes of hands reached into the center of the circle, resting on Coach Abraham's clenched fist. Players who were around the perimeter of the circle place their hands on the nearest shoulder.

"Unity, on three. One, two, three... UNITY!" hollered the Jaguars in one voice.

With renewed enthusiasm, the team dispersed from the practice field, overjoyed to have completed their most grueling practice yet, and looking forward to tomorrow's practice when "football" truly began.

One player, however, exited the practice field like a torpedo blasting from a battleship. Choosing to forego any customary post-practice banter with his teammates, he immediately distanced himself. Dejected by his disappointing performance at offensive guard, Pete longed for some type of outlet for his frustration.

He headed straight for the locker room, grabbed his duffle bag from Locker #18, and violently slammed his locker shut.

I was horrible today. What do the coaches think of me now? How could I pull the wrong way on that trap? And then I jumped offsides on the very next play. I stunk! Why did all my teammates look directly at me when Coach Allen was talking about a lack of leadership? I let my coaches and teammates down. That's why. If I keep this up, this will be my last season of football. There won't be any colleges interested in me.

Instead of taking his things and walking home, Pete went directly to the Jaguar weight room. For the most part, weightlifting had ended last week, but the weight room was always open after practice for an hour or two for anyone willing. There weren't too many football players interested in lifting after a three and half hour practice, however.

Pete opened the door and turned on the lights. Next to the stereo was a poster with one of his favorite sayings: "Winners do the things that losers refuse to do."

Over in the far corner of the weight room, Pete's favorite bench awaited him. He tossed his duffle bag against the wall and laid down on the bench. Grabbing the 45 pound bar, he cranked out 30 quick repetitions; his back began to cramp up after the 20th repetition. After completing his set, he hopped on to his feet and loaded a 45 pound plate to each side of the bar. He immediately laid back down and pressed the bar off his chest 10 times. Pete felt tired and weak. Following a long visit to the drinking fountain, he added a 25 pound plate to each side of the bar and pressed it eight times. Feeling a little stronger and bolder, he loaded the bar to 225 pounds. He cranked out six slow-but-steady reps. After the sixth rep, his lower back began to cramp again, but he forced out two more reps.

Pete was about to rack the weight when he heard the words, "Okay, Pete, two more reps. You can do it."

All of a sudden, he was staring directly upwards into the face of Roger Collins, who was leaning over him, his hands ready to grab a hold of the bar if needed. Pete sharpened his focus, and with added determination, inch by inch, he pressed the bar off his chest, holding the bar for a few extra seconds in the locked position, hoping to have enough strength remaining for one last rep.

"Come on, Pete. This is the one that really counts. It's all yours, Pete. I'm not going to help you. I know you can do this," encouraged Roger.

Pete slowly lowered the bar to his chest and thrusted the bar off his chest with all the force he could muster. It stalled about halfway up. Pete waged all his strength upon the 225 pounds, but the bar was just suspended in mid-air, for three to four seconds. Pete refused to surrender, adamantly opposed to begging Roger's assistance.

"Come on, Pete. Finish the rep. Lock it out. It's all yours," shouted Roger.

The cramp now felt like an ice pick that had pierced six inches into his lower back. If he didn't get this over with soon, the bar would concede to gravity and come crashing down upon his chest. This was Custard's Last Stand; it was now or never. Squeezing the bar with all his might, he pushed, pushed, and pushed... And his elbows began to lock as the bar reached its final destination. Pete racked the weight, letting out a groan as he lifted his knees up to his chest to relieve the cramp in his back.

"Great job, Pete. You didn't need my help at all. Now get off the bench, so I can do a set," said Roger.

Pete dragged himself off the bench and returned to the drinking fountain.

What in the world is he doing here? He's the last person I'd expect to see. Maybe I ought to go stuff his face into my duffle bag so he can get a taste his own medicine. But what if it wasn't him?

Better not make a fool of myself by jumping to the wrong conclusion.

After slurping down huge gulps of water, Pete watched his teammate. Roger was cranking out warm up reps with 95 pounds on the bar. His technique was all right, and it appeared that he was working hard. To be sure, he wasn't here to show off. Pete grabbed a pair of 50 pound dumbbells and carried them over to the incline bench next to Roger. He set them on the floor, and said, "Okay, Roger, how much do you need for your second set?"

"Throw on a couple of ten pounders, I guess."

"All right then," replied Pete, "A ten and a five." He loaded both sides of the bar for Roger and then stepped behind the bench to spot him.

"If you get stuck, though, don't expect any help from me, Roger. After all, I owe you one, you know."

Chapter Eight

Following Wednesday's practice, Coach Allen felt like he had endured a two hour root canal, minus the Novocain.

Just what had gone wrong? He had promised himself that this year he would not lose his cool again on the football field. How could he ever expect his players to respect him?

A football coach had to earn a certain amount of trust from his players. When it's fourth and inches, the game is on the line, there's time for one more play, the last timeout has been called, all the players are huddled around him, eyes looking to him, anxiously awaiting the play that will either win or lose the game... When it came down to that crucial moment, would the players have faith in him? Would they trust him to keep his cool, to remain level-headed, and to make the right call? Would they believe in his mental capacity to project what the adversary's defensive coordinator might be thinking and to then counter with the most effective play?

It wasn't like playing a video game. You couldn't just hit the reset button to delete a game that didn't go your way. The score was permanent, and the consequences determined your destiny in the conference standings. Furthermore, standings determined playoffs or no playoffs. But what was of far more significance was the reality that the game would forever be etched in your memory—for better or worse. Over the course of fourteen seasons, there were a number of failed opportunities that stuck out in Coach Allen's memory. Moments where—given a second chance—he would have called a play-action pass instead of the inside trap, or he would have put the ball in the hands of his more powerful fullback instead of the highly-talented but hesitant-to-run-between-the-tackles Prima Donna halfback.

One more incident of losing his composure and the team would lose confidence in him for good. As a result, Jim bolted for the seclusion of the meeting room where he could be free from further contact with players and where he could gather his thoughts before the staff meeting where he would surely be called into account for his actions on the field. Reaching into his pocket, he grabbed his wallet, pulled out a couple dollar bills, and purchased a couple of Diet Cokes from the vending machine. Then he remembered their new comrade, Coach Oliver, and purchased a regular Coke for him. He balanced the three cans in his hands and retreated to the table where all his football notes were still spread out from the morning's team meeting.

Jim's exhausted body slumped into the hard plastic chair, and he brooded over the sparse number of plays they had put into their offense thus far: four running plays and two passing plays. Looking through his notes from the previous season, he noted that after their first three practices last year, they had already put in 10 running plays and five passes. Bottom line? If they were to play a game today, they would have only six play options for moving the ball toward the opponent's end zone, and that didn't even call into question their limited ability to execute the plays properly. Coach Allen imagined the defensive coordinators throughout their conference licking their lips with anticipation as they awaited the opportunity to reap vengeance upon their traditional arch enemy, the mighty Juddville Jaguars.

A few minutes passed before Coach Abraham entered the room—Coach Oliver was still out on the field, working with the long snappers.

Keith removed his hat from his head and removed the whistle from around his neck. Sitting down in the seat next to Jim, he asked, "Everything all right, Jim?"

"I'm sorry I lost my cool out there again, Keith. I was way out of line. I don't know what I was thinking. I blew a gasket, and then shortened team offense. I come in here after practice, and then have the audacity to be upset that we've got so few plays in."

Patting him on the shoulder, Keith responded, "You're putting too much pressure on yourself, Jim. We can only work with what we've got. This isn't the same group of kids we had last year. You've got to remember that most of last year's starters were two year starters. That gave them a huge head start on this year's team. We expected to have to go slow the first week. You've got to give it time. We've got a completely new backfield; it's going to take time for them to get their timing down."

"I realize that, Keith. But I'm just really falling apart out there."

"Is everything okay at home?"

"Yeah, pretty much... I guess. You know... the usual."

Suddenly, the door opened and Coach Oliver entered the room.

"Have a seat, Gary. I got you a Coke," said Jim, relieved at the opportunity to change the topic of their conversation. "Here's your Diet Coke, Keith."

"How come I got the Diet?" joked Coach Abraham, winking at Coach Oliver as he sat down next to them.

Gary set his clipboard down and snapped back the tab of his Coke. "Thanks, Coach."

Changing to a lighter subject, Coach Abraham said, "Tomorrow when we start hitting, we'll find out what kind of chances we'll really have this season. I say—after a brief warm up—we go right to our hitting drills. Let's limit live contact only to individual group drills, however. I would prefer to hold off going live during team scrimmage until Friday or even Monday, if need be."

Coach Allen responded, "I think that tomorrow we should scale things down offensively. I would prefer not to add any new plays. It seems foolish to introduce something new when we can't run what we already have in. Let's just polish what we've got in so far. At quarterback, I think I'm going to stick with David Riley for the time being. I have to admit, though, I liked what I saw out of Roger today. But he'll have to prove himself over the long haul before I put him back in charge of the offense."

"Defensively, I think things went well today," said Coach Abraham. "The kids really worked hard in drills."

Turning to his rookie volunteer assistant who generally deferred to the wisdom and experience of his mentors and who thereby chose to remain virtually silent during their daily "skull" sessions, Keith said, "I think we'll be okay up front, don't you, Gary?"

"Yeah, I think we've got three, maybe four decent prospects. You've certainly got an all-conference linebacker in O'Connor. What an animal! I can't wait to see his first hit tomorrow."

"How do you think Pete's working out on offense so far, Keith?" asked Coach Allen, a look of concern in his eyes. "He was having a rough time out there today during team offense. You don't think we're asking too much from him, learning a brand new position without much warning."

"I think he'll be all right, Jim," answered Keith. "Put it this way, if Pete can't carry the load offensively, we're in really big trouble because there is no else with enough strength, smarts, and speed to be our pulling guard. He'll develop. He has to. Just give him some time."

When Pete opened the door to his trailer, he slammed his duffle bag on the floor and went straight to the refrigerator. Jerking open the door, he grabbed the half-empty jug of milk and a loaf of bread. He checked the fruit drawer and noticed a couple of Red Delicious apples, and grabbed the biggest one—even though it appeared slightly bruised. Next, he grabbed the extra-large jar of Jif peanut butter from the cupboard and a knife out of the silverware drawer. He laid out six pieces of bread on the cutting board and spread generous helpings of butter and peanut butter on the bread. He stacked the three sandwiches on a plate along with his apple and sat down at the kitchen table. In between bites of sandwich, he swallowed huge gulps of milk right from the jug. Within five minutes he had devoured his sandwiches, an apple, and a half-gallon of milk.

Pete picked up his duffle bag and went to the laundry closet. He took out his white practice pants—nearly gagged on the scent of urine—and threw them in the washer along with some dirty athletic socks, underwear, and his supporter. He measured out a ½ cup of detergent, set the washer for Hot/Cold Rinse, and silently prayed that his pants would come out unstained. Then he thoroughly washed his hands with ample amounts of soap.

Feeling the physical effects of the morning's practice and his after-hours workout in the weight room, he decided to lie down on his bed and read his new UFL Preview magazine. As he paged through the magazine, he scoffed at the majority of articles highlighting the UFL's star athletes—all the pretty boy quarterbacks, the trash talking wide receivers, and of course, the you-can-throw-my-way-but-please-don't-run-my-way defensive backs. Finally, hidden way in the back, he located the article that had prompted him to buy the magazine in the first place: "Kent Karchinski: Dragon of Distinction or Extinction?"

With disbelief, Pete read the disparaging comments about his hero that had been written by some pencil-necked sportswriter whose head could—Pete supposed—most likely fit inside a thimble. What did he mean Karchinski was "washed up and never would return to his former level"? Sure, his favorite player was coming back from a serious shoulder injury—the second surgery on that shoulder, as a matter of fact—but the operation had been way back in January, and Karchinski had worked out relentlessly for the past six months, meeting teammate Kirk Maitland in the Dragon weight room at 6:00 a.m., six days a week.

Pete recalled previously reading about how Maitland was once 15 minutes late for his workout. Apparently Karchinski had slapped 300 pound Maitland three times before he could explain that he had been pulled over by a cop for driving 65 in a 35 mph zone. According to Kirk, his face felt like it had been shoved into a pot of boiling water for thirty seconds; what Maitland remembered the most, however, was being totally surprised to see Karchinski suddenly break out in laughter. When he asked Kent what was so funny, his response was, "You've got a perfect white hand print of mine on your face." Kirk had to run over to the nearest mirror, and sure enough, there was the white chalk imprint of his teammate's hand. Needless to say, Maitland was never late for a workout again.

It had always been Pete's dream to one day meet his hero in person. In fact, he visualized heaven as a place where he could workout with his idol, Kent Karchinski. He could imagine the resounding clang of 45 pound plates rattling on the Olympic bar as he cranked out an UFL record 35 repetitions with 225 pounds in the bench press. Or how special would it be to have the honor of giving a lift off to K.K. as he maxed out with 450 pounds. Karchinski had been crowned the UFL's Strongest Man each of his first five seasons in the league. Even after two surgeries, he still had made the top five.

Above Pete's dresser was a poster of his hero: number 54 of the New Jersey Dragons. Karchinski was crouched in a hitting position; his jersey ripped above his right shoulder, all dirtied with soil and blood; his neck bulled; his eyes glaring straight ahead; his biceps bulging; and his massive legs coiled, ready to unleash his superior power upon whoever would be foolish enough to run his way.

Karchinski was everything a football player should be. And when he walked off the field, he was a family man. He had a wife of ten years—his high school sweetheart—and a five year old daughter and two year old son. Karchinski often spoke of his family as his absolute treasure; he was as devoted a husband and father as he was a football player. On the field, he was an uncaged lion, but off the field, he possessed the loyalty of a teddy bear.

Setting the magazine down, Pete looked up at an old photograph of his family on top of his dresser. They were sitting on a picnic table, his dad on his right, his mom on his left. They had been on a camping trip. His dad wore a white tank top, denim shorts, a worn pair of Nike running shoes on his feet, and a can of Budweiser in his right hand. His mom was dressed in a blue tee-shirt, white shorts, brown sandals, and a cigarette in her right hand. Pete was snuggled between them wearing a New Jersey Dragon t-shirt, blue shorts, filthy bare feet, and a football tightly clenched in his hands. A green tent was propped behind the picnic table.

So many years ago... back before his dad was incarcerated. Now Pete had no idea what his father even looked like.

Rising up from the bed, Pete walked over to the dresser. He opened the top drawer and pulled out an old, wrinkled envelope that he kept inside the mostly-ignored Bible his grandma had given him for his thirteenth birthday. He remembered how she had said, "This book will give you hope when the world offers none." Setting the book aside, he stared blankly at the envelope he had opened hundreds of times over the past six years. Holding it up to his nose, he tried to recapture the scent of his father. Not a trace.

A couple years ago, Pete had been snooping in the back of his mom's closet when he came across an old cardboard shoe box; he discovered an old news clipping with a picture of his dad during the trial. His father, dressed in a state-issued, orange jump suit, bound by handcuffs, head slumped down, staring down at the floor. He was accompanied by a Billington police officer. The headline read "Paul O'Connor: Guilty of Two Counts of Manslaughter". Several days after discovering the article, Pete garnered up enough courage to ask his mother about the clipping. Her callous response was, "Forget you ever seen it."

Six years later, Pete had stayed clear of his mother's closet, choosing instead to hang on to the last official correspondence from his father. It was the letter he could actually recite from memory:

Dear Pete,
    I can't tell you how much it hurts to think about how I have let you and Mom down. The shame I feel haunts me every moment of the day. The two boys who lost their lives because of me are always on my mind.

I have no memories of the horrible accident. All I can remember is waking up in a jail cell and being told that I was being charged with manslaughter, the result of my third drunk driving offense. This time my irresponsible actions hurt more than just my family. I wish it would have been me that died, not two innocent boys. How I wish it could have been me.

I love you and your mom very much. She deserved much better than me. So do you, Pete. It would be better for you if you carry on your lives without me. By the time I am released from prison, you'll be a young man. I have pleaded with your mom to divorce me and take a second lease on life. You'll be better off never hearing from me again. I have already done enough damage.

If you remember one thing, Pete, learn from my mistakes. Stay away from the booze. It has cost me everything. And it snuffed out the lives of two innocent boys.

For that I can never forgive myself. Take care of your mom.

Love,
Dad

Pete set the letter down, clenched his blanket tightly in his hands, closed his eyes and tried to sleep. The first time he read that letter, he had come so close to shredding it to pieces. Now—with the exception of the photo on his dresser—it was his only memento of his father.

Every once in a while he would sit down and write a letter to his father. Disappointment would always follow. A week would pass. His mom would hand him the envelope, marked in red rubber stamp, "Return to Sender". She tried in vain to conceal her pain and disappointment, but her eyes never lied. Her words remained the same: "Let him go, Pete. Let him go. It's what he wants."

At 4:30, Cindy O'Connor found her son asleep on his bed, clutching the letter from his father in his right hand. She sat down on the bed beside him, gently running her fingers through his hair. How she wished things could have been better for her son.

After Paul had received his minimum 10 to 15 year sentence, Cindy had packed up all their belongings, headed

35 miles east on US 81 to Juddville, in search of any available employment and an opportunity for a new life.

Over the past six years, she had worked three different jobs; her current job was a factory job, working second shift. Her paycheck was barely enough to cover the rent for the trailer, buy clothes for her and Pete, and put food on the table. With only a high school diploma, she had very few options. With no leftover money for tuition at the local community college, she would never have the opportunity to fulfill her dream of getting a nursing degree.

Outside of working 50 hours a week, and keeping the trailer clean, Cindy didn't have much of a life. One night a week Cindy and a couple of girlfriends from work would stop at Ernie's Pub and have a drink. There was never another man in her life. A few months back, she had actually contemplated signing the divorce papers, but she kept putting off setting up an appointment with the lawyer. Finally, she dropped the idea altogether. It wasn't that she had hopes of ever getting back together with Paul; he had shattered any hope of that…She just couldn't fathom ever being able to love again.

Her mind drifted back to that infamous Monday so long ago. All by herself, she had driven the 150 unspectacular miles to the Carson City State Penitentiary. Cindy had felt like she was on death row as she anxiously waited for him in the visitor's room. Over and over in her mind, she had rehearsed her final plea. Reaching down deep into her emotional reservoir, she pretended to be happy, pretended to feel optimistic that her prayers might actually be answered.

When Paul finally sat down across from her, he barely made eye contact through the glass window. She had wanted so much to cheer him up, but she could see right away that there was very little life left in him. For a few minutes, they had engaged in small talk. Updates on how Pete was doing, how her job was going—choosing to ignore any discussion of how they were behind on nearly all their bills. Then from out of no where, Paul stuck a dagger deep into her soul.

Cindy would never forget the look of hopelessness in his eyes. His voice was quiet and raspy, "I don't want you to come and see me anymore. You must…" Paul's eyes searched the walls above and behind her. "You must divorce me... as soon as possible. Get on with your life, Cindy. Start a new life without me."

Rising to his feet, Paul extended his hand up to the glass partition and whispered, "Good bye, Cindy." Then he turned and exited the visitor's room, and the life of her soul came bursting out like air from a punctured balloon.

Cindy had been taken completely off guard. She buried her wet, stinging eyes into her hands, impervious to her surroundings. Who knows how many minutes passed before a prison guard tapped her on the shoulder, coldly informing her that visiting hours had expired.

The reality of Paul's message weighed heavily upon her. She knew that when her husband made up his mind, there was no turning back. It was a done deal. Since Paul was now securely locked up behind the cold, steel bars of the state penitentiary, there was no hope of her ever being able to reach him. Cindy was helpless. Most distressing, however, was the undesirable task of passing on the devastating news to their eleven year old son, who was waiting eagerly at home for any form of positive news about his father.

During the drive back from Carson City, all she could do was cry, cry, and cry. She knew she had 150 miles of driving to get it all out of her system. By the time she reached Billington, she would have to regain her personal strength and mental fortitude. Pete required a mother and a father now. She would have to do her best to fill both roles. Her tears must forever be hidden away.

Six years later, Cindy and Pete were survivors, living new lives in the town of Juddville. No one knew about Pete's father, and true to his word, he had totally removed himself from their lives. Although there had been no official divorce, all communication had ceased, and thus, so had the relationship.

Yet not a day passed when neither Cindy nor her son failed to think of him. So many of Pete's mannerisms reminded her of Paul: his quiet resolve that she had been drawn to when they had first started dating; his love of exercise and hard, physical labor; and occasionally, the traces of Paul's unique brand of humor—not much of a talker, yet often catching people off guard by an amusing one-liner or semi-crude comment.

Eventually, Cindy came to accept the painful reality that there would never be another man in her life. Circumstances beyond her control had removed Paul from her life, yet she was hopelessly in love with him, for better or for worse—in her case, worse. Her best friends, Tina and Gayle, had long since given up trying to set her up with a date. Cindy's response was always the same, with no exception: "Not interested."

Furthermore, she had allowed her natural beauty to fade. She rarely wore makeup anymore though the need was increasingly present. When she looked at herself in the mirror, she couldn't avoid noticing the bags under her eyes, or the way her black hair draped lifelessly down her shoulders. The expression on her face was stuck in neutral, unresponsive to neither the compulsion to move forward nor the temptation to stare backward. Once in a great while, she might break out into a fit of unrestrained laughter, but those occasions were rare and unexpected.

Yet the sleek shape of her body was the envy of her friends who were for the most part each carrying around an extra ten pounds for each child brought into the world. Cindy's gaunt appearance was more the by-product of restless nights and her unconquerable addiction to nicotine which generally squelched her appetite for food and minimized her need for sleep—generally four to five hours a night on a good night. Smoking was the only pleasure in her life, and it didn't bother her that it might one day kill her. As long as she lived long enough to see her son get to college, she wasn't concerned.

Now as she sat next to her son on his bed, she caressed his shoulder, relishing the rare opportunity to gaze upon this little boy who had so quickly become a man. The whole manner in which he had been able to cope with life, in the absence of his father, had truly amazed her. Many boys his age—who had also been deserted by their fathers—were already just one step away from prison. Gangs, shoplifting, drugs, sex, guns, and knives were the pitfalls just waiting to prey upon these vulnerable, fatherless boys. And there was always the threat of alcohol. As far as Cindy knew, Pete had kept a distance from alcohol. Times were not much different from when she was a teenager, however. Yet if anyone was aware of the consequences of drinking, it was her son.

71

Fortunately, Pete had chosen a different path, and every night she bowed down at the foot of her bed and prayed that this football season would fulfill each and every one of her son's dreams. All summer long he lived in the weight room; at night he ran wind sprints by himself on the high school track. A couple of those nights she went with him to keep him company. She was astonished by his commitment. Back and forth across the track, he sprinted. First, 100 yards, five times; next, 80 yards, seven times; then, 60 yards, nine times; and finally, 40 yards, eleven times. Cindy almost vomited just watching him.

Not wanting to disturb her son who appeared to be resting so peacefully, she quietly crept out of his room and decided to smoke a quick cigarette, and then surprise him by preparing his favorite meal. If there was one thing Pete could not resist, it was cheeseburgers on the grill and corn on the cob—washed down with two large glasses of milk—that would be a wonderful meal, indeed.

Chapter Nine

One by one the 29 Juddville Jaguars emerged from the locker room in their black mesh jerseys and alabaster pants. Fully-dressed in their shoulder pads for the first time, even the scrawniest of players looked poised for battle. It was amazing what a $100 pair of shoulder pads could do for a teenager's ego.

The largest player on the team, Larry Moore, looked as big as a trailer. Unfortunately, he moved like one, too—all he needed was a "Wide Load" sign hanging from his rear end. Tommy Schultz—a recent convert to the sport of football—strutted back and forth, lower back arched, chest sticking out, nervously trying to psyche himself up for his first experience with full-contact. Mike Owens stood in the center of a circle of five players, his helmet off, tossing a football into the air, boasting of his numerous accomplishments the year before on the jayvees. His thick, curly brown hair screamed "total neglect", and his socks were pulled all the way up to his knees. In addition, his football armor included black elbow pads, Nike wrist bands, and authentic UFL receiver gloves—just like the gloves of "Showtime" Shaun Jackson of the Miami Raptors.

"Remember the Billington game last year when I ran for three touchdowns. On my 60 yarder, I stiff-armed the corner and sprinted down the sideline. There was no one within 20 yards of me," bragged Owens. "I would have gained 300 yards if Coach Stockton wouldn't have taken me out of the last quarter."

All of a sudden, Pete bumped his way into the middle of Mike's huddle of worshipers. "Hey, Mike, let me remind you of one thing: this isn't the jayvees anymore. You might actually have to take a hit this year. And let me tell you. You *will* feel it. There won't be anymore powder-puff tackles."

"How would you know, Pete? Can't say as I remember you carrying the ball much last year," retorted Mike, his admirers joining in, providing backup laughter.

"Well guys, that was then, and this is now. If I were you, I would be more concerned with the now. And I would offer a word of advice to you all: make sure you've got your chinstraps on tight."

Pete delivered a friendly openhanded smack to the shoulder pads of Mike and said, "See you out on the field, boys." Then he trotted over to Coach Abraham who was just about to blow his whistle.

"Bring it in, men. Let's make sure we do a good job stretching in warm-ups today. I know you're all excited about hitting, but we don't want to lose anyone before we get to the fun. Around the tree, and lineup for cals," barked Coach Abraham.

As the 29 Jaguars bolted for the tree, a noticeably different attitude emerged. Players were howling with enthusiasm. Big Larry Moore let out a gigantic, "Yeeeeeh, Hawww!" as he circled the tree.

Warm-ups went quickly and without incident. During form run, players were starting to huff and puff a bit. The coaches were not surprised, however, for it would take some getting used, carrying an extra 25 to 30 pounds on their backs. By water break, the wild and raucous energy had begun to wane, and as the team split into offensive groups, the players were starting to become impatient for their first taste of contact.

Unfortunately, the first taste for the offensive linemen would begin on the torturous five-man sled; the backs would be taking on the infamous two-man sled.

Coach Abraham divided his men into five lines before initiating them into what would become their routine blocking progression. The entire routine lasted more than 20 minutes, followed by a quick water break. When the linemen returned, they reviewed the inside trap and halfback power blocking schemes versus a 5-2 defense.

Finally, Coach Abraham introduced the first "live" blocking drill. He placed two full-length blocking dummies on the ground, parallel to one another, creating about a four yard running lane between them. Then he divided the linemen into a line for blockers and a line for tacklers. As a bonus, one lineman would get the rare privilege of touching the football by assuming the role of running back.

To no one's surprise, Pete stationed himself in the front of the blockers' line. Across from him on defense was 235 pound Gary Osborn. Coach Abraham stood directly behind the tackler, holding up two fingers to signal the count to the blocker and running back.

Pete crouched down into his three-point stance, his muscles poised to explode like a rocket ready for blastoff. On the other side of the line of scrimmage, Osborn bent down in a four-point stance, growling like a starving lion that slept through feeding time.

Coach Abraham began the cadence, and a nervous junior who inherited the honor of carrying the ball first, prepared to meet his doom. The four yards distance between him and his blocker in front of him seemed like a quarter mile.

He offered up a silent prayer: *Please get a piece of him, Pete.*
"Red 22... Red 22... Set... Go... Go..."

On the second "Go", Pete exploded from his stance, striking Gary just above his thigh pads before he had even taken a step. Pete dug his cleats into the turf, chopping his feet, driving his hips forward, slipping his helmet to the right hip of Osborn, and thereby creating a huge, four foot hole for the much relieved running back. Pete dropped down to his hands and finished the block by crabbing on all fours, taking Gary's feet out from underneath him.

Lost in a momentary state of reverie, Coach Abraham unnecessarily blew his whistle though the play had concluded several moments earlier. "That's the way to drive block, Pete."

And then looking to the rest of his linemen, "Did you see that? Low man always wins, no matter what the size of your opponent!"

Pete rolled out from underneath his behemoth opponent, resisted the temptation to taunt him, and jogged over to the defensive line. While some players unsnapped their chinstraps and removed their mouth guards while waiting in line, Pete kept his helmet secured and mouth piece in place as he eagerly awaited his next battle.

After waiting in line through six one-on-one confrontations, it was finally Pete's turn to go on defense. Pete lined up about three yards from Craig Daniels—the number one center on the depth chart. Craig went about 205 pounds, had decent speed, and used excellent blocking technique. Pete knew this would be a good match up. He crouched into his "Kent Karchinski" linebacker stance: his legs spread apart at shoulder's width, knees slightly bent, arms flexed at his sides, biceps bulging out of his tight-fitting jersey, and his laser-like eyes glaring right through Craig to the running back cowering four yards behind him. Pete listened to the count, but he focused intently for the first sign of movement in either Craig or the back. On the first "Go", Craig sprang out from his stance.

Pete stepped forward with his right foot and thrust out both hands into the lower edge of Craig's shoulder pads, driving him back a half step. He felt pressure to his right, so he slipped his hands to the outside of Craig's shoulder pads, flinging him to his left. Instantaneously, Pete located the ball carrier running straight toward him; Pete dipped his shoulders and uncoiled every ounce of power from his legs into the running back.

A thunderous crack echoed across the practice field as Pete's shoulder pads drove upwards into the unprepared running back's mid-section. Lifting him off the ground, Pete wrapped both arms tightly around him like a python, and dropped him flat on his back. This time Pete was unable to hide his exuberance; he popped up from the ground, adrenaline rushing through his veins, and an unavoidable grin of satisfaction upon his face. He could not help but yell out an unabashed, "Yes!"

Regaining his composure, Pete grabbed the football to take his turn at running back. Meanwhile, his teammates were still hooting and howling, as if they were seeing fireworks for the first time.

That hit would have even impressed Keith Karchinski, Pete thought to himself.

After about 20 more minutes of man-to-man combat, the offensive linemen joined the backs for team offense. Even though they were not going to scrimmage live today, they would be blocking full-force against a shielded scout team for the first time. All of the defensive linemen and linebackers would be wearing over-sized forearm pads; they would assume their normal defensive postures, would carry out their proper defensive techniques, but would stop short of tackling the running backs. The defensive backs wore no extra padding so their arms could be free to play the ball on any pass attempts. Basically, the action on the line was live; you just couldn't tackle the ball carrier. And once the running back got into the secondary, the defensive backs would just try to wrap up the ball carrier if they could get to him.

Instead of alternating plays between the red and white units, the red unit would run their plays first while the white unit ran scout defense. About half way through team offense, they would then switch.

The red offensive unit assumed their huddle positions while David Riley received the first offensive play from Coach Allen. David trotted nervously to the huddle, crouched to a kneeling position, and called out the first play. It was a 34 trap. The offense broke out of the huddle and ran to the line of scrimmage.

The quarterback began the cadence. "Blue 28... Blue 28... Set... Go!"

Daniels snapped the ball crisply into Riley's hands and joined Wilcox in a double-team block on the nose guard. Right tackle, Osborn blocked down on the linebacker. The unblocked play side tackle—Jimmy Smith—stepped across the line, licking his lips as he set his sights on the fullback who had just received the ball and was coming his way. All of a sudden—from out of nowhere—Pete O'Connor scraped behind the double team, his arms pumping and legs churning. A massive collision was inevitable.

Jimmy could not remember if he had gotten the wind knocked out of him from Pete's initial trap block or if it occurred after Pete landed on him. The only thoughts crossing his mind were, *Who am I? Why did I ever want to play football in the first place?* Desperately, the rookie defensive linemen gasped for his next breath as he rolled back and forth like a ship being tossed about on a violent sea. The pain that had begun in his midsection had now spread throughout his body.

After a tense minute or two, his breath returned, but his teammates were now jeering at him, aghast with delight. Suddenly, the wounded warrior felt Pete grab hold of his right hand, lifting him to his feet.

"It's okay, Jimmy. That happened to me at least once a day last season. Eventually, you'll learn how to read the trap, and then you'll be ready for me next time."

Pete rejoined his teammates in the offensive huddle, ignoring the adoration from his peers. What had been lost in the play was the route of Mike Owens carrying the ball down the field. Coach Allen hadn't missed the error, however.

"Mike, you run that play North and South, not East and West. That play hits right up the middle of the field. Don't try to break to the sideline as you get through the hole. You'll run right into the cornerback. Next time, run that ball straight up the gut."

As Riley got the next play from Coach Allen, Mike sneered to the rest of huddle, "I'd like to the see the corner bring me down."

"Shut up, sophomore," warned Pete.

The red offensive unit ran several more inside traps and halfback powers. For the most part, the plays were run correctly although there was a ton of room for improvement in the area of speed and proper blocking technique. The next play Coach Allen called was the quarterback keep.

As the offense broke from the huddle, Riley looked to his right. Roger Collins was the play side cornerback. Now was his chance to solidify his position at quarterback. On the third GO, Craig snapped the ball into David's hands. As he received the snap, he lifted his left foot, pivoting 90 degrees on his right foot. Owens sprinted by him, faking the inside trap. Riley brought his right foot around, his back facing the line of scrimmage. He thrust the ball into the abdomen of left halfback Bast, riding the fake for a full count. Next, he pulled the ball out from Bast just as two defenders were descending upon the halfback like vultures upon fresh road kill. David hid the ball behind his right hip and dashed around the right halfback's hook block on the outside linebacker. Out in front of him was the pulling guard. He could almost smell the end zone now.

Suddenly, from out of no where, Collins snuck behind the pulling guard, knocking David off his feet with a forceful two-hand shiver. The ball skipped away from Riley who was still lying on his back in a state of bewilderment. The pulling guard—Pete O'Connor— alertly dove on the ball, preventing a turnover. The defense was euphoric as Collins strutted back to the defensive huddle like the king of the jungle.

"You've got to get to that block, O'Connor," shouted Coach Allen. "Look to the inside as you pull around the end. It doesn't matter if the corner's cheating up or even if he's blitzing. You've got to get to him or our quarterback's dead. And Riley, you can't cough up the football like that. That's one lap around the field after practice. There's no excuse for turning over the football... EVER!"

David returned to the huddle with the next play. Same play. This time when David broke from the huddle, he stared straight ahead, not wanting to tip off the play to Collins—the extremely perceptive scout team cornerback who was also, coincidentally, the current backup quarterback. On the second GO, David received the snap, pivoted deep into the backfield, faked again to Bast, placed the ball on his hip, raced around the end, holding his breath, and...

Instead of seeing Roger darting across the line of scrimmage, David saw the back of Pete's shoulder pads. Hidden from Riley's view was Collins who was backpedaling so fast it looked like he must have been wearing roller skates. Pete drove him 15 yards and buried him a couple feet from the sideline. Riley brought the ball up under his arm pit and sprinted up the field 35 yards to the end zone, not a single defender in sight.

Pleased with Riley's recovery and curious about his young quarterback's ability to throw under pressure, Coach Allen decided to air it out on the next play. Once again, he chose to pick on his "favorite" cornerback: Roger Collins. The red offensive unit broke from the huddle, excited to run their first pass play of the day.

Riley took the snap, faked again to Bast and rolled out to his right, behind the pulling guard's block. Halfback Jeff Nash was covered deep, so he looked to the tight end Dan Hardings in the flats. Dan was sprinting to the sideline about four to five yards upfield with Roger chasing him, a step and a half behind.

David released the ball quickly, but the ball hung in the air, and Roger leaped in front of Dan, intercepting the football. When Riley came up to tackle him, Roger easily stiff-armed him and sprinted up field for an easy touchdown. Coach Allen whipped his hat to the ground in disgust.

"Riley, that's another lap after practice. We won't be able to throw the ball at all if you're going to throw floaters. My daughter could put more zip on the ball. Both receivers were covered—which means our faking was pathetic. But the run was wide open. Never force a pass into tight coverage like that, David. Turnovers change momentum. Momentum is difficult to obtain even harder to steal back."

Meanwhile, Roger was whooping it up. The entire defensive unit had surrounded him, fighting for their turn to high five him. He was really beginning to enjoy playing on the defensive side of the ball. The red unit finished their offensive series of plays with an inside trap. This time Owens ran the ball straight up the field, cutting perfectly off the end's downfield block on the safety.

After a quick water break, it was the white offensive unit's turn. Roger was given complete charge today. Coach Allen sent him to the huddle with the first play; a 36 inside trap.

"Let's go, white," encouraged Roger, "Concentrate on your assignment and don't forget the count... 36 trap on one... 36 trap on one... Ready... BREAK!"

The white team turned from the huddle and sprinted to the line of scrimmage. Roger approached the center, looking to his left and then to his right. When everyone was set, he put his hands under the center and barked out the command.

"Blue 18... Blue 18... Set... Go!"

Roger received the snap and pivoted to his right, placing the football into the mid-section of reserve fullback Tommy Schultz. Roger released the ball, faked to the right halfback and sprinted around the end, drawing the attention of cornerback with a perfectly executed fake.

The ear-piercing shrill of the whistle caused Roger to turn and look back, completely unaware of what had happened with the football. Tommy lay on the ground about a yard behind the line of scrimmage, cradled around the football.

"What happened with the handoff?" screamed Coach Allen.

Hustling back to the huddle, Roger interceded, "My fault, Coach. Poor handoff. Won't happen again."

A bit shocked by his backup quarterback's new sense of responsibility, Coach Allen calmly responded, "Okay, let's get it right next time. That's one lap after practice, Collins. And one for you, Schultz."

The white unit struggled through their running plays. The majority of the linemen were juniors, many playing their positions for the first time. The backfield was even less experienced and very timid with the football. On their eighth play of team offense, Schultz ran a beautiful trap, straight up the field. Once he slipped through the seam created between the tackle's down-block on the linebacker and the pulling guard's trap on the down lineman, there was a sea of green before him, and Tommy didn't hesitate to shift into high gear, outrunning Mike Owens who was pursuing him in vain from the backside cornerback position.

"Great execution, white offense." Looking over to the defense huddling around the ball, Coach Allen continued, "You see how Tommy ran that ball straight up the field, Owens? That's what I mean by North and South."

Sophomore Mike Owens, leaning over in the huddle with his hands on his knees, cursed Coach Allen under his breath.

The white unit had already consumed 20 minutes just to run eight plays. Most of the plays had been run twice as there was always at least one breakdown in the blocking scheme. Repetition was the primary method of instruction. If a play was not run to the approval of the coaching staff, the play would be repeated as many as 15 times in a row if needed. Coach Allen had scripted 15 plays for both units. The red unit had barely gotten through the script in their 25 minute segment of practice.

Wanting to test Roger's arm before the conclusion of team offense, Coach Allen called the 22 halfback power pass. With excitement pouring through his veins, Roger sprinted to the huddle to call the play. Approaching the line of scrimmage, Roger noticed Owens was the playside corner. Riley was at safety.

Placing his hands underneath center, he began the cadence. "White 44... White 44... Set... GO!"

Collins received the snap awkwardly, regained control of the ball, reverse-pivoted to his left, faked a handoff to the left halfback, and rolled out to his right. Unfortunately, the backside guard forgot to pull, so the outside linebacker was unblocked and charging upon him with a full head of steam.

Roger pump-faked a pass, causing the linebacker to slow his charge and lift up his arms to block the pass. Meanwhile, Collins ducked beneath him and headed towards the sideline. Both receivers were covered closely, so Roger put the ball under his arm pit and sprinted up field. 25 yards later Roger was run down by Mike Owens who pushed him out of bounds.

Coach Allen blew his whistle and ordered the white unit to lineup on the ball. Starting with the right end, he went over the assignment of each player, pausing when he got to the left guard.

"What do you do on this play, Mike?"

The junior guard answered, "Pull three steps to the right and lead up the two hole, Coach."

"Mike," responded Coach Allen with a touch of sarcasm in his voice, "did you happen to notice the word 'pass' immediately following the words '22 power'? It wasn't a run; it was a pass. Huge difference, don't you think? Instead of leading up the hole, you have to pull all the way down the line and seal off the edge. Otherwise, our quarterback is going to be ground beef! Furthermore, you are a lineman. Linemen can't go down field on pass plays.

"Roger, you made a smart decision to run the ball there."

Coach Abraham's voice suddenly took command. "Okay, players. After a water break we're going to defense. We'll start with position groups and then come together for a live tackling drill. Go ahead, get your water. Hustle!"

Each of the defensive groups went through their agility drills. The down linemen and linebackers reviewed gap responsibilities and stunts for the 5-2 while the defensive backs reviewed pass coverages. About 20 minutes elapsed, and then the entire Jaguar team gathered at midfield.

Coach Abraham blew his whistle. "Okay, this is one of my personal favorite hitting drills. It's called ICE BREAKER."

He pointed to four full-length dummies laying on the ground parallel to one another. There was about a two yard gap between each dummy:

DP

I I I I

RB

Coach Abraham continued, "It's really simple. On the whistle, the ball carrier runs through one of the gaps, and the defensive player shuffles down the line, reads the running back, and comes up to make the tackle. Make sure you use good tackling technique. Your head should be up, eyes on the ball carrier. Neck bulled. Feet shoulder width apart. Knees bent. Aim your shoulder pad at the ball carrier's waist. Rip your arms upward as you make the tackle. Lock your hands behind the running back. Pull his legs into you and drop him in his tracks. This is where we find out who the hitters are. Most of all, have fun. You don't get to do this type of thing your whole life, you know."

At the front of the tackling line was none other than Pete O'Connor. There was a bit of commotion in the running back line as no one was all too eager to be tackled by him. Mike Owens was near the back of the running back line.

Surveying the order of players in the running back line and irritated by the apparent lack of courage on the part of his backfield, Coach Allen quickly spoke up. "Hey, Owens. You like to run the ball, don't you? Why don't you go first? I'm sure you're not intimidated by varsity hitting, are you?"

Mike's face turned a few shades of red as he slipped his mouthpiece into his mouth and trotted to the front of the line. Grabbing the football tightly with both hands, he moved his right foot back and assumed a sprinter's stance, ready to accelerate from zero to 50 at the sound of the whistle. Cautiously, he looked into Pete's eyes, hoping to discover at least a slight trace of fear—or at the minimum—a hint of respect. Unfortunately, Pete was grinning at him, like he was a steak dinner.

The air became still. The only sounds Mike could hear were his beating heart and quickened breath. The whistle pierced the silence, and Mike stepped straight ahead towards the gap between the first two dummies. Pete shuffled to his right, completely zoned in on the sophomore running back.

Instead of plowing through the first gap, Mike dipped his inside shoulder and swiftly shifted his hips to the left, making a wide cut left, hoping to elude Pete with his speed and shiftiness. This move had paid huge dividends last year on the jayvees, usually leaving would-be-tacklers diving at Mike's ghost, with nothing but blades of grass in their fingers.

But as soon as Mike reached the third dummy, he could hear the pounding of footsteps, and by the time he rounded the fourth and final dummy, he felt his leg violently chopped out from beneath him.

The next thing he knew, his face was staring at thick, green turf, and the ball was pinned beneath him. Mike rolled over, on his back, gasping for his next breath.

Coach Abraham ran over to him and asked him if he was alright. Realizing that Mike had had the wind knocked out of him, he carefully grabbed hold of the top of his pants and lifted his hips up from the ground; nothing could alleviate Mike's pain or embarrassment, however.

Pete popped up from the ground, bright green grass stains on his practice pants, and jogged nonchalantly over to the ball carrier line. Even though he knew he had made a decent open-field tackle, he was disappointed that he hadn't hit his target a little higher. When you take out a running back's legs, they fall forward. But if you hit them at the waist or higher, you're able to lift them off the ground and propel them backwards, laying them out on their backs, resulting in serious negative yardage. And as a bonus, you get to land on them.

Next time around, he'll be laying on his back, staring at the clouds, vowed Pete.

After a few moments of anxiety amongst teammates and coaches, Mike regained his wind. Coach Abraham instructed him to get some water and rejoin the drill whenever he felt ready. The players in the tackling line were snickering as Mike hobbled gingerly to the water trough."

"Welcome to the varsity, Mike," jibed Craig Daniels, unable to resist the urge to comment.

Pretending not to hear, Mike continued across the field, choosing not to look back at the drill that had already resumed.

Next up were the heavies: Gary Osborn, 235 pounds, in the running back line; and super-heavy, Larry Moore, outweighing Gary by over 50 pounds, in the tackling line. As they lined up across from one another, it looked more like a Sumo wrestling match than a football drill. Nevertheless, they had the attention of the entire football team, minus one.

On the sound of the whistle, Gary chose the nearest gap—the one requiring the least amount of running, naturally—and tried to bowl over Larry. Nothing doing, the behemoth tackle had other ideas. Larry wrapped his mammoth arms around Gary, standing him straight up. The undersized running back attempted to keep his legs moving, but to no avail. Larry had him in his grasp like he was the last piece of chicken from the bucket. Suddenly, Gary became one with the earth as he was completely enveloped by his sweaty monster-sized teammate.

Gary made a mental note to try to outrun his adversary next time instead of running right into his clutches.

Several minutes passed, and there were a few solid, bone-crunching tackles, but most were forgettable or mediocre, at best. Tommy Schultz had just tackled David Riley, and it became immediately obvious to everyone that last year at this time, Tommy had been practicing his free throws and not playing football.

"Did someone hit the mute button?" inquired Coach Allen. "I must be losing my hearing or something. If you're going to hit like that, Schultz, you might as well leave your pads in the locker room."

Humiliated, Tommy disappeared to the back of the running back line, embarrassed by his first tackle of the season.

It was Pete's turn to run the ball next, and the next player in the tackling line was Roger Collins.

Perfect, thought Pete. *Prepare for blast off, Roger.*

He stared down Roger, and his heart was beating like tom toms.

I'm going to hit you so hard, you'll be peeing in your own pants.

His mind refocused.

Everyone's expecting me to plow right over him, but I've got something special planned.

On the whistle, Pete took three quick steps as if to sprint for an outside lane, but then he abruptly planted his left foot, and cut directly back into Roger. Nevertheless, Roger was not caught off-guard, as Pete had anticipated.

Bent down in a hitting position, legs poised and balanced, Roger uncoiled the hit of the century upon Pete.

CRACK went the sound of the pads. Shoulder pad on shoulder pad.

Pete was dead in his tracks; he dug his cleats in the ground and desperately tried to pump his legs, but he was moving no where. Roger's arms were locked around his waist, and he was trying with all his might to lift Pete and finish him off correctly.

Not wanting to surrender to defeat, Pete tried spinning out of the tackle.

Sensing that he wasn't going to put Pete on his back, Roger slid down to Pete's knees, wrapped both arms around his ankle and rolled him to the ground.

As Roger jumped to his feet, he pulled his facemask back around so he could see again. A stirring round of applause awaited him.

"Way to bring him down, Roger," shouted Coach Abraham, amidst a chorus of hooting and hollering.

Pete caught up to Roger, slapped him on the buttocks, and said, "Nice hit, Roger," and jogged to the back of the tackling line where he silently prayed for one more opportunity to collide with a teammate before Coach Abraham's whistle called an end to the "Drill of all Drills".

Nevertheless, disappointment came minutes later when Pete was next in line for tackling.

There will be plenty of opportunities to come, Pete reminded himself.

After a quick water break, the team assembled for special teams. Today's specialty was punting. The first couple of snaps were low as the centers were unaccustomed to snapping while wearing their bulky shoulder pads and helmet. But since they were not facing a live punt block opponent, they were able to get the punts off and were able to cover the punt with relative ease.

By this point in the week, Roger had clearly established himself as the number one punter on the team. All of his kicks sailed at least 35 yards downfield, and he mastered the trick of putting a spiral on the ball which was a lot more difficult to achieve off of your foot than with your fingertips.

After the red unit and white unit each had five punts, Coach Abraham blew his whistle. "Everyone on the goal line for sprints. Hustle, hustle, hustle. Spread out, and give yourself some room. A lot of you seem to be really huffing and puffing out here today. You're not used to carrying around the extra weight of your pads. We're almost done with our first week of practice. We've got a scrimmage next week and our first game is in two weeks. There is no time to lose. The time is right for pushing yourselves. You can't leave anything on this field. Do you hear me?"

"Yes, Sir!" responded the beleaguered Jaguar team, ready to put today's conditioning behind them.

Back and forth the 29 players trampled. The sun was now directly above them; sweat was pouring down their faces, stinging their eyes, adding to their misery. Their minds were fixed on two things: the count of the impending sprint and the fantasy that practice might be over sometime soon.

After they had completed their first set of ten 40 yard sprints, Coach Abraham gave them a very brief water break. He blew his whistle after exactly one minute, announced the next sprint would be on "two" while the last group of stragglers hurried to get back in their places as he started the cadence.

As they progressed through the second set of sprints, Roger Collins dropped further and further behind the pack.

Coach Allen—who was also under the influence of the high noon temperature—was the first to call attention to Roger's decline. "Collins, what are you doing back with all the beefers? Get your rear end up front where it belongs."

First one leg buckled, and then the other, as Roger dropped to his knees. He was only five yards from the finish line. Coach Abraham sprinted over to him and immediately called for the trainer. The trainer—a trainee from nearby Lakeland Community College—drove over on the golf cart.

Collins awkwardly stood up, and the trainer tried to get him to lie back down.

"I'm alright. I'm okay. I'm fine."

"Have a seat on the cart, so I can make sure. We can't take any chances in this kind of heat," said the trainer.

"You listen to the trainer, Roger," ordered Coach Abraham.

The trainer drove Roger over to the shade of the rarely appreciated oak tree as Coach Abraham rejoined the team for the completion of conditioning. Meanwhile, Coach Allen paced back and forth along the opposite sideline.

After removing Roger's helmet, the trainer grabbed a wet towel that had been soaking in an ice bucket, and placed it directly on the top of the weary player's head. Then he gave Roger a water bottle and instructed him to drink several sips of the cool water.

"You feeling better, kid?" asked the trainer.

"Yeah, I have a bit of a headache, though. I was starting to feel like I was going to pass out there for a minute."

"It's the heat. You've got to make sure you are drinking plenty of water before, during, and after you exercise on days like today. Keep that towel on your head. When they're done with sprints, you can walk over and rejoin them. But in the mean time, drink plenty of water."

After about five more minutes, conditioning was finally over. Coach Abraham called the team around him.

"Before you grab a knee, remove your helmets and shoulder pads."

After about a minute, the players were breathing normally again, their shirts were soaked, and their bare arms were glistening with perspiration.

"I think you can all see that we've got a lot of work to do, men. But we *are* making progress. Today we had some fun out here in the hitting drills, but believe it or not, the hitting in an actual game is going to be even more intense. If any of you got bumps and bruises, make sure you ice them. If you think you may have been injured, see the trainer immediately after practice. It got pretty hot out here again today. You have to make sure you're drinking plenty of fluids. If you feel yourself getting dizzy—at any time—don't try to be a hero; get some water and then get back in the drill as quickly as possible."

Coach Abraham stepped back, signaling to the rest of his staff to come forward to say a few words. Coach Allen stepped to the middle of the circle, removing his sweat-soaked hat from his head before beginning.

"I was really impressed with some of the hitting I saw out there today. Football is an extremely brutal game, involving collisions at top speed. It's important that you assume the role of the hitter and not the hittee. If you use the techniques we teach, and you go full-speed, you will find this game to be very enjoyable. Some of you are still way out of shape. We've got one more practice this week, and a full week of practice next week before the scrimmage on Friday. Then our first game is the following week. We do not have a lot of time on our side, fellas. Make sure you get refueled and rested up for tomorrow's practice. We need to build on what we accomplished today."

Coach Allen stepped out of the circle, and Coach Abraham looked over to the youngest member of the staff. "Coach Oliver, why don't you send them off?"

The rookie coach stepped into the circle, raised his fist, and said, "We're starting to look more and more like a team. Get your hands in here. The name of the game is football. On three, FOOTBALL."

The players were quick to respond, layering hand upon hand over Coach Oliver's fist.

"One...two...three... FOOTBALL!" shouted the Jaguars as their fourth official practice came to conclusion.

In groups of twos, threes, and fours, the team dispersed the sweltering practice field, relieved to be getting off the field before the mid-afternoon sun reached its peak level of intensity. One player stayed behind, however. Roger.

Alone. With no instructions from the coaching staff, and certainly without the approval of the trainer, Roger began running up and down the field. Forty yards at a time.

Coach Abraham—the last coach on the field—
noticed Roger's efforts and called out to him. "I'm
impressed by your determination, Roger. Just don't
overdo it, though."

Not sure of how many sprints he had missed, Roger
ran a total of twelve 40 yarders. All on his own volition.

Chapter Ten

As Coach Abraham walked off the practice field, he felt much
better about the progress of his football team. The first day of
hitting was always his favorite. There was one practice, however,
that was even more special: practice on Thanksgiving Day.
Unfortunately, Keith had only experienced two such practices over
the course of his twenty-five years of coaching.

Each year there would be eight teams privileged enough to
begin their Thanksgiving Day with a high intensity, high-spirited
pre-game practice, only then to be followed by their traditional
feasts at home. In fact, on such occasions, these proud teams would
be poised for the game of their lives to take place the next day.

There were four divisional championship games: Class D
Finals, facing off at 11:00 a.m.; Class C Finals, at 2:00; Class B
Finals, at 5:00; and Class A Finals, at 8:00—Class A being the
schools with the largest enrollment, and Class D the smallest.

Last season, the Juddville Jaguars played in the finals for the
second time in school history, winning the championship by a
decisive score of 21-0. The victory earned Juddville their first state
championship in any sport. Approximately 9,000 of Juddville's
12,874 citizens made the three hour trek across the state to cheer on
their Jaguars. The game was played on Astroturf in the gigantic,
state-of-the-art UFL Stadium of the New Haven Eagles.

The shining moment of Coach Abraham's career was holding
the Class B State Championship Trophy above his head. The
moment was beautifully captured in a full-size color photograph on
the front page of the Juddville Gazette. The victory had been the
culmination of years of studying countless volumes of football
books, of picking the brains of hundreds of successful high school
and college coaches, of analyzing thousands and thousands of hours
of video, and of opening up the weight room three days a week in
the off-season—even during the two weeks of Christmas Break.
Coaching football was a year round, full-time job; as a result, Coach

Abraham had very little energy left to devote to his part time job: teaching history.

As much as Coach Abraham wanted to savor the sweet taste of last year's state championship, the harsh reality was that last year's success was, indeed, ancient history. Some of the spoils that came with the championship trophy were the obnoxiously-large championship ring that he proudly wore on the ring finger of his right hand and, more significantly, the inevitable surge in notoriety amongst his coaching peers. In the off-season, dozens upon dozens of coaches had approached him, asking for advice in building a championship football program, pleading for any elite coaching tips for installing his 5-2 defensive package.

Yet, after 25 years of coaching, and witnessing the constant fluctuations in talent and commitment from year to year, Keith knew that the game was still played by teenage boys. Last season was a once-in-a-career season; Juddville virtually had no weaknesses; in fact, at many positions, they had players ready to come off the bench who would have started at any of the other schools in their conference. Furthermore, Coach Abraham's memory was still sharp enough to remember his humbling beginnings when he first took over the helm at Juddville, back when there were barely enough boys on the roster to conduct a practice.

In the game of football, you play 11 on 11; in order to simulate game conditions in practice, 22 players are required. There were a couple of seasons, early in Coach Abraham's reign, when he had only 20 to 21 players suited up. When those smaller teams hit the field on Friday night, to the unknowing fan or biased parent sitting up in the bleacher they might look like run of the mill football players, but to anyone who might have seen them report to the locker room in street clothes 60 minutes prior to kickoff, such players would never be branded as the coach's *meal ticket*. The painful reality of high school football was that high school coaches could not recruit, draft or trade players like in college or the UFL; nevertheless, they were still expected to maintain the community's winning tradition or else.

Even though most of the Juddville faithful wouldn't choose to bet their mortgages on Jaguars' chance of duplicating last year's unprecedented championship season, the expectations for them to qualify for the playoffs was a given. On the other hand, Coach Abraham knew there were a number of local skeptics already writing off their season as a rebuilding season, but Keith refused to be taken captive by their pessimism.

90

This year's team had loads of potential. Talent? Yes. Leadership? Not yet. Experience? No comment.

Therefore, the mission was crystal clear to Coach Abraham: simulate game-like conditions as often as possible while supplying ample motivation. At the same time, it was becoming increasingly apparent to him that the coaching staff must try—as much as possible—to refrain from expressing excessive criticism. There was a fine line between refining a player's technique and destroying his confidence, a fine line between building a team's intensity and crushing their spirit. Therefore, Keith would have to lean heavily upon his 25 years of experience to establish and protect that boundary. An equally difficult challenge would be to insure that his coaching staff abided by that line, particularly his offensive coordinator.

One of the most important lessons he had learned early in his coaching career was that negativity breeds more negativity. If you repeatedly tell a team how bad they are, in no time at all, you'll have them all convinced. The key to success in coaching has always been teaching the fundamentals within a positive environment. It would be most detrimental to this year's team for Coach Abraham to depart from this time-tested philosophy.

After meeting with his coaching staff from 1:15 to 2:30, Coach Abraham spent another hour completing Friday's practice plans. Before leaving for home, he had to return a call to Mike Owens, Sr. who had left a message earlier in the day. He decided to call him from the central office in the high school.

Not sure of what to expect, Coach Abraham punched in the numbers, hoping the conversation would be brief.

"Hello," answered an unfamiliar woman's voice.

"Hello. Is this Mrs. Owens?" asked Keith.

"No, this is Sarah. A friend of Mike's."

"This is Coach Abraham. Mike left a message for me to call."

"Oh, he's in the swimming pool talking to Mike, Jr. Just a minute, please."

Keith leaned back in the chair of one of the school secretary's and tried to relax. It was already going on 4:00. Sitting alone in the dark, unoccupied office—for what seemed like at least five minutes—Mr. Owens's voice finally broke through the silence.

"Hey, Coach Abraham. I wanted to talk to you about Mike. He came home from practice today pretty discouraged." After a brief pause, he continued, "I asked him how the team looked, and he just shrugged his shoulders and gave me one of those, 'Okay, I guess' responses. That's not like him, Coach. He used to love football. I know these aren't supposed to be the most enjoyable days of football. I still remember back when I was playing football at Central University. Three practices a day in the sweltering heat, no water breaks. Any ways, I know it's not supposed to be a birthday party, but a lot of people are saying Juddville will be lucky to win half their games this year. What I really want to know about is Coach Allen. Mike says he's always on his case."

Upon hearing the mere mention of the name of his comrade, Coach Abraham cut into the conversation. "Mr. Owens, I have complete confidence in all of my coaching staff. I think our success over the years speaks for itself. Mike's going to have learn that the varsity is going to be much more intense than jayvee football."

Interrupting Keith, with a sudden flare in his voice, "Let me remind you of one thing, Coach. There are a couple other schools in the area where Mike could play, you know. Yeah, I know he's only a sophomore, but it's never too early to begin thinking about college. If you aren't going to appreciate his talent, we may be forced to look around. You know as well as I do that Division I teams only look at players coming out of winning programs."

"Mike, calm down, would you, please. It's the first week of the season. Last year's state championship was an incredible experience, but it's not what we're all about, you know. There is so much more to be gained from football than trophies. I think in the next three years, you'll be glad that your boy was part of our program."

"Coach, that's all good and wonderful, but last season's championship is over and done with. And if you would have been thinking more about the future, you might have considered bringing Mike up for the playoffs last year to gain some experience for this season. I know he was only a freshman but..."

On and on, Mike, Sr. rambled. Coach Abraham felt the blood in his veins turn to ice as his heart grew so cold he doubted whether he would be able to breathe and to respond to his critic at the same time. Nine months ago, he was hoisting the ultimate trophy above his head, and now he was getting second-guessed by some arrogant, brainless loser. Keith looked at his watch.

4:30

Enough was enough.

One more time Coach Abraham cut in, "Mike, sorry I gotta go. I appreciate your feedback, but I can't talk anymore. I'll do my absolute best to help your son get a college scholarship when the time comes, but right now I've got 28 other players to look after, as well. We're trying to put the best people in each position while developing some unity and enthusiasm. It's pretty early to be casting predictions about the future of this team. Believe me, Mike, we're doing all we can. We'll come around, though. You'll see. In the mean time, tell your boy to hang in there. Nice talking to you, Mike."

Click.

"Uh..." stuttered Mr. Owens, not quite ready to end the conversation.

Keith Abraham was absolutely livid.

What a jerk! Division I prospect? Mike Owens? Not in a million years. He's got too much of his father in him.

When it comes to the athletic ability of their children, some parents have unbelievable imaginations. Mike Jr. had decent 40 yard dash speed as a sophomore, but if that was the only requirement to play college football, Coach Abraham would have produced dozens of NFL stars over the last two and a half decades.

After viewing a potential recruit on film, the first thing college recruiters would invariably ask is, "How is Johnny's character?" and then "What kind of grades does Johnny get?"

Mike Jr. had been ineligible during two weeks of the basketball season last winter—failing both English and Algebra. He had also come pretty close to being ineligible during his jayvee football season. His reputation for being lazy in the classroom also extended to the practice field.

The decision to bring Mike up to play on the varsity this season had not been unanimous. The first point Coach Allen always made about Mike was hard to ignore: Mike was the best running back in the program, jayvee or varsity. But the maturity level and off-season commitment of Mike was sub par. Yet another year on the jayvee might exacerbate the problem further. If the varsity talent level had not been so depleted, Mike's name would never have been considered for promotion to varsity. The bottom line was that if the Jaguars were to have any chance of being competitive this season, they would have to take a chance on Mike.

Overall, Mike had met the expectations of Coach Abraham up to this point. For sure, Keith was not using the same measuring stick he had used for his starting running backs the previous season. And to be fair, Mike could not do anything about the father fate had dealt him. Who knows? It might just end up working out in his favor. One day he might rise up out of bed and realize that if he was to follow in his father's foot steps, he would inevitably find himself reaching the same dead end. Surely, if anyone had witnessed the consequences of laziness and an inflated ego, it was Mike Sr.'s own son.

Prior to the aforementioned phone call, Mike had been the least of Coach Abraham's worries. He still had bigger worries at the position of quarterback. Who would be at the helm? Riley or was there still hope for Collins? He knew Jim had probably made up his mind, but Jim was prone to making hasty judgments. Nevertheless, Jim was the offensive coordinator, and Keith trusted his assistant implicitly. He would never question Jim's decision making, especially on personnel.

Coach Allen had been his partner now for 13 seasons. Each of those seasons, he was no doubt probably closer to Jim than to his wife Carol. Together, they had fought many battles, and what was so amazing was how many times Keith would know "word-for-word" what Jim was about to say. But aside from their close relationship, the reality was that there was not another offensive coordinator in the state that Coach Abraham would prefer over Coach Allen.

15 years ago Jim had been hired into the Juddville District to be the head jayvee football coach. At the time, Jim looked like he could play in the UFL. His fiery intensity was unmatched. In his first few seasons, Jim had lost control of his temper a few times, and his choice of language had landed him in trouble with a few mothers and administrators, but Jim had never laid a hand upon a player. To be sure, Jim had come a long way over the years.

Keith loved to remind his apprentice of his first football clinic as a member of the Juddville Staff. It was the annual state high school clinic held in a large Hilton Hotel in New Holland. There were a few notable college coaches and successful high school coaches speaking. The clinic began at 2:00 p.m. on Friday, yet the hotel's lounge was always jam-packed by noon.

For the most part, coaches from winning programs would be seated in the front rows of the conference hall taking notes on everything from blocking schemes, defensive back drills, to even building support in your community. Other coaches would be roaming through the vendors' exhibits in the adjacent, triple-sized conference room, where all the latest in football equipment and communication gadgetry were on display.

At 10:30 p.m., after the all the speakers had finished, the beer bash would commence. Nearly a thousand coaches would congregate throughout the large ball room, sharing stories, opinions, and vulgar jokes, while trying to avoid having beer spilt on them by yet another 275 pound line coach trying to carry five full cups of Budweiser in his pudgy hands.

Since this particular clinic had been Jim's first, he had followed the lead of Coach Abraham and the rest of the Juddville Staff—that is, until the beer bash began. A couple of the Juddville Coaches were enjoying a beer—but not Coach Abraham—so Jim migrated towards his comrades that were sharing the same thirst as him.

After consuming a couple drafts over the course of about an hour, Jim bumped into an old teammate from Warren College. They made their way immediately in the direction of the kegs, and Jim managed to double his intake of alcohol for the evening in about a half an hour's time.

At midnight, Coach Abrahams and his assistant Coach Olsen—who was in his early sixties—retired to their room for the evening, desiring to find refuge from the increasingly loud and belligerent atmosphere developing at the "social". Once the two varsity coaches were out of the picture, Jim finally began to cut loose.

The next morning at breakfast, Keith heard all about the exploits of Juddville's newest football coach. The bash ran out of beer at 1:00 a.m., so Jim and his buddy Russ moved on to the lounge where they could order a few stronger drinks. It seems that Jim and his friend had developed an affinity for Tequila back in their Warren College days. So with salt and lemon in hand, they proceeded to drain a half a dozed shots a piece.

At about 9:30 the next morning, Jim woke up in his friend's room on the bathroom floor, snuggled around the toilet. Jim had, in fact, made several offerings to the Porcelain Goddess in the wee hours of the morning. As he staggered to his feet, he thought someone must have sunk a hatchet three inches deep into the center of his forehead. Jim caught up to the rest of the Juddville staff in the conference room at about 10:15.

Although Jim tried to pretend otherwise, it became quite obvious to the rest of his colleagues that he was nursing one severe hangover. At the luncheon, Russ came over and sat down in a vacant seat next to Jim and the rest of the Juddville staff. Much to Jim's dismay, his old buddy proceeded to retell the highlights of Jim's exploits the previous evening. Coach Abraham wasn't sure if the red tint in Coach Allen's face was more from the previous night's over consumption of alcohol or from embarrassment.

Such was the first official coaching clinic of Jim Allen. For awhile, Coach Abraham had been more than a little concerned about Jim's drinking habits, but it seemed that over the years, Jim had begun to mellow in that regard. At last year's clinic, Jim had only consumed one token beer before retiring to their room at 11:30.

But last year's clinic was truly special. For one, every coach in the state had wanted to congratulate them. As the reigning Class B State Champions, Coach Abraham and Coach Allen were as close as they would ever be to achieving celebrity-like status. It was difficult not to get taken in by all the compliments offered up from literally hundreds of their coaching peers from around the state. Pride swelled up inside Jim's chest as he swaggered around the clinic wearing his Juddville State Champion sweatshirt. So by the time 11:30 came around, they were exhausted from all the attention and just wanted to go back to the room, order a pizza, and perhaps, find a basketball game to watch on television.

Another reason last year's clinic would be forever etched in Coach Abraham's memory was because one of the most bizarre incidents he had ever witnessed occurred on the drive home. Whenever Keith retold the story, he got tears in his eyes.

In favorable weather, Juddville was approximately a 90 minute drive. The jayvee coaching staff was packed in the back seats of Coach Abraham's van, and Keith and Jim were sitting in the front, conversing about personnel for the upcoming season.

All of a sudden, Jim spied a pen on the dashboard. It was some type of novelty pen. Nonchalantly, he picked up the pen and removed the cap. Then Jim proceeded to unleash from his left nostril the largest, crustiest booger ever unearthed by man. Keith was speechless, uncertain how to respond to such an act of immaturity.

Seemingly disappointed by the lack of response from his travel mates, Jim delicately placed the booger into the cap of the pen before restoring the cap back upon the most unfortunate pen. The jayvee staff in back didn't know whether to gasp in horror or laugh aloud in approval.

Next, Jim held the pen up to his ear and shook it as if he might be able to hear it rattle. Proud of his work thus far, he set the pen back on the dash and eyed his companions who were all in awe of his handiwork.

That was when things became really scary. The groans from the other coaches had dissipated and their attention had drifted elsewhere. Alone in his thoughts, Jim was just sitting there in the passenger seat, staring at the pen on the dash. Meanwhile the gears within his mind began to really kick into action. An idea popped into Jim's mind that was so bizarre and so original that there was no doubt in his mind that not one of the billions of human beings that had ever populated Earth could possibly have ever conceived of it.

Embracing his destiny with a sense of boldness and cool confidence, Jim reached out with his left hand and pushed in the cigarette lighter. After about ten quick seconds, he removed the cap from the pen—holding the cap upwards in his right hand—and reached over with his left hand to pull the lighter out of its housing. The next move was one for the history books.

Jim slowly brought the cap directly above the lighter—its coil already bright orange—and tipped the cap upside down, gently tapping the top of the cap with his index finger, coaxing the behemoth booger out of hiding, as it gave way to gravity and rolled from its temporary lodging into the burning belly of the lighter.

The booger sizzled slowly before becoming violently engulfed into a cloud of greenish-gray smoke. Within seconds, the front seat of the minivan was filled with the booger's pungent aroma.

Meanwhile, Coach Abraham had to pull the car off the road. The minivan was actually shaking because of the intensity of everyone's laughter. Jim couldn't wipe the tears from his eyes quickly enough. The younger jayvee coaches' mouths hung wide open in amazement until the cloud proceeded to drift towards the back of the vehicle. Their cheers were replaced by jeers as they quickly covered their mouths, gagging from a scent most fowl and unimaginable.

Keith was trying to simultaneously roll down the window and bury his face in the crook of his arm. He was laughing so hard; his chest was caving in and out, and his ribs were beginning to cramp. He was fairly certain that he had never laughed nor cried so hard in his four decades of life.

Coach Abraham was grateful for the temporary comic relief of this memory that Jim had provided him on this simmering August afternoon. It had been another long day and he was glad he could trade the time-consuming hassles of head coaching for the comforts of home. He was looking forward to a relaxing evening at home with his family. His youngest daughter Julia was leaving for college this weekend, so tonight they were planning to take her out for dinner at her favorite Italian restaurant.

97

Chapter Eleven

Pete was feeling pretty good; it was already Thursday afternoon. What a practice! Man, did he love to hit. So far, he was pretty happy with his progress at offensive guard, and he was beginning to believe there was hope for his teammates. Considering where they had started on Monday morning, the coaching staff had brought them a considerable distance.

He would never have dreamed he would be lining up as guard. Granted, the position was not the same adrenaline rush as receiving a handoff and dashing around, through or over the onslaught of eleven blood-thirsty defensive players. But there was a special satisfaction gained from providing a running lane for your dependent teammates. Another bonus was that as a lineman one could expect physical contact each and every play; whereas in the backfield, you were often required to carry out a fake or run a pass route where there would be no contact whatsoever. Often times, the whistle would blow the play dead, and the running back would return to the huddle having neither touched the ball nor the opponent. Linemen were afforded no such luxury.

As a result, there was a distinct "blue collar" mentality that went along with playing on the line. Gone, for sure, was all the glory of playing running back, but in its place was a promotion into the *Battle in the Trenches.* At the end of every play—be it touchdown, short gain or turnover—the blocker and blockee would retreat to their respective huddles, and one would know he was the victor while the other would know that on that particular play, his opponent had gotten the better of him. Pete was intent upon becoming a dominant force in the trenches—one who would never fail to earn the distinction of "victor"—and he was willing to pay whatever price was demanded.

After a quick bite to eat and a cat nap, Pete had to work at the Pancake House from 4:00 p.m. to 10:00 p.m. Until school began, he had consented to continue working one weeknight—Thursdays—in addition, to his regular 11:00 to 7:00 a.m. graveyard shift on Saturday nights. During the months of June and July, he averaged 40 hours a week, washing dishes and busing tables whenever he was needed. Pete had hoped to save as much as he could to buy a car and to be able to insure it for at least six months in advance.

Some kids his age would most certainly complain that all the late nights at work would cut into their social lives. But Pete needed the money. Nevertheless, he would occasionally join his buddies at the parties and local "hot spots". Because of Pete's steady summer income, he always had spending money; besides, if he didn't work, he would be too broke to have any fun.

As a result, on Saturday nights, he would hang out with friends for a couple of hours before reporting to the Pancake House. On Friday nights and Sunday nights, however, he was free. Sometimes, they would catch a late movie, or if they were looking for girls, they'd hang out at a party. Even though Pete refused to drink during training—which was basically year-round—his friends didn't seem to mind. If his friends had too much to drink, they always had a designated driver in Pete—a role he never minded filling.

Right now, Pete didn't have his eyes on any specific girl, but that didn't mean his eyes weren't open. During the season, he tried to avoid any serious relationship with the opposite sex; there simply wasn't enough time to devote to a girlfriend. Yet, it was during football season that the majority of girls seemed to swoon towards the elite status of the Juddville Jaguar Football Team, and they were often times willing to offer whatever services necessary to gain their affection.

Pete's looks would not be described as "Hollywood", but he was more attractive than most, and what set him apart from the rest of his peers was his physique; he possessed more muscle mass than most college-aged men. At more than a few parties, his physique had captured the eyes of some mildly-intoxicated girl. On most occasions, he had chosen to ignore their aggressive advances.

From the lion's share of locker room chatter, it seemed that the only thing most guys wanted from their girlfriends was sex. Apparently, the majority were not being left empty-handed either. But what about love? It seemed to Pete that if there wasn't going to be love, the relationship was pointless. Like playing football without keeping score. Why bother? Besides, there were way too many potential negative consequences with fooling around: diseases, unwanted pregnancies, and etc.

For a while, Pete thought he was in love with Melanie. But she had clearly had something different in mind. The first time he found out that she was cheating on him, he forgave her. He could still vividly remember how she had managed to manufacture one tear after another as she begged for his forgiveness.

"I didn't know what I was doing, Pete. I was drunk," she repeated over and over.

According to his trustworthy friends who had been at the party where her indiscretion occurred, she had only gotten as far as kissing the impostor. If she had gone any further, there was no way Pete would have forgiven her, nor her partner, for that matter.

What was most painful, however, was that at the time, Melanie had been Pete's closest friend. She knew many of his secrets—they had dated for nearly nine months. Because Pete was accustomed to forgiving those whom had wronged him, he gave her a second chance.

When word got back to him that Melanie had cheated on him a second time, he nearly went ballistic. His torn heart gave birth to a depth of anger so potent that it required every ounce of Pete's self-control to restrain it. It was like trying to run down a steep, slippery hill while carrying a vial of nitroglycerin. Naturally, he refused to speak to her again.

His phone call was brief: "Melanie, this is Pete. We're finished."

Click.

She tried to call him back, but he hung up on her. When she continued to call, he just took the phone off the hook. Pete had given her a second chance. There were no third chances in Pete's playbook.

Over the next few months, Pete's training was fueled by the unfaithful acts of Melanie. As a result, his bench press jumped from 245 to 280, and his squat increased 100 pounds to a max of 475.

Each time he approached the loaded barbell for the heaviest set of the workout, all he had to do was close his eyes and picture Melanie. His whole body would begin to quake like he was the Incredible Hulk. His heart vigorously pumped out rage to each cell of his body as he pushed himself to unprecedented levels of sheer power and strength. The other lifters in the gym would stop right in the middle of their sets to observe Pete's latest frenzy.

Pete had been a free man for six months now, and he still refused to talk to Melanie. It wasn't that he was afraid he would fall back in love with her; no, it was the fear that he might lose his mental edge, which had first manifested itself in the weight room and was now on tap at the local football field. In fact, as far as Pete was concerned, Melanie could go right ahead and sleep with every guy on the team, and it wouldn't bother him; it would just provide him with all the more fuel for battle.

As he pedaled his beat-up bicycle into the parking lot of The Pancake House, he had already worked up quite an appetite. Maybe, he would have one of the cooks grill him up a quick cheeseburger before the dinner rush began at 5:30. One of the fringe benefits of working at a restaurant was free food and drink. He could eat whatever he wanted, whenever he wanted—as long as it wasn't in front of the customers. On most nights, he would consume close to a gallon of milk.

Entering the restaurant from the back door, he punched in and immediately reported to the kitchen where he put in an order for a cheeseburger with fries. Then he walked out into the restaurant to see how many tables needed to be bused.

Thursdays were generally a pretty slow week night. Pete had no trouble keeping up with the tables and washing the dishes in the back. At about 8:00, he began his cleaning duties: bathrooms, sweeping and mopping floors, emptying the garbage, and etc.

Before punching out at 10:00, he devoured a three-egg ham and cheese omelet. Exhausted, he avoided the temptation to hang around the restaurant and flirt with the waitresses. Instead, he pedaled his bike home at a brisk pace.

When Pete got home, he found a note on the kitchen counter from his mother.

Pete,
    I have to work late again tonight. I am a sucker for overtime. Can we have lunch tomorrow after practice? I miss you.
                                        Love,
                                        Mom

Opening the refrigerator, Pete grabbed the half-gallon of Neapolitan ice cream and then a spoon from the silverware drawer. He sat down at the table and proceeded to shovel multiple mouthfuls of ice cream into his mouth, barely taking the time to savor the sweet blend of chocolate, vanilla, and strawberry. After consuming nearly half of the box, he returned the ice cream to the freezer, brushed his teeth, set his alarm clock for 6:45, and instantaneously collapsed upon his pillow.

During the night, he dreamed deep dreams. At first, he was at football practice, and the first two times the offense broke from the huddle, he ran up to the line of scrimmage thinking the play was on *one*, but the rest of the offensive unit was waiting in their stances expecting the play to be on *two*. But instead of getting yelled at, the coaches said, "It's okay, Pete. Don't worry about it.   You'll get it right next time. We know you're trying your best."

Then when he would get back in the huddle, his teammates were sneering at him. "What's the matter, Pete? Afraid you're going to get knocked flat on your ass?" asked Roger Collins, who was the starting quarterback again.

Mike Owens added, "Hey, Pete. Too rough for you up on the line?"

Then Roger added one more insult. "Hey, Mike. How far around the team do you think Melanie will get by the end of the season? I had my turn last night."

After about five seconds had elapsed, Pete was unable to restrain himself from kicking the crap out of Roger. He jumped on him and started pummeling him in the midsection with one punch after another. Coach Allen pulled him off Roger before Pete had thoroughly beaten the snot out of him.

Coach Abraham blew his whistle. With cold, accusatory eyes, he said, "Get off this field, Peter. You don't belong on this team. You're a loser, just like your father. We know all about him. We know why he's in prison. We don't want you on this team anymore."

As Pete walked off the field, his head hanging down in shame, all of a sudden Melanie appeared. She meandered up to him, put her arm seductively around his neck, and whispered, "You know what? Roger was better!"

Then she broke free from him, laughing hysterically before skipping over to the team that had already resumed practicing as if nothing had happened.

The dream shifted to the Pancake House where Pete was in the back washing dishes. The manager's voice abruptly blared over the intercom, "Pete, could you come to the front, please. Your father is here to see you. And could you bring a tray of water glasses with you, too."

My dad? He's here?

Pete grabbed the steaming tray of glasses that had just come out of the dishwasher and backed himself through the swinging door into the dining area. Walking through the waitress station, he observed that all the waitresses were staring at him. Then they started to point at him, bursting out in laughter.

Completely clueless as to the reason for their laughter, Pete pressed onward, looking desperately from table to table for his father. When he got to the hostess station, the manager—who was ringing up an order on the cash register—pointed downward to Pete's lower extremities and bursted out, "Pete, you're butt naked!"

When Pete looked down, he suddenly realized that from the waist down, he was naked, indeed. He lowered the tray of glasses to cover up his privates and ran to the back of the restaurant. Lying on the rubber matting in front of the dishwasher, he found his work pants. He frantically tried to pull them back on, but for some reason, his left pant leg was caught on his shoe. No matter how hard he yanked or twisted, his pant leg just wouldn't come up.

I've got to hurry or I'll miss my dad.

Tears welled up in his eyes as his heart beat uncontrollably.

Pete's room was pitch dark when his mother came in and shook him firmly by the shoulders.

"Peter, Peter. Your alarm is going off. Don't you have to get up for practice?"

When he opened his eyes to the look at the alarm clock, he noticed that it was already 6:45.

"I'm sorry, Mom," pausing to be make sure of his whereabouts, "I was having a terrible nightmare."

"Are you okay, honey?"

After taking a few moments to consider, Pete responded, "Now I am. But I better get moving."

"Did you see my note about lunch, Pete?"

"Yeah, that'll be fine. Thanks for waking me up."

When Pete got out of the shower, he was fully awakened and primed for football. He gulped down a large glass of orange juice and grabbed a banana for the road. In order to get to the locker room by 7:30, he had to walk at a quicker pace. He wanted to make sure that he had plenty of time to get his football pants on and get his football equipment all together.

Usually, Pete was the first one in the locker room, but today Adam Foster—the transfer from Billington—was just a few minutes ahead of him.

"Hey, Adam," said Pete, as he entered the musty smelling locker room.

Adam looked up at Pete, and looked away.

Pete spun the dial of his lock back and forth until it popped open.

"How do you like Juddville Football so far?"

"Okay," mumbled Adam.

"I know you're probably not too impressed with our team right now, but we've got excellent coaches. It's just a matter of time, and they'll have us ready to kick some butt. You'll see."

Pete waited for Adam to speak, but there was no response. He searched his mind for something else to say. "How good is Billington this year?"

"A lot better than this team."

Startled by boastful tone in Adam's voice, Pete retorted, "We'll see."

Adam began to pull on his grass-stained football pants as several juniors entered the locker room.

Pete was relieved to finally be in the company of a few teammates that had a personality and had Jaguar-blue blood running through their veins.

"Hey, Pete. You think we'll get to scrimmage today?" asked David Riley.

"It's hard to tell. Maybe, for a few plays at the end of team offense," replied Pete. "You're looking pretty good out there at quarterback, David. Keep it up, and you'll have a starting position in the bag."

"I hope so, I hope so."

The next group of players to enter the locker room was led by Roger Collins.

Dan Hardings—one of Roger's shadows—stopped at his locker next to Pete and blurted out for the entire team to hear, "Hey, Roger, the party's starting at 8:00. I'll pick you up about 7:00, so we can cruise around for awhile beforehand."

Roger looked over at Pete, a mild look of embarrassment on his face, and then responded, "You go ahead, Dan. I'm not sure I can go yet. Don't wait for me. If I can get out, I'll just meet you there."

Pete glared at Roger.

"What's up, Pete?" asked Roger.

"Football. What else is there?"

"Right."

"How you feeling today? Still seeing stars from our big collision?"

"I was a little dizzy last night, but I feel okay this morning. How about you?"

"I'm fine. It'd take a lot more than that to take me out. Not a bad hit for a quarterback, though."

"Well, from the looks of things, I don't think I'll be playing much quarterback."

Pete wanted to suggest that Roger find a new crowd to hang out with, but he didn't want to go too far. Even though Pete couldn't stand Roger, and even though there was a certain debt that he was still waiting to repay, he knew that in the best interests of the team, it was essential that he do his part to keep the peace with his teammates. You just can't go into battle with sworn enemies in your own huddle. No doubt about it, Roger was a spoiled punk who had everything money could buy, and he was the epitome of a "pretty boy". Yet Roger had stood up to him on the field yesterday. There weren't too many of his teammates willing to go toe-to-toe with him; that had earned him Pete's partial respect, for the time being anyway.

As for the practice pants, Roger was still Pete's number one suspect, but he was beginning to wonder if the culprit was someone else. Consequently, he was in no hurry to administer justice. Instead, Pete was content to wait until he was absolutely certain of the criminal's identity; in the meantime, he would pretend like nothing had happened, and perhaps, let the perpetrator sweat it out a bit.

After a brief thirty minute team meeting, the Jaguars hit the field at about 8:30, giving them about 15 minutes to work on specialty skills—snapping, punting, kicking, receiving skills, and etc. Coach Abraham blew his whistle at 8:45, and the 29 Juddville Jaguars ran for the tree with a renewed vigor and enthusiasm, for they could almost taste the conclusion of the first week of training camp.

Calisthenics and form running went quickly and smoothly. Group offense was shortened to 30 minutes. Most of the time was spent blocking dummies. The last ten minutes were spent putting in two new plays: the quarterback bootleg and the wingback counter.

At exactly 9:30, Coach Abraham called the team together for team offense.

"Men, we're going to start out with the first offense. If things go well, we'll toss the hand dummies off the field and go live for about 10 plays." His voice rising over the exuberant hoots and howls of his players, he took the scout defense aside.

"We want a good look from you today. Play tough on the line of scrimmage and try to get to the ball carrier and wrap him up. Now is the perfect time to show us if you can play defense or not."

Calling back to other side of the line of scrimmage, Keith added, "Coach Allen, we'll stay in a 5-2 today, but we may stunt an occasional linebacker, so you linemen better be ready."

"All right, offense," barked Coach Allen, "Let's look sharp today. Show me what you've learned this week."

The offense formed a tight huddle around center Craig Daniels.

Coach Allen called the first play.

"34 trap. Make sure we make a good fake to the halfback."

Inside the huddle, David Riley knelt down on his right knee and called the play. Breaking from the huddle, the offense rushed eagerly to the line of scrimmage.

Riley began the cadence. "Blue, 28... Blue, 28... Set... Go!"

Daniels snapped the ball crisply into Riley's hands; David pivoted 180 degrees on his right foot as Pete pulled to his right. David placed the ball firmly into the arms of Owens. Pete smashed into the defensive tackle's mid-section, driving him backwards three yards while Mike Owens sprinted through the gaping hole. Riley pivoted another 45 degrees and placed his empty hands into the bread basket of Rob Bast. Rob's arms clasped around the imaginary football and sprinted up field. David pulled out his hands and put them on his right hip as he took off for the sideline. The inexperienced outside linebacker bit on David's fake, dashing foolishly after him. Roger Collins was also deceived, converging on the quarterback and shoving him with two hands after realizing he didn't have possession of the ball.

Coach Allen blew his whistle. "Outstanding faking out there, David and Rob." Mike Owens all alone with the football, 35 yards down field, turned back to the original line of scrimmage, waiting for his portion of deserved praise. But when he returned to the huddle all he heard was Coach Allen commenting on Pete's block.

"That hole was so huge; a UPS van could drive through it."

Riley returned to Coach Allen and received the next play: 11 QB Keep. Again the offense sprinted to the line of scrimmage.

"Blue, 22... Blue, 22... Set... Go!" As soon as the ball was snapped, junior nose tackle Greg McDonald drove out from his stance, forcing his hand dummy underneath the center's pad, knocking him a step into the backfield. Pete—who was pulling to his right—bumped into Daniels. And David, pivoting to his left, bumped into both of them. He tried to regain his footing while maintaining control of the football, but the ball squirted loose. Pete and David simultaneously smothered the football before a defensive player could recover it.

"Run the play again from the line of scrimmage," instructed Coach Allen. "Daniels, you've got to hold your ground. You can't get pushed backwards like that. We want to play the game in their backyard, not in our own."

The offense reassumed their positions at the line, and David started the cadence again.

"Blue, 28... Blue, 28... Set... Go."

This time Daniels snapped the ball a half a second sooner and fired out of his stance in just enough time to obtain leverage

106

beneath the nose tackle's pads. Pete pulled behind the center, running in a crouched position behind the right side of their offensive formation. As he scraped around the right halfback's hook block on the outside linebacker, his eyes were searching to and fro for a defensive back to pulverize. Meanwhile, Riley had faked to Owens, faked to Bast, and was sneaking around the edge with the ball on his hip.

Pete found the corner—moreover, Roger found him—and was immediately in his facemask. Unable to block Roger to the inside, Pete tried to drive him towards the sideline. He managed to budge him a step or two before Roger submarined him, creating a pileup and very narrow running lane for David to cut up through.

David transferred the ball from his hip into the more secure area of his right arm pit, dipping his shoulder as he planted his right foot, cutting sharp left into the hole. David gained about three yards before the backside safety was all over him, wrapping his arms up high around David's shoulder pads as Coach Allen blew the whistle.

"Freeze. Everybody freeze."

Twenty-nine pairs of eyes scoured the field, paranoid of the possibility that their blunder was about to exposed.

Coach Allen's voice broke through the momentary silence with a pitch capable of piercing glass.

"Owens… look who finished that tackle! Guess who? That's right. The safety. From all the way across the field. Now look where you are, Mike. About three yards up field. You're supposed to carry out your fake a minimum of 30 yards. I don't think the safety ever looked at you. If you carry out your fake, the safety will at least have to acknowledge you, and that gives us enough time to spring the quarterback around the end. How many times do I have to tell you? You've got to run the same way when you're faking as you do when you actually have the ball."

The red offense ran 10 more plays against the dummies, and then they did a walk through with the 22 and 48 counter. Coach Allen was hesitant to run the counter play "live" on the same day it was introduced because it involved a lot of misdirection in the backfield, so it required a significant amount of repetition to get the timing down correctly. Until all eleven players are going to the right place at exactly the right time, there can be some nasty collisions: backs running into backs, guards pulling into fullbacks, and etc.

Finally, Coach Abraham blew his whistle. With much anticipation, the Jaguars awaited his next command.

"All right fellas, get rid of the dummies."

Immediately, seven dummies flew in the direction of the sideline. At the same time, there was a noticeable surge in intensity in both the offensive and defensive huddles.

"Let's open us some holes, now," shouted Pete, in a state of extreme euphoria. "This is what we've been busting our butts for."

David reported to the offensive huddle with the next play. "Let's break this one for a touchdown, guys. 36 trap, on one."

Pete interrupted, "Let's go on two, David. I guarantee will catch at least one d-lineman jump."

"Okay, 36 trap on two. 36 trap on two. Ready... Break!"

The Juddville Jaguar offense assumed their positions at the line, poised to run their first "live" play of the season.

"Red, 19... Red, 19... Set... Go..."

The nose tackle—as predicted by Pete—jumped across the line of scrimmage, and the entire offensive line snickered. Coach Abraham blew his whistle and shouted, "McDonald, why are you moving? You respond only to the movement of the ball, not the cadence. That's one lap after practice."

The offense rehuddled and David called the same play. Again, it was on two.

Riley crouched beneath the center and began the cadence. "White, 22... White, 22... Set... Go... Go."

Taking the snap from the center, David pivoted on his left foot and handed the ball off to Owens. Right guard, Steven Wilcox, pulled to his left, and collided with the left offensive tackle Joey Miller who was clogging up the hole, unable to get through to the near side linebacker.

Owens—unable to see any daylight inside—juked to his left and tried to break it to the outside, but the outside linebacker was there to meet him, and wrapped him up high while the corner hit him low, taking his feet out from beneath him, forcing his facemask into a lush sea of green.

Mike hobbled back to the huddle, pulling fresh sod from his face mask. "Come on, line... how about blocking someone?"

"Shut up, sophomore," retorted Pete. The other offensive players in the huddle looked at Pete and then at Mike. The only sound was heavy breathing.

Coach Allen broke the silence. "Joey, you've got to step quickly with your inside foot or you'll never get to the linebacker. If you don't get to him the play won't go. You've got to get off on the count. That is supposed to be the offense's advantage. You're too slow out of your stance."

Not quite finished yet with his critique of the play, Coach Allen added, "And Michael, you lost three yards trying to break it outside. Granted... there wasn't much of a hole inside, but we'll take a one yard gain over a negative three, any time. Second down and nine leaves us with a lot better options than second and thirteen."

Coach Allen sent David off with the next play. "22 power, on set. 22 halfback power, on set. Ready, break." Pete hustled to the line of scrimmage, eagerly anticipating his next collision.

"White, 48... White, 48... Set!"

Daniels snapped the ball crisply into David's hands.

Pete stepped to his right.

David reverse-pivoted to his left, faking a handoff to Mike.

Pete took a cross-over step with his left. And another step with his right foot and then planted with the same foot before cutting 90 degrees upfield.

David handed the ball off to Rob Bast.

Pete dipped his left shoulder and cut up the two hole, scraping the double-team block on the defensive tackle. He could hear the hoof beats of the running back directly behind him.

Pete's eyes zoomed in on the backside linebacker who had read the play and was in hot pursuit of Rob. Unfortunately, the young linebacker neglected to see if anyone else was coming. Pete crouched low and exploded into the unseasoned linebacker, driving his hands under the would-be tackler's shoulder pads and propelling him flat on his back.

Meanwhile, Rob sped past the disabled defender and cut back into the center of the field, setting up the backside end's block on the safety. Rob continued up field for another 20 yards until he heard Coach Allen's whistle. Trailing ten yards behind Rob was Mike Owens, who was carrying out his fake.

"Great job, offense. That's the way it should look every time," shouted Coach Allen, trying to keep his praise in check.

Pete grabbed the hand of the fallen linebacker, helping him up on his feet before sprinting back to the huddle.

Now this is football, Pete thought to himself.

Coach Allen decided to air it out the next play, and he called a 22 halfback power pass. David wiped the perspiration from his hands onto his practice pants. The sun was already beginning to reach its peak, and the young quarterback felt that all eyes would be on him this play. He nervously called the play in the huddle; the butterflies in his stomach were impossible to ignore.

"Dan, be looking right away," said David as they broke to the line of scrimmage.

Daniels snapped the ball on one, and David reversed-pivoted to his left, faked to Owens, turned another 90 degrees and faked to Bast who stutter-stepped—exaggerated his fake—before attacking the blitzing outside linebacker. David put the ball on his hip and rolled to his right. Pete was pulling on the play and had inside position on the outside rushing linebacker. Pete broke down into a pass blocking stance and hooked his man, pushing him—with some assistance from left halfback Bast—all the way into the center of the trenches.

David was all alone, sprinting out towards the right flats. He waited for Hardings to release into the wide-open banana route. Meanwhile, right halfback Jeff Nash was streaking past the safety—who had badly bit on the outstanding fake of Bast. Nash had ten yards on the safety. Nevertheless, David threw off his right foot, and the ball flew with a tight spiral, hitting Dan Hardings between the numbers.

Dan caught the ball and was about to turn upfield. Safety, Adam Foster, whose man had just burned him deep, had read David's eyes. Instead of trying to catch up to the halfback behind him, Foster gambled on the quarterback throwing to the shorter route. Luck was on his side this time, and just as Hardings turned upfield, Adam plastered him up high, putting his helmet directly on the ball, jarring the ball out of the surprised receiver's hands. Hardings fell to the ground and rolled back and forth, wincing in pain.

Oblivious to his teammate's pain, Adam picked up the ball, holding it above his head like it was the Stanley Cup Trophy. Then he skipped back to the huddle, handed it off to the nose tackle who placed the ball on the 40 yard line. The rest of the defense was giving high fives to the Billington transfer, congratulating him for delivering such a humongous hit. Coach Abraham ran over to Hardings to see if he was okay. Coach Allen took his inexperienced quarterback aside.

"David, didn't you see Jeff wide open downfield? It was a guaranteed touchdown. You made a hero out of Foster instead of a goat. I want you to throw the high percentage pass to the short receiver most of the time, but when the deep receiver is so wide open, we've got to take advantage of their blunder and go long. It doesn't even need to be a perfect pass; all you have to do is get the ball to him so he can catch it."

"Okay, Coach. I'll get it to him next time."

Dan Hardings was on his feet and being helped to the sideline by the trainer. Coach Abraham took Adam Foster aside.

"You know you got lucky on that one, son. Most of the time a quarterback will throw deep and take advantage of the wide-open receiver. Don't forget to read your keys. The right halfback released downfield immediately. If you're taking your read steps, thinking 'Pass, Pass, Run', you should have been able to identify that he wasn't coming to block you. He was looking to burn you deep. And if the quarterback would have thrown it to him, that's exactly what would have happened."

Instead of looking into Coach Abraham's eyes, Foster was staring over at the offense, who were still in the huddle.

"Did you hear what I said, Adam?" asked Coach Abraham, growing a bit perturbed by the lack of response from his safety.

Still looking away, Adam put his mouthpiece back into his mouth and mumbled a barely discernible, "Sure, Coach."

Coach Abraham retreated to his spot about 15 yards behind the defense, increasingly dismayed by the attitude of his transfer student from Billington.

What is this kid's problem, he thought to himself.

The red offense ran five more "live" plays, and then the white offense ran 10 plays against dummies. Although Roger performed decently at quarterback, the rest of the players on the second unit were too inexperienced to go live at this point in training camp— especially, since they would be up against most of the first teamers who were now over on scout defense.

The last play for the white offense was a 22 halfback power pass. Roger called the play and analyzed the secondary as he approached the line of scrimmage. Owens was at strong safety, Riley at strong corner, and his biggest concern—O'Connor—was all over the field at linebacker.

Roger placed his hands under the center. He realized that this was his last opportunity this week to impress the coaching staff with his quarterbacking skills.

"Blue, 34... Blue, 34... Set..."

The ball snapped firmly into Collins's hands. He faked quickly to the reserve fullback Schultz, faked to the reserve halfback Greene, and rolled to his right. The unblocked outside linebacker was charging directly for his Adam's apple. Collins ducked inside of him, regained his balance, and then cut back to the outside. The corner and safety were both coming up, expecting Roger to tuck the ball under his arm pit and run. But Roger released the ball just as Owens was about to wrap him up. The ball sailed 35 yards downfield with a perfect spiral. The ball proceeded into and out of the outstretched hands of the right halfback.

"Johnson," hollered Coach Allen, "Where'd you get those hands? The lumber yard?" The entire team bursted out laughing. Coach Allen jogged over to the young athlete and patted him on the back of the shoulder pads. "Nice try. Great route, Billy. You'll catch it next time."

Roger also ran over to Billy, smacking him on the rear end, saying, "It's okay, Billy. I think I overthrew you a bit."

Coach Allen looked over to Coach Abraham and gave him the nod. Keith blew his whistle, signaling the conclusion of their first official "live" scrimmage. It was nearly 11:30, and the sun was now at full-intensity.

After a much needed water break, the team broke off into defensive groups. Coach Oliver reviewed gap responsibilities in a 5-2 Normal, and the 5-2 Eagle—where the defensive tackles slide down into B gap, head up on the offensive guards, creating a 3-man wall in the middle. The inside linebackers then slid out into C gap. Inside Stunts and Mike Stunts were reviewed, followed by a few agility drills: bear crawling and rolling, then shuffling through a 6 bag obstacle course. The defensive linemen finished with some work on the tackling sled.

Meanwhile, Coach Abraham reviewed linebackers stunts and pass coverage: dropping back into hook zones and covering backs out in the flats.

Coach Allen reviewed Cover 2 and Cover 3 defensive back responsibilities versus the pass and the run. Then they worked on backpedaling, man-to-man coverage, and tackling technique.

At exactly 12:00, Coach Abraham blew his whistle for specialty. "Today, we have put together a tentative punt team. If you are not on the punt team, you are rotating in on the other side of the ball, giving us a good look trying to block the punt."

Roger Collins was the first team punter, Daniels the long snapper, reserve back Billy Johnson earned an up-back position, but everyone else was from the first offensive unit. Bryan Cox was the backup punter, switching in every third punt; Pete O'Connor and Dan Hardings alternated as back up snappers every third punt. Daniels, however, was by far the superior snapper; he had been long-snapping since the fourth grade. O'Connor and Hardings were still working on achieving a spiral while snapping with both hands.

On the first few punts, there was very little rush coming from the defense. Harding's snap even bounced twice, and no one even came within two feet of blocking the punt. Naturally, the attention of Coach Allen was invoked.

"What the heck is going on over there, defense? Are you boys too afraid to block a punt? Afraid it's going to give you a tummy ache?"

The defensive huddle became silent.

"I want 10 people on the line of scrimmage. I'll buy anyone a Coke after practice who can block a punt."

A sudden spike in passion arose on the defensive side of the ball as 10 thirsty bodies crowded the line of scrimmage, anxiously awaiting the snap of the ball. Adam Foster crouched into a sprinter's stance, shading the outside shoulder of the left offensive end. Adam tilted his head to the inside, eyes focused on the snapper.

Daniels hunched over the football, his hands tightly grasping the pigskin. He looked backwards—through his legs, of course—at Roger who was exactly 13 yards deep. When the line and backfield were set for a count, Roger called out the signal.

"Set..." Daniels waited about three seconds before snapping a perfect spiral. The ball flew on a line for Roger's midsection. He caught the ball, took three quick steps, and released the ball to his right foot.

At exactly the same time as the ball was about to make contact with Roger's right foot, Adam Foster—arms outstretched like Superman—entered the geographical vicinity. A loud thud echoed throughout the sweltering humidity, and the ball ricocheted off Adam's midsection, bouncing four yards behind the punter. Adam hopped to his feet, picked up the ball, and sprinted downfield for a touchdown.

"Johnson! Johnson! Who the hell did you block? Didn't you see Foster coming?" barked Coach Allen. "If there's no one coming from your inside, you've got to get a piece of the man coming like a raging bull from the outside. You've at least got to get a hand on him."

Coach Allen then shifted his attention to the punter. "Collins, you took too long getting the punt off. You need to either take a one step or two quick steps to punt the ball. If the man from the outside is getting to the kick, we're taking too long."

Turning his attention over to the defense, Coach Allen added, "Great look, defense. Way to sacrifice your body and make a play, Foster. Blocking a punt is the most exciting play in football. Adam, I owe you a Coke after practice. Now let's see if anyone else wants to drain my wallet."

The punt team reassembled in their huddle. After receiving the play from Coach Allen, Roger entered the huddle.

"Okay, guys. This time we're going to run the fake punt pass. Dan, you run a short flag. Rob, you run a 5 yard out. Be looking right away, you'll both be wide open." Roger looked each of the 10 players in the eye before continuing. "Give me some time. Fake punt pass, on snap. Ready... BREAK!"

The punt team bolted to the line and crouched down in their two point stances. Ten defensive players hugged the line of scrimmage, eager for the opportunity to earn a free pop from Coach Allen.

Roger waited two seconds and barked out the command, "Set."

Daniels fired the ball back to Roger with another perfect spiral. Hardings sprinted out of his right end position, breaking at a 45 degree angle when he was exactly seven yards upfield. Bast swung immediately out into the right flats, turning his head back to Roger who was rolling out to his right. Then the punter/quarterback drilled a strike 20 yards downfield, hitting Hardings between the numbers. Dan turned upfield and gained an additional 15 yards before the lone deep back pushed him out of bounds.

Behind the play, Roger was watching the trajectory of his pass. All of a sudden—from Roger's blind side—Adam Foster speared him in the small of his back. Pete saw the whole incident out of the corner of his eye. Without a moment's hesitation, Pete got right into Adam's face, lifting him off the ground before pummeling him to the grass.

"What do you think you're doing, moron?" screamed Pete. "That's your teammate."

Coach Abraham blew his whistle. Roger was rising slowly to his feet, trying to conceal the pain flaring up his lower back.

"Coach Allen, why don't you get the team started with conditioning while I have a conversation with these two."

"Sure, Coach. All right, everybody spread out on the goal line. Give yourselves plenty of room."

Coach Allen located Roger who was in the middle of the pack, with his right hand behind him, trying to support his lower back. "Roger, are you okay? Do you need to see the trainer?"

"I'm okay, Coach. I'll be fine."

Meanwhile Coach Abraham escorted the two dissidents to the opposite end of the field which the junior varsity team had vacated nearly a half hour earlier.

114

"What's this all about, Adam? You knew Roger had already released the football."

"I... I couldn't stop," responded the Billington transfer, showing no sign of remorse in neither his voice nor his body language. "I didn't think it was an illegal hit."

"It was a cheap shot, you..."

"That's enough, Pete," interrupted Coach Abraham. "I didn't ask for your opinion. Let me handle this. I don't need you making matters worse by retaliating. You try that in a game, and you're the one that gets ejected. Not only for the present game, but the next game, as well."

Pete grew cold to a chill. He couldn't imagine a more severe torture than to be suspended from playing football.

Coach Abraham considered his next words carefully as he looked down at the opposite end of the field where the rest of the team was completing a 20 yard sprint.

"First of all, Adam. Your late hit would have given the other team an automatic first down even if they hadn't completed the pass. And you might have been ejected from the game, also. I will not tolerate dirty play on this team. You will need to demonstrate self-control if you want to be a member of this team. Do you know how awful you would feel if you were forced to sit out two games, Pete? Is that how you want to spend your senior year? On the sidelines?"

"No, sir," looking directly into Coach Abraham eyes before turning to his teammate. "I'm sorry, Adam," extending his right hand to demonstrate the sincerity of his apology.

Several awkward moments later, Adam reluctantly reciprocated by offering his own right hand. There was no eye contact on the part of Adam, however; his eyes were glued to the ground. All of a sudden, Foster lifted his head, projecting an unmistakable beam of severe loathing in the direction of his teammate.

Pete was startled by his teammate's expression. He broke eye-contact and turned to Coach Abraham. Pete's blood regained its near-boiling temperature as he waited impatiently for the impending punishment.

Coach Abraham broke the silence by announcing, "Here's what you guys are going to do for me." He walked over to a yellow scrimmage vest lying on the ground. He picked it up with his right hand and tossed it to Pete, and then continued his instructions. "You two are going to run the length of the field. 100 yards. Up and down. Twenty times. You will both be holding onto this mesh as you run, so you will have to work together as a team. If either of you lets go of the mesh, you will both start over. Understand?"

"Yes, sir," answered Pete, wanting desperately to get the humiliation over with.

True to form, Adam nodded without saying a word.

Fortunately, for Pete, at least, his running partner was in decent shape. Pete and Adam had very little difficulty hanging onto their end of the mesh, for neither of them wanted to have to run any further than the amount already assessed.

By the time they completed their last 100 yard sprint, the rest of the team had already heard the coaches' final remarks and were now long gone; only the coaches remained, and they were still talking at the far end of the practice field.

"Did you see how quickly Pete came to Roger's aid?" asked Coach Allen. "I wouldn't have predicted that in a million years."

"I'm very concerned about this Foster kid. He's a strange bird," said Coach Abraham. "He never looks you in the eye. Hardly ever speaks a word. He seems like he's angry at the world. I'm going to check his file next week when the counselor starts enrolling new students. The only thing I know about him is he's from Billington."

"Has anything good ever come out of Billington?" joked Coach Oliver.

"Good point, Gary," responded Keith.

"We should ask Coach DeWitt if he remembers him from last year. He probably started for the Bulldogs somewhere; I would imagine in the secondary. I'll try and catch up with him before the jayvees are done meeting," said Coach Allen. "I better hurry, though. You know how those jayvee coaches like to get an early start on the golf course on Fridays."

Coach Allen trotted across the parking lot to the high school's south entrance. Coach Abraham shifted his attention to Coach Oliver who was standing silently by his side.

"Well, Gary. What do you think after your first week of coaching?"

"I sure have a lot to learn, Coach. I thought I knew the ins and outs of our system, but there is a heck of a lot more to it than I imagined. The biggest challenge is being patient with some of these kids. It seems like they're taking forever to get their technique down. As soon as the ball's snapped, they want to stand straight up instead of playing low. I just wish I could put the pads on and show them exactly what's going to happen when they play high."

116

"That wouldn't be very wise, Gary. We're already short enough on linemen as it is. Unfortunately, most of them have zero lower body strength because they refused to step one foot into the weight room during the off-season. Now they're paying the price.

"On Monday, we'll start bringing them into the weight room. On the field, you've just got to run them through drill after drill, forcing them to stay low. If they still don't get it, you can always institute duck walking into their daily routines."

"Coach, I couldn't. I still remember the time you made us duck walk. I was sore for three days."

"Did it teach you to play low, though?"

"It sure did. I remember threatening the other defensive linemen in the middle of a game. I told them I was going to step on their backs if I had to, but there was no way I was going to do another duck walk."

"See what I mean?"

By this time, Adam and Pete had soaked their heads under the water trough for several minutes, slurping down more than a half gallon of water before starting for the gate.

Coach Abraham shouted out to them, "I expect we won't be having any more discipline problems from the two of you again, will we?"

"No, sir," responded Pete. Adam just lifted his head apathetically, glancing back at Coach Abraham and Coach Oliver with a vacant stare.

"Have a good weekend, and stay out of trouble," warned Coach Abraham.

Chapter Twelve

As soon as Pete had passed through the gate, he immediately distanced himself from Adam Foster. He needed to create as much as separation as possible before he ripped him to shreds. The best possible medicine right now—Pete assured himself—was to rip off his football gear in exchange for a pair of shorts and a tee-shirt, and then head for the weight room to burn off some steam. He hadn't worked out since Wednesday, and his muscles already felt like they were beginning to deteriorate.

Halfway across the parking lot, a car suddenly pulled up behind him. The horn honked three times, jostling Pete from the privacy of his own mind. He turned to see his mother pulling up beside him, driving her rusted-out Ford Ranger.

Then it dawned upon him that he was supposed to go out for lunch with her today. The sight of his mom's smiling face wiped away any thoughts of having a post-practice workout.

"Hey, stud. Buy you some lunch?"

"Depends what you got in mind."

"Anything you want, Pete."

"Give me a minute to change out of my gear."

Pete jogged the rest of the way to the locker room. When he arrived at locker #18, he froze in his tracks. Hanging from his Master padlock was a yellowish, flemmy loogie.

"Shit," exclaimed Pete, smacking the top of his locker with his open right hand. He started for the paper towel dispenser just as his new acquaintance from Billington was exiting a bathroom stall. Pete grabbed about three feet of paper towel, dampened a corner of the towel at the sink, and returned to locker #18.

Adam was taking off his cleats; he looked up at Pete, through his greasy brown bangs.

Pete eyed his teammate with semi-accusing eyes.

"Did you see who did this?"

Several moments of silence followed. Adam looked downward and pulled on his high-tops.

Then he replied, "I didn't see nothing."

"I bet you didn't. You got some bone to pick with me, Foster? Did I do something to you? What the hell's your problem, anyways?"

Adam lifted his head and swept the hair out of his eyes. His freckled face was beaded with sweat. He stared at Pete through his dark brown, almond-shaped eyes. Pete felt a frigid gust of hatred rush from him.

A dichotomy of emotions swirled within him. His heart enticed him to lash out at Adam and administer quick and absolute justice, but his conscience reminded him of his allegiance to the team, and his pledge to Coach Abraham to avoid further trouble. Nevertheless, it was just Adam and Pete alone; at least, he could put a scare into him by picking him up and slamming him into the lockers.

Just as Pete was about to take a step toward him, the locker room opened, and in walked Coach Allen.

"What are you two doing here still? You guys going to kiss and make up or what?" joked Coach Allen.

The coach's weak attempt at humor was met by a hollow silence.

"You guys are going to have to start acting like teammates," he commanded, looking first toward Adam and then to Pete. Coach Allen could sense that there was still something brewing between the two players.

"What ever is going on between you two is not as important as the success of this team, so you'd better bury the hatchet. I'll be back in five minutes, and I better see both of you cleared out of here. Do we have an understanding?"

"Yes, sir," answered Pete.

A slight nod was the only acknowledgement from Adam.

Coach Allen turned and exited the locker room, and Pete finished wiping the nasty spit from his padlock. His feeling of abhorrence for Adam was expanded in his chest, like a balloon filling up with helium. He wanted to punch him in the worst way.

After getting dressed in his denim shorts and Juddville Jaguar tank top, Pete slammed the locker and secured the lock, spinning the dial to make sure it wouldn't fall open. Before leaving the locker room, he walked right up to Adam to share a few choice words of warning.

"I don't know what kind of game you're playing, but I should remind you that football season doesn't last forever. If you survive the season, you'd better hope my memory of this day fades away. In the mean time, if I catch you near my locker, I'll kick your ass on the spot. I don't care if Coach makes me run a marathon every day after practice; it will be worth it."

Adam's face turned cherry red as he attempted in vain to conceal his fear. He breathed a heavy sigh, and the fear on his face dissipated—only to be replaced by a cold, loathsome gaze. Pete felt the chill emanating from his teammate, and it reminded him of the walk-in freezer at the Pancake House.

Feeling quite certain that his message to Adam had been received, Pete exited the locker room, sticking his chest out, flexing his triceps as a final warning.

The torrid sun nearly blinded Pete as he stepped out of the high school into the 90 degree temperature. He let out a yelp when the flesh on the back of his thighs made contact with the burning vinyl seat on the passenger side of his mom's truck. His mother smiled at him, and inquired, "What took you so long?"

"Oh, I had to clean up a few things?"

"How was practice?"

"We're starting to come along, I guess. It's too early to tell, though. But I think we've made a heck of a lot of progress since Monday."

"How are you doing so far?"

"Did I tell you I got moved to offensive line?"

"No, you didn't," responded his mom, a sense of outrage in her voice. "You've worked so hard. Why in the world would they want to put you up on the line where you'll never touch the ball?"

"The coaches didn't have much of a choice, Mom. We don't have a lot of muscle on the line, and I was the only one in the backfield that might be able to help."

Pete's mom maneuvered her way through the parking lot and turned right onto Henry Street.

"Where are we going to eat, Mom?"

"What sounds good to you?"

"I don't care. As long as it isn't the Pancake House."

"I'd like to go somewhere we can talk. I got some news about your dad that we need to talk about. How about Paul's Steakhouse?"

"That's a little expensive, don't you think?"

"It'll be all right, honey. I've been working quite a bit of overtime lately, and I'm not going to have that many more opportunities to take my most favorite person out for lunch."

"I guess if you put it that way. And I haven't had a good steak in a long time," responded Pete with a gleam of excitement in his eyes.

Ten minutes later and they were pulling into Paul's Steakhouse. It was about 1:30, and the lunch crowd was breaking up. Pete's mouth was salivating as he imagined his first bite of a 14 ounce Porterhouse, smothered with mushrooms.

The hostess seated them in a booth in the corner. Pete didn't even need to open his menu. He studied his mother as she glanced at the menu. She had certainly weathered her share of storms raising him by herself these past six years; beneath her hardened exterior, however, she was fairly attractive for a mom. Back in the day, she must have turned a lot of heads.

The waitress returned with two glasses of ice water. Pete grabbed his glass and instantaneously drained it. The waitress looked down at Pete and asked, "A little bit thirsty, are we? I'll get you another right away."

Noticing his Juddville State Championship t-shirt, she added, "How's the team look this year? We going to the Dome again?"

Pete's face turned bright red as he tried to compose a diplomatic response. He would feel foolish hearing himself predict a repeat state championship, yet he could not in good conscience give a doomsday forecast, either.

So he responded, "Oh, it's a little early for making hotel reservations in New Haven, but I think you can count on us being pretty decent."

"Well, what can I get for you today, son?"

"Mom, you can order first."

"Sure, I'd like a chicken salad with Ranch dressing, please. And could I have a Diet Coke with that?"

"And how about the football star?"

"Who me?" blushed Pete. "Just bring me a Porterhouse—medium-rare—baked potato with butter and sour cream, and a salad with blue cheese dressing, please. And could I also have a large milk, too?"

"Certainly. Your order will be up in just a few minutes." The waitress collected the menus and added, "I'll be right back with your drinks."

Pete quickly interjected, "And could I have another water, please."

"Anything you want, sugar."

Cindy O'Connor reached into her purse and pulled out her pack of Marlboro Lights and her butane lighter. She slid the ash tray in front of her and nervously lit up her cigarette. Tension swept across her face as she exhaled, blowing the smoke upward, away from her son—as much as possible.

"Peter, I received some news about your dad yesterday. It seems they're running out of space in prisons these days. As a result, the parole board is sending a lot of inmates home early. Your father may get an opportunity for early release. His case is coming up next Friday. The only problem is that your father isn't interested in an early release. He is insisting upon serving his full sentence. I don't think they'll take his wishes into consideration, however."

She paused a half a minute to allow for the news to sink in. Pete was speechless; his eyes wide open in disbelief, and his fingers nervously rolling his fork back and forth. There was neither joy nor anger in his expression.

"Of course, I have no idea where he'll go if he is released. He might move back to Billington, or I suppose, he might choose to just wander about for awhile. Whatever he decides, I would expect he might want to see his family again, but I would never be foolish enough to think that I could ever predict what your dad might be thinking. And as much of a bombshell as it might be for you and I to finally get to see him again, I expect it might be an even greater shock to him. He's been away a very long time, and while he's been gone, his little boy has grown into a fine young man."

Cindy smiled at her son, hoping to help ease the tension. But her attempts were in vain, for she could see by the way Pete was white knuckling the fork that he was anything but relaxed.

"You do you want to see him, don't you, Pete? I know he's been out of our lives for some time, but he is still your father."

Pete was dumbfounded. This was more than he could handle. His dad out of prison? He had given up all hope of ever speaking to him again. Six years ago, his dad had literally deleted Pete and his mom from his life.

He refused to write. He declined family visitations. How was Pete supposed to feel? And if he agreed to see his father, then what? Would his dad take one more swipe with his serrated dagger, driving it deep into the fragile hearts of the only ones in this world desperate enough to love him?

Breaking the silence, Pete responded, "Mom, I can't give you an answer right now. I've got to focus on football. This is my big chance. This is what I've been working so hard for. I don't think I can deal with this until after the season. If you want to see Dad, go for it. But I can't right now. He cut me from his life when I needed him most. I don't want to see him or hear from him—now or probably forever."

Cindy had been afraid her son might respond this way; in truth, she felt responsible—to some degree—for his callous attitude. She had been an effective teacher. He was merely echoing much of her sentiment over the past six years.

Looking him straight in the eyes, she spoke in a deep, solemn voice. "I have to see him." Extinguishing her cigarette butt in the ash tray, she continued, "When I decided to marry your father, I made a vow to stay with him till death do us part. When your father first suggested that I divorce him, I told him I could never even consider it until we could meet face-to-face, outside of the prison walls. In spite of his obvious shortcomings, my soul is still joined to his.

"Right now, I know it's important that you pursue your dream. You know I support you and have always supported you 100%. But I've been holding on to my dream for these last six years. As crazy and irrational as it seems, my dream is that we can become a family again. I just can't give up on this dream. Can you possibly understand?"

Cindy's eyes began to tear up as she lit another cigarette. "I am still hanging on to this hope... I understand how you are angry with your father. But please don't hold it against me if I hold out a little bit longer on my dream."

Pete grabbed his mother's hand and spoke with a shaky, uncertain voice, "Mom, you are all I've got. You and I have always stuck together. Do what you gotta do, Mom. Just leave me out right now. I don't have room for him in my life. I don't need him... I don't want him in my life, period. That's exactly what he wanted, remember? If he gets released, tell him I wish him well, but he can stay the hell out of my life. I've made it this far without him, and I can make it the rest of the way on my own, too."

The sharpness of her son's words startled Cindy, but she figured that it might take Pete a little time to adjust to the unexpected news. The natural yearning that a son has for his father must still be buried somewhere deep down in her son's heart. No one had expected Paul to be released for at least another four years. She had anticipated Pete being in his early twenties and that they would have had the luxury of perhaps a few months to maybe even a year to prepare themselves mentally for their reunion with Paul. Now their entire world was being suddenly overturned, and—for the time being, at least—she would have to face this challenge alone.

Cindy's mind was in turmoil.

I wonder what Paul is thinking? Does he still have feelings for me? Does he have any idea where he'll go when he walks out that prison gate? Is he worried about whether he'll fall back into his old addictions? What are his dreams for the rest of his life? Do they include me?

So many unanswered questions, Cindy wished that she had someone that she could go to with her problems, someone who might listen to her, someone who could just tell her that everything was going to be fine.

Seeing the anger enflamed within her son's eyes and not wishing to spoil the remainder of their lunch date, Cindy forced her overpowering thoughts back into the recesses of her mind and changed the topic back to a safer topic: football.

"Tell me about the team this year, Pete. Who is the quarterback? Do you feel more pressure to win after last year's state championship? How is Coach Allen holding up? Has he gone ballistic yet?"

Pete smiled at his mother. She was always interested in what was going on behind the scenes. Whenever there was a special feature during the pre-game of a major athletic contest on television, she would almost immediately be drawn into the drama—whether it involved a member of an athlete's family facing an incurable disease, or an athlete's humble beginnings in a extremely rural community. Without exception, Cindy rooted for the underdog. That's what he loved most about his mom, and that was why he was confident she'd always be his biggest fan. The mood returned to a more peaceful one as Pete answered each of his mother's questions between bites of steak and baked potato.

Deep in her heart, Cindy treasured this rare moment alone with her son, fully expecting that next year at this time, Pete would be on his own somewhere, playing football while receiving a free college education.

Chapter Thirteen

Meanwhile the Juddville Jaguars Varsity Coaching Staff was just wrapping up its coaching meeting. Overall, there was a feeling of guarded optimism over the progress achieved in five short days of practice. Coach Allen had been able to rundown the head jayvee coach; when Jim asked him if he remembered an Adam Foster from last year's Billington's squad, Coach DeWitt's mind drew a blank. He promised Jim he'd pull out last year's scouting report over the weekend, however. In the meantime, Coach Abraham left a message in the counseling office requesting Adam's file as soon as it arrived from Billington.

It was 3:30, but they had already accomplished quite a bit in their meeting. First, they had reviewed the depth chart, making a few significant changes. For one, Adam Foster would now be backing up Jeff Nash at safety. The coachability and attitude of Adam were suspect after the last two days of practice, and the coaches resolved to send an unequivocal message to Foster—and to the rest of the team, for that matter—that if you refuse to respect your teammates, you will see very little playing time at Juddville. Furthermore, it was decided that if Foster took one more cheap shot at a teammate or an opposing player, he would be done for the season.

Practice plans for the next week focused on preparation for the 4-way scrimmage on Friday. On Monday through Thursday, they would attempt to put in the rest of their scaled-down offense, would spend a lot more time on team defense, and would continue to hone their specialty teams. Weight training would resume on Monday and Wednesday, and the level of intensity in conditioning would be doubled.

The scrimmage was going to be held at 10:00 a.m. on Friday at Juddville. The same day at 4:00 p.m, they would be scouting their first opponent: the Pennington Pirates.

Coach Allen was the first one to begin packing up his things, cramming his practice plan files and notes into his briefcase. He couldn't wait to get home to give his mind a much-needed break from football. By the end of the meeting, Jim had developed a moderate migraine, and he had already begun formulating a strategy for appeasing his unwelcomed cranial discomfort: specifically, an ice cold 12 ounce adult beverage that he would be cracking open the minute he stepped into the kitchen.

The challenge of facing three different opponents on Friday was a bit unnerving. None of their scrimmage opponents were on their regular schedule, and there was always an element of surprise as far as what type of defense to expect from your opponent in a scrimmage. Their opponents might come out in a 6-2, a 5-3, a 5-2, or even a 4-3 defense. Some coaches change defenses from year to year as often as 16 year old girls change hairstyles.

In Juddville's first week of practice, they had faced only one defense: the 5-2, the same defense they—no coincidence—happen to play. As a result, they would have to cover blocking adjustments for at least 3 to 4 new defenses in next week's four practices. With an experienced group of football players, that would generally represent no problems; in fact, it would be like a review. Unfortunately, this year's group would require a lot of explaining and repetition.

All of these concerns could be conveniently be placed on the back burner in about 30 minutes when Coach Allen would be at home, sitting in the shallow end of his swimming pool with an ice-cold Budweiser in his hand. So with an Oscar-like performance, Coach Allen pretended like he was ever so reluctant to have to leave the meeting. He slowly pushed his chair back from the table, looked at his watch while sighing, "Coach, I better get going. Mary needs my help with the kids this afternoon. Is there anything else you need from me before I get going?"

Coach Abraham had been diagramming a drill for Coach Oliver on the white board. He looked behind him to Coach Allen and said, "I think we're all set. But you haven't given me an answer yet about tomorrow, though."

"Oh, yeah." Jim had been hoping that Keith had either forgotten or perhaps, he might have observed the not-so-subtle clues Jim had directed his way that he wasn't really interested in spending one of his last Saturday mornings waking up early to attend some kind of men's breakfast at his church.

Nevertheless, Jim responded, "Well, I've talked it over with Mary, and it's okay with her, so I guess I'll see you there. What time does it start again?"

"8:00 a.m."

Ugh. The last opportunity to sleep in on a Saturday morning for the next three months, and he was going to church.

Maybe, I'll be home by 10:00 a.m., anyway, thought Jim optimistically.

Reading his Jim's mind, Keith added, "It should get over by 10:00... 10:30 at the latest."

"Great, it will give me an excuse to take an extra long nap tomorrow afternoon," joked Coach Allen. "Anyways, we'll see you guys later. Excellent job coaching this week, Gary. You've really been a huge help to us."

"Thanks, Coach," responded Coach Oliver. "Have a good weekend."

"You, too, Gary. See you tomorrow morning, Keith."

Jim felt about 15 pounds lighter as he walked out of the meeting and was met by the warm August air. He felt like he had accomplished quite a bit in his first week and was ready to reward himself with an afternoon of leisure, Budweiser style. As he pulled out of the school's parking lot, his mind shifted scenes instantaneously. He visualized the crystal-clear refreshing pool and smelled the tangy barbecue chicken on the grill. A little Whiffle ball in the front yard, and maybe a little late night loving with Mary after the kids were put to bed.

Gary Oliver was the next coach to check out from the meeting. His official plans were to take his girlfriend out for dinner and a movie. Overall, the first week of his coaching career had been about what he had expected. He was no stranger to the intensity of Juddville Football. As the new kid on the block, however, he was left out of most of the strategizing and the major decision-making, so his responsibilities were relatively few. One day he hoped to earn a greater role on the Juddville Staff, but for now, he was grateful for the opportunity to learn from two of the best.

126

Furthermore, in a few short weeks, Gary would be busy enough when his student teaching assignment began.

After Jim and Gary had been gone about an hour, Keith looked at his watch and noticed that it was quickly approaching dinner hour. He had one stop to make on his way home: Jerry's Sporting Goods. He had promised Coach DeWitt that he would pick up a pair of XXL shoulder pads for a jayvee lineman. If he put it in high gear, he could still make it home by 5:30.

On his way to Jerry's, Keith began to worry about how his team would perform in Friday's scrimmage. True, it was only a scrimmage—no one kept score, except for the dads—but doing well against their three opponents was often a confidence builder going into the regular season, especially for an inexperienced team like this year. And no one needed to remind Coach Abraham that the first two opponents on Juddville's schedule were going to be tough competition.

The Pennington Pirates were under their first year with Greg Patterson, former defensive coordinator of Bellview, a state powerhouse from the other side of the state, a team that went undefeated two years ago, allowing only one touchdown in four playoff games. Coach Patterson would have a tough time turning the program around in one year—Pennington was primarily a "basketball" town—but everyone was expecting a significant immediate improvement, especially on defense.

What worried Coach Abraham the most was their second opponent, however. This was not the ideal year to play Juddville's most fervent rivalry—the Billington Bulldogs—on the second game of the season. Last season they had faced the Bulldogs on the eighth date, and Juddville had scored three quick touchdowns in the first half, due to several costly turnovers committed by Billington's shaky quarterback. Not willing to call off his players too early, Coach Abraham and his Jaguars ran the score up to 45 to 0 by the end of the third quarter. Juddville's reserves gave up two touchdowns in the fourth quarter, but the damage had already been done. The final score was 45 to 14, the worst defeat in Billington's proud history. The disgruntled Billington fans were calling for Coach Callaghan's head for the next few months. Needless to say, the outcome of this year's match up against Juddville would most likely determine the future of Coach Callaghan's career at Billington. The advantage Billington held over Juddville this year was that they lost only three seniors; therefore, the majority of this year's team would be highly motivated to avenge last year's humiliation.

Meanwhile, Coach Allen was tossing a ball around in his pool with his two boys while his three year old Katherine was playing in the shaded sandbox. Mary walked out onto the deck, calling out to him, "Jim, what time are you going to start the coals?"

"A few more minutes, honey. The water is great."

"Just let me know so I can start boiling the water for the corn."

While Jim's gaze followed Mary back into the house, the rubber football suddenly smacked him in the side of the head.

"Luke, was that you? You're going to get it now," warned Jim as he plunged under water like a great white shark in search of its prey. Luke kicked desperately for the edge of the pool, but not before *Jaws* got a hold of one of his ankles. One moment his head was above water, the next moment he was being tugged underwater. The sea beast let go of him after a few seconds. As Luke ascended above water, he was met by his dad who lifted his entire body out of the water and tossed him three feet into the air. After making a gigantic splash in the deep end of the pool, Luke quickly bobbed back up to the surface with an uncontainable grin on his face.

"Do that again, Dad," begged Luke.

His younger brother also chimed in, "Me next, Daddy. Throw me, too."

"All right... all right," agreed Jim as he waded over to his four and a half year son Kevin who was wearing bright orange swimmies around both arms.

"One... two... three!"

Kevin's eyes squinted tightly as he sailed through the air. After submerging about a foot below the surface, he popped back up with an ear-to-ear grin. "Throw me again, throw me again, Daddy."

"No, me, Dad. It's my turn," yelled Luke.

"Take turns, Kev. You each get five throws, and then I've got to start the grill. You guys are getting so big. I'm going to throw my shoulder out."

As the drum beat of the forthcoming football season grew louder and louder, Jim felt melancholy over the necessity of his having to spend so much time away from his "home" team the next three months. He wished that the job of coaching football was less of a drain on Mary and the kids, but he knew that wasn't possible. The commitment the sport of football demanded had much to do with why it was so special, so full of passion.

After completing the ten mandatory throws and having to decline several times the invitation for ten more throws, Jim crawled out of the pool and toweled off. Luke and Kevin hopped out of the pool behind him. Jim grabbed another Budweiser out of the poolside cooler as his two boys followed him to the grill.

"Can I help?" asked Luke.

"Maybe when I put on the barbecue sauce, son. Why don't you two go in and change out of your wet suits and tell your mother I'm starting the grill?"

"Okay," answered the boys in unison as they raced against one another to the deck.

After lighting the coals, Jim checked up on Katherine who was still playing in the sandbox. "Are you having fun, Katherine?"

All covered with sand, like a cinnamon donut, Katie answered with an irresistible smile, "Uh, huh... but Daddy, will you play dolls with me?"

"I can't right now, sweetie. How about I put you to bed tonight, then you can show me your dolls, okay?"

"Okay, Daddy."

Picking up football equipment from Jerry's always seemed to take a lot more time than anticipated. It would be a rare occurrence, indeed, for Coach Abraham not to bump into another coach, a former player, or a parent. And this particular Friday afternoon would be no exception. His first conversation was with Jerry—the owner—who wanted to get the lowdown on this year's Jaguars. Next, a conversation with Mitch Vermeer, a former player who was now coaching his son in the youth football league. Finally, a father of one of last year's seniors had to give Keith a complete update on their boy who was currently holding a part-time construction job while taking two courses at Lakeland Community College.

At 5:15, a brand new pair of Wilson Shoulder Pads in his arms, Coach Abraham exited Jerry's Sporting Goods and quickly hopped into his Honda Civic. He was now fully aware that he was going to be late. About two miles from home, he passed Faith Community Church on his right and noticed Pastor Larry Jenkins who was opening the driver's door of his silver four-door sedan.

Larry waved enthusiastically when he recognized the automobile. Not wanting to be rude, Keith pulled over, his car adjacent to Pastor Jenkins. Rolling down his window, Keith called out, "Hey Pastor. Everything all set for tomorrow's breakfast?"

"All systems ready to go, Coach. Your committee did most of the work." With a gleam in his eyes, he added, "I'm praying for a 100 men to be here tomorrow. The office has been swamped all day with phone calls."

"That's awesome, Pastor. Could you offer up a special prayer for my good friend and assistant coach, Jim Allen? He's planning on attending, and I really hope that he'll be receptive to the message."

"Why don't we pray for him right now, Keith?"

"That's a great idea."

For the next five minutes, Coach Allen and Pastor Larry prayed for the Lord to speak to each man who would be attending the breakfast. They specifically prayed for Coach Allen, asking that the power of God's love might be felt deeply in his heart tomorrow morning.

Coach Abraham thanked Pastor Jenkins for praying with him and said goodbye. At five minutes to six, Keith pulled into his driveway where he noticed that his daughter Julia's car was missing from its usual parking place.

"Carol," he called out, as he jerked open the front door. "Where's Julia? I thought we were taking her out to dinner tonight?"

Mrs. Abraham was sitting comfortably in the blue leather couch, reading the front page of the Juddville Gazette. "Keith, she was here at 5:30 to gently break the news to you that she had new plans. This is her last weekend with Brian, so they're going out for dinner. Naturally, she knew better than to ask if you'd be interested in joining them."

"You're kidding me, right? We made plans with her first. This is our last weekend with her, too."

"Keith, you made plans. You never asked her, remember? Anyways, we're going to have to change our plans now because our reservation was for 6:00, which is in about three minutes."

Sitting down next to Carol on the sofa, Keith put his hand upon his wife's and said, "I'm sorry, Carol. I guess I got sidetracked on the way home. Do you still want to go out, just the two of us?"

"Can we talk about something besides football?"

"I'll try."

Getting up from the couch, Carol assumed control over the dinner plans with a renewed sense of command, "Honey, go get yourself cleaned up while I call to see if we can get a later reservation."

Fatigue began to settle upon him as he slouched back on the couch.

"Keith, do you think I'm all dressed up like this to go LuLu's Diner?"

Suddenly Coach Abraham became aware of Carol's stunning appearance. Her turquoise blue summer dress that stopped just above the knees, revealing her athletic legs; her shiny golden-brown hair resting on her tan, sexy shoulders; her enchanting hazel eyes; and her soft, seductive perfume emanating from her neck brought about an abrupt change on his state of mind. He had no idea how Carol did it, but she had been able to keep her youth and beauty through 24 seasons of marriage; he often shuddered to think where he would have ended up without her.

It would be an injustice to Carol to focus entirely on her physical attractiveness, however; she was without a doubt, his very best friend, his confidant. When he needed a sounding board, when he needed advice, she was usually the first and unfortunately, sometimes the last person he turned to. It didn't matter if the issue was football, teaching, politics, finances, or spiritual matters. Keith valued his wife's input, for she was intelligent and not afraid to speak the truth. Every morning during his time alone with God, the first thing he would thank Him for was his one of a kind, much-depended on wife.

Unfortunately, Carol had often been the object of neglect. Each autumn, she assumed the status of football widow. But she knew how important coaching football was to her husband, and she even tried to enjoy it. Unlike many coaches' wives who try to find a safe seat on Friday nights—somewhere out of harm's way—Carol preferred to sit in the midst of Keith's most vocal critics where she could challenge them to match her boisterous enthusiasm. When the criticism got really bad, her favorite reaction was to rise to her feet and cheer like the quarterback had just thrown a 60 yard touchdown.

Carol had deserved much more than Keith had given her. And now she was all he had left, as Julia was off for college on Sunday.

Then it would be just the two of them. It suddenly dawned upon him that Carol had more reason to be frightened at the prospect of becoming an empty nester than he did. From now on he would really have to make it up to her during the off-season.

Chapter Fourteen

By the time Pete's mother dropped him off at home on her way to work, he had made up his mind that he would have to go to the Body Shoppe to get in a workout, or he would go absolutely

131

nuts. It was 4:00, Friday afternoon, and it would take him no more than fifteen minutes on his bike if he pedaled like a madman.

Without even going inside his trailer, he went right to his 10-speed bike, unlocked it from the fence, and sped off so fast his tires were about burst into flames. His stomach was a bit bloated from his huge porterhouse, but his legs felt rested and surprisingly strong.

Pete's mind, however, was darting all over the place. As if he hadn't had enough on his mind with football this week—being a team captain, learning a new offensive position, trying to figure out who had been messing with his locker, how to overcome his intense desire to beat the crap out of Adam Foster—now he had family issues to contend with, issues that he had thought were put to rest.

Dad? Free to come home?

Four years ago, Pete would have been ecstatic. Now he just wished his dad would stay away.

One of the lessons Pete had learned from athletics was that you can't let anything, any one come between you and accomplishing your goals. This was the worst possible moment for his dad to come barging back into his life. So much of his future was riding on the next few months.

What if I lose my mental edge? I can't mess this season up. I've got to be strong... focused.

As much as he tried to deny it, however, Pete yearned for his dad. There was no getting away from it. Most of the time, the impulse was like a flickering light, barely visible, but never fully extinguishable.

Frustrated by the amount of thoughts already consumed by the news of his father, Pete forced his mind to concentrate on his impending workout. Because it was almost 4:30, he could workout about an hour and a half. Since his legs got a decent workout riding his bike, he decided he would focus on upper body. He had just enough time to blast his chest, shoulders, and arms before hopping back on his bike to return home by 6:30. Pete hurriedly locked his bike in the back of the dilapidated two-story house that had been converted into a dungeon for physical pain.

The Body Shoppe was everything a gladiator would want in a gym. First and foremost, it was loaded with literally tons of free weights—not sissy machines. On the main floor were three benches, an incline bench, a decline bench, and a two-tiered dumbbell rack, loaded with dumbbells ranging from 10 to 120 lbs. There were two plate-loaded lat machines, two chinning bars, a t-bar apparatus, two preacher curls benches, and a sit up bench.

A plate rack was located in each corner. The floor was covered with a dingy green carpet that was wearing thin in high traffic areas. A square wooden box containing blocks of chalk was situated in the middle of the room. A desk—almost always unoccupied—was located by the main entry. On top of the desk was a spiral notebook—for signing in—and a few bodybuilding magazines.

Pete signed his name underneath the 23rd signature—he was the 24th—and laid the daily workout fee of $2 next to the notebook. Since there was no cost to lift at the high school's weight room, he had no reason to pay for a monthly membership at the Body Shoppe. The high school weight room had limited hours, however, and it was never open on the weekends. If Pete had his way, he would do all of his lifting at the Body Shoppe although he would never admit this to Coach Abraham. The atmosphere was superior; the vast majority of members came to lift not to socialize. The best part was that there was competition. He wasn't even close to being the strongest lifter, like he was at school. In fact, there were a couple of powerlifters who could bench over 400 pounds, one guy who could squat 700 pounds, and one behemoth was deadlifting more than 800 pounds.

Pete walked immediately to the basement where he could relieve himself and weigh himself on the scale. 193 pounds. He had lost 5 pounds this week.

It could have been worse, he thought to himself. He recalled how he had lost a shocking 10 pounds during the first week of football his previous season.

He walked by the treadmills and exercise bikes, pausing a moment to take in the phenomenal amount of power on display in the squat and deadlift area. There were three powerlifters squatting and one deadlifting. The sound of 45 pound plates clanging on the end of an Olympic bar was one of Pete's favorite songs. One squatter had four 45 pound plates on each end of the bar, and the reps were so easy it looked as if he was squatting the bare bar. Each time he exploded out of the bottom, the bar would bend like a horseshoe as he ascended to an upright position.

Pete now wished that he had the time and energy to squat today—even though he would more than likely be discouraged by the decreased amount of weight he would be able to lift. One of the side effects of football was that your strength in the squat would go down more than 50 pounds during the season. One might think that all the crouching, running, and driving of sleds, would be a benefit to one's leg strength. Unfortunately, all the endurance and speed

133

work recruited a different type of muscle fiber—slow twitch rather that fast twitch. Bottom line, however, was the fact that the amount of weight a player was able to squat was not nearly as important as his ability to move quickly and aggressively from sideline to sideline. The upside for players concerned about the their long-term lifting progress was that it took only about three to four weeks to regain one's strength once the season had come to an end.

Once Pete was on the main floor again, he got a quick drink from the drinking fountain and immediately went to work. He started out with five sets of bench press. Then he grabbed a pair of 50 pound dumbbells and did three sets of incline bench. Next, he did three sets of flies with 35 pound dumbbells. His chest was now fully pumped, so he proceeded to the next muscle group: shoulders. He began with three sets of upright rows, then returned to the dumbbell rack for three supersets of lateral raises and bent laterals.

Pete refilled his tank with H20 and took a brief four minute break before attacking his arms. He started with four sets of biceps curls with a straight bar. Then he went to the preacher curl bench and cranked out three more sets to exhaustion. The skin on his biceps was so taut it felt like the muscle was about to burst right through it. He proceeded to the pulley machine where he did four sets of triceps pushdowns. The muscle on the back of his arms was now becoming fully engorged with blood.

As he walked over to the dumbbell rack, he couldn't resist taking a quick peak in the mirror. His arms looked like they were a good two inches larger in circumference, and he felt so powerful. He grabbed a 60 pound dumbbell and returned to the preacher curl bench where he sat down with his back to the bench in order to perform three sets of French presses. On the last set, he nearly lost control of the dumbbell as he attempted to raise it above his head. He brought the dumbbell forward, slamming it clumsily down on the floor.

Jim—the majority owner of The Body Shoppe—was preparing for his next set of close grip benches. He looked over at Pete with an annoyed look on his face, "Easy on the floor, kid."

"I'm sorry, sir. I'll be more careful next time." Pete's face turned to crimson as he returned the dumbbell to the rack before taking one last drink from the drinking fountain. He cautiously looked back over at Jim who was finishing a set on the bench. Three 45 pounds were on each side, and he had just cranked out 10 reps like it was a box of Kleenex.

What I would give to be able to bench that much weight...
Jim sat up from the bench and noticed Pete gawking at him.

Pete was star struck. "Uuh, thanks for the workout, Jim. See you next time."

The gym owner looked him in the eye and replied, "You bet, kid. You worked hard today. Haven't seen you around much lately, though."

"I'm playing football right now."

"Enjoy it while you can. A lot of us would give an arm and leg to suit up again. Say 'hi' to Coach Abraham from Big Jim, would ya?"

"I sure will." Pete reluctantly turned to the door, and then added, "See ya, Jim."

As he descended the concrete steps, Pete felt physically exhausted, but he was happy, for he had been able to spend an hour and a half in one of his favorite places, a place where many of his heroes resided.

His chest and arms were still pumped, and the warmth of the early evening August sunshine felt like healing balm to his fatigued muscles. The remainder of the evening would be spent just kicking back and relaxing.

When he walked around to the back of the building, he immediately sensed something wrong, however. His bike was twisted in the opposite direction from the way he had left it, and both tires were completely flat.

Pete cursed loudly at his damaged bike. Five miles from home and no transportation. No gas station within sight. Pete's temperament returned to a volcanic fever. He had no choice but to start hiking. His mother was at work by now, and he had no one else to call.

After about 15 minutes of brisk walking, Pete felt like he had tacks sticking in the bottoms of his feet. But if he could continue at his current pace, he was confident he would be home in time to see the kickoff of tonight's UFL game.

*If I **ever** find out who let the air out of my tires...*

Someone probably thought it would be funny, but Pete had experienced enough "jokes" this week, and he feared he was rapidly approaching his breaking point. His mind flashed back to the putrid smell of urine in the bottom of his locker, and then he recalled the disgusting loogie hanging from his lock. Adam would pay for the latter offense after football season. But Pete still wasn't sure who showered his locker with urine. In a way, he hoped he never would find out. If he ever laid hands upon him, it could be very, very ugly.

Nevertheless, the prank his father was trying to pull on him right now was much larger by comparison. A six year hiatus from Pete and his mom's life, and now they were supposed to just open up the front door and let him back into their lives. What about the stack of 50 unanswered letters he had written? Oh but no, all alone in his miserable cell, Paul O'Connor chose to barricade himself from the rest of the world, refusing to communicate with the ones who really loved him and so desperately missed him. And what about his mother? Did he have any idea how much he hurt her when he refused to see her when she came to visit?

Hey, Dad, if you are really out there. It's too late—plain and simple. You made your choice, now live with it. Somewhere else, please.

Though the sky was robin's egg blue, Pete somehow sensed a storm on the horizon. First one, then another tiny teardrop emerged from the corner of his eye.

"Just leave me alone," Pete shouted—fully aware of how foolish he probably looked carrying on a conversation with himself as he walked along the street.

Suddenly, he heard a car honking behind him. He looked back and saw a burgundy sedan pulling off to the side of the road. After the car rolled to a complete stop, Roger Collins jumped out of the driver's seat with a wide grin across his face.

"What in the heck are you doing, O'Connor? You need a lift somewhere?"

Talk about adding insult to injury, thought Pete. Just thinking about accepting help from Roger gave him stomach pains. Nevertheless, Roger owed him, and picturing himself stretched out upon his couch in five minutes instead of 45 painful minutes was a proposition too irresistible to refuse. Sometimes you had to compromise your standards to get ahead in the world.

"Sure, I would really appreciate a lift right now. I was just working out at the Body Shoppe, and when I was ready to leave, I discovered some moron let the air out of my tires."

Pete moved quickly to the passenger side, opened the door, and let out a huge sigh of relief as he collapsed into the comfort of Roger's air-conditioned car. Immediately, the sweat on his skin began to evaporate. Roger turned down the volume of his FM stereo.

After a few moments of uncomfortable silence, Roger broke the ice. "You didn't have to go after Adam like that, you know. I would have paid him back sooner or later. I felt bad when Coach

Abraham made you run. I tell you, though. That kid is pretty freaky. Do you think everyone from Billington is like that?"

Choosing to leave the last question unanswered, Pete responded, "I figured I might catch a little bit of heat for laying him out, but you can't let a guy get away with taking a cheap shot on your teammate. And we can't afford to have you getting hurt like that. You're okay, aren't you?"

"I'm a little stiff in my lower back, but I'll be fine." Roger's eyes focused on the road as he asked his next question. "So how do I get to your house from here?"

A slight hesitation in his voice, Pete answered, "I live in Maple Village. You know where Henry and River Avenue meet, just before the high school."

Roger drove silently ahead, trying to think of something appropriate to say. "You know, I think we should be pretty good this year. I think our D is going to be tough, and once our offense gets going, we'll start putting points on the board."

Pete looked over at Roger and said, "David is doing a decent job at quarterback, but he'll never have the arm that you have."

"I hope I get another shot, but I'm kind of enjoying getting to play defense. I love coming up from my corner position and putting a big sting on someone."

"Well, don't give up on quarterback. We may need you before this is all over."

Pete turned on to Henry Street, passing the high school on his right. He noticed Adam Foster walking all alone across the parking lot.

"There's our buddy from Billington right now," said Roger, looking over at Pete with a look of mischief on his face. "What do you say we stop and say hello?"

"I'd rather not, Roger. I would just as soon stay as far away from trouble as possible. I don't trust myself around him."

How ironic! A couple days ago Pete had wanted to rip Roger into pieces with his bare hands. He had been certain that Roger had been the one who had urinated in his locker. Now he wasn't so sure. Surely, Roger wouldn't appear to be so at ease right now if he had committed such a despicable deed. Perhaps, it had been this Adam Foster punk. But what did Adam have against him anyway? Why would he want to start something? Pete was beginning to feel like he had enemies all around him. And all he wanted to do was play football. Was that too much to ask?

Roger drove past their unpopular teammate, choosing to ignore him this time. A few blocks down was the entrance to Maple Village.

"You can let me out right here at the entrance. I'll walk the rest of the way."

"It's okay. I can take you home. It's no problem."

Turning left onto Strawberry Lane, Roger came upon a group of elementary kids who were swerving their bikes back and forth in front of him, forcing him to abide by the 10 mph speed limit. They seemed completely unaware that someone was behind them. A couple of older men were tuning up a Chevy pickup; one was smoking a cigarette while his partner was under the hood. The next trailer was Pete's

Roger had never been in a trailer park before. He was shocked by the size of the lots and the trailers. He could fit three, maybe four trailers inside of his home.

As he pulled into the short driveway in front of Pete's trailer, he asked, "So what are you up to this weekend, Pete?"

"Tonight I'm just going to kick back and watch the football game on TV. I've got to work graveyard tomorrow night, but I'll probably do something beforehand."

"There's a big bash tomorrow night at the Pit. Maybe, I'll see you out there."

"We'll see. Behave yourself, though, would ya?"

"Don't worry, Pete. I'm just going out there to see if there are any hot looking babes in need of some company."

"Thanks for the ride, Roger. I don't know if I would have ever been able to walk the whole distance."

"No problem. See ya around, Pete."

Pete stepped out of the car and walked up the sidewalk to the front door of his trailer. He was so relieved to finally be home. Tomorrow he would borrow his mom's pickup to retrieve his bike. All he wanted to do now was eat and watch some football—and put his feet up, of course.

Slowly, he reached down to pick up the newspaper. He placed it under his arm, reached into his pocket, pulled out his key, and opened the door to an empty trailer—like he had hundreds of times over the past six years.

Entering the compact-sized living room, Pete sunk into the soft, heavily-worn sofa while immediately turning to the sports section of the Juddville Gazette. His primary interest was the televised sports schedule for the weekend. A much needed smile emerged on his face as he read the following listing:

138

Less than an hour until kickoff. Normally on Friday night, Pete would give his buddies Nick and Dave a call. Tonight, however, he had a date with his 26 inch RCA color television. He set the paper down on the couch and scurried to the kitchen and put a frozen Tombstone pizza in the oven. Suddenly remembering that he still hadn't showered after the morning's grueling practice and the afternoon's workout at the gym, Pete indulged himself with a steaming-hot 10 minute shower.

He could hear the timer for the pizza ringing as he stepped out from the shower. Wearing only a towel draped around his waist, he sprinted to the kitchen and removed the pepperoni and sausage pizza—another minute and the cheese on top would have browned. He set the pizza on the stove and returned to the bathroom to finish toweling off. After putting on a clean pair of Lee cut-offs and a t-shirt, Pete returned to the kitchen where the aroma of a sizzling hot pizza awaited him. Cutting the pizza into eight pieces, he could hardly wait to sink his teeth into one of his favorite snacks. To satisfy his intense thirst, he filled a 16 oz glass with milk, and carried the milk and pizza into the living room. As an after thought, he went back to the kitchen to double-check if he had turned off the oven, and grabbed two lengths of paper toweling to serve as a napkin.

The first piece of pizza was devoured in two bites—singeing the roof of his mouth; two huge gulps of milk chased the scalding tomato sauce down his throat, but the damage had been done. Pete turned on the television to see if he could catch the preview for tonight's game at the end of the local news broadcast. Pieces #2, #3, and #4 descended into his stomach in rapid succession. Piece #5 was interrupted by an introduction to the sports news. Jack Wagner, the local sports media guru, spoke directly into the camera, "Coming up next, News from the PGA, and an exclusive preview of the Eagles' first exhibition game."

Pete polished off his fifth and sixth pieces of pizza during the commercial break. In the one quick swallow, the glass of milk was drained, and he had been contemplating refilling his glass before Jack Wagner reappeared on his TV set.

"Tonight's matchup between the New Haven Eagles and the New Jersey Dragons will be a big test for both teams. Free agent signee, Dan Hayford, will be the leading the Eagles at quarterback. But the star quarterback will be without the services of All-Pro wide receiver Mike Simmons who is in the midst of a contract holdout. The rest of the starting offense should be intact, however, so tonight should be a good test for the Eagles.

"The Dragons' defense, led by All-Pro linebacker Kent Karchinski, is eager to reestablish their dominance from a year ago. Karchinski is coming back from extensive surgery on his right shoulder that gave him so much trouble the second half of last season. Reports from the Dragons' training camp are that Karchinski is as close to 100% as he probably ever will be in this stage of his illustrious career, and that he is on a personal mission to disprove critics who have been calling for him to end his career.

"The Dragons will also be suiting up without former Juddville gridiron star Jimmy Harrison, the playmaking tight end who retired at the end of last season. Needless to say, the Eagles' Preseason Kickoff should be a great contest."

Switching to the weather, Pete clicked the television off, setting the sports page on his lap as he grabbed the last piece of pizza. There wasn't any news about Karchinski in the paper, but there was an interesting article about Jimmy Harrison. Apparently, he was scheduled to speak tomorrow at a local church.

The story on the New Haven Eagles included a quote from Coach Fazio: "We're coming off an intense week of practice and we're eager to put our new offense on display. Hayford will play the entire first quarter and possibly one or two series in the second quarter." Fazio went on to predict that their defense should be one of the most dominant in the league. Since the first roster cuts were on Tuesday, the second half of the exhibition game would be devoted to evaluating personnel in game situations.

Pete finished off the last bite of pizza as he scanned the paper for other news around the UFL. Before tossing the paper into the magazine basket, he checked the television sports schedule a second time; he noted there were televised games on Saturday afternoon, Saturday night, and Sunday night. Pete smiled, and asked himself, *Is there any better time of the year?*

Chapter Fifteen

It was 12:30 a.m. when Jim Allen crawled out of bed and walked quietly to the kitchen. After some rare time alone with his wife, Jim and Mary had drifted peacefully off to sleep. It had been the perfect ending to a wonderful evening, and they were well-aware that this was to be the last Friday night together as a family for the next two to three months.

Now Jim was wide awake. What was on his mind wasn't football, but instead, this ridiculous breakfast he had been pressured into attending. Why did he ever agree to spend his last "free" Saturday morning of the summer cooped up in some stale church basement, listening to a bunch of squares talking about the evil world they had barricaded themselves from? He wished Mary had objected. In fact, he had been counting on it. Instead, she was supportive—even enthusiastic—about his going.

Of course, there was no way he could have lied to Coach Abraham either. Although Keith was ignorant about much of Jim's past and of his private life outside of school and football, their day-to-day communication as coaches was built upon a foundation of honesty with one another. When Coach Abraham wanted Jim's opinion regarding Xs and Os, Jim felt compelled to be 100% truthful, even if his opinion was 180 degrees contrary to Keith's. But when it came to political issues or God issues, Jim preferred to keep his views private. On several occasions Jim had to back off from becoming too emotional over a heated argument with Coach Abraham regarding issues such as Mary working part-time or whether it was a sin to drink an occasional beer. On most social issues, Keith saw things as either black or white. Jim acknowledged that there were certain issues that had a clear right and wrong, but he felt the vast majority of social issues contained a gray area where neither side was absolute. For instance, did a person have to be a member of a church in order to go to heaven? Jim wanted to believe in God and to learn more about Him, but he chose not to be a part of the "country club" atmosphere of church.

What really irked Jim even more than having to give up his last free Saturday morning was this: he didn't like to be manipulated or coerced into doing something he didn't want to do. Jim did not want to become a member of Keith's church, and he felt that this was just another attempt of Keith's to wear down his reluctance. Jim had a lot of doubts, a lot of questions, and a lot of fears about church. Nevertheless, he had given Keith his word that he'd be there, so there was no backing out now.

Maybe I'm making too much out of it, thought Jim, as he treaded softly from his bedroom, down the stairs, and into the kitchen.

His destination was the freezer where he retrieved the half gallon container of Neapolitan ice cream. Late night ice cream binging was an indulgence Jim was having great difficulty giving up. Ever since he had become a married man, he had ended just about every evening with an over-sized bowl of his favorite ice cream. Tonight he had fallen asleep relatively early, so it was appropriate for him to interrupt his sleep for a brief midnight snack. Besides, ice cream always helped him fall asleep.

After serving himself three giant-sized scoops, he returned the almost-empty container to the freezer compartment, and carried his bowl down to the basement. He turned on the television and automatically turned to the sports channel. The majority of news this evening pertained to baseball which he suffered through in order to get to the reports on the first night of exhibition football. Jim's eyes were becoming heavy by the time the New Haven Eagles report began, but he managed to hear that they had won, scoring all their touchdowns in the second half. The first offense had produced only three points in the first half. Hayford had quarterbacked all but the last series of the first half, and ironically, the final series of the first half was when the Eagles had scored their 47 yard field goal.

So much for high-priced free agent quarterbacks, thought Jim as he watched the reports on three other exhibition games before noticing that it was already 1:00 a.m., and his alarm would be going off in another six hours. Without making any noise, Jim tiptoed upstairs to the kitchen, and rinsed out his bowl and spoon in the sink. Then he gingerly walked up the carpeted stairs. Stopping just outside of Luke's bedroom, Jim could hear the sound of his soft breathing; he couldn't resist the temptation to go in and have a look at his oldest son. The New Haven Eagle football helmet nightlight cast just enough light for him to see Luke's head resting peacefully on his pillow. How could it be that Luke was seven years old already? In another two years, he will have used up half of his years living under their roof.

Jim knelt alongside his bed and kissed him gently on the forehead. Then he went to Kevin's room, and finally, Katie's. Before sliding back under the coziness of the down comforter covering their king-sized bed, he double-checked the alarm clock to see if it was set for 7:00 a.m. The cool breeze blowing in from the bedroom window had created an ideal temperature for sleeping, and it was only minutes before he was back to sleep.

Keith Abraham was awakened by a loud thud coming from the kitchen. Peering through fog-covered eyes, trying to locate the red digital numbers on his alarm clock, he was eventually able to discern the current time: 3:13.

142

*Is that Julia? Where in the world has she been? I'll have to
have another father-to-daughter conversation with her tomorrow.*

Mindful of tomorrow morning's busy agenda at church, Coach
Abraham rolled back over on his stomach and immediately fell
back to sleep.

Meanwhile, Julia gently lifted the stool back up to its proper
position. She went to the cupboard to the right of the sink, grabbed
a large glass, and filled it with ice from the freezer; then she filled
the glass with water from the dispenser outside the refrigerator
door. She took two huge gulps, refilled her glass, and then crept
upstairs to her bedroom where she stripped off her clothes and
pulled on a night shirt.

Cautiously poking her head from the doorway of her room,
she deduced that her parents were both asleep, so she walked to the
bathroom where she brushed her teeth and gargled with mouthwash.

She frowned at her reflection in the mirror. Her eyes were
tear-stained, her dark brown hair disheveled. For the past four
weeks, Julia had been treated like someone truly special. All of her
life she had wanted someone to adore her, someone to make her feel
like a MVP.

Along came Brian. Not exactly on the same career track as
her and certainly not anyone that she would have ever seen herself
falling for—she had always tended to avoid older guys for they
generally had only one thing on their minds. Yet there were
obvious advantages to having an older boyfriend—particularly, one
who had reached the magical age of twenty-one and could legally
buy alcohol.

Brian Taylor was an assistant manager at the Sub Shoppe, and
in the winter he was going to start taking classes at the local
community college; his goal was to earn an associate's degree in
business. Julia had been seeing him for over a month now; most of
their dates had been to movies or to parties. Brian treated her like
royalty.

Tonight, however, he had made her feel somewhat
uncomfortable. He had hinted at the idea of getting a room at the
Best Western Hotel tomorrow night. Julia had entertained the idea
only for a brief moment; then she turned him down for a number of
good reasons. For one, she didn't want to give away her body to
someone she was only just starting to get to know. Second, she
would be leaving for college on Sunday so she intended to get a
good night's rest in her own bed the night before—not rolling
around in some cheap hotel bed. Finally, her parents would go
ballistic if she stayed out all night. It wasn't usually a problem if

she stayed out past midnight on Saturdays—as long as she was able to get up for church Sunday morning. The last thing she wanted to do was rock the boat her last night home and have to sit before the Abraham grand jury the next day.

Julia had tried to explain all this to Brian with infinite gentleness, but he became real quiet at the mention of the words "leaving for college the next day".

His only response was simply, "I thought you really liked me."

On the drive home, he didn't speak a word, but Julia could feel the anger radiating from him. By the time they pulled into her driveway, their relationship had all of a sudden become a perilous airplane slipping out of control, both engines failing, headed for imminent disaster.

Taking Julia completely by surprise, Brian turned down his stereo, put his hand upon her shoulder, and said, "Julia, I'm sorry. I shouldn't be acting this way. You don't deserve this. I'm just mad at the idea of having to let you go. I've never been so close to a girl before, and I'm paranoid that you'll find someone else when you're off at school."

Julia was quick to respond. "Oh, Brian, I won't be looking for anyone else... Believe me, I wish I didn't have to go. It's just..."

Brian wrapped his arms around her, and kissed her before she could say another word. Then he pulled back and said, "You better go. We've still got one more night before you leave, don't we?"

"Yeah, I guess," she muttered, and before she could get any more words out, she began to choke up. Embarrassed by her uncharacteristic outbreak of emotion, she stumbled out of his car and quickly waved goodbye.

How could she leave behind the one person in this world that she could be herself around and actually be appreciated? Sure, Brian had a few rough edges. All of her friends had been in a state of shock when she started dating him. Their most frequent criticism was that he was still working in a restaurant after graduating more than three years ago. And Julia would never forget the poisonous words of her ex-best friend Amber who said, "What kind of loser still hangs out at high school parties when he could be hanging out at bars with people his own age?"

Julia's immediate rebuttal was, "If we didn't have guys like Brian, who would we get to buy for us?"

Never one to concede the last word, Amber responded, "Just because they buy for us, doesn't mean we need to start dating them."

Her parents had been far more critical. Naturally, her father's criticism pointed towards football. On dozens of occasions, he had reminded her that Brian had been kicked off the jayvee squad for stealing money out of teammate's locker. Then he would usually proceed down his list of bullet points:

- "What is he doing now, Julia? He's working in a fast food restaurant."
- "He's three years older than you. He should be a senior in college."
- "What about his faith? Is he a Christian, Julia? We know you're old enough to make your own decisions, honey, but..."

Julia had heard the sermon over and over. She only wished that her parents had had an opportunity to see the side of Brian that she knew. But that would never happen now.

In one sense, Brian wasn't much different from any of the other boys she had dated. Most of her previous boyfriends had felt intimidated around "the Coach", and it didn't matter if they were one of his "golden boys" or a non-football player.

As Julia rested her weary head on her pillow, her feelings toward Brian became overshadowed by her dread of college. The mere thought of going off somewhere all alone was terrifying. Why couldn't she just work for a year like so many of her friends were doing? When she brought up that possibility with her parents, they put a kabash on that idea once and for all. "If you want us to help pay for your college," they had insisted, "You're going to get started immediately." There was absolutely no possibility of her postponing college for a year. It felt like they couldn't wait to get her out of the house.

Julia wasn't even sure why she was going to college in the first place. She had no clue as to what career she was interested in, and she had barely met the entrance requirements at Tyler College. Her SATs were a bit low; it was only because of her B average and because both parents were Tyler Alumni that she was admitted.

The thought of moving 120 miles from Brian and rooming with a complete stranger petrified her. Furthermore, Tyler was a small Christian college located in a nothing town out in the middle of no where. What kind of social life could she hope to find there? Tears began to soak her pillow case as pulled her blanket tightly around her and drifted off to sleep.

Jim jolted out of bed at exactly 7:00 a.m. He desperately wanted to turn off the alarm and enjoy a few more hours of peaceful slumber on this sacred Saturday morning. But his mind alerted him of the obligation that awaited him—it was nearly as bad as a wedding—and he limited himself to only 10 more minutes of sleep by hitting the snooze button just once this morning. When he jumped back into bed and cuddled up next to Mary, she seemed impervious to him and to the alarm clock.

When the alarm went off again at 7:10, this time Jim turned off the alarm for good and navigated himself in the direction of the master bathroom where he treated himself to a steaming hot, ten-minute shower. After meticulously drying himself off, he dressed casually in a pair of khaki shorts, a white golf shirt, and loafers. He figured that many of the men would be wearing long pants, a button shirt and tie, but Jim refused to make an already uncomfortable experience "unbearable".

Harboring virtually zero enthusiasm for the morning's proceedings, he walked downstairs into the kitchen and made a half pot of coffee. While waiting for the coffee to finish brewing, he walked out to the mailbox and grabbed the Juddville Gazette. When he had returned to the kitchen, the coffee was almost done.

Close enough, he thought to himself as he grabbed his favorite mug from the cupboard, filling it to the brim with his early morning necessity.

Since it was going on 7:30, he proceeded directly to the sports page, perhaps he could catch up on the rest of the news later. He had just enough time to finish one cup of coffee while skimming through the brief summaries of last evening's exhibition games. By 7:45, Jim had filled his travel mug and was begrudgingly heading out the door, praying that the next two hours would go by as quickly as possible.

When he arrived at Faith Community Church, he was hoping to find a parking space close to Keith's, but there were already more than 50 cars in the parking lot. Naturally, Coach Abraham must have been the first to arrive, for his car was right next to the church's side entrance. Jim settled for a parking spot closest to the exit. He envisioned himself being the first to his car in an *optimistic* ninety minutes.

His heart began to quicken and his lungs became tight as he slowly got out of his minivan. A thin-scalped father accompanied by his teenage son—the latter, suffering from major bed-head—entered the building just before him. A simple sign was posted on the door, **Men's Breakfast: Enter here.** Jim followed them down the corridor to a large meeting room where there must have been at least 50 circular tables, each surrounded by a half-dozen folding chairs. About two-thirds of the tables and chairs were already filled. Jim frantically scanned the room for Keith or for any familiar face.

Not surprised in the least, he located Keith directly in front of the podium; he was proudly wearing his new Juddville Jaguar game shirt. As Jim maneuvered between the crowded tables to the front of the room, he avoided making eye-contact with the hundred-or-so faceless strangers, assuring himself that there couldn't possibly be anyone here that he might recognize or that he might want to talk to should there be a break in the morning's activities.

At a table to the right of Keith's, he was surprised to see David Riley sitting along side his dad with their backs to him. Jim put his hand on David's shoulder, speaking abruptly, "Hey, David. What are you doing up so early when you could be sleeping in?"

Turning to face his coach, "Hi, Coach Allen."

David's father offered Jim a firm handshake, "Coach, I'm Jack Riley. It's a pleasure to meet you."

"The pleasure is mine, Jack. You've got a fine boy."

"Thank you. David's told me a lot about you."

Jim couldn't keep from blushing as he recalled some of the "choice" quotes David might have shared from the first week of practice.

Mr. Riley continued, "David says he's learning a lot about the game of football. I want to thank you for your willingness to coach. I know it's pretty tough these days to find good coaches willing to put in the time and willing to put up with all the harassment."

"Well, thank you, sir." He wasn't sure what else to say. Jim wasn't accustomed to receiving such heartfelt appreciation. As a result, he generally avoided getting "chummy" with parents; they generally had a not-so-hidden agenda, and it always seemed to revolve around how much playing time their son was receiving.

"David's really working his tail off. What I like about him best is his attitude and character."

Out of the corner of his eye, Jim could see Keith approaching with a mammoth-size grin. "Hey, Coach Allen, I am so glad you could make it. I saved you a seat up front."

Looking over to the Rileys, Keith added, "Good morning, Jack. Good morning, David. Did you get your running in this morning, David?"

"Sorry, Coach. I'm not planning on running until about noon when it's hotter."

"Well, it's 7:59. We should be getting started. Why don't we have a seat, Jim? There's coffee at our table, and I can't wait to introduce you to Jimmy Harrison."

I sure hope it's caffeinated, Jim thought to himself as he approached their table with mild apprehension. It didn't take a genius to identify the only person seated at their table having broad enough shoulders to have played in the UFL. He was sipping coffee from a Styrofoam cup. His hands were gigantic, capable of holding two or three cups in one hand if he wanted.

"Jimmy, I'd like you to meet my assistant coach, Jim Allen."

"Good morning, Jim. If I might say, you've got an excellent first name, Coach."

Jim was too afraid not to laugh, so he pretended like it was the funniest joke he had ever heard. Shaking the former UFL player's hand, Jim responded, "It's a pleasure to meet you, Jimmy."

"How did your first week of practice go, Coach?" asked Jimmy.

Just as Coach Allen was about to answer, the conversation was interrupted by Pastor Jenkins who was ready to begin the breakfast with a brief welcome and opening prayer.

As Jim bowed his head to pray, his appetite was on full-alert as the tantalizing smell of pancakes and sausage wafted up to his nose. He couldn't help but peek at the cinnamon rolls and assortment of fresh melon sitting before him.

Hurry up, Pastor, he thought to himself. He couldn't wait to hear the word "Amen".

At the conclusion of the prayer, Coach Allen was a man on a mission as he proceeded to inhale two helpings of sausage and pancakes, pausing just long enough between bites to drain a glass of orange juice and two cups of coffee. When he finally pushed himself back from the table, he decided he needed a quick bathroom break.

On his way back to the table, Jim was surprised by all the chatter and enthusiasm at such an early hour of the day. Evidently Jimmy was about to be introduced, for Pastor Jenkins was working his way up towards the podium.

Coach Allen was shocked by the ordinary appearance of the UFL star. Dressed in plain blue jeans and a loose fitting golf shirt—XXL, no doubt—he didn't look like a millionaire. His only symbol of prestige was the championship ring on his right hand. It probably weighed a couple pounds; every time he lifted his fork to devour another bite of pancake, the diamonds sparkled like an ice-covered pond in February.

Aware of all the attention his ring was drawing around the table, Jimmy said—with a sheepish expression on his face—"This is my Super Bowl ring. Can you believe the size of it? A bit extravagant, don't you think? You want to know the funniest part? The insurance premium I have to pay on it is more expensive than the premium on my car."

Coach Allen stared at the ring in awe. It was enormous. Masterfully engraved were the words *Super Bowl Champions: New Jersey Dragons*. The ring probably was more expensive than most of the automobiles in the church parking lot.

While everyone was gawking at Jimmy's ring, Coach Abraham decided to get in on some of the attention by removing his Juddville State Championship ring and holding it up for the rest of the table to view. It was like comparing a VW bug against a BMW. Coach Allen was glad he had left his ring at home. Even though it was much smaller than Jimmy's Super Bowl ring, it was still quite bulky. Consequently, Jim chose to display his ring in his trophy case at home, and he was comforted by the fact that he didn't have to worry about anyone breaking into his home to try to steal it.

Coach Abraham leaned over to Jim and said, "We'll have to order bigger rings next time, Coach. Did you get enough to eat?"

"I'm stuffed." Patting his bloated stomach, Jim added, "I'm usually not much of a breakfast person—usually just a few cups of coffee—but when I get the opportunity for a feast like this, I go all out. Those pancakes were out of this world."

"You got plans for the rest of the weekend, Jim?"

"Probably just relax by the pool… play with the kids, you know."

"I've got to bring Julia up to Tyler College tomorrow, so I'll be gone most of the day. I was wondering if you might have some time later today to go over a few defensive adjustments I've been toying with."

Before Jim could make up an excuse, he was rescued by Pastor Jenkins who was beginning his introduction with great fervor. While the pastor rambled through his summary of Jimmy's accomplishments, Coach Allen couldn't help but notice Juddville's most famous son nonchalantly slipping off his ring, stealthily placing it in the front pocket of his blue jeans.

As Pastor Jenkins enumerated the athletic accomplishments of the featured speaker, Coach Allen surveyed the large meeting room and noticed that all of the tables were filled; in fact, a few tables had been added at the last minute. There was even a photographer and reporter from the Juddville Gazette. Jim was amazed by the number of men who had been willing to rise out of bed at such an early hour on a Saturday morning.

Finally, the introduction had come to its conclusion. When Big Jimmy elevated from his seat, it seemed like he just kept getting taller and taller. He looked like one of those mechanical extension ladders on fire trucks; he must have stopped extending at the height of about 6'8''. The people seated in the back of the room would have no trouble seeing the speaker on this occasion. Nevertheless, Coach Allen noted a slight degree of nervousness in the former UFL player as he began his speech.

The attention of the audience was fully engaged. Jimmy Harrison looked at his audience and then began:

"On any given day, you can pick up a copy of a newspaper and read yet another story about the moral failure of a professional athlete. Maybe it's possession of drugs, or maybe drunk driving, or soliciting a prostitute, or perhaps, domestic violence. And you wonder, how does this happen? Why would someone who has it all, do something so stupid, something so fundamentally wrong?"

Jimmy paused, and looked down at his notes with a very grave expression on his face.

"Yet those are, I am afraid, only the stories of those who have been caught in their sin."

Raising his eyes again to meet the audience, "If the truth were known, most of us have a lot of garbage in our lives that the world would love to read. I—for one—have made a colossal amount of mistakes in my lifetime. And I shudder to even think about the possibility of my children ever hearing about them.

"Today I want to tell you about the turning point in my life. It occurred at a time in my life when I was truly living a double life. And when you are living a double life as a professional athlete, the pressure is unbelievable. You see, there was one side of me that the press and all of my fans saw: the strength, the swagger, the confidence, the total package of success. But the other side of me—the dark side, if you will—the side most people never see, the person I was at home in the presence of my wife and family, that person was entirely different.

"I was angry, full of lust, bored with everyday life, always looking for some new thrill. What was most troublesome was the perception I had towards the people around me. I trusted absolutely no one, and I suspected those around me as leeches—only by my side to gain something for themselves. Though I was constantly surrounded by all kinds of people, I felt secluded, devoid of what

150

the rest of the world enjoyed and took for granted: true companionship.

"Then I was introduced to someone who knew everything about me: the good, the bad, and the wicked. Although He did not condone my selfish attitude and sinful actions, He still loved me and accepted me, regardless."

As Jimmy went on to describe his first encounter with God, he spoke about how it wasn't about him becoming religious; instead, it was about having a relationship with the Creator of the world. The point of Jimmy's message that really caught Coach Allen's attention was when Jimmy admitted that his biggest obstacle to entering into a relationship with God was his UFL-sized super ego.

Though every cell in Coach Allen's body resisted even the idea of surrender, he knew he had been making such a mess of his life that maybe it was worth a try. All of his life Jim had abided by the following rule: no one tells me what to do. Unfortunately, he was all too familiar with seclusion, with loneliness, and with a life void of purpose. The distinguished speaker was certainly speaking about an issue to which Jim could truly relate.

"Today I would like to give you an invitation to join a team that is destined for the ultimate victory. A team that has an MVP quarterback. His name is Jesus Christ, and He is in direct contact with His Father, the Creator of this game called life. If you are willing to put your trust in Him, and to run His plays—even if it requires you to put your life on the line in the most treacherous trenches—I assure you that you will experience the ultimate victory.

"The journey will not be easy—if you think you'll be able to carry the ball across the goal line without meeting adversity, you're fooling yourself. The enemy has a middle linebacker who is constantly on the prowl; staring us down from the other side of the ball, trying to cast fear and doubt into our minds. He wants nothing more than to knock you and me down, to strip the ball from our hands, and to send us off the field on a stretcher. Moreover, he will do anything to deceive us into switching uniforms… into coming along side him on evil's side."

The analogy between life and the game of football was impossible for Coach Allen to ignore.

"You need to shut your ears to Satan's relentless taunting and listen instead to the clear cadence of our MVP quarterback. You need to open up our Creator's playbook and begin to commit it to memory. You've been running plays from the enemy's playbook for too long; they are filled with deceit, destruction, and despair.

Oh sure, they look good on paper, promising you swift victory and instant gratification. But they will leave you spiritually bankrupt and mortally wounded.

"Open your heart to Jesus; even now he is waiting for you, right by your side. He's reaching out with his nail-pierced hands, waiting for you to grab hold, so He can lift you up on your feet again and lead you back onto the playing field. Take a look at His uniform; do you see how it is so bloody and tattered? Do you know the beating he took for you? Do you know why? The Bible says, 'By His wounds, you have been healed'. Accept his helping hand before the clock runs out. It's the fourth quarter, the two-minute warning. There is no time to waste. Won't you join Him for this fantastic finish?"

Jimmy paused for a moment, casting his gaze across the room, the sincerity and intensity of his eyes too powerful and impossible to avoid.

"Let me tell you something else—for all you go-it-alone John Waynes out there. The plays designed by the Creator won't work if you try to execute them all by yourself. For one, without your All-Universe quarterback, you don't have a prayer. Secondly, you need teammates to help you in the trenches. One of Satan's most deceptive plays is to entice you into a remote corner of the playing field, all by yourself, where no one can help you fight off the enemy's constant barrage of blitzes.

"The truth is you need a few teammates to run interference for you, a few teammates to steady you when you start to lose your balance. You need a few trustworthy, battle-tested men you can trust, men who will point you back to the huddle where the Captain is waiting to recharge you with His supernatural power.

"Solomon—in his infinite wisdom—wrote in Ecclesiastes 4, 'Two are better than one because they have a good return for their work; if one falls down, his friend can help him up. But *pity* the man who falls and has no one to help him up... Though one may be overpowered, two can defend themselves. A cord of three strands is not quickly broken'."

Coach Allen took a moment to sip from his water glass; for the first time in his life, he felt like his eyes were truly open. He was relieved to see Pastor Jenkins walking towards the microphone.

Is it possible that the message is already over? Nobody wants to be out of here sooner than me, but Jimmy seems to be just getting started. Let him speak awhile longer, thought Jim.

Not to worry. Pastor Jenkins was only announcing an intermission. Jim was appreciative of the opportunity to visit the restroom and refill his coffee cup if time permitted. All of a sudden, Jim felt a hand on his shoulder.

"Hey, Coach. What's your impression so far?" asked Coach Abraham.

"Pretty powerful message, Keith. He's got my mind racing in all different directions." Jim looked down at his watch. "How much longer will he speak?"

Jim was conditioned as a teacher and as a coach to be constantly tuned-in to his watch. Everything had to be organized into neatly divided increments of time, just like television.

It was already 8:45, and Jim was expecting to be home by 9:30—10:00 a.m., at the latest. Then he could plan the next activity for the day—most likely a nap. Unfortunately, Jimmy's message was already beginning to slip from his consciousness.

"Oh, I think it's probably half-time, Jim." Changing the subject, Coach Abraham boasted to a crowd of men who had begun to flock towards the podium, "You would not believe what a freight train Jimmy was for us. Nearly impossible to bring down. By far, the best player I ever coached. I think you started at Juddville the year after Jimmy graduated didn't you?"

Coach Allen nodded. His thoughts were split between his conversation with Keith and the fading remnants of Jimmy's message. Jim broke for the bathroom while Coach Abraham continued to reminisce.

"Jimmy played tight end and defensive end that year. Teams would actually start the game trying to block him with a running back. Then they'd try a tackle or a pulling guard. When that didn't work, they'd send a back and a lineman, and it still was doomed to failure. Our only problem was that we didn't have a quarterback that could throw to him. It was still a lot of fun that year, though. We knew Jimmy would have a good shot at playing Division I football because he was being heavily recruited already as a junior. But I never dreamed he'd make it to the pros."

Their conversation was abruptly interrupted by Pastor Jenkins who had assumed his position behind the microphone. Jim had returned with a full cup of steaming coffee.

"I hope you all had a chance to stretch out your legs for a few moments. We really have to keep this morning's program rolling. I know I can't wait to hear more from our prestigious guest speaker. Once again, Jimmy, we are so grateful for you to be here with us this morning."

Jimmy cleared his throat before resuming.

"Did you know what your most important role as a man is? Think about that for a minute. What comes to mind? Provide for your family? Protect your wife and kids? Discipline your children? Well, those are certainly a few of the important roles of a father, but did you know our most important purpose is to do everything in our power to bring all the people we love along with us to heaven. It's our most important mission. The only one that lasts forever.

"How are you doing in this area? Do you know if your wife and kids are going to heaven? Are your actions bringing them closer to heaven or are you driving them away? Too often our families get the short end of the stick—even in well-intentioned Christian families, I might add. Men are quick to devote their time and energy to their jobs, and to their hobbies, and sadly, even to their ministries, but we often have nothing left in the tank to give to our families. By our actions, we are, in effect, choosing to ignore and neglect the beautiful woman and the most precious children that God has entrusted to us. Is it any shock then that they often end up being spiteful towards God?"

Raising his voice several decibels louder, Jimmy's eyes pierced deeply into the gaze of his audience.

"Men, this is no time for us to abandon our sons and daughters, even if it is for a noble cause such as serving God's Kingdom. Don't serve up your children to Satan. He's ready to snatch them from us if we aren't awake.

"Do you know why our role as fathers is so vital? Here's a truth I've found that will make you stay awake at night. Did you know that the image we form of our Father in Heaven is patterned on the relationship we have or have had with our Earthly father? Think about your father for a moment. Was he distant, hard to reach? Is that the way you feel about God? Was your father cruel or abusive? Do you think God is cruel, unjust? Maybe you felt that you could never seem to get your dad's attention or his approval. Perhaps, you can still hear your dad ridiculing you after every baseball game, putting every error under the microscope while completely ignoring every play you made that was exceptional. If so, chances are you've always believed you needed to earn God's love. Somehow you've always been convinced that there must be something you're not doing that must be disqualifying you from earning God's favor. Privately, you beat yourself up because you don't quite measure up to this elusive standard of perfection that your daddy once held up for you.

"Well, let me put your heart to rest. No amount of good deeds will ever get you into heaven. And let me pass on to you another reminder: Jesus died for you when you were drowning, when you were up to your neck in your own cesspool of sin.

"Some of you might be wishing that you could have had any kind of earthly relationship with a father because your father died when you were young. Or even worse, he took off and left your mother to raise you. Is it any wonder you doubt the existence of God? Or maybe you had a phantom father. Rumor had it that you had a father that lived with you, but in reality, he was so rarely at home, and when he was home he never had a moment's time for you. And to make matters worse, your dad loved to offer up an Old Country Buffet's worth of promises, such as 'Son, after dinner let's play catch. I just have to make one phone call and I'll be right out.' So you sprint to the garage and grab your glove and your dad's glove and a baseball, and you go to the backyard and wait. You begin to throw yourself pop-ups. Your arm begins to tire and you wonder if your dad is coming. A half hour later you go back into the house and find your dad in a near-comatose state on the couch. You know from experience that it is not a good idea to awaken him. So over the years you learn to accept the fact that he is there, but he really isn't. And you begin to believe that maybe you don't need him after all."

Coach Allen had to take a deep, deep breath for that one. He was on the verge—no he was already there—of breaking down into tears.

Jimmy Harrison continued, "Is it any surprise that you view God as disconnected, completely uninvolved with the affairs of men? Sometimes we prejudice God by calling Him *Father*. With that name, we in some cases, place a label on Him that prevents us from ever wanting to open ourselves up to Him. But did you know that He is the Father of the fatherless. He has a special affection for you. The love He has for you is so great that He has provided a way for you to come back to Him. In fact, right now He is waiting for you to make that phone call home. You will never get a busy signal. The Bible says He never sleeps nor slumbers.

"The relationship He desires to have with you will fulfill you like no other. You can meet with Him at any hour of the day, as often as you like. In fact, you can meet with Him every morning for breakfast for the rest of your life. Furthermore, He'll never grow tired of your company. He can handle hearing all about your problems… all about your pain. And He won't try to dominate the discussion and try to make it all about Him. If only you'll open your heart to Him. If only you'll open your mind to His Word. The relationship He promises will far exceed any you might have once dreamed to have with your earthly father.

"One day, He will be waiting for you to join Him in Heaven. And you will get to hug Him; you will get to high-five the nail-pierced hands of His Son. It will be a celebration like no other."

Tears streamed down Jim's face faster than he could wipe them. At first, he was ashamed of his inability to turn back the flood of tears, but as he looked around him, he was at least comforted by the fact that the majority of men in the room were also crying unabashedly.

This experience had to qualify as the most bizarre of his life. He had no sense of this coming. He felt completely embarrassed yet delirious at the same time. For the first time in his life, he felt like he was breaking free, that he was somehow heading down a new path. A path with purpose. A path pointing to real victory.

Jim's attention drifted back towards the podium.

"God wants to be that Father you missed out on when you were growing up. He wants to lift you up on His shoulders and to show you the world from His view. He wants to give you advice on how to live, He wants to show you how to love, and show you how to be a real man, not some artificial, macho wimp. If you give Him the opportunity, He'll teach you how to become a real man, a man like His Son Jesus."

At this moment in Jimmy's message, the pastor walked back up to the podium and stood next to the gigantic guest speaker. Sitting at the table just a few feet away, Coach Allen's mind was spinning in circles. The message had scratched open many aged-old wounds. In contrast to most of the audience around him, Jim was not a churchgoer, and he didn't need to hear Jimmy's message to be reminded of his sinful condition. Each day of his life provided him with more than a few snapshots for his photo album of failure. That was the biggest sticking point for him. Time after time he had tried to change his bad habits, and he had always failed. He had long ago reached the point where it was hardly worth trying anymore.

Take his anger, for instance. Every time Jim made a conscious decision to put a lid on it, a new opportunity for failure was waiting for him just around the corner. It might be the car in front of him on his drive to work, driving five miles below the speed limit, seemingly immune to fact that it was occupying the express lane. Or maybe it would be the 14 year old boy in the front row who continues to come to class tardy with no book, no pencil, and no completed assignment to turn in. Within a blink of an eye,

Jim would be shouting profanity at the unknown driver or publicly lambasting the despondent teenager, cutting him to pieces with his ultra-sharp sarcasm. Moments later his conscience would be right beside him, whispering, "I told you so, you'll never change," into his ear.

But what troubled him the most were his mood swings around the house. He looked at Keith who was seated to his right. Jim had always envied his friend's ability to cope with the pressures of teaching and coaching. Sometimes, he wondered if Keith was human. It all seemed so easy for him.

Jim's thoughts were interrupted by the pastor who had assumed authority of the podium. "Now we're going to shift the focus of our program..."

Oh my gosh, thought Jim, *I thought this had to be the end!*

"... We've just heard a very challenging message from Brother Jimmy, and if you're like me, I'm sure he struck a nerve of yours at some point. We're going to spend a few moments in accountability before we dismiss. Otherwise, how can we be sure we'll act on our convictions? So what I'd like everyone to do in the next minute is to partner up with at least one if not two other men. In exactly 60 seconds, I'll give you further instructions."

I think the pastor had a little too much caffeine, thought Jim. *What was this all about anyway?* The last thing Jim wanted to do was get all touchy-feely with someone he hardly knew. And his mind began to formulate excuses for making a quick get-away.

My daughter has a doctor's appointment... No, it's Saturday.

Luke's got a soccer game... Not in August.

I have to pick up Mary's car from Baker's Auto Repair... That could wait until this afternoon.

His mind was reaching desperately for one legitimate excuse. The clock was running, he was out of timeouts, and he was about to get a delay of game.

Jim looked over at Keith. He didn't seem to look too overjoyed either.

What the heck. Maybe he'd even hear a good story or two. In another hour, it would all be over, and he'd be back in his car on his way home with the whole afternoon ahead of him.

Naturally, Jim chose to pair up with Keith. He hadn't expected the featured speaker to join their huddle, however.

"Powerful message, Jimmy," said Coach Abraham, reaching out to offer a congratulatory handshake.

Coach Allen added, "Sure gave me a lot to think about."

Jim felt awkward sitting in a group with two Super-Christians. He knew he had a lot to confess, but what could Keith possibly share? Obviously, they had just spent the last hour listening to the confessions of Jimmy. Whatever struggles this UFL star had faced in the past, he certainly must have earned compensation in heaven for his message this morning.

Jim felt an unavoidable pressure from his two partners to go first. Not much question in his mind about where to begin. Without going into too much detail, he made a sincere request for prayer for dealing with his anger.

He cleared his throat as his eyes began to water. "I'd also like to be totally honest with you guys about this salvation thing. It's just that I have a really hard time believing that all the humiliating, hurtful things that I've done in my lifetime can all be forgiven… completely swept clean from my record… just like that. It doesn't seem fair to me. Why would God make His Son pay for all my screw-ups?"

"I think you know the answer to that question, Jim," responded Jimmy, "It's His amazing love. None of us have earned it. None of us deserve it. It's a gift. It's the kind of love that could only come from Heaven."

Throughout the entire huddle so far, Coach Abraham had remained uncharacteristically quiet. His mind seemed to be vacationing in some distant, far away place. Meanwhile, Jim and Jimmy conversed back and forth, talking plainly, talking about God and about life, as if they were old high school buddies.

Then Coach Abraham unexpectedly excused himself from the huddle without offering any explanation.

Finally, their conversation came to a halt about 15 minutes later when Pastor Jenkins brought the morning's activities to a close by offering up a prayer. Usually, when Jim shut his eyes to listen to a prayer, he felt like he was eavesdropping on some heartless ritual. On this occasion, however, he could feel an electrifying sensation, a sense of euphoria, far greater even than the way he felt last season when the last second had ticked off the clock and the Juddville Jaguars had been crowned state champions. It was like the way his heart once felt like it was about to burst with joy and relief when Mary had agreed to marry him.

At the conclusion of Pastor Jenkins's prayer, Coach Allen opened his eyes and noticed that Jimmy was staring at him.

Jimmy leaned forward, rested his elbows on the table, his hands folded together.

"Can I ask you a personal question, Jim?"

"Sure, Jimmy," not nervous at all about his new friend's sincerity and trustworthiness.

"Have you ever prayed to receive God's gift of salvation?"

"Well, to be honest with you, Jimmy, I can't remember for sure. It could have happened when I was younger, back when my mom would bring me along with her to church. But it was so long ago, and if I did, I'm not sure I really was aware of what I was doing."

"Would you like to say that prayer right now?"

A smile broke out from the face of Coach Allen that was as brilliant and passionate as a July sunrise.

"Yes," Jim answered. "I'd like that."

For the next few minutes, the ex-UFL football star led Jim Allen through a prayer of confession, a prayer of submission, a prayer of great thanksgiving. When they opened their eyes, most of the men had cleared out, including Coach Abraham. Jim and Jimmy exchanged phone numbers, and Jimmy gave his new friend a mammoth-sized bear hug.

Finally, Jimmy Harrison said with the utmost sincerity, "If you ever need to talk or if you ever need anything, don't hesitate to call, you hear me, my friend?"

"Thank you, Jimmy. I can't thank you enough."

"No, thank Him. He's the man... the Son of Man," said Jimmy pointing to the cross at the front of the room.

As Coach Allen exited Faith Community Church, his feet felt so light he wanted to see if he could jump up and dunk a basketball with two hands.

Who would have figured, thought Jim. *Who would have figured? I wonder where Keith could have disappeared to in such a hurry.*

Chapter Sixteen

Pete slept in until 10:30. Generally, his mom got in later than usual on Fridays; her attendance at *Ernie's Pub* on payday was mandatory. It was the social highlight of her week, which meant staying up till at least closing time—even later if she and her girlfriends chose to go out for a late night breakfast afterwards. As a result, Pete had been conditioned to tread quietly across the floor of the O'Connor trailer on Saturday mornings.

On this particular morning, Pete had an additional incentive for not awakening his mom: he fervently wanted to avoid any resumption of the conversation they were having at lunch about his dad. As far as he was concerned, the possibility of his father being released from prison was a lost dream that he had stopped wishing for a long time ago. Furthermore, there was no way it could possibly be true. His dad was sentenced to a minimum of 10 years. So Pete dismissed the idea to the furthest recess of his mind.

After helping himself to two large bowls of Cheerios, an oversized Dole banana, and a large glass of orange juice, Pete retrieved the Juddville Gazette from the porch. It was lying on the heavily-trodden, dingy-green welcome mat. With extreme gentleness, he closed the front door, preventing even the slightest noise from intruding upon the tranquility of the morning hour. Sitting down on the couch in the living room, Pete scanned through the sports section, looking for the write-up of last night's exhibition game. He read a couple of other sports stories before dressing for his Saturday workout.

Ever so quietly he slipped on his gray Jaguar state championship tee-shirt, a pair of navy blue shorts, a clean pair of white athletic socks, and his Nike running shoes. Over his shoulder he carried his football cleats which he joined together by the laces.

Pete figured he would reach Raymond Sanders Stadium by 11:30. In the time it would take him to walk to the high school, his relatively-light breakfast would have had about an hour to digest. Although there was a slight degree of soreness in his pecs and triceps from yesterday's workout, his legs felt relatively fresh, and the prospect of getting his running out of the way before noon motivated him to walk faster. After his workout, he would have the rest of the day to enjoy before reporting to work at 11:00 p.m. for the graveyard shift.

As he walked through the trailer park, he passed several kids at the playground. A couple of boys were racing up the slide the wrong way; another handful of kids were swinging on the swing set; a larger group was playing a game of touch football—four on four. When Pete passed the latter group of youngsters, their game came to a momentary halt as they stared in awe at one of their heroes.

"Hey, guys. Toss me that ball a minute," said Pete.

The oldest boy looked nervously down at the ball in his hands, wondering if he would ever get the ball back if he offered it up to Pete. Not wanting to face the potential consequences of disobedience, he reluctantly tossed it to Pete. The ball fell a few feet short. Pete took a few steps towards the boy and picked it up.

He carried the ball over to the boy who had thrown him the ball. "Place your fingertips along the threads of the ball. Then when you release the ball, you roll your fingers off the ball, and you should get a pretty decent spiral, like this."

Then he threw the ball to a freckled-face boy who was standing timidly about 30 feet away. The ball made a loud thud upon his ketchup-stained tee-shirt, and he managed to pin the ball up against his chest before smiling proudly.

"You guys keep practicing hard. It won't be too long and you'll be the ones carrying the Jaguar tradition. Let me tell you. There's nothing better than strapping on the black and blue Juddville helmet on Friday nights and going to battle under the stadium lights."

The small tribe of boys nodded in agreement, and then the older boy who had thrown Pete the ball asked, "We gonna be state champs again this year?"

"We're gonna try," answered Pete, trying to sound more confident than his heart truly felt. "I'm going to get my running in right now, so I'll see you guys around."

"See you, Pete," answered the boys in unison.

By the time Pete had walked through the trailer park and had reached Henry Street, he could already feel the ruthless August sun searing his shoulders. He had to remind himself, however, that it wouldn't be too long before the days would grow short and the temperature would begin to drop to a more ideal temperature for the game of football. For now, he would have to do what everyone else was expected to do: just endure the heat. Besides, the one advantage of the extreme temperature was that it would enable him to get in the best possible shape faster.

Before long Pete was walking across the Juddville High School parking lot towards the front gate of Raymond Sanders Stadium. Even though he had played on the field dozens of times and sat in the bleachers as a spectator more times than he could count, he still couldn't help but stare in awe at its sheer size. For a town the size of Juddville, they had erected a monstrous football facility. It was the largest, best-maintained football field in their conference. The home bleachers alone held over 3,000 spectators, and the visitor's bleachers seated another 1,000. For the really "big" games, there would be another thousand fans lined up five-deep around the perimeter of the field. The town was simply obsessed with football; it was simply the most revered season of the year.

Pete sat down on the inside lane of track by the closest end zone and laced up his cleats. Then he stretched: first, the hamstrings, then the groin, followed by his quadriceps, and then finally his lower back. When he popped up onto his feet, he felt loose and ready to begin his rigorous running routine.

Starting at the goal line, he jogged the first 20 yards, the next 40 yards about a 75% sprint, and the final 40 at about 90% speed. He ran five yards past the goal line, turned around, walked up to the goal line, paused for about 15 seconds, and ran back to the original goal line. That was a warm-up.

Next, Pete ran a total of five, all-out 100 yard wind sprints. Then he gave himself a 60 second break. His lungs were on fire by this time, and the sweat in his eyes was beginning to sting. For the next set of sprints, he walked to the 20 yard line. For the second set he would be running seven 80 yard sprints. On the first sprint, he always appreciated the "shorter" distance of each set, but as for the remainder of the sprints, he couldn't feel any noticeable difference. Considering the fact that he had just completed a full week of intense football practices, he was disappointed by how much fatigue and discomfort he was feeling.

During his seventh 80 yard sprint, Pete began to feel dizzy, and he was beginning to zigzag as he approached the finish line. He decided it would be wise if he jogged over to the drinking fountain to replenish his water reserve before starting the third set. Just as he was bending over to get a drink, he heard a familiar voice calling out his name.

"Hey, Pete."

He turned around and spotted David Riley entering the front gate of the stadium. Pete was pleasantly surprised as he wasn't accustomed to having a running partner.

Gathering up enough breath before responding, Pete muttered, "Hey, David. What's up?"

"Not much. Mind if I run with you?" the emerging quarterback asked, feeling confident that Pete would want some company—after all, misery loves company.

"Sure, the more the merrier, I guess."

"I'll do a quick stretch and catch up with you."

In less than two minutes, David was up on his feet and running onto the game field where Pete had purposefully put off his next set of sprints, so he could have someone to push him.

"What are we running?" asked David.

162

"I've got nine 60's and eleven 40's left," answered Pete, eyes cast downwards at his feet.

"Well, what are we…?"

Before David could finish his sentence, Pete broke out of his two-point stance. By the distance of thirty yards, the teammates were neck and neck. With less than 10 yards to go, David passed his partner, finishing a full stride ahead of him.

Pete was clearly irritated at himself and immediately turned around and lined back up for the next 60 yard sprint. David hurried to get back up to the line.

"Ready?" sneered Pete.

David nodded. Again, the captain led the way.

Though David's legs were fresher, Pete stayed even with him for the next seven sprints. For the final 60 yard sprint—with only 20 yards to go—David blazed ahead of Pete, finishing more than five yards ahead.

Pete crossed the finish line and collapsed to one knee. He had tried as hard as he could to match his running partner's final burst of speed, but he had come up short.

I'm already beginning to run like a lineman, he thought to himself.

Lifting up the mid-section of his tee-shirt, Pete wiped the sweat from his eyes. Suddenly, his stomach began to contract, and before he could do anything about it, not less than a quart of oat mush spewed violently from his mouth. The bitter taste combined with the salty perspiration cascading down his face was unbearable. He spat repeatedly on the ground.

David stood beside him, cautiously waiting for the right moment to intrude. Finally, he spoke, "Are you going to be alright, Pete?"

Hearing his voice, but choosing to ignore him, Pete staggered to his feet.

"Hey, Pete. Are you okay?"

Slowly, he turned his head 90 degrees towards David, and as his eyes adjusted on his teammate's face, he could see the sincerity in his eyes.

Pete cleared his throat and then responded. "Yeah, I'm okay. I guess I overdid it on breakfast. Let's move up 20 yards to get away from my Cheerios."

As they neared the new starting line, Pete was already feeling better.

"Okay, we've got eleven 40's, and then we're done. This time you're blowing chunks, Riley."

"Bring it on, bring it on, O'Connor. Now I know what the O's in your last name stand for."

"You're real funny, Prima David."

Jim had just polished off a bologna and Muenster cheese sandwich—smothered in Hellmanns—some plump green grapes, and a large glass of 2% milk. The kids were still inside finishing off their Spaghetti-Os while he stretched out on his favorite lounge chair, hoping to fall asleep reading the latest Tom Clancy thriller. Just as the words from page 73 began to blur, he heard the sliding glass door open and his wife's voice calling out.

"Jim, Jim. Phone call for you."

"Just take a message, for crying out loud," snapped Jim. "Can't you see I'm sleeping?"

"It's Keith."

After an uncomfortably long period of silence, Jim finally responded.

"All right, I'll be right there."

Irritated to a point just shy of resentment, Jim lifted himself up from his chair, walked up the deck, and grabbed the phone from Mary's extended hand. Observing the empathy in his wife's eyes, he winked at her before proceeding.

"Hey, Keith."

"Jim, sorry to bother you, but I was doing some thinking about Monday's practice, and I wanted to run a few ideas past you."

Mary studied her husband's face. His eyes began to grow stern. Quietly, she shut the sliding door, secretively cursing the insatiable demands of the coaching profession.

Rather uncharacteristically, however, Jim cut him off before he could even get started, "Coach, I'm sorry, but can we talk about this tomorrow? We were just on our way out the door."

Feeling a little self-conscious about lying but desperate for a much-needed break from football, Jim added, "How about I call you tomorrow sometime?"

"Uuh… Let me see. Yeah, tomorrow's okay, I guess. Wait a minute… no, I almost forgot. I'm dropping Julia off at Tyler College tomorrow."

Keith began to feel lightheaded. Once again he had been painfully reminded that today was the last day his youngest child would be living under his roof. Tomorrow, a new chapter began in Julia's life. Then life in the Abraham house would return to just Keith and Carol, the nest officially emptied. Today was his last opportunity to enjoy the company of his little girl. Last night she

164

had gotten in quite late and hadn't rolled out of bed until just a few minutes ago. At the moment, she was taking a longer than normal shower.

Maybe she would be up for a movie or a trip to the mall? Not my favorite place in the world, but I could let Julia decide for a change.

Growing impatient for an exit from this unwanted and increasingly awkward conversation, Jim interjected, "Keith, I'm sorry. How about if you give me a call tomorrow night when you get back from Tyler? I should be down in the basement working on football until about 11:00."

"I know I shouldn't have bothered you this afternoon, Jim. It was nothing urgent. You should be enjoying this day with Mary and the kids. I'll see you Monday morning."

"Are you sure you don't want to talk tomorrow night? I'll still be up. I'm sure of it."

"No, it's not anything too... too important."

"Okay, then. By the way, you made a quick get away this morning. One minute you were at the table, the next minute you were gone."

"Oh that. Yeah, I guess I felt... I don't know. All of a sudden I felt like I needed some fresh air. I was getting a little light-headed."

"I hope you're not coming down with something. We can't have you out of commission this time of the year! You better get some rest this weekend. You hear?"

"You're absolutely right, Jim. I'll see you on Monday."

And before Jim had a chance to say goodbye, Coach Abraham terminated the conversation.

Hanging up the phone, Jim breathed a sigh of relief. He had feared the worst. In his mind, he had begun to visualize the two of them confined to his basement—on one of the last sunny Saturdays of summer—watching and rewinding and re-watching game tape from the previous season, analyzing their opponent, speculating what they might do differently, losing track of time, isolated from their families, impervious to the rest of the world. Somehow, however, Jim had found the nerve to prevent an unnecessary intrusion upon the Allen family, yet there was something very troubling about their conversation. In the all the years Jim had known Keith, not once did he ever hear his voice tremble. It almost seemed like he was about to breakdown.

No... not Coach Abraham. Never, thought Jim.

As Pete and David crossed the goal line for the final time, concluding the final dose of self-induced torture, they collapsed to their knees, speechless for nearly two minutes, desperate to resume normal breathing patterns. Finally, David broke the silence.

"Hey, Pete, if you're not doing anything tonight, do you want to come over and play video games? I've got the new UFL football game. You won't believe the graphics. It's like the real thing, man. Crowd noise and everything."

A fifteen second pause. "Uh... David, I'd really love to, but I've got to go into work at 11:00 to work the graveyard shift. Nick and Dave and I were planning to go out to the party at the Pit beforehand. Don't worry; I'm not going there to drink. I just heard there's going to be a lot of babes hanging out. You can come with us if you want."

"Thanks, but I'll pass. I'm not really into parties like that..." With a slight tinge of embarrassment, he added, "And if my father ever found out, I'd be grounded for life."

"I understand," lied Pete, not having a single memory of his dad ever disciplining him in their limited time together, not to mention the fact that his mom hadn't laid a finger on him since way-back-when—probably about the same time he could first bench his body weight. Nevertheless, Pete knew that if need be, his mom could muster up the necessary physical strength to discipline him. But Pete had made a vow several years ago to never add to his mother's hardship and burdens.

Without a doubt, however, Pete appreciated the unlimited freedom his mother granted him. There were boundaries, of course, but most of them were self-imposed. It was his own choice not to smoke, not to drink, not to blow off his education. Life's lessons had shown him all too clearly where those paths would lead him.

"How about this afternoon then?" counter-offered David.

Several moments passed while Pete considered. He really wanted to check out that video game—everybody on the team was talking about it—but Pete had so much on his mind. What he really needed right now was some time by himself where he could begin to come to grips with the grim possibility that life at home with Mom was about to become radically different.

Unable to disguise the guilt in his voice—and knowing it— Pete fabricated a spur-of-the-moment excuse, "You know, David, my mom needs me to help her out with a couple of jobs around the house this afternoon. I'd really like to hangout sometime, though. Can I take a rain check?"

"You bet."

After changing out of his Nike cleats, Pete draped them over his shoulder and began walking towards the gate. He still had that sour taste in his mouth, and his stomach felt a little funny. He turned back to look at David who was trailing behind in Pete's footsteps.

"Hey, David, see you on Monday."

"Can I give you a lift? I've got my dad's car."

"Nah, I need the exercise." Pete looked to the ground before adding. "Hey, don't tell anyone about me spraying on the field today, okay?"

"Oh, don't worry, Pete. As soon as I get home I'll be calling up the *Juddville Gazette*."

"Don't even think about it," laughed Pete.

"Sure you don't want a ride?"

"No, I'm sure."

"All right. See you then."

When Julia had showered and dressed, she found her dad sitting quietly at the kitchen table. Her mom was outside, on her knees weeding one of her many flower beds, earnestly trying to cope with the reality that her baby girl was going off to college the next day.

After a steaming-hot shower, Julia put on a pair of designer jeans shorts and a white spaghetti strap shirt. She bursted into the kitchen with a renewed sense of vitality. It was amazing what shopping could do to lift a girl's spirits. Opening the refrigerator, she looked for a cold carbonated drink. In the lower shelf she found a half-full 2 liter of Sprite. Out of the corner of her eye, she spied her dad sitting alone at the table. Remarkably, there was no newspaper, sports magazine, or game plan in front of him.

"Hello, Jules," said her dad.

"Hi," she responded uneasily, startled by the sound of a nickname she hadn't heard for several years.

An awkward void of silence swelled between them. Coach Abraham had about a thousand things he wanted to say but couldn't articulate a single one of them. He stared at her in wonder and disbelief. He wanted to ask if her if she was nervous about going off to school the next day. He wanted to ask if she was feeling alright and why she had gotten in so late last night—but he knew that would be the absolute worst question right now. He wanted to ask if she might spend some time with him this afternoon. He wanted to ask her how she really felt about him. He wanted to ask her if she had felt neglected all these years. And he wanted to know

167

if he could ever possibly make it up to her. But he spoke nothing—fearful that he might appear weak, that he might appear vulnerable before his daughter.

Julia poured herself a glass of Sprite and asked, "Would you like some, Dad?"

"No thanks. Did you have fun last night? I must have been asleep when you got home," fibbed Keith.

"Yeah, it was sort of late, I guess."

"We were hoping to have one last dinner with you before you left. I'm afraid we're running out of opportunities. Any chance for tonight?"

"Sorry, Dad. I've already got plans."

"Well, how about lunch then. Are you free for lunch?"

"Don't you have football to work on today?"

"Nothing that can't wait."

"I'm so sorry, Dad. Jessica and I made plans to go shopping a week ago. She didn't happen to call why I was in the shower, did she? We're going to the mall. I've got a couple things to pick up before tomorrow."

"No, no phone calls." His heart felt like an inner tube that just had all the air squeezed out. He felt like he lost the big game, only this time the outcome really mattered: the affection of his daughter.

Julia rinsed out her glass in the sink and placed it on the top shelf of the dishwasher. She couldn't help but notice the uncharacteristic gloominess in her father, and she wished that she could postpone her plans with Jessica, but it was too late.

Keith stared out the kitchen window, absorbed in his thoughts. *Perhaps, I am being served up a taste of my own medicine. I wonder how many times Julia has wanted an opportunity to spend time with me only to be told—time after time—that I was too busy?*

"Do you know where Mom is?"

"She's outside working in the yard." Desperately, yearning to be of some value to her daughter, Keith offered, "Honey, do you need some money for shopping?"

Julia looked at her dad who was pulling out his wallet from his back pocket.

How could she possible say no? Sure, Dad, I'm sure I can use a little extra cash."

"Here, Julia," handing over a couple $20s. "I can't have my daughter going off to college tomorrow short on supplies."

The youngest Abraham daughter reached out and grabbed the money from her father's hand. Then she kissed him on the cheek, giggling as she imagined how she might spend the money shopping or—better yet—on a bottle of Schnapps that evening.

Turning her back to him, she crossed the room to the phone and quickly dialed Jessica. Keith slowly lifted his tired body from the stiff wooden chair and retired to his bedroom, hoping to sleep off the sorrow of one of his all-time worst defeats. It seemed like the enemy had stripped the ball from him and was taking great delight in running up the score.

Have I lost her forever?

Chapter Seventeen

Adam Foster made himself a peanut butter and grape jelly sandwich, grabbed a 12 ounce can of Pepsi, and sat down in front of the television to watch another movie on his favorite movie channel. It was the premiere of *Vengeance is Fine.* Since the movie was rated R, he hadn't been old enough to see it in the theatre—why would his mom want to get up off her fat butt to take him to a movie that he might actually want to see?

Angel Foster didn't go for the violent, macho-hero movies; instead, she preferred the steamy romance flicks, the ones where male tooshes were exposed, and she had never thought twice about bringing her teenage son to such movies, even if they were rated R. Romance, sex? Why not? Violence and adventure? Not this time.

Adam despised going to movies with his mother, but he didn't dare tell her so. His mother's grip on him was just shy of suffocating. She was an all-powerful python. The more Adam struggled to break free, the tighter she squeezed.

If it wasn't for all the overtime required of his mom at her job as a receptionist at JB's Grocery Warehouse, Adam would be under surveillance 24 hours a day, 7 days a week.

Back in Billington—when Angel had been laid off for six months—life had been unbearable: home all day long, her buttocks glued to the couch, non-stop soap operas and talk shows, choking down one Marlboro Light after another. Every time Adam had worked up enough nerve to ask her for permission to play with a friend, the answer had always been the same: "Honey, I don't think that's such good idea. Why don't we see if there's a good movie in town, instead."

Although he couldn't stand being around Angel, she was all that he had. Adam's father had run off to Chicago when Adam was still in diapers. His childhood was spent in Billington where the rest of Angel's family lived. When the economy had taken another turn for the worse, his mom decided—against the wishes of her family—that it was time to go where the jobs were. So after school got out in June, Angel and Adam packed up all their belongings in the back of their beat-up station wagon and set off to find a better life in Juddville. She knew—as far as her family was concerned—that she was moving into enemy territory, but she had to do something to put food on the table and to pay the cable bill, for that matter.

During the first two months of the summer, Adam had been confined to the trailer during the day while his mother was at work. He could watch all the television he wanted, he could help himself to anything in the refrigerator, but he was not to step one foot out of the door until she got home. To make sure he abided by this rule, she would call once in the morning and once in the afternoon—never at the same time, of course. It wasn't until the week before football began that Adam had finally started to sneak out of the trailer while Angel was at work.

Desperate for company, Adam one day ventured across the street where he made the acquaintance of Josh Evans, a 19 year old, who owned a Yamaha YZ 250. Josh was currently unemployed, smoked Camel cigarettes, and lived with his mom, also.

On that iniquitous day in July—after Angel had left for work—Adam boldly stepped outside his trailer and sat down on the top step of his porch. A few minutes later, Josh came speeding down the road, revving his throttle to achieve as much attention as possible before parking his bike in front of his trailer. When he saw Adam staring at him, he said, "What are you lookin' at, punk?"

Before Adam could turn to go back inside his trailer, Josh said, "Wanna go for a ride on my bike, kid?"

Bewitched by fear and curiosity, Adam stuttered, "Sh-sh-shure."

"Well, get over here and hop on," commanded Josh.

So began Adam's relationship with his neighbor across the street. For a little over two weeks now, Adam would wait until his mother left for work before sneaking out of the trailer to hangout with the coolest friend he had ever met. It didn't matter to Adam that Josh was 19 years old. It didn't matter that Josh didn't work. Nor did it matter that he had recently been incarcerated—everybody makes mistakes. All that mattered to Adam was that someone had actually taken interest in him and wanted to be his friend.

During the past week, Adam couldn't hang out with Josh until after he got out of football practice. It didn't seem to bother Josh for the most part although he often asked Adam why he would want to spend so much time playing a stupid game that had so many rules.

Consequently, Adam was beginning to rethink his decision to play football. As was true for most boys growing up in the town of Billington, he had grown up with the dream of one day donning the crimson red and ivory white Bulldog uniform. For the most part, Adam enjoyed playing the sport, especially defense. He loved to tackle and was pretty athletic, so he could do a pretty decent job defending the pass.

What was most ironic, however, was his mother's insistence that he play football. Angel's family had contributed greatly to the rich football heritage in the town of Billington. The Foster name was synonymous with football. Angel's brother Rich was a legendary quarterback back in the 70s. As a matter of fact, he led Billington to two consecutive state championships. Uncle Rich held nearly every quarterback record in the school's history. He went on and played four years of college football at a Division II school where he switched to defensive back. If it hadn't been for football, Uncle Rich would never have made it to college. Football had been his ticket, and he had made good use of that opportunity, earning a business degree and high enough grades his last two years to make the prestigious Dean's List.

After graduating from college, Rich returned to Billington and married his high school sweetheart, Martha, who had been waiting for him, along with a promising share of her father's local Ford dealership. In a very short period of time, Martha provided him with two sons, and Rich eventually bought out his father-in-law's share of the business, renaming it Foster Ford.

Life rolled smoothly along for the legendary quarterback until one day tragedy came knocking at their door. Fate determined that their two sons—who were destined for gridiron greatness—would be run down by a senseless drunk driver in broad daylight. Rich and Martha had been sitting on their front porch when the policemen arrived to tell them there had been a terrible accident. Needless to say, the lives of Rich and Martha were turned upside down.

The pain extended beyond the boundaries of Rich and Martha. Rich's sister Angel had always been very close to her brother. He had been there for her after her boyfriend fled town after finding out Angel was pregnant, leaving her all alone to raise Adam.

While Angel was pregnant, Rich had made a few contacts to find her employment. When she needed help coming up with enough money for a deposit on her apartment, Rich immediately wrote out a check, never once asking for reimbursement. With the help of her older brother, Angel was able to get her life together, hold a job, and raise her boy as a single mother.

Rich and his two boys often took Adam under their wings, providing him with the only thing she couldn't provide: male companionship. At least one weekend a month, Rich would call over to her place and invite Adam to go along with them on a fishing trip or to see a ball game in New Haven. Not only would Adam get the attention he so desperately craved, but Angel would also get a much appreciated break from looking after him.

When Angel heard the news about her two nephews, she was devastated. If anyone could come any where close to feeling the depth of Richard Foster's pain, it was his sister Angel, and she would have done anything to help ease her brother and sister-in-law's sorrow.

After a mournful period of six months, Angel volunteered Adam to spend time with her brother, hoping that Rich could resume being a male role model for her son, and perhaps, help fill the void left by his two deceased sons.

As a result, Uncle Rich became like an adopted-father to Adam, and instead of spending one to two weekends a month together, Adam began to pedal his bike over to Uncle Rich's nearly every night after dinner.

What Angel didn't realize, however, was how much pressure her brother was putting on Adam. Almost immediately, her son was forced to carry the tremendous burden of trying to accomplish all of the unfulfilled dreams of his two deceased cousins.

Most every night, Adam could be found playing catch with his uncle after supper, perfecting his spiral, practicing pass routes, and preparing for his jayvee season. Uncle Rich's goal for his nephew was for him to be moved up to the varsity as a 10th grader, but by July, he had realized Adam wasn't quite ready for varsity football.

Though the pressure was heavy at times, Adam was extremely grateful that an adult had taken such interest in him. What he enjoyed most about hanging out with his uncle was hearing all the old stories of Billington's glory days back when Uncle Rich had been the star quarterback. The legendary 13-0 perfect season, and especially, the night his uncle completed 21 out of 24 passes for 320 yards and four touchdowns. When he looked at his almost four-decade old uncle, it was sometimes difficult to imagine him as a superstar; yet whenever his uncle gunned the football at Adam from a distance of 40 yards, the ball nearly wrenched his fingers right out of the socket.

On the morning when equipment was distributed to sophomores, Uncle Rich took the day off from work and brought Adam to the high school. On their way to the locker room, they just so happened to coincidentally pass the trophy showcases in front of the gymnasium. Sure enough, right next to an old red Billington football jersey, right next to an old leather football with the numbers 13-0 painted in white, and right next to a state championship trophy was an 8x10 glossy of Uncle Rich. He looked so young, so handsome with his dark black lamb chops. Could that really have been twenty years ago?

Unfortunately, the joys of that summer had been quickly trumped by disappointment and defeat. All the hours of practice with his uncle had not transformed Adam into a budding superstar. It did help earn his nephew a starting position on defense, however. The high point of Adam's sophomore season was an interception in the third game of the season against Reedsville. It came just before the end of the first half bringing the Rockets scoring drive to a screeching halt at Billington's 15 yard line. Adam had made the pick on the 10 yard line and was forced out of bounds after a 5 yard return. Naturally, he was ecstatic at the end of the game. For one, Billington defeated Reedsville 21 to 20; secondly, Adam couldn't wait to hear Uncle Rich's reaction.

The post game tradition was for parents and friends to wait in front of the entrance to the locker room to meet their favorite player.

Uncle Rich caught up to his nephew just as he was stepping off the field.

"Adam, what happened after that interception?" screamed his uncle. "You could have broken the game wide open if you wouldn't have chickened out and ran the ball out of bounds."

His uncle's comments caught him completely off-guard. Tears burst out like an April shower. Unable to hold back his tears and thoroughly embarrassed for crying in front of his teammates, Adam bolted in the opposite direction of the locker room. He crossed the parking lot, sprinted two blocks to Winding Creek Park on the outskirts of town, and claimed the first available picnic table to hover over and release all of his disappointment and humiliation.

He had given his best effort, hadn't he? It was a great pick. So what if he didn't take it the distance? It still changed the game's momentum and prevented a score. Yet it hadn't been good enough for Uncle Rich.

It was at this moment when the possibility of quitting had first entered Adam's mind. He didn't need football. And perhaps, he didn't need his uncle either. If Angel didn't understand, then to Hell with her, too.

Adam stayed at the park for about an hour before walking home in complete darkness. When his mom asked him what was bothering him, he walked right past her, went directly to his room, and slammed the door. Adam had decided he would tell his mother in the morning that he was done with football. His mind was made up. Maybe he would get a job and start earning some money for some wheels.

In the morning, however, his mom woke him up at 7:00. She had cooked him breakfast—a rarity for a school day—and it was his favorite: a three-egg, ham and cheese omelet. Then she caught him by surprise; she apologized to him for Uncle Rich's reaction the night before. Evidently, he had called Angel after Adam had gone to bed; her intuition enabled her to perceive the nature of her son's frustration. As a result, she began to wonder if it might be best for her and Adam to find a way out from under her brother's command.

While Adam gulped down his omelet, Angel tried to explain to him how all of Uncle Rich's hopes were wrapped up in watching his nephew play the game that he loved. Since he couldn't relive those memories through the lives of his two deceased sons, Adam was all he had. But when Adam told her he was thinking about quitting, she went absolutely ballistic.

"You're thinking about WHAT?"

"About quitting."

"There is no way my son is going to quit football. Your uncle may have gone a little overboard last night, but you owe it to him and to yourself to finish this season. You worked too hard over the summer to quit now. That's exactly what your father did when he found out I was pregnant. Don't you even think about quitting, young man. Don't you dare do this to me!"

Faced with no alternative, Adam agreed to finish out the season, and Angel assured him that she would talk to Uncle Rich about backing off for awhile and giving him some space.

By the end of the season, Adam had actually earned limited playing time on offense at quarterback—maybe there was at least a feint hope of him getting an opportunity to compete for the position of signal caller on the varsity next season.

But that dream would go unfulfilled. When his mom got laid off in January, and she had been unable to find a new job over the next six months, she was forced to look elsewhere for employment once the unemployment checks ran out.

As a result, Angel started looking at job postings in the nearby Juddville Gazette, and she was able to interview and secure a job in enemy territory. But a job was a job. Adam had never imagined transferring to Juddville, but the move wasn't all bad. At least he could be free from his uncle's dominion.

Chapter Eighteen

After rinsing off his plate and glass in the kitchen sink, Pete walked up behind his mom, placing his hands gently upon her bony shoulders. He leaned around and kissed her on the cheek.

Dinner had been uncomfortably quiet. Pete didn't usually say a lot during dinner; his mom generally carried the conversation for the first five to ten minutes while Pete devoured not one but two platefuls of food. Only then Pete would push his chair back from the table to make room for his bloated stomach before interjecting his opinion on the topic at hand.

Tonight his mom had prepared one of his favorite meals: spaghetti and meatballs with garlic bread. Pete had gulped down his customary two helpings while his mother had barely touched hers. For most of the meal, she had propped her head up with one hand while she sullenly swirled a couple of noodles around her fork.

She had tried to be gentle in broaching the subject of Pete's father, but as soon as she mentioned his name, her son's entire upper body became dangerously tense, so much so that she feared he was going to burst right out of his tight-fitting tee shirt. Cindy was an experienced enough mom to know that her son needed more time before she reintroduced the subject of his father's parole. Instead of inflicting further agony upon Pete, she tried to gracefully shift the conversation to football before her son began to completely shut down.

After a few minutes of silence—while his carbohydrate-rich supper began to digest—Pete's conscience began calling out to him. Across the table sat his one loyal friend and his only family—not to mention the fact that she had just prepared for him his favorite meal. Now she sat dejected, alone, and certainly afraid of the days

175

ahead. It suddenly dawned upon Pete that her pain was surely greater than his own. As a result, he could not in good conscience allow his resentment towards his father to overshadow the love and admiration he had for his mother. For the time being, he would choose to deliberately hold his bitter feelings in check.

Although Pete had been just about ready to get up from the table to set out for his abbreviated Saturday night out with Nick and Dave, he instead opted to enjoy a few additional minutes alone with his mom. He looked across the table at her and couldn't help but notice the fatigue and years of disappointment etched in her face. A slender tear drop emerged from the corner of her eye.

Reaching across the table, he grabbed her hand reassuringly, wishing he could somehow make things better for her. He wanted to make her smile again. He wanted to hear her breakout in one of her trademark fits of laughter.

Life in the O'Connor home had been somewhat stable over the past two years. Together, Pete and his mom were surviving albeit barely making ends meet. And now—finally, for God's sake—it was football season, the best time of the year. If anything could come into their home, open wide the curtains, and let in some much needed sunshine, it was football.

But now there was a sudden change in forecast. Potential severe weather could be blowing in their direction.

Nevertheless, Pete forced himself to smile. Staring into the eyes of his mother, he confided, "Mom, just give me some time with this. I know you've never let go of Dad, but to me, he's been dead for years. I don't see how I can bring him back into my life again... I'm sorry... He's dead and buried. And I just can't deal with this right now."

"Peter, sooner or later, you will *have* to deal with it. Maybe not tonight, maybe not this weekend, and maybe not even this season, but eventually we will both have to face the reality that your father is going to walk out of that prison someday soon. And I would so much like to face this challenge like we have faced every other challenge over the last seven years. One last time, will you stand by my side on this one?"

Pete nodded his head slowly and rose from the table, pushing the chair back into place.

"Mom, I'm going out with Nick and Dave before I go to work. You want me to put some gas in the Ranger?"

"It's already half-full, Pete. Just don't take it across the state and back, and you'll be fine."

A smile suddenly cracked the surface of Cindy's face as she began to prod, "Hey, I've been meaning to ask you. Have you heard from Melanie lately?"

Pete shot an ice cold glare towards his mother, "Don't even go there, Mom. Don't even go there. Besides, who's got time for a girlfriend during football season?"

"Oh, I bet she'll just be killing herself up in those bleachers this fall. What was she thinking letting the star of the Jaguar football team slip right through her hands?"

Yeah, that's exactly what I hope she'll be doing, thought Pete.

"I'll see you in the morning, Mom. It's gonna be nice to sleep in tomorrow for a change, but don't let me sleep past 1:00, okay? I've got to get up and get going so I can get my workout done before the gym closes at 5:00."

"Sure, honey. Have a good time tonight and be safe."

Pete kissed his mom on the forehead and grabbed his work clothes on his way out of the trailer. Tonight was going to be fun. Pete could hardly wait to get out to the Pit. Before picking up Nick and Dave, he stopped at DJ's Convenience Store to buy a couple 16 oz bottles of Coke. It was pretty difficult to stand around at a party with nothing in your hands to drink while everyone else was consuming one plastic cup after another of keg beer. Most of his classmates didn't mind that Pete didn't drink; they actually respected his commitment to Juddville football. Anyways, Pete didn't really care much about what his peers thought. Only a few of his classmates were foolish enough to make fun of him. The last one to try had been Roger, and Pete had just about dislocated his Adam's apple. And if they only knew how alcohol had messed up his family, they wouldn't be so quick to make fun of his decision to be alcohol-free.

The Pit was an ideal spot for underage drinking. The only drawback—which was ironically what made it so popular, in the first place—was the incredibly long hike from the parking area of Lakeside Park to the hidden alcove nestled between three sand dunes, also known as The Pit. The reason for the 15 minute walk was obvious. What donut-bloated police officer would walk a mile through heavy sand just to bust up a teenage party?

No one was sure whether the cops had ever suspected any illegal activity going on out at the Pit or if they even wanted to know. As long as everyone at the party was back to their cars prior to 11:00—the park's official closing time—there was never any trouble. Yet they had to at least be suspicious of the 25-plus cars

177

parked at Lakeside nearly every Saturday night of the summer, even though the park during this time was practically void of people. Perhaps, the police figured that kids would be kids, and it was better to have them away from the general public having their fun, as long as no one was getting hurt. At least the kids weren't cruising the streets downtown, disrupting the peace with their loud music.

At 8:00 p.m., on one of the last Saturday nights in August, many of the inhabitants of Juddville would invariably make the obligatory stop at the Cone Shoppe before the favorite summer establishment closed for the winter, or else they might choose to enjoy the peace of their own backyards, spraying themselves with insect repellant, inviting their neighbors over for one last bon fire. Most of the Juddville teenagers, however, were extremely conscious of the fact that the end of summer was drawing dangerously near, and the official beginning of another torturous year of school was already breathing down their necks.

So when Pete and his buddies pulled into Lakeside Park, there were already 30 vehicles parked. As soon as Pete shifted his mom's truck into park, his companions were already jumping out, energized to begin the long trek across the sandy shores of the Big Lake to this most revered of teenage hangouts, an oasis that promised them cold refreshments on a warm summer evening.

After five minutes at a hurried pace, Nick and Dave were struggling to keep up with Pete. The *squeak, squeak* of the sand meeting rubber tennis shoes, barely muffled the huffing and puffing of their breathing.

Pete was lost in thought. Wearing a clean Juddville State Champions tee-shirt and his favorite pair of faded Lee blue jeans, he hoped that his muscular build would not go unnoticed at the party. With all those cars parked back at Lakeside, he expected to find at least one or two attractive girls that were currently in the market for a boyfriend. Not the prissy, popular type of girl either, he hoped, but more the down-to-earth, simple type; the type of girl whose spirit reminded him of his mother—although he would never dare to admit this to anyone. She shouldn't wear much makeup, and maybe just a touch of perfume, especially to help cover up the smell of tobacco smoke if she was a smoker.

The last thing Pete wanted was a relationship with some spoiled, pampered, life-size Barbie doll. Instead, he was looking for someone like Melanie, who lived in a modest-size home, on a limited budget, in an environment where she would have to work hard to earn any privileges. Often times a girl's face communicated all that was needed to be known: many of the "In" girls coated themselves each day with layer upon layer of makeup before parading around the hallways in their designer clothes with forced, artificial smiles forever on display.

Yet on a rare occasion, if you looked long enough and were willing to cast your vision in unexpected places—like in the library or in the music wing of the high school rather than at the table of high privilege in the cafeteria—sometimes you might come across a yet-to-be-discovered gem who was both genuinely happy and naturally beautiful. What Pete was looking for was a girl who smiled when she was happy, not one who smiled pretending to be happy—like it was just part of a staged performance.

He had once believed that Melanie had been that type of girl, but history had proven differently. Anytime she had a few drops of alcohol in her, within an hour she could be found draped all over the nearest willing boy. As far as Pete knew, her flirting had never led to anything beyond some intensely theatrical French kissing. Nevertheless, her loose living had earned her the unflattering reputation of a slut.

It really didn't really matter to Pete how others chose to classify Melanie. To him she would always be "that two-timing bitch".

On this particular Saturday night, Pete had resolved to stay as far away from her as possible. Instead, he would just toy around with some of the underclassmen girls—nothing below the 10th grade, however. Nothing serious, of course, just some casual flirting before he had to report to work.

About ten minutes into their hike, Nick and Dave were fighting for their next breath of oxygen. Nick, a 6'4'' reserve center for the Juddville basketball team protested with more than a hint of sarcasm in his voice, "Hey, Super Pete! Can you pick up the pace a bit? There's a small corner of my shirt that's not soaked with sweat yet."

Pete countered, "Oh come on, you basketball wuss. You afraid a little sweat's going to scare away Jennifer?"

"Naaah, she loves sweat. For our one month anniversary, I gave her a small vial of sweat that I squeezed out of my workout shirts after basketball camp."

"If you've been working out so much, where did that little pot belly come from that you've been carrying around all summer? You're going to have to work on that, or your rear end's going to be glued to the bench all season."

"At least my brain will be fully-functioning which is more than I can say for you, you pigskin moron."

"Ooh, that's a good one; don't you think so, Dave?"

"I'm staying out of it. You know I abhor violence," huffed Dave, his mind completely focused on the cold draft beer that awaited them. "If you really want my opinion, however, I think you're both a couple of dumb jocks."

If Pete was a lion, and Nick was a giraffe, then Dave would have to be an elephant. At nearly 235 pounds, Dave could maybe jump over a two-inch thick phone book. Unlike Pete and Nick, Dave was in no way concerned about working up a sweat on the way to one of the most anticipated social events of the summer. For the most part, he spent the larger part of each day drowning in sweat. He even broke a sweat when he sat down on the toilet to release his daily Loch Ness monster into the porcelain playground. With all that size, many of Dave's classmates assumed he must be a football player, but he never had any aspiration for doing anything athletic. He liked to watch high school sports, and he even watched professional sports on television, but he was not about to go and do something crazy like committing to the rigorous practice regimens required of most competitive sports.

So why would a football player and a basketball player choose to hangout with a classmate with such low ambition? There was no one funnier in the entire senior class than Dave; his mind was so spontaneous and imaginative. Sure, his physique and athleticism often made him a target for mocking, but there were very few souls brave enough, for they would have to endure the obligatory comeback that was sure to follow. As for girls? There was only one motivation that would inspire Dave to walk this mini-marathon, and it came in a 14 oz plastic cup, but if a girl came his way and was showing an interest, then let nature take its course. Consequently, he was thoroughly baffled trying to understand his friend Pete's reason for journeying out to the pit; nevertheless, he liked hanging out with the football freak, and he could not help but admire his commitment. Besides, if he ever had a run-in with someone who didn't appreciate his quick wit, there was no one better to have in his corner than Pete.

As the unlikely trio of friends descended the slope of the sand dune, they immediately noticed that the party was in full force. Voices were shouting back and forth; there was laughing and screaming, and someone had even brought a tune box which was currently cranking out a tune from one of Pete's favorite groups, AC/DC.

Nick and Dave proceeded directly to the older looking guy who was holding a stack of cups in one hand and a wad of bills in the other. The face somehow looked familiar, but Pete couldn't attach a name to it. He clearly looked older than the rest of the crowd, however.

While Pete waited for Nick and Dave to purchase their cups, he surveyed the party. Most of the faces were familiar, but there were a few former Juddville students that he hadn't seen in a while. The girl who was standing next to the guy selling cups looked a lot like Coach Abraham's daughter. Instead of drinking beer from a plastic cup, she was drinking straight out of a pint of Peach Schnapps.

She can't be possibly be with him, can she? thought Pete.

A few minutes later, Nick and Dave returned with their cups filled to the brim with draft beer. Dave took a big sip, smiling with deep satisfaction as he wiped the foam from his lips.

"Who is that selling cups?" asked Pete.

"That's Brian Taylor. He graduated three years ago. And that's Coach Abraham's daughter with him. How do you think he would react if he caught his daughter hanging out with that loser?" asked Nick.

"I think it would make even one of Coach Allen's legendary outbursts pale in comparison. By the way, you guys, you should have seen Coach Allen go after Roger Collins this week. It was one for the ages. But anyways, I don't get why anyone who graduated three years ago would be wanting to hang out at a high school party."

"I don't care if he's 60 years old," commented Dave. "If he's providing the beer, tonight he's my best friend."

"I wouldn't say that too loud, Dave, or you just might become his next girl friend," joked Nick, elbowing his buddy in the ribs.

"Well," said Dave, in his best effeminate voice, "he is kind of cute, but no one could ever take your place, honey bun."

"Get away from me, you sick pig," responded Nick.

All of a sudden, their playful conversation was rudely interrupted.

"Hey, Jocko. Yeah, you with the Juddville tee-shirt. You buying a cup or what?" asked Brian Taylor, a menacing look on his face, taking a step toward Pete as he handed the bottle of Schnapps back to his girlfriend.

Pete held up his bottle of Coke and answered unashamedly, "I'm not drinking."

"Yeah, I bet you're not," then with an antagonistic tone he added, "I catch you drinking off this keg, and you're buddies will have to carry you home on a stretcher."

181

"Ha, ha, ha," laughed Pete, appreciating the absurdity of his arrogant adversary's imagination.

Julia Abraham grabbed Brian's arm and tried to pull her boyfriend away from an imminently ugly confrontation with one of her father's prized football players.

With a look of alarm in her eyes, she pleaded, "Come on, Brian. He's cool. Leave him be. He's not looking to cause any trouble."

Brian pushed her away, saying, "Get your damn hands off me. What is it? You don't think I can take him because he's one of your daddy's football studs?"

"No, that isn't it at all. Just leave him alone. I don't want him to ruin our last night together. That's all. Just let it go. Please, Brian."

Brian glared back at Pete. He wanted so desperately to go over and knock that smirk off his face.

Pete stared right back at him. Eyes like lasers, just waiting for his prey to make the first move.

The rest of the party became uncomfortably quiet. A couple graduates came over and stood next to Brian.

The bulky looking one asked—in a voice loud enough to be heard over the music—"Is there a problem here?"

Pete recognized him immediately. It was Al Baker, graduated two years ago. He was a two-way starter: defensive end and offensive guard. Pete nodded to him.

Al walked over to Pete and slapped him a high five. The tension of the moment diffused, and the crowd resumed their prior conversations.

"How's it going, Pete." Then taking him aside, he spoke in a barely audible voice. "If I was you, pal, I would keep your distance from Brian. He's not worth the trouble. Then Al put his bulky arm around Pete, ushering him even further away from the keg. "So you guys going to be any good this season?"

"Oh, I think we'll be pretty tough. Everyone is expecting us to win another state championship, of course. They've got me playing guard right now. I never knew that playing on the line could be so much fun. You really get to crush people."

"Man, I can't tell you how much I miss playing football. Enjoy it while you can, Pete."

"How come you're not playing college football somewhere?"

"I went out for the Lakeland Community College team last year, but I knew I wasn't going to get much playing time, so I decided to hang them up."

"What are you doing with your time then? You still working out?"

"I've got a job. Taking a few night classes. Not much time left for working out." Al's voice then lowered to a whisper. "Let me give you a little friendly advice, Pete. Stay clear of Brian. He's got kind of a short fuse, and when he gets a little liquid courage in him, he gets a little psycho."

"I'm cool, man. I don't want any trouble. He was just giving me a hard time about not buying a cup, that's all. I just came to have a good time before I go to work. I'm not looking to start anything."

"With Brian, you won't need to start anything, so you better just keep your distance, okay, Pete?"

Meanwhile, Brian was engaged in a private conversation with another older friend. He looked relatively scrawny in his weathered black leather coat, his unshaven face and unwashed hair—probably hadn't seen a comb in several days. As Brian whispered into his ear, his companion dragged on a cigarette, nodding his head in agreement.

Nevertheless, Dave was in need of a refill, so he boldly converged upon the keg. After refilling his cup, he rejoined Pete. "You know who that is next to Mr. Keg Man, don't you? It's Josh Evans. He just got out of prison for a couple of breaking and entering convictions."

At the mere mention of the word *prison*, Pete twitched involuntarily. The word carried more weight for him than most kids his age. To him, it was an enormous cage holding the most decadent of creatures. There was no rehabilitation, only further degradation for most. Pete's dad once made a serious mistake, but it was prison that transformed him into an uncaring, selfish fiend. What could possibly induce a man to wholeheartedly turn his back on the only two people who stood by his side, who loved him unconditionally, and still yearned for his presence in their lives?

A chill of air swirled through the pit, alarming several of the partygoers.

"Whew, did you feel the temperature just drop?" said Dave, tilting his cup back to enjoy its last few drops. "I better get a refill to warm me up."

"Slow down, Dave. You don't want to be blowing chunks the whole walk back," cautioned Pete.

"Don't worry about me, big boy. I'll be fine. You just take care of yourself."

By 9:30, it was completely dark; fortunately, someone had actually brought a Coleman propane lamp, placing it conveniently alongside the keg. Altogether there were at least 50 young adults now congregated at the Pit, the majority of high school age, with a handful of graduates and dropouts.

Pete had finished his Coke and was talking to an attractive sophomore named Cathy. She had long, curly-blond hair and sparkling blue eyes. Her older brother Ken had graduated the year before. Pete remembered getting tackled by him in practice on a number of occasions. Naturally, Cathy had a much sweeter disposition than her brother.

It hadn't been all that difficult for Pete to avoid coming into further contact with Brian Taylor since he had no need for visiting the keg. For the most part, Pete had forgotten all about the incident, letting it roll off his shoulders. One thing was certain, Pete had very little energy to engage in any physical altercation; he had spent himself in his workout earlier in the day. What ever energy remained he wished to conserve for walking all the way back to the truck and for working the graveyard shift at the Pancake House.

Thus, his conversation with Cathy was reluctantly cut short, and Pete scouted out Dave and Nick who were hanging out at the keg, most likely anticipating the dreadful spitting sound of a keg going dry.

"Hey guys," said Pete. "You got a ride home tonight, right?"

"Oh yeah," affirmed Nick, pointing over towards Jennifer and her homely-looking best friend Emily, who were keeping tabs on Nick and Dave from about 10 yards distance.

Pete wanted to comment on the prospect of Emily hooking up with Dave, but he decided to bite his tongue, for Dave might actually be interested in her, and he didn't want to scare him off.

A series of groans erupted around the keg as it began to spit. Dave, who was next in line, let out the biggest sigh of disappointment. Nick sensed his friend's pain and poured out half of his freshly-poured brew into his companion's empty cup.

"I could kiss you, my friend," said Dave.

"That won't be necessary," replied Nick.

From out of nowhere, Melanie suddenly appeared. Up until this point, Pete hadn't even been aware of her presence. But now, here she was, front in center, breaking his two foot comfort zone. He could smell her familiar perfume as she nervously brushed her hair back with her fingertips.

With a slight look of embarrassment on her face, she asked, "Is the keg dry already?"

"Afraid so," responded Nick.

The conversation went quiet while Nick and Dave and Pete communicated back and forth with only their eyes. Melanie focused her manipulative gaze upon Pete, trying in vain to encourage him to send away his friends. When her ex-boy friend had the audacity to turn his back to her, huddling up close to his friends, leaving her standing all alone, facing the backs of their heads, she finally picked up on the message.

Then Pete casually asked his buds, "Where are you guys heading once the party breaks up?"

"I'm not sure. Hey, Nick, what do you say we head to McDonald's? Or do you and Jennifer have other plans?"

"You know me, Dave. I'm all for food. Then once we have taken care of our essential needs, we can pursue other forms of entertainment," joked Nick, peeking over his shoulder to make sure Jennifer didn't hear him.

Melanie had rejoined her girlfriends who, in typical dramatic fashion, were consoling their shot down girlfriend.

Meanwhile, the time was rapidly approaching 10 o'clock, and Pete realized it was time to hit the road.

SMACK. Pete felt the impact of someone's hand thrusting forcefully down upon his right shoulder. He turned around swiftly and observed Roger standing behind him, leaning slightly to his right with an awkward grin on his face.

"Hey, bud. How's it going?" slurred Roger.

"I'm good. You look like you're enjoying yourself a little bit too much, though. Doesn't the team mean anything to you, Roger?"

"Sure, it does. But it is Saturday night, isn't it? Don't we deserve a little down time after all that suffering?"

"Not the kind of fun that's going to put the team's chances for success in jeopardy. Can't you ever think about anyone besides yourself?"

Sidestepping the question and attempting to get on the good side of Pete, Roger responded, "I heard you had some trouble earlier. I wish I would have been here then."

Pete paused and reflected a moment before proceeding. He didn't really want to bring the topic up again.

Not really having much choice, however, Pete answered, "Oh, that. Well, it was really nothing." If Pete considered Roger a real teammate, he might have provided a detailed account of his conflict earlier in the evening. Since Roger was flying pretty high right now, there wasn't much reason to get into it; he wasn't going to remember any of it anyways.

Growing annoyed by the unwanted company of one of his least favorite teammates and becoming a little antsy about departing for work, Pete said, "I was just about ready to leave for work."

"Are you serious, man? You've got to be crazy going into work at this hour!"

"Hey, man. It pays the bills, what can I say? It pays the bills."

"That's a bummer," stammered Roger. "This is a pretty awesome party."

"You better be careful, Roger. I hope you're not driving, are you?"

"Are you kidding me? I'm not driving. Melanie's driving me home."

Pete grabbed hold of Roger's collar—for the second time this week, but this time not quite so tightly.

"Just kidding, man. It was a joke. I'll be okay. I'm at my limit for the night." Wanting to prove himself to his teammate, Roger added, "I guess I won't need this one then," and he dumped his nearly full beer on the sand.

Dave—who had been engaged in a private conversation with Nick nearby— hastily dropped to his knees, crawled a few paces towards Roger, and pretended to lap up the beer-soaked sand as if he were a dehydrated dog.

Looking up at Roger, Dave reprimanded him saying, "You villain. You brainless beast. Have you no sense? No soul? How could you commit such a wasteful, dastardly deed?"

After the laughter subsided, Roger turned to Pete and asked, "You working out tomorrow, Pete?"

"Yeah, I'm hoping to get to the gym by 3:00."

"Mind if I join you?"

"Yeah, sure, why not?"

Pete looked around the party and noticed about half of the gathering had already disappeared. Checking the time on his watch, he said, "I've got to get going, or I'm going to be late. Be careful, Roger. We can't afford to lose you."

"Don't worry. I'll be okay. Promise."

As Pete turned from the party to begin the journey back to his truck, he hoped his teammate would sober up sufficiently during the long walk back from the Pit.

A half-moon shone dimly upon the waves gently rolling onto the shore. Pete walked as close to the water as he could without getting his feet splashed. In front of him—about 100 yards or so—he observed three dark silhouettes. They were walking at a pace slow enough that he would probably overtake them before reaching the parking lot.

If Pete was going to get to work on time, he was going to have to hustle.

All of a sudden he heard a voice shouting his name from behind him. It was Roger, sprinting to catch up to him.

"Hey, wait up."

What the heck is going on with Roger? thought Pete. *All of a sudden he thinks he's my best friend.*

"I've got to hurry or I'll be late."

Roger was gasping for oxygen, a strong scent of beer on his breath.

Fighting the temptation to slouch over his knees to regain his breath—thus, appearing weak in the presence of his teammate—Roger put his hands up behind his head, taking deep breaths as he struggled to keep up with Pete.

With the exception of the rhythmic pattern of Roger's breathing, the two Juddville teammates walked in silence. Suddenly, a loud shriek arose from somewhere amidst the patches of beach grass and pine trees along the base of the dunes. The scream was followed by a loud smack.

Pete and Roger sprinted about 75 yards across the sand to where two dark shapes were wrestling. As they got closer, Pete yelled out, "Hey, break it up. Break it up."

"Get the hell out of here!" commanded the person who was holding down—what now appeared to be—a girl, who seemed to be helplessly under the other person's control.

Pete immediately recognized Brian Taylor's voice, so he concluded the female companion had to be Coach Abraham's daughter. Slowly but surely, Pete advanced towards Brian and Julia.

As he got nearer, the reason for the screaming became obvious. Julia's shirt was ripped open; her pants unsnapped and pulled down to her knees. Self-conscious about her half-nakedness, Pete was reluctant to move any closer. Her hair was disheveled, but not so much to conceal that she was crying and holding the left side of her face.

Brian put his arm around her and glared at Pete, "You take one more step towards us, and someone's going to get hurt."

Pete took two bold steps toward him and responded, "It looks to me like someone's already hurt, douche bag. You must be a real tough guy to beat up on a girl like that."

Brian jumped to his feet, and Julia rolled away from him, tugging on her pants in desperation.

"Are you okay, Julia? I heard you scream."

Julia was now sobbing hysterically, attempting in vain to calm herself down so she could speak. Roger was standing back about twenty feet behind Pete, unsure whether to stand back in the shadows or come to the aid of his teammate.

"Hey, dumb ass," called out Brian, who had obviously had more than his share of the keg. "I'm not going to tell you again. You and your buddy better mind your own business and hit the road before I start to get mad."

Pete looked back to Roger who was slowly retreating into the shadows. "It's Coach's daughter. We can't just leave her like this."

Turning his attention back to Brian, "I'm not leaving until she tells me she's alright."

Taking a step towards Pete, Brian sneered, "You should have run when you had the chance."

Dropping both hands to his sides, and clenching them into fists, Brian began to circle around the Juddville captain, crouching into a fighting stance, ready to pounce at the first favorable moment. Not generally prone to patience or prudence, Brian impulsively made the first move, lunging towards Pete with a weak left jab.

Pete easily ducked the errant punch and waited for the optimum moment. While keeping an eye on Brian, Pete glanced back towards where his teammate had been standing. Roger was nowhere to be seen.

That figures.

Taking one more glance down at Julia who was sobbing, all curled up in a ball on the sand, Pete knew exactly what he must do.

Like an armored tank suddenly shifting into overdrive, Pete rammed into Brian, grabbing him by the collar with both hands, lifting him off the ground, and then pummeling him into the sand.

"Don't," garbled Julia. "I'll be alright."

Pete paused for a moment, turning his head back towards Julia who was now staggering to her feet, holding her face with one hand. Pete turned his head back to his adversary, but not quickly enough to avoid being sucker punched.

Falling to one knee, he was upset with himself for letting down his guard, thereby allowing the slime ball to get a free shot.

188

He hoisted himself up off the ground, regained his balance and wiped his nose, checking for blood.

"Is that your best shot, loser?"

All of a sudden, Brian seemed to have experienced a surge of adrenaline and self-confidence for he was now prancing back and forth like he Muhammad Ali.

"I've got some more for you. You ain't seen nothing yet," taunted Brian.

A kaleidoscope of emotions rushed through Pete's mind as he lifted both of his fists for battle:

Urine-soaked football pants.
Spit drooping from my lock.
Flat bicycle tires.
Melanie, the unfaithful one.
Adam Foster, pain in buttocks.
Melanie...
Old man up for parole...

Pete stepped towards Brian, grabbed him by his collar with both hands, drove him backwards into the sand, and pinned him to the ground. While maintaining complete control of his prey with his left hand, he began to slap him with his open right hand.

"Didn't your momma ever tell you not to hit a girl?"

SLAP

"Didn't your momma teach you to treat your girl like a queen?"

SLAP

"Didn't your momma ever warn you that some day you were going to piss off the wrong person?"

SLAP

At this point in the lesson, Pete faced the dilemma of either to finish the job with Brian or get to work on time. Although Pete was feeling relatively confident that a small portion of tonight's lesson was already beginning to sink in, he was absolutely certain that in order for the lesson to really take hold, the teacher would need to provide further enrichment. Unfortunately, the time allotted for tonight's lesson had expired, and this particular pupil wasn't worth losing his job over.

Pete pushed himself off his feeble opponent, turning toward Julia who was hunched over on her knees, wiping her mouth with her sleeve after vomiting upon the sand.

"Can I give you a ride home?" asked Pete, fully realizing that he would now most definitely be late for work.

189

Before Julia could formulate a response, Pete felt two hands reaching from behind, grabbing him around the throat. Pete leaned forward and flipped the assailant over his head.

Back for seconds, I see, thought Pete.

Brian rolled over and struggled to his feet.

Pete blocked a weak right hook with his left forearm and countered with a quick jab to Brian's nose.

CRUNCH

His enemy staggered backwards, leaning forward, holding his nose.

"You mother…"

A thin stream of shiny dark fluid began to flow down from Brian's nostril. He wiped the blood with the side of his hand and approached Pete with renewed fervor. He crouched down like a mountain lion and then unleashed a swift kick with his left foot.

But it wasn't nearly swift enough. Pete grabbed his foot, flipping him backwards onto the sand. Now the sand was beginning to stick to Brian's bloody nose. This time there would be no pity.

Pouncing on his prey, Pete began to slug him unmercifully.

Left.

Right.

Left.

Right.

Brian's head tossed back and forth like a windshield wiper.

In only a few moments, he had drained all the fight from his foe. Pete lifted himself back up on his feet. His knuckles were stinging and beginning to bleed. His breathing was heavy, and he had even worked up a sweat.

Brian moaned as he rolled over on his side.

Julia was still on the ground, curled up like a crumpled up piece of paper. Pete was unsure how to approach her; ever so gently he reached out his hand, placing it upon her shoulder.

"Come with me, Julia. Everything's going to be all right now."

She brushed back her tangled hair, exposing her tearful eyes. As she looked into Pete's eyes, some of her terror began to dissipate. Then all of a sudden, she turned away and began to vomit again.

One heave, followed by another, and yet another.

Now what am I supposed to do? She's too drunk and too beaten to just leave here. I am already in big trouble at work. And sooner or later, Brian'll be up on his feet again, too stupid to know when enough is enough.

After a few minutes, the vomiting subsided, so Pete reached his hand out, and said, "Come on, Julia. Let's go."

Julia wiped off the bitter slime dripping from her mouth and looked up at her protector. Grabbing hold of his hand, she lifted herself up.

"You know my name?"

"Are you kidding? Everyone knows who you are."

"Of course, they do. The Coach's daughter."

"Name is Pete O'Connor."

"I guess the Coach's daughter had too much to drink at her going away party," confessed Julia. "Just get me away from him, would you?"

Pete heard voices approaching. Looking back in the direction of the Pit, he saw two shapes approaching. Judging by the sheer mass of the lead person, he concluded it had to be Al Baker, the former Jaguar he had spoken with earlier.

"Hey, Al. Over here."

Al walked over to Pete and Julia, his companion trailing behind.

"We had a little trouble." Pointing to the body twitching back and forth on the sand about 50 feet away, Pete added, "Brian was getting pretty rough with Coach's daughter."

"Is he okay?" asked Al.

Ignoring his question, Pete continued, "I heard a scream and I thought I'd better see what the trouble was. I had another teammate with me, but I guess he chose to stay out of it."

Al turned back to whisper to his companion who immediately swore, removed his coat, and whipped it to the ground.

"Calm down, Josh. We have no idea what happened."

"What are you talking about? It's plain enough to me. Brian's lying on the ground, and there's Mr. Big Shot with a dumb smirk on his face, and now he's with Brian's girl. Now if you're not going to do anything about it, I'll have to take care of it myself," promised Josh, the convicted felon, who was trying to burn a hole through Pete with his smoldering laser eyes.

Pushing him in the shoulder, and backing him up three steps, Al looked his companion straight in the eyes, "You listen to me good right now, Josh. You ain't going to do nothing, you hear me? You're on probation, remember?"

"That's right. But since you aren't willing to make things right, what choice do I have?"

"I tell you what. Let's go check on Brian. See what he has to say." Then lowering his voice to almost a whisper, Al added, "If need be, we can always catch up with Pete later."

Josh nodded his head in agreement and then reached down to pick up his coat, brushing the sand from it, before pointing his finger back towards Pete.

"Don't think you're going to get away with this, punk. You'll get your due."

Al grabbed Josh by the arm and tugged him in the direction of Brian. Al looked back towards Pete, and with his eyes, sent him an If-I-WERE-YOU-I-WOULD-GET-OUT-OF-HERE telegram.

Pete could hear Brian whimpering like a whipped puppy.

"Let's get going, Julia. How about if I drop you off at your house on my way to work?"

"On your way to work?" asked Julia in disbelief.

As they started their walk back to Lakeside Park, Pete heard the voice of Al Baker exclaim, "Holy shit! Would you look at his face? It looks like it got trapped in a bees nest."

Chapter Nineteen

By the time Pete and Julia reached the parking lot, it was pitch dark. There were only a few cars left, and Pete couldn't help but notice the police car with its interior lights on, occupied by two members of the Juddville Police Department.

Pete felt his pulse quicken as he opened the passenger door of his truck for Julia. As he walked around the front of his vehicle, a powerful flashlight shone upon him. He got to the driver's door and quickly opened it. When he heard two car doors open simultaneously, he feared trouble on the horizon.

In a state of near panic, Pete attempted to start his engine, but it stubbornly refused to turn over. On his second try, the engine started; just as he was about to put the transmission into reverse, he heard a heavy knock on his window. He looked out and observed an officer shining a flashlight at him. To his right, another flashlight shone upon Julia from her window.

All thoughts of reporting to work on time had now deteriorated; Pete rolled down his window to address the police officer.

"Would you step out of the car, son?" asked the policeman. The officer looked to be about 6'3", at least 230 pounds. His Juddville Police Department hat covered a Marine-length buzz cut.

With much apprehension, Pete opened the door and slowly stepped out of the truck. Using his flashlight, the officer scanned all the way from Pete's face down to his toes.

"You been drinking tonight, son?"

"Not a drop, sir."

"I would hope not. I'm sure Coach Abraham wouldn't be too pleased to hear one of his boys was out breaking training rules on the weekend."

At that moment, Pete remembered he was wearing a Juddville tee-shirt. Julia had slumped in her seat at the mention of her father's name.

"Can I see some identification, please?"

Reaching into his back pocket with his right hand, Pete pulled out his wallet, swiftly located his license, and handed it over to the officer. Meanwhile, Julia had been asked to step out of the truck, and she was now being closely inspected by Officer Daniels.

After examining his license carefully, Officer Kane asked, "Can you tell me where all those blood stains on your shirt came from, Pete?"

Desperately trying to think of an appropriate response, the other officer brought Julia around to the other side of the truck and whispered into his partner's ear.

"Your friend appears to be slightly intoxicated, Pete. Does the blood on your shirt have anything to do with her? She appears to be wounded."

Julia stood next to Pete. He waited for her to respond, but she was silent. All of a sudden her weight shifted, and she awkwardly regained her balance as she was about to stumble to the ground. Officer Daniels grabbed hold of her arm and said, "Young lady, you'd better come with me," and escorted her to the squad car, sitting her down in the back seat.

Pete was about to offer an explanation when he was interrupted by voices coming up the trail from the beach. Three individuals emerged from the shadows into the parking area.

"Would you follow me, Pete?" Quickly, Officer Kane shuffled Pete into the back of the squad car, seating him next to his extremely intoxicated, recent acquaintance.

Instead of joining his partner in the front seat, he turned on his flashlight and headed in the direction of the approaching voices.

Fearing the worst, Pete leaned forward, covering his eyes with both hands, agonizing over his decision to stop and help Julia. He suppressed the urge to turn and look out the rearview window. His heart was racing, and he felt a trickle of sweat roll all the way down his arm pit to his waist.

His fear suddenly was overshadowed by anger as he realized that he would not just be late for work: he would most likely not make it into work at all. Pete couldn't believe what was happening.

What in the world am I doing sitting in the back of a police car? Is this the reward I get for helping Coach's daughter?

Unable to resist the temptation to turn and look any longer, Pete twisted around and observed Officer Kane talking to Al Baker and Josh Evans. He appeared to be taking notes as he spoke with them.

A third person was seated on the ground next to them. Pete's body temperature dropped 10 degrees as the officer knelt down and shined the flashlight on him. The person was none other than Brian Taylor, all bloodied, both eyes swollen shut.

Then Officer Kane returned his focus to Al and Josh. He was now on his second page of notes. Al seemed to be doing most of the talking; occasionally, the officer would turn to Josh—the ex-con—who would nod his head and speak a word or two. Pete hoped that the officer would be alert enough to do a background check on Josh before accepting his testimony. Meanwhile, the officer seated up front remained silent. Pete hoped he could not hear his heart thumping.

What have I done? Am I going to jail now? And for what? Protecting someone who was defenseless? So what if Brian got the snot kicked out of him? Didn't he deserve it? What was I supposed to do, just keep walking? Call the police when I got to work 20 minutes later? What is Al telling him, anyways? It's just my luck that the one I tried to protect is sitting right next to me—inebriated, deaf, dumb, and... blonde.

Whether it was the Schnapps, shock, or fear, it was a mystery why Julia had suddenly clammed up. Other than Julia, Pete had no other witnesses. Except for Roger. But he was long gone. Even if Roger was still here, Pete wasn't so naïve to believe that his teammate would actually stand by his side. He had already demonstrated his cowardliness earlier.

Pete checked the time on his watch.

11:05 p.m.

He had now been detained for more than a half hour. Officer Kane was still questioning Al and Josh; he seemed to be filling up page after page of notes. Brian was still sitting on the ground beside them. Finally, the officer closed his notebook, offered a final word to Brian who was now being lifted back on his feet by Al and Josh. Then he dismissed the three young men before approaching the squad car.

Pete was on the edge of his seat; the tension was so great, he felt like his intestines might rupture if someone didn't break the silence.

Officer Kane nodded to his partner and then turned around to the occupants of the back seat. "Pete and Julia—your Coach Abraham's daughter, aren't you?"

She nodded.

"We're going to have to take you both into the station. Officer Daniels, any word out of the young lady?"

"Not a word, Officer Kane."

"I hope she perks up by the time her daddy arrives at the police station."

"Pete, we're going to have to contact your parents, too. Your mom and dad at home, I presume?"

"Excuse me, sir. But I'm supposed to go into work tonight. I'd really hate to bother my mom at this hour. Can I at least tell you my side of the story, first?"

"Son, you'll get your chance…" snapped Officer Kane, "but I think you're going to want to have at least your mom there with you when we start the questioning."

Officer Kane flicked on his headlights, started up the engine, and zoomed out of Lakeside Park while two captives sat soundlessly in the back, their bodies stiffened by fear.

This is crazy. This isn't happening to me. Get me out of this mess, someone.

Chapter Twenty

For most of the families in Juddville, it was a typical Sunday morning. That could not be said of the O'Connor home, however. Hardly a sound could be heard except for the sporadic, mostly-subdued sobs of Cindy O'Connor who was sitting alone on the couch in the living room with a half-emptied box of Kleenex at her side.

The Abraham home was also in disarray. Coach Abraham had been up all night after picking up Julia from the police station at

12:30 a.m. Once they had returned home, he and Carol spent the next hour trying to get answers out of their less than coherent daughter. But their attempts were fruitless, so Carol finally led Julia to her bedroom just before 2:00 a.m.

For the next hour and a half, Keith and Carol discussed what to do about their youngest daughter, whose life was now in complete disarray. They even contemplated calling their older daughter Mary who was pursuing a career in marketing in New York City. Their oldest daughter had maintained a fairly regular correspondence with Julia, calling her once a month, and sending a letter every once in awhile. They were quite sure, however, that Mary would not be able get away from her new job without suffering any repercussions, however.

It was still unclear to the elder Abrahams, what had actually happened to Julia. According to Pete—who still commanded the complete trust and respect of Keith—he heard her scream, and when he went to investigate, he found her lying on the beach, holding the side of her face, about to be raped. Unfortunately, neither Julia nor Brian was able or willing to corroborate Pete's story.

What was clearly irrefutable, however, was the fact that Brian Taylor had been on the receiving end of one severe beating, served up by the most important player on this year's Juddville football squad. Consequently, the Juddville Police Department was pursuing assault charges against Pete. Of course, Keith's number one concern was the welfare of his daughter, but he could not turn his back on his team captain and his potential legal troubles.

Nonetheless, Julia was foremost on Keith's mind. On the eve of what was supposed to have been her departure for college, her life had been violently derailed, and Keith could not help but feel that he was at least partly to blame.

When Carol went to bed at 3:30 a.m., Keith sat all alone in his living room. For the next hour and a half, he was on his knees, crying out to God, pleading for his daughter, and begging for mercy and forgiveness for his obvious failures as a father.

At 5:00 a.m., Coach Abraham rose from his knees, made a pot of coffee, filled up his travel mug, and went on a long walk with his dog Muffy. When he returned home an hour later, it was still too early to call Pastor Jenkins, so he hopped in the shower.

The hot water brought momentary comfort to his fatigued body, but did nothing to remove the stain on the Abraham reputation from the previous evening. At approximately 6:20, Keith picked up the phone in the kitchen and dialed the pastor's home phone, praying that he might already be awake. Pastor Jenkins answered the phone on the fifth ring, and tried his best to convince Keith that he hadn't roused him from bed. The coarseness of his voice suggested otherwise, however.

Overruling the protests of Keith, Pastor Collins insisted on meeting with him immediately—regardless of any last minute preparations still required of him prior to the 9:30 worship service. Within in 15 minutes, Keith was sitting in his pastor's kitchen, his hands wrapped around a warm mug of coffee. Coach Abraham—clearly not his typical upbeat self—tried to explain his family's predicament, and the complications it presented for Julia's immediate future. The exact details about the altercation at the beach were still vague. Keith was hoping his daughter might be more forthcoming in the morning after several hours of sleep, but he feared her memory would most likely be blurred from her excessive alcohol consumption.

When his early morning house guest had concluded his story, Pastor Jenkins bowed his head and prayed for his friend. After their time of prayer, he advised Keith to delay bringing Julia to Tyler College for at least a few days, if not a week or two. In addition, he set up a time to meet with the Abraham family that evening.

It was 8:00 a.m. when Keith departed from his pastor's kitchen—still too early to call on Coach Allen—yet it was urgent that he speak with his assistant as soon as possible. Ideally, he would prefer to take care of football business while his wife and Julia were still sleeping. He felt it was his duty to be there for them when they awakened.

By 8:15, Coach Abraham was rapping on the screen door of Coach Allen. Miraculously, Jim was already up and seated at his kitchen table, holding his daughter Katie snuggly in his arms.

The look of shock in Coach Allen's eyes was impossible to miss. As he opened the door, Coach Abraham wasted no time.

"Jim, I hate to bother you on a Sunday morning, but something has come up."

Opening the door with his free hand, Jim welcomed his friend, "Come on in, Keith. What happened? You look like you've been up all night. Can I get you some coffee?"

"Sure, Jim. That would be great."

Keith walked over to the kitchen table and sat down in the nearest chair. The Sunday paper was spread out, covering most of the table with the different ads and mostly ignored sections of the Sunday paper. Jim was wearing an old Juddville tee-shirt and some loose fitting shorts. Over the counter he poured a fresh cup of

197

coffee into a Juddville State Championship mug and placed it before Keith.

"Thanks," said Coach Abraham, smiling to Jim for his choice of mugs. "You know that little girl in your hands is more precious than anything else in this world. Make sure she always stays Number 1 on your depth chart."

With that introduction, Keith began to tearfully relate to his friend all that had transpired in the last 24 hours. Throughout the narrative, Keith would insert, "It was all my fault," or "I can't blame Julia for…" When he reached the point in the story involving their team captain, he was able to speak with a little more composure.

"I don't know what I can do to help Pete right now under the circumstances. For Julia's sake—as well as Pete's—it's probably best that I try to stay out of the picture as much as possible. If I try to get involved in the legal process, people will accuse me of trying to bail out one of my boys, or even worse, that I'm just trying to cover for him because of my daughter's involvement.

"You should have seen his face, Jim. He was in complete shock. Then they fingerprinted him and everything."

"And there were no other witnesses?"

"Apparently not. Julia hasn't been able to tell us anything yet, but it's very clear that her feelings for Brian have suddenly changed 180 degrees. She didn't show any concern about Brian's injuries. I am quite sure she was somewhat aware of what was going on, but now if she suddenly comes out and backs up Pete's story, I know the accusations will be that she's just protecting one of Daddy's best players. I just don't know what to think. It's a real mess, Jim."

"Let me bring Katie up to Mary a minute, Keith, and we can talk some more."

Jim exited the kitchen and walked quietly upstairs to his bedroom. Meanwhile, Keith looked out the sliding glass door and surveyed the Allens' backyard. He admired the in-ground swimming pool and the lush, well-maintained lawn. Outside of the fenced in area he could see the top of a jungle gym, complete with two swings, a bright red slide, and various climbing apparatuses.

If only I could go back and start all over again.

Coach Abraham's thoughts were cut short as Jim reentered the kitchen. "Can I get you a refill, Keith?"

"No thanks, Jim. I've had my fill this morning. Do you have any suggestions for how we can help Pete?"

"Well, I was thinking I could go over and visit Pete and his mom this afternoon. Do you know what the specific charges are?"

198

"Officer Kane said he was being charged with assault."

"Aren't they interested in finding out who organized the party and who furnished the alcohol? I know Brian must be 21, isn't he? But your daughter and—I imagine most of the party—were underage."

"The police made no mention of extending their investigation outside of the assault. When they gave Pete a breathalyzer test, the results showed he hadn't consumed a drop of alcohol, just like he had said.

"You know what makes me feel even worse? Did you know Pete's father is incarcerated? You should have seen how devastated he looked when he finally got a hold of his mom on the phone. To add insult to injury, she had to borrow a car from a friend so she could pick up Pete from the station."

"Wow, I didn't know about his dad. What is he doing time for?"

"Manslaughter. He plowed into a couple of kids while driving under the influence. After he went to prison, he completely cut himself out of Pete and his mom's life. They have had zero contact with him for the last five years."

"Keith, I think I would like to pay that boy a visit today. He needs to know there are people who are going to stand *with* him. What is this going to mean for Pete and football?"

"Well, I'm sure we'll have to follow the athletic handbook which means he'll be suspended unless he's cleared of the charges."

Jim felt the pit in his stomach become twice as heavy.

"What ever happened to 'innocent until proven guilty'?"

"That doesn't apply to football players, Jim. One other thing. I'm afraid there's a very good chance I will have to miss practice on Monday. We were supposed to be dropping Julia off for college today, but all those plans have been thrown into disarray. Right now, taking care of her is my first priority. She was really messed up last night, and I don't know what kind of shape she is going to be in today, but for once in her life..."

Keith's voice began to tremble.

"For once in her life, I want to be there for her."

Keith cleared his voice, and continued, "I hope to be at practice for the meeting on Monday so I can explain a few things to the players, but nothing is certain at this point. We may be spending most of the day at the Juddville Police Department, trying to sort this whole thing out. No doubt, once the media gets wind of this story, it's going to spread like wildfire."

"Don't worry about the team, Keith. We've faced challenges like this before. Is there anything Mary and I can do to help?"

"Yes, there is Jim. You can pray for us. I never really got to talk to you yesterday about Jimmy's message at the men's breakfast. That part about neglecting your children hit me right in the forehead like a two-by-four. I only wish I would have heard that message about fifteen years ago."

Jim reached over and placed his hand upon Keith's shoulder, "Hey, don't worry about the team. Coach Oliver and I've got it covered. Julia needs you right now. And I'm sure she'll be fine. She's got a good head on her shoulders."

David Riley and his family were ushered down the center aisle to the front of the worship center. They were seated in the fifth row from the front—where the Rileys always sat—two rows behind Coach Abraham. But on this day, Coach was not seated in his customary seat, and David hadn't seen him chatting in the narthex where he usually had a swarm of people about him, inquiring about the status of his boys.

He must be out of town or speaking at another church, thought David.

Pastor Jenkins began the service with his standard welcome, and then led the congregation in the singing of a few hymns. After the last hymn, "Great is Thy Faithfulness," Pastor Jenkins proceeded immediately into a time of prayer. When he neared the end of his prayer, David was jolted into attention:

".... and we ask, Dear Father, that you would especially be with the Abraham family right now. Give them guidance and comfort, Lord, and give them Your grace to face the challenges before them. In the name of Jesus, we pray. Amen."

For the remainder of the service, the majority of people in attendance at Faith Community Church found themselves imagining what type of difficulties Coach Abraham and his family were now facing. Was there an illness? Marital problems? Death in the family? Who would know? Naturally, any news would stay confidential.

During coffee time, after the service, the congregation was abuzz. Their concern about the Abrahams was motivated by only the best intentions, but in secret, many of the parishioners couldn't wait to get home to feed their curiosity by calling their most dependable contacts on the Rumor Wagon network.

After church, David and his family sped home for their much anticipated Sunday dinner. This week his dad was grilling barbecued chicken to complement his mother's signature potato salad—heavy on the eggs, with just the right amount of cucumber, radishes, and carrots, with extra mayo, of course. It was 1:00 before they were able to sit down at their picnic table to begin devouring their Sunday feast. For dessert, there was a juicy, ripe watermelon.

When the Rileys were done with their meal, Mr. Riley suggested they offer up a prayer on behalf of Coach Abraham and his family.

David volunteered and prayed, "Father, be with Coach and his family. We don't know what's wrong, but we trust that You will keep them in your care. Thank You. In Jesus's name. Amen."

At the conclusion of the Riley's Sunday afternoon backyard picnic, David and his sister Karen quickly cleaned up the table. The paper plates and plastic cups were discarded, and the leftovers were secured in Tupperware containers and placed in the refrigerator. Then David decided to spend some time in his room where he could lay down and read his new Sports Mag: UFL Preview. His sister went over to a friend's house to play while Mr. and Mrs. Riley retired to the living room for their customary Sunday afternoon nap.

A couple hours later, David woke up from his nap and looked at his alarm clock. It was 4:30; he looked out from his bedroom window; the sun appeared to be beating down on the dry, withered grass; and there wasn't a single cloud in the sky. There wasn't any breeze coming through his window. His oscillating fan was doing its best to create some airflow in his room. In the corner of his room lay David's football cleats. A favorite slogan of Coach Abraham came to mind: *Winners do the things that losers refuse to do.*

Compelled to lift himself out of his post-nap comatose, David changed into a pair of running shorts, a tank top, and a pair of clean athletic socks; and in a few short minutes, he was walking out to the garage, his dad's keys in his hand, determined to get his workout over and done with. At the last second he decided to grab a football just in case there might be a few other players hanging out at Raymond Sanders Field. It was probably too late in the day to bump into Pete O'Connor, though.

Maybe I should call him, thought David. Not wanting to be distracted from his present course, however, the Jaguar quarterback decided to go at it alone instead.

Maybe next time.

Roger Collins came to life at about 1:30 p.m. His mother usually let him sleep as late as he wanted on the weekends. She would usually make him eggs or a sandwich as soon as he rolled out of bed.

After taking a scalding 15 minute shower and washing down two Tylenols with a large glass of ice water, Roger was feeling rejuvenated. He was thinking about heading to the beach for one last hurrah. Maybe, he would run into a couple of teammates and play a little catch with the football. What better way was there to show off in front of girls?

Unfortunately, his mom was perched on her favorite chair, in the sun room adjacent to the kitchen, elegantly sipping her ice tea while reading the Sunday paper.

"Hey, Mom," said Roger.

"You get in late last night?"

"Not too bad. Where's Bill?"

"He's in the den, fussing on the computer. You know what today is, don't you?"

"Yeah, I think it's the usual day that comes after Saturday and just before Monday."

"Don't get cute with me. You know today is back-to-school shopping day. I made your favorite sub: roast beef and provolone. As soon as you're done eating, we're heading to the mall. I can't have my baby walking around in rags when he returns to school in one week."

"Aw, Mom. Can't we do this some other time? I just got new clothes for my birthday. This is one of the last chances I'll have to go to the beach."

"What do you mean, 'go to the beach'? Judging by all that sand you tracked in last night, I'd say you spent enough time at the beach last night."

His mom's sobering reminder quieted him for a moment, and then he went back on the defense. "Mom, the summer's almost over. I'm not wasting one of the last days of summer walking around the stupid mall."

"Roger, I promise it won't take more than an hour or two. I don't have to remind you that Bill was willing to set aside time from his busy schedule just for this occasion, and we don't want to disappoint him do we, honey? He's been looking forward to this all week."

"No, Mom."

"I won't take 'no' for an answer, Roger. If you stop your whining, maybe we can stop at Bim's Music on the way home. I'm sure we can pry a couple of twenties out of Bill's wallet."

"But I don't want any new CDs. I just want to hang out at the beach with my friends."

"Come on, Roger. You were just there last night."

"Mom, why do I have to do this? I'm not a kid anymore. Can't I just pick out some clothes on my own after practice some day this week? I'm sure Bill would rather be doing something else, too. Doesn't he have some work to catch up on?"

"You are the most ungrateful son in the whole world. If it wasn't for Bill, we'd be living on the streets. Your father only provides us with the bare-minimum in child support. If it wasn't for Bill, we'd be living in a trailer. So what if Bill isn't the kind of man who spends all his time watching sports on TV or playing golf or going fishing or whatever it is you expect him to do. My point is that he *wants* to spend time with us today, so if you want any new clothes or any new CDs, today is the day. And that's final, Roger."

Realizing that his mother wasn't going to budge on this one, Roger decided the best course of action was to get this shopping spree over as quickly as possible.

In five minutes flat, Roger had inhaled his sub sandwich. After a quick trip to the restroom, Roger snagged the keys to Bill's Lincoln Continental and raced out to the garage. In no time at all, he was revving the engine, beeping the horn, waiting impatiently for his mom and Bill to join him.

The digital clock in Bill's car reminded him of the time. It was already going on 2:00. Perhaps, they could be done by 4:00 if he was lucky. At least he didn't have to worry about anyone on the football team seeing him shopping with his parents. No one in their right mind would ever think of going to the mall on a day like this.

Finally, Bill and his mom walked out of the front door, his mom—without any hint of reservation—assumed the passenger seat next to Roger while Bill was relegated to his usual back seat status.

Always a little nervous about letting his teenage step-son take the wheel of his pride and joy, Bill stammered, "You just make sure…" then captured by the radar gaze of his wife, "What I mean is, Roger, you take us where ever you want to go first. You are the boss this afternoon, Kiddo."

Every time he heard Bill call him "Kiddo" it made him want to puke. His step-dad was such a suck up. Roger wondered what type of deal he set up with his mom. Surely, there must some payoff coming. "Wall Street" Bill was all about making deals. He must be profiting from today's sacrifice somehow.

As they departed from their luxurious home in North Shores Estates, Roger quickly accelerated to the speed of 60 mph. The speed limit was 45 mph, but he wanted to see how irritated Bill could become on this spoiled Sunday afternoon; besides, what cops would be out on a lazy Sunday afternoon, anyways?

Up ahead, about 30 yards, was a sharp left turn in the road, and Roger saw a cloud of dust blanketing his half of the road. Immediately, he began to apply pressure to the brakes, slowing down to 15 mph. A pickup truck had gone into the ditch.

"Whoa, look at that truck, Mom."

Roger began to pull off the road.

"Stay put, Roger. Just pull up along side them, and we'll see if they're okay," ordered Bill.

Roger decreased their speed to 5 mph. As they approached the vehicle, he observed the truck's front end had smashed into an old wooden fence. The driver's door was hanging open, and the driver had emerged. A husky male with dark straggly brown hair and an unkempt beard was attending to a dirty blonde haired woman who was leaning forward in the passenger seat.

Her hands were covered with blood, but she appeared to be conscious.

As Roger was about to bring the car to a complete stop, he heard Bill's voice from behind, "Keep going, Roger. Keep going. They'll be fine. Just some minor bumps and bruises. Look there's someone coming out of that house with a phone in her hands. Help's on the way. There's nothing we can do."

Out from a beige ranch house, walked a middle-aged woman, talking into her portable phone.

"Mom, what should I do? The woman looks like she needs help?"

"Bill, maybe we should make sure everything is..."

"Kate, this is no time to play Florence Nightingale. We're not doctors. An ambulance will be here any moment. Besides, did you see that driver? That redneck's probably got a shot gun in the back seat. Let the police and the rescue unit handle it; that's what they get paid for."

Reluctantly, Roger pulled back onto the road, trying to erase from his mind the frantic look in the eyes of the injured woman. His stomach began to feel nauseous, and he felt himself become light-headed. Not wanting to appear weak in front of Bill, Roger took a deep breath, and refocused his thoughts on the road.

A few minutes later they were at the mall. Roger parked the car, relieved to be on his feet again, desperately yearning to distance himself from his self-centered, cowardly step-dad. His conscience was under a rapid fire attack:

That poor woman, I hope she's alright.
We should have stopped to help.
Why did we have to bring Bill along anyways?
I should have stopped.
But I had no choice.
Bill made me keep going.
Pete would have stopped.
Who?
That's right, Pete.
But not you.
Two times in the last 24 hours.
Two women in distress, and you left them to suffer.
I'm just like Bill.

The shopping trip was a disaster. Roger intentionally made it his mission to be uncooperative and unruly at every opportunity. Every time his mom asked him to try on a pair of pants or a shirt, he'd respond, "I'll never wear that."

His mom's reply would be, "Just try it on, Roger. Let's just see how it looks."

"Preppy. That's how it looks. I'd get laughed out of school."

"Oh, come on, Roger. You have to dress for success. I bought Bill a shirt like this, and he wears it all the time."

With that comment, the possibility of that shirt ever touching his body immediately received an irrevocable death sentence.

"You like it so much, Mom? Then you wear it. I won't even let it hang in my closet."

His mother finally conceded that her boy was no longer her "Ken" doll that she could dress up, like she had enjoyed so much when he was in grade school. Roger managed to drag his mom and Bill into a sporting goods store where he picked out a West Shores University sweatshirt and a pack of Nike athletic socks.

On their way out of the mall, Roger relinquished the car keys to Bill. He vowed to never drive in the company of his step-father again. The ride home was ghastly silent save a minimum of small talk between Bill and his mom. When they passed the area where the accident had occurred, Roger covered his eyes in shame.

Later that afternoon, Pete and his mom were about to receive an unexpected visitor. Coach Allen had parked his minivan behind the O'Connor's truck, about a foot of his minivan protruding out into the road. With great anxiety, Jim approached their front door. He had absolutely no idea what he was going to say. He was not in the habit of praying, but on the drive over, he had earnestly pleaded to God for some divine assistance.

Cindy O'Connor opened the door to greet him. Standing behind her was Pete, a look of despair chiseled on his face.

"Hi, I'm Cindy."

"I'm Jim. Pleased to meet you. Hey, Pete."

Pete nodded, his hardened look beginning to soften slightly.

"Why don't we have a seat in the living room? There's not a lot of room, just enough for me and Pete."

Jim lifted up a magazine from the recliner before sitting down. Pete and his mom sat on the couch.

"The new UFL preview edition? I haven't gotten a chance to read mine yet."

Observing the article and accompanying photo where the magazine had been opened to, Jim commented, "Karchinski... reminds me a lot of the way you play the game, Pete."

Pete's eyes brightened, he began to blush as he fixed his gaze upon the floor.

"He's a modern-day gladiator. Everyone seems to have written him off after his shoulder injury, but he's still standing. Isn't he, Pete?"

"He's my favorite player, Coach."

"No kidding."

Attempting to shift the conversation tactfully to more urgent matters, Jim cleared his throat and began, "Well, Pete, I want you to know that the coaches and the team are behind you 100%. Coach Abraham needs to be with his daughter Julia right now, or he would be here too, but he wants you to know how much he appreciates what you did. We feel terrible that you have been dragged into this awful mess when all you were trying to do was respond to someone's cry for help.

"We want you to know that we will assist you in anyway we can. At the moment, however, Coach Abraham wants to make sure he doesn't complicate the situation. Unfortunately, anything he does right now involving his daughter or with you—one of his football players—is going to be perceived negatively by the public and the media. Yet he is confident there are ways he can help that won't attract any attention from the media or public eye.

"For one, I am not personally involved, and I will do everything I can to help. If you don't mind, Pete, I didn't get a lot of the details from Coach Abraham this morning. Can you fill in a few of the gaps for me?"

"Sure, I guess. What do you want to know?"

"First and foremost, are you sure there were no other witnesses. I mean, there wasn't anyone else there that could vouch for you?"

A pained expression swept across Pete's face. He became lost in thought for a few moments. After taking a deep breath, he spoke slowly with carefully measured words. "I was at a party with a few friends at the beach. I had to leave early to go to work. As I was walking back to my truck, I heard a scream for help. At the time I didn't know it was Julia, but I could tell it was a girl. I couldn't just keep walking. She sounded like she was being hurt.

"I walked over to where the scream came from and found Julia and her boyfriend. The next part is kind of embarrassing, Coach, but Julia was half-naked. She was trying to escape, but he was holding her down on the ground. It was then that I recognized she was Coach Abraham's daughter. He started to make threats to me, and I refused to leave until I knew Julia was going to be alright. I guess what happened next... Well, I don't know, Coach. Some people might say I took things too far, but I think he had it coming. What do you think?"

Coach Allen was concentrating so intensely—trying to visualize the scene exactly as Pete described it—that he had inadvertently missed Pete's question.

"Coach, do you think I went too far?"

Jim cleared his throat, and felt a rush of blood flow to his head as he tried to think of the right words to say. He had to make sure he wore his "educator" hat since he was speaking to a student/athlete. He wanted to tell him, man-to-man, that he had been hoping for quite some time now that Brian Taylor would get his due. He remembered when the jayvee coaches told him about a player getting caught stealing money from the locker room. In a perfect world, the players would have just dragged him out onto the field to administer justice the old-fashioned way.

"Pete, I know one thing for sure. There aren't many young men in the world today that have your courage and your character. I know without a shadow of a doubt that you did the right thing. You did what I and Coach Abraham and any other man would have wanted to do. I only wish there was someone else there who could verify your story."

Pete stared at the floor.

If I say that Roger Collins was there, too, he will only deny it. Besides, what would Roger say? "Yeah, I was there. But I was too drunk to help, so I decided to save my own skin and run!" It doesn't matter. Roger's not going to come forward, anyways.

"You look exhausted, Pete. You must not have gotten any sleep."

Mrs. O'Connor intervened, "Maybe about two hours or so, Coach. When I picked him up from the police station, we had to drive back and get the truck. Then Pete insisted that he go into work. It was almost 2:30 in the morning by then, but he refused to leave the restaurant without a busboy for the bar crowd. He usually works until 6:00 a.m., but after punching out at his regular time, he stayed around and worked for another hour, so he could finish the rest of his cleanup duties. That's the kind of person he is…"

Pete's mom suddenly excused herself from the living room as tears were pouring down her face. After grabbing a box of Kleenexes from the bathroom, she returned to her spot on the couch by Pete's side.

"Let me explain to you the situation from the school's perspective. The athletic handbook says that any athlete charged with a felonious crime shall be suspended indefinitely from all practices and competitions until the athlete is cleared of wrong doing. If convicted, the duration of the athlete's suspension will be ascertained once the student/athlete's sentence has been determined. Unfortunately, the bottom line is that unless the police decide to drop the charges against Pete, he will be suspended from all practices and games until the case goes to trial."

"But whatever happened to 'Innocent until proven guilty'?" asked Cindy.

"Good question, Mrs. O'Connor. There's nothing we can do to change the school board's policy at the moment. Coach Abraham has an enormous amount of friends in the community, however. Officer Kane, the police officer who is handling Pete's investigation, can expect a tremendous number of phone calls and letters in the coming days. In addition, Coach has a trusted friend from his church who is a respected lawyer in town, and if the police go ahead with these charges, rest assured, we will make sure you get the very best legal counsel. And you won't have to worry about legal fees, Mrs. O'Connor. They will be taken care of.

"In the meantime, Pete. I want you to go over in your mind everything that happened last night. If you can think of anyone who may have seen anything, either during the altercation or even before hand, that might help your defense, I want you to write their names down. We need to do all of our homework on this one. Pete, you need to stay strong and hang in there. Do you have any questions or concerns, Cindy?"

"Is there any chance the police will drop the charges against Pete? For crying out loud, Pete says Coach Abraham's daughter was getting raped. It seems to me the police are investigating the wrong person!"

Jim couldn't ignore the extreme irony of the police's efforts. The name Brian Taylor was familiar to most of the teachers and principals in the Juddville Public Schools system. Unfortunately, the troublemakers were the students whom were nearly impossible to forget. It was a constant source of frustration when Jim would bump into a former student and recognize the face but be completely dumbfounded of his or her name. But it wasn't so for those who were constantly disrupting class, for those who were regular visitors to the principal's office; no, there was never any name recognition failures when it came to students of ill-repute. Such was the person Brian Taylor.

"You're absolutely right, Cindy. If Brian Taylor is anything like he was when he was in school, I am quite sure he's got to have some type of criminal record by now. As a matter of fact, the police ought to be investigating whether Brian had any involvement in furnishing alcohol for the party. Why else would someone his age be welcome at the party? It certainly wasn't for his charm.

"Anyways, I know I don't really have to say this, Pete, but it is imperative that you keep yourself away from any place or any person that could bring any more trouble our way. We need to keep this contained. I want to make this as clear as I possibly can, Mrs. O'Connor. You and Pete have the complete support of the Juddville Coaching Staff. If you need anything, if you ever have any questions or concerns—no matter what hour of the day or night—I will give you my phone number. Coach Abraham intends to call you tonight. He is in a difficult spot right now because of the involvement of his daughter. But he wants you to know you have his support and his gratitude."

The frustration on Mrs. O'Connor's face was mounting, and she had to interrupt. "But where is he right now? Isn't he the head coach?"

"I know what you're thinking, M'am, but his situation at home right now is about all he can handle. His daughter was supposed to be leaving for college today. But instead, she is right smack in the middle of a criminal investigation involving her boyfriend and one of her dad's most valuable football players. What is most frustrating about it is that she hasn't been able to articulate any type of response to the police. At this point, it isn't clear whether her lack of response is due to the amount of alcohol she consumed at the party or to shock over her boyfriend's attempts to take advantage of her.

"Coach Abraham is trying to help Julia come to grips with the incredible horror of last evening. And as much as he would like to go to bat for Pete right now, he worries that if the public sees him getting involved in your defense, it will not help your case, and it will bring all kinds of accusations of meddling and favoritism upon himself. His daughter is really in rough shape right now, and she needs the full attention of both her parents."

"Coach, I understand he is preoccupied with his daughter. I just want what my son deserves. This is his dream that is being shattered. All for coming to the defense of his daughter. Please help us get him out of this mess.

"Pete doesn't have much of a father, you know. His dad's incarcerated and chose to take himself right out of our lives. You and Coach Abraham are his role models. I don't know what he would do if he didn't have football."

"Try not to worry, Mrs. O'Connor. These things usually work themselves out once all the emotions cool down. When all is said and done, I'm confident that Pete will be fully exonerated."

Coach Allen rose to his feet, doubting whether he had done anything to encourage Pete and his mother. He put himself in Pete's shoes and wondered how he would hold up under such dire straits. Jim looked around the trailer and observed that there didn't seem to be any appliances broken and no apparent holes punched into the walls.

"I just want to say that I am going to do everything I can, Pete. Hang in there. If it's okay, I'd like to stop by tomorrow."

"Yeah, sure. Hopefully there will be better news by then," responded Cindy.

Pete nodded in agreement. His eyes conveyed a less favorable forecast, however.

On the drive home, Jim could barely keep his attention on the road.

Why did life have to be so unfair? Pete is one of my all-time favorite players. He has such a passion for the game. He's a lot like me when I was in high school. What did he do to deserve this? It's just not fair. Look at all the trouble I escaped growing up. There were so many times I could have been suspended from school or found myself behind bars. So many things I'm ashamed of; most of them buried in the past.

What was so incomprehensible to Jim was that for some odd reason, God had just used him to try to lift the spirits of someone less fortunate, someone whose dad had deserted him. Someone who was feeling right now like the whole world was against him.

As Coach Allen pulled into his driveway, he noticed the digital clock inside his car.

Could it be 6:30 p.m., already?

The usual Sunday evening football anxiety compounded with the additional, extreme challenges facing the Juddville Football Program right now nearly overwhelmed Jim as he entered his home. Mary and the kids were sitting around the table eating one of their favorite weekend snacks: chips smothered with melted cheddar cheese. Katie had a string of cheese hanging all the way from her chin down to her plate.

"Hi, honey," said Jim walking over to Mary to kiss her on the cheek in between chews.

"How did it go, Jim?"

"Not so good, I'm afraid." Reaching into the refrigerator, Jim pulled out a cold Budweiser and sat down in his spot at the head of the kitchen table.

"You want a plate of your own?" asked Mary.

"No, I'll just have a few chips. Then I've got a ton of work to do."

Jim had accepted the reality that there was no way Keith would be at practice the next morning. As a result, the responsibility for tomorrow rested entirely on his shoulders. At least he would have some assistance from Coach Oliver. From what he could tell so far, Gary was going to be an excellent teacher and coach. He did a great job with the kids in drills, insisting that the kids use the proper technique. Not too bad of a motivator either.

"Look, Daddy. I'm having beer, too," giggled Luke, his oldest boy, who was lifting up his half-emptied glass of foamy root beer with a grin that stretched nearly the distance of a first down.

"That's not beer, son. That's root beer."

Jim was unable to escape the coy look upon Mary's face, halfway hidden behind her own mug of beer. She set her mug down and smiled at him, appreciating the spontaneous humor of their children.

"How is Cindy holding up?"

"Under the circumstances? Better than I would be, that's for sure. We'll have to wait to see what happens tomorrow. It breaks my heart to see this happening to Pete. He doesn't deserve this. It's so unfair."

Jim shrugged and took a deep sip from his beer.

"What's wrong with Peter, Daddy?" asked Luke.

"Oh, it's nothing, son," changing the subject. "Well, guys, this is the last week of summer. Then it's back to school for Daddy, Luke and Kevin. You ready to start preschool, Kev?"

For the next fifteen minutes, the discussion went around and around the table like a merry-go-round as the Allens plotted the events of their last week of summer. Then Jim dismissed himself to the basement while Mary got the kids into the bathtub and ready for bed. At about 8:30, he came upstairs to read *The Cat in the Hat* to young Katie. After kissing her goodnight, he went to the boys' room and tucked them into bed. Mary was just finishing reading a Curious George story.

Jim had been hoping to get a workout in this evening—either jogging a couple miles or a quick workout with the weights in the basement—but he was completely drained. So he changed into his pajamas, set the alarm clock for 4:30 a.m., and plopped into bed. He was even too tired to wait up for Mary who was in the kitchen balancing the checkbook. Only one week into the season, and the lives of the Allens were already held hostage by the demands of football.

Chapter Twenty-one

His heart beat frantically as he proceeded down the freshly waxed floors of the corridor leading to the boys' locker room. Holding his breath, he slowly opened the locker room door, yearning to find it empty. The clock on the far wall read 7:05.

After one week of practice, he had observed that most of his Juddville teammates arrived at about 7:30. The only players who reported earlier than that were those needing to see the athletic trainer—and, of course, Pete O'Connor.

The lights were turned off in the locker room—a good sign— so this first year Juddville player was pretty confident that he was the first player to report to the second official week of practice. His mind fully-focused on completing his mission—not the least bit burdened by any sense of guilt or apprehension—he boldly stood before locker number 18, lowered his shorts, and emptied his full bladder. By the time he was finished, the urine was beginning to stream out from the vents at the bottom of Pete's locker.

Satisfied with the achievement of his objective, he sprinted through the locker room and exited out the back door before any teammate could see him. Then he walked back around to the front of the high school where the bike rack was located. For the next 10 minutes he fussed with his bicycle lock until a significant number of his teammates had shown up.

By 7:30, ten or more teammates had entered the school to prepare for the first practice of scrimmage week. For a Monday morning, there was a considerable amount of chatter throughout the locker room. Instead of the typical bragging and exaggeration concerning who dated whom over the weekend, the conversation was centered upon one of their captains. Strangely, no one seemed to notice the puddle in front of his locker, though a few players had just missed stepping into it.

At exactly 8:00, Coach Allen called the team meeting to order.

"I know you're probably all wondering where Coach Abraham is this morning, but he's not going to be at today's practice. I want you to remember all the way back to the beginning of last week when Coach was talking about priorities. Well, Coach Abraham is tending to a family crisis today. The situation is very private and personal. He may choose to disclose additional information to you when he returns to practice tomorrow, but I am going to ask for you all to keep him and his family in your thoughts and prayers.

"On a separate issue," continued Coach Allen, clearing his throat while he grabbed a prepared statement from the top of his pile of practice plans. He lifted the paper up close to his face to read, but then decided to return it to the pile.

"You may have noticed Pete O'Connor's absence this morning, as well. Pete was involved in a legal matter this past weekend. I am really not supposed to divulge any of the details, but Pete got involved in an altercation. He was defending someone who was defenseless, someone who was in a very vulnerable predicament. The police were involved, and at the moment, it appears that Pete may face charges. According to our athletic handbook, any athlete facing felony charges shall be automatically suspended from all practices and games until the legal matter has been resolved. If any of you have information about this incident, I urge you to contact Officer Kane of the Juddville Police Department."

The room was as quiet as a funeral. No one dared to speak a word.

Roger Collins's head slumped into his folded arms, desperate to bury his shame, to bury his humiliation from deserting a teammate.

I was there, too. I was right behind him—for a few moments. That Brian punk was all over Coach's daughter. She had cried out for help. Pete had run over to help; I followed. But then when things got a little scary, I bolted.

Roger had attended more than his share of parties at the Pit that summer, and he had seen the Coach's daughter on several occasions. But he had never seen her as drunk as she was on Saturday night, and her boyfriend seemed intent on taking full advantage of her.

All of a sudden, Roger's head snapped upwards as a revelation pierced his chest with a sharp, cramp-like sensation.

I did exactly what my father would have done. Someone truly needed me, and what did I do? I turned my back on them and fled.

Coach Allen made a quick transition to the next item of business. "As you all know we have a scrimmage this Friday, so we have a huge amount to accomplish in the next four days. Today, we'll focus on offense. Before we put in a few new passes and a reverse, I want to take a few minutes to review our base plays from last week…"

At exactly 9:15, the whistle of Coach Allen signaled the beginning of practice. Upon completion of the warmup lap, the Jaguars lined up into six lines for calisthenics. Only one captain from the previous week remained: Mike Owens.

Faced with an unprecedented number of challenges the week prior, the coaching staff had inadvertently neglected to discuss team captains. Usually that decision was made before the first official practice. Captains were selected according to their football ability, their off-season commitment, and their leadership potential. This season, only one player's name had ever been discussed; unfortunately, this player was currently under suspension.

All of a sudden, as if following a script, Mike Owens vacated his spot in front of the team, filling an empty spot in the second row. Then twenty-six players took a knee as David Riley and Steve Wilcox left their spots in line and slowly approached Coach Allen.

"Coach, we were talking as a team on our way out to the field, and we have decided that we don't want any captains out front leading cals. Pete's our captain. If he can't be up there, there's not a single one of us that is capable of filling his shoes. For the time

214

being, we would like to stretch as a team—without any designated leader. We'll all work together to try and fill the void."

The first impulse of Jim was to reprimand them for stepping outside their boundaries, for naively believing that it was within their job description to make a decision of this nature rather than the coaching staff's. He wanted to point out the foolishness of their idea: every team, every organization needed leadership. Yet when he sensed the noble and profound sincerity in their request, he couldn't help but concede.

Clearing his throat, Coach Allen stared deep into the eyes of David and Steve. "Okay, men. I respect your decision for the time being. But we're going to need an extra dose of leadership in drills and especially, in the huddle. I'm sure you two know the stretching routine by now. We'll go through the routine quietly, under your direction from your regular spots in the front row."

As the team progressed through their modified routine, Coach Allen informed Coach Oliver of the team's decision. He then reminded Gary that they would go group offense until 10:15. Afterwards, they would join together for team offense.

When the team was done with their last stretch, Coach Allen led them in a couple of spirited exercises: jumping jacks and breakdowns. Then they split into form running lines. Typically, Monday practices were a lot like Mondays at most places of work in the U.S.—lots of idle chatter, low energy, very little productivity. Much to Jim's surprise, however, the Jaguars were pushing themselves at an extraordinarily brisk pace.

After a set of 20 yard backward runs and finally, a set of all-out sprints, Coach Allen blew his whistle for a water break. While the players flocked to the water hose, Coach Allen grabbed a couple of footballs and headed to the middle of the practice field while Coach Oliver positioned himself upon the 5-man sled.

At the conclusion of the water break, Coach Oliver put the linemen through a rigorous blocking progression on the sled: right shoulder block, left shoulder block; pull right, pull left; reach right, reach left; and finally, five yard fire outs, once with a right shoulder, once with the left. Then he divided the linemen into two groups, taking the opportunity to announce that juniors Greg McDonald and Mike Simpson would be vying for the vacant guard position. Greg and Mike were both guards on the second unit, so they would be alternating plays with the first unit and alternating at the same position with the second unit. Mike was not as aggressive, but he knew his assignments better. In contrast, Greg was having a very difficult time learning his plays, but he loved to hit.

Both the first and second units reviewed the inside trap, halfback power, the counter, QB Keep, and the bootleg. With ten minutes of group offense remaining, Coach Oliver set up "Kiss the Maiden", a favorite drill of Juddville linemen for many, many years. Three offensive linemen stood in single file, five yards separating them. About five yards behind the last linemen was a self-standing blocking dummy with a football resting on top of it—symbolizing the head of the precious maiden. Lined up face-to-face across from the first blocker was a pass rusher, who had to fight his way through the three blockers before tackling the maiden.

Pass Rusher
↓
Blocker

Blocker

Blocker

Maiden

Daniels, Wilcox, and Osborn assumed their places as blockers while McDonald was first in line for Pass Rusher. On Coach Oliver's command, Greg fired out of his three-point stance. Daniels utilized his superior upper body strength and invaluable experience, quickly obtaining leverage beneath McDonald's shoulder pads, knocking him back onto his gluteus maximus. Greg hopped back onto his feet, sidestepping Daniels, lowering his shoulder this time as he rammed into the pads of Wilcox. Wilcox was ready for him, however, forcing Greg to work exceedingly hard to advance five yards to the final behemoth who was waiting in the wings to protect the fairest of maidens. Gary Osborn was licking his chops as he awaited the unwelcomed insurgent. McDonald chose unwisely this time as he foolishly attempted to attack the Ox below radar. If he had been running on a full tank of gas—instead of just fumes—his low to the ground approach may have worked. Unfortunately for Greg, the Ox was an honor roll student quite adept in the sciences—particularly in physics—and he took full advantage of Newton's law of gravity, squishing the exhausted McDonald's nose straight into the turf, and burying his victim beneath 235 pounds of cheeseburger until hearing a cry for mercy. Greg dug his cleats and fingers into the turf, trying in vain to claw his way to freedom.

"Let him up, Ox," interceded Coach Oliver. Reluctantly, Gary released his prisoner as Greg bear-crawled the remaining three yards to the Maiden, toppling the ball from its perch.

Greg staggered to his feet and assumed the first blocker position while Daniels and Wilcox shifted back a spot. Osborn waltzed to the back of the rusher line, basking in all the glory. The next one in line to attack the Maiden was Simpson.

For the next ten minutes, each lineman was afforded at least one opportunity to rush the Maiden. The enthusiasm generated from this drill did not go unnoticed by the running backs who were monotonously reviewing plays until each of the two backfields could run every play without a single error.

"Can't we play Kiss the Maiden?" begged Mike Owens.

"Kiss the Maiden? You think we've got time for that? I don't think so, Mike. Besides, I think it might get a little rough for some of you," sneered Coach Allen, biting into his whistle before signaling the official end of group offense.

After a five minute water break, first offense huddled around Coach Allen. McDonald assumed Pete's vacant guard position while Simpson was waiting in the wings over on scout defense.

"Coach Oliver, can you set up the defense in a 5-2? And go ahead and start blitzing linebackers as soon as you're ready. Have the d-linemen wear flippers to begin. If all goes well after the first 15 scripted plays, maybe we'll toss the flippers and go live a bit before second offense."

Coach Allen gave David the first play. "34 trap. Be crisp now, offense."

David relayed the play, and the offense broke the huddle with a spirit of guarded enthusiasm.

"Blue 28... Blue 28... Set... Go!"

Daniels snapped the ball into Riley's hands; he reversed-pivoted to his left, handed the ball off to Mike, continued his pivot, faked to Rob Bast, and sprinted around the right side of formation, his hands on his backside hip, feigning possession of the ball.

David heard the whistle immediately. Looking back to the interior of the line, he observed a throng of bodies swarmed around the fullback. No net yardage for play number one.

The offense hustled back to the huddle as Coach Allen tried to maintain his cool. With a semblance of patience, he commented, "McDonald, that's your trap. You've got to pull on that one. We aren't going to have much of a running lane if our trapping guard forgets to pull."

Riley returned to the huddle with the next play. "22 power. We're going on 'two' this play."

Before calling for the break, David discretely reminded Greg to pull this time. The offense scurried to the line of scrimmage as David analyzed their opponents on the other side of the ball. The left inside linebacker was cheating up to the line of scrimmage like he was going to blitz.

"White 36… White 36… Set... Go…"

Before the second go could even form upon David's lips, Greg McDonald jumped prematurely from his stance, colliding with Riley just as he was about to call for the snap between the center's legs with the second Go. The whistle of Coach Allen screeched through the humid air.

"Simpson, switch with McDonald," commanded Coach Allen. "Your audition is over for the day, Greg. You can't play offense and make mental errors."

Mike assumed the vacant left guard's position in the huddle and readied himself for his first play.

"34 trap, on one," called out Riley.

The offense lined up for their third play, their confidence beginning to wither.

"Blue 28… Blue 28… Set… Go!"

Riley received the snap, handed off to the fullback who followed Simpson to the 4 hole before cutting straight up field, squeezing between the trap block on the tackle and the down block on the linebacker, advancing upfield for a gain of 15 yards before a safety wrapped him up.

Coach Allen clapped his hands enthusiastically. "That's the way to execute a trap block, Simpson. Now just bring a little more power into that block, and we'll have a humongous hole. Hardings, you've got to get your rear end upfield on that safety. If we get a block from you, that play goes the distance."

The offense had limited success the next ten plays, breaking a few long runs for would-be touchdowns. They managed to avoid any *major* mental breakdowns and were gradually gaining confidence.

"Are you guys ready to go LIVE?" inquired Coach Allen.

The response was an emphatic "Yes".

"Okay, Coach Oliver. Have the d-linemen get rid of their flippers. Defense, you can now tackle the running backs. Go ahead and blitz one linebacker every play, Coach. We've got to start working on picking up stunts."

Coach Allen put a hand on David's shoulder and called the next play. "22 Power Pass. They'll never see it coming. Make sure you carry out your fakes, and it's an automatic touchdown."

David took a knee inside the huddle. His stomach began to feel queasy.

This is it. Here's my chance to show the coach I can throw the ball. I've got to throw a strike.

Riley called the play. As the offense broke from the huddle, he wiped his perspiring hands on his pants. Crouching under center, he barked out the cadence.

"Red 48... Red 48... Set... Go... Go..."

David received the football, reverse pivoted to his left as Owens sprinted by, pretending to receive the handoff. McDonald was blitzing, and Mike collided with him head on, putting an immediate halt to his quest to get to the quarterback. David continued his pivot around to the halfback who exaggerated his fake with a few stutter steps.

The defensive end and cornerback bit on the faking halfback. Meanwhile, David had the ball on his right hip and was rolling out behind Simpson, the pulling guard. Downfield, Jeff Nash was streaking wide open, at least 10 yards behind the safety. Hardings, the tight end, was breaking free into the flats with no one on his tail.

David opted to go deep, lofting a fluttering pass 25 yards downfield into Nash's hands. Jeff caught the ball, turned upfield and sprinted for a touchdown as the safety, Adam Foster, dived at his ankles, grabbing nothing but grass.

As David raced down to congratulate his receiver, he felt like he could stretch out his arms and fly. When he reached Nash, they celebrated their touchdown with a sky-high five.

Coach Allen complimented the team as they regrouped in their huddle.

"That was a great job faking. If you don't fill for that pulling guard, Mike, that play gets blown up from behind. Excellent protection, line. Way to pull it in, Nash. The throw wasn't pretty, David, but it got the job done."

The next play was a 36 trap. Again McDonald was blitzing. Simpson was supposed to chip block from the nose tackle to the backside linebacker, but he never got there because McDonald knocked him two yards into the backfield, creating a pileup that neither Wilcox—the pulling guard—or the fullback could wade through.

"You can't be tentative firing out of your stance, Simpson," shouted Coach Allen. "There's no way the defense should ever beat us to the hole. We know the count. You've got to be quicker!"

The next play was the Wing Right 11 QB Keep. This time the right linebacker was stunting through the playside guard/tackle gap. The playside end was not alert to the stunting linebacker, but fortunately, the blitzing backer bit on the fake to the halfback. Furthermore, Roger Collins—playing strong corner—cheated inside also, setting up an easy hook block for Simpson who was pulling from the backside. Roger recognized the QB Keep too late, trying desperately to free himself from Simpson's block.

David sprinted free for twenty five yards. The safety—Adam Foster—trailed about seven yards behind.

Coach Allen blew his whistle, and David slowed to a trot. Foster kept running and speared David in the small of his back. Coach blew his whistle again. This time the piercing shrill lasted for five seconds and was followed by a hasty rebuke.

"Foster, are you deaf? Can't you hear a damn whistle?"

All of a sudden, Roger Collins jumped his teammate from behind and started pummeling Foster with hard blows to the stomach. Coach Allen sprinted to the fracas, immediately grabbing the right arm of Collins and yanking him off Foster.

"Foster, you can get your ass off this practice field right now. You are done for the day—if not the season. You will report to the meeting room tomorrow morning at 7:15 a.m. In the meantime, the coaching staff will meet to determine if it's in the best interest of this team to keep you around any longer.

"Collins, you can start circling the field until I get tired."

In the back of Jim's mind, he worried if he had done the right thing making Collins run laps around the field considering all the flack he received from Roger's mom the last time he made her son run. He stuck to his guns, however—this was no time for indecision—he would just have to face the music later. There was no complaint from Roger, though; he seemed to be taking his punishment in stride.

"Huddle up, offense. You all right, David?"

"I'm fine. That's why quarterbacks wear rib pads isn't it?"

The first unit ran eight more plays before Coach Allen called for the second offense. It was no coincidence that Jim blew his whistle and instructed Roger to conclude his long distance running and hydrate himself before reporting to the offensive huddle.

Under normal circumstances, he would have found a substitute for Roger, but if the truth were known, Coach Allen was mighty proud of Roger for putting a few good licks on Foster. The kid from Billington was a cancer on this team; the longer they kept him around, the more damage they would surely suffer.

"You okay to run the first play, Roger?" inquired Coach Allen, aware of his backup quarterback's labored breathing.

"Sure, Coach... I'll be okay."

The second half of team offense began slowly—a multitude of errors necessitated a steady stream of correction from Coach Allen and Oliver. The offensive line struggled to open holes against the defensive front, yet each time the group returned to the huddle, Roger somehow kept their spirits fully-charged. When Tommy Schultz—the backup fullback—started belly aching about the lack of holes to run through, Roger told him to keep his mouth shut and worry about his own assignment.

Not willing to be the field general responsible for initiating a massacre of massive proportion, Coach Allen chose to refrain from allowing the second unit to go "Live". After all, the majority of the best players were currently on scout defense. It just wouldn't be fair, nor prudent; furthermore, they just couldn't afford to have another player go down to injury.

Nevertheless, Jim did allow his second unit an increased number of plays. They were able to review all their base plays to both sides of formation. By the end of their portion of team offense, they seemed to be exuding a lot more confidence, and they were able to open a few holes while avoiding any blatant blunders.

At 11:20, Coach Allen whistled for water break. In light of Coach Abraham's absence, they had to restructure their usual approach to defense. Instead of breaking into three position groups, the coaches split the team in half to work on tackling technique. Coach Allen started his group with form tackling on the tackling sled while Coach Oliver put his players through an angle tackling drill. After 10 minutes, the groups switched. Then the group rejoined their original coach for another tackling station: this time Coach Allen worked on sideline tackling while Coach Oliver worked on goal line tackling. Again, after 10 minutes of repetitions, the groups switched.

By the end of the extensive tackling session, the sun was at high noon, and the players were starting to show their fatigue. For 10 minutes, they reviewed punt team assignments with the first offense filling most of the spots. Coach Allen explained a few critical variants of the punting game: pooch punting to pin the team inside their 15 yard line; quick-kicking; and punting from your own end zone.

221

The attention spans were quickly fading. Coach Allen even caught David Riley's eyes gazing off into the distance.

"All right guys, enough is enough for one day. Gather around me. Today we're going to run cross country. You can remove your helmets and shoulder pads for this run." Coach Allen's instructions were interrupted by shouts of elation as they immediately began unsnapping their helmets, stripping away their sweat-saturated jerseys and tossing them into piles.

After a half a minute had elapsed, Coach Allen resumed his instructions, "Here's where we're going to run today. We are going to start out by running around the entire field, corner to corner. Then head out the main gate, turn right and run along the sidewalk all the way to the middle school parking lot. Go straight to the softball field and circle behind the backstop, then around the softball field. Follow the sidewalk back to our field and then touch me. Are you ready? Go!"

Just over six minutes later, Roger Collins was passing through the gates and touching Coach Allen on the shoulder.

Wow! This kid's beginning to amaze me, thought Coach Allen. *I better stop making him run or the cross country coach might start recruiting him.*

The second player to emerge through the gate was David Riley, followed by Mike Owens and Rob Bast. Coach Allen and Coach Oliver waited in anticipation, wondering which linemen would finish first and assume Pete O'Connor's first-among-linemen status.

The fifth player to finish was Mike Simpson, the front runner—judging by today's practice—to fill Pete's offensive guard position.

One by one the members of the Jaguars Varsity passed through the gate. Coach Allen was now deep in thought, grasping for the most appropriate, most inspiring words he could offer to his downcast-but-not-defeated team. Suddenly, a tremor of excitement sparked through the huddled players who were waiting for the rest of their team to finish.

The cause of their excitement was most unexpected; Larry Moore was rounding the North East corner of the field. Slowly but surely, he trudged across the blistering sidewalk onto the practice field.

Seconds later, he was tapping Coach Allen's shoulder before receiving an exuberant chorus of praise from his teammates. Embarrassed by all the attention, Larry dropped to a knee, anxiously awaiting the exit speech from his coaches.

The team grew somber as Coach Allen removed his hat. Jim had expected the worst when he had first realized he would be leading practice without his long time friend Coach Abraham. Further complicating the matter was the highly sensitive conditions behind Keith and Pete's absence. With the exception of the repeat incident initiated by Adam Foster, this had been one of the most animated, unifying practices of his coaching career—including last season's state championship season.

What could he say now to affirm their efforts and to encourage them to stay positive through their present tribulation? Uncharacteristically, Jim closed his eyes and took a moment to ask for favor from the One looking down from above. Then Jim somberly began:

"I want you all to know that this has been a very difficult practice for me. You know, Coach Abraham is more than just a coach to me. We have been through a heck of a lot of battles together..." As Coach Allen thought carefully about his next words, he began to choke up as his eyes began to produce a number of unwelcomed tear drops.

Desperate to regain his formidable composure, he quickly wiped his eyes on one of the last dry portions of his tee-shirt.

Having now regained his composure, Coach Allen continued, "What Coach Abraham is going through right now as a father and as a husband is very much like a goal line stand, only the stakes are much higher than giving up 6 points to your opponent. So I want you to remember him and his family today in your thoughts and prayers. Secondly, I want to compliment you for the awesome job you did filling the void left by Pete's absence today. It really breaks my heart thinking about what Pete must be going through right now. There is not a doubt in my mind that—at this very moment—Pete is agonizing over not being out here with you today. So if you get a chance today, please let him know how much he was missed today. Let him know how much his teammates care.

"I know I should probably say more," continued Coach Allen, "but I'm going to leave you to yourselves to finish off this practice. I am very proud of you, men. After you've had a few private words together as a team, you are free to go."

With that brief benediction, Coach Allen looked over to Coach Oliver, nodded his head in affirmation, and proceeded to walk off the field to the much anticipated shade of their meeting room. Jim had hoped to see Coach Abraham's car parked in front of the meeting room, but his customary parking spot was vacant. Meanwhile, the players had circled around quarterback David Riley and center Craig Daniels, who had assumed the leadership of the team meeting.

From the classroom window, Coach Allen and Coach Oliver covertly eyed their team. About five minutes later, the 27 survivors reached their hands into the center of the circle, listening to the charge of Craig Daniels. The words were not discernible, but as the team dissembled, the message was abundantly clear.

On this most disastrous of Mondays, facing some of the direst circumstances a team could possibly imagine, this assembly of young men was being transformed into a squadron of battle-hungry warriors. Only three more practice days, and the Jaguars would be hosting three untested teams in a scrimmage before the watchful gaze of half the town of Juddville.

Chapter Twenty-two

Pete paced back and forth across his living room carpet. All morning long he had felt the rage building inside him. He was incensed at the world, infuriated by the sudden turn in his life's circumstances.

His mom was sound asleep in her room; she had finally consented to taking her sleeping medication at 1:00 a.m. Having to listen to her incessant sobbing for nearly three hours after Coach Allen's visit had made conditions unbearable for Pete. Normally, his mom was pretty thick-skinned. The impenetrable shell that had amassed around her heart the last seven years had enabled her to endure many job disappointments and the ensuing financial burdens of raising a teenage son without even a dime of assistance from her incarcerated husband. Up until now, the promise of football had always been there to help appease the sorrow, to help provide a convenient escape from all the misery of her disastrous life. It was so easy to lose herself in all the drama of a Friday night showdown between the Juddville Jaguars and a worthy opponent. And this was the year when her son was finally going to take his place center stage as team captain and two-way starter. All of Pete's hard work was finally going to pay dividends; all of his dreams were coming into fruition. But now the dream was being stripped right out of his hands.

Cindy had called in sick Sunday evening; her shift would survive without her. She had promised to take Pete out to lunch Monday. At 1:00 p.m., they would be meeting the lawyer that Coach Abraham had recommended.

Slowly, Cindy was drifting back into consciousness. Her eyes opened and she became aware of the time on her alarm clock.

10:25 a.m.

Pete heard his mother's alarm going off, and he felt a nervous sweat form upon his brow. In a few moments, she would emerge from her room. Not wanting to face her just yet, he opted to quickly vacate their morbid premises where he had been confined for more than 24 hours. It would be better for both his mother and himself if he got some fresh air by going on a long run.

He was already dressed, so he was out the door in five seconds flat. Not wanting to have to explain where he was going, he very gently closed the door behind him. Normally he would stretch for about five minutes, but today he did not have that luxury. Instead, he chose to start out in a slow trot for a minute or two. Then he would kick it into high gear.

As he proceeded down Strawberry Lane, his mind immediately began to picture his teammates out on the practice field, working their tails off in the intense heat of a sweltering August practice. He felt so ashamed for not being there with them.

Paranoid of being recognized out in public and of being lambasted for missing practice, Pete had chosen to cover his head with a black and white bandana; in addition, he wore dark-tinted sunglasses, confident that he would be able to complete his run incognito without any unwanted encounters with neighbors or any other familiar persons he might cross paths with on this most gloomy Monday morning.

Since it was only 10:30 a.m., he figured he could easily get in four miles without the threat of running into any teammates.

Under different circumstances, Pete might have noticed the gorgeous sky above him: painted baby blue, it formed a playground for the handful of fleecy clouds who seemed ecstatic to have the whole sky to themselves. Though the temperature was already 80 degrees, there was very little humidity. Pete felt a slight breeze on his face as he readied himself for physical pain.

His inner turmoil began to boil over like a raging inferno; he accelerated to maximum speed, not worried about pacing, not concerned about slipping. His arms pumped furiously; his thighs were moving like giant pistons. He imagined himself carrying a football and running over the many maple trees he passed along the way.

As he exited the trailer park, he headed West on Henry—away from Juddville High School. Pete figured if he ran hard enough he might be able to elude the torment bubbling deep inside his soul. Then his mind abruptly journeyed into the land of "What Ifs".

What if I had skipped the party and hung out with David Riley instead?

What if I had chosen to go into work an hour late and walked back to the parking lot with Nick and Dave? I know they wouldn't have run off like Roger. They would have told the police the truth.

What if I had left the party 15 minutes earlier? I wouldn't have even heard Julia's scream.

What if I had just ignored her scream? Kept going. Minded my own business.

What if I wouldn't have kept pummeling Brian's face until it swelled up like a beach ball?

What if I would have kept punching him until his brain went numb... until his breath went still?

The possibility that he had momentarily lost control out on the beach was too frightening for him to consider, yet the idea seemed to be taking root in the dark recesses of his conscience. Properly channeled anger had always been Pete's ally on the football field and in the weight room. In a football game, however, there was always a referee's whistle to signal the end of the play. Out on the beach Saturday night, Pete hadn't heard any whistle. What he heard was a voice directing that ferocious jaguar within him to finally break free from its cage.

As Pete reached the corner of Diamond Avenue and Henry—his normal turn around point—he noticed a police car hidden in an alcove of trees, using a radar gun to nab speeders. Turning his back to the squad car, Pete felt an unexpected chill as he set out to complete the last half of his run at a feverish pace. He half-worried that he might be under surveillance.

The timer mode on his digital watch showed that he had run his first two miles in under 16 minutes. Pete was on pace to break his four mile record of 31 minutes. He began to lengthen his stride while deliberately trying to slow his breathing.

His tee-shirt was soaked almost all the way down to his navel. The sweat in his eyes was beginning to sting, so—without stopping—he removed his sunglasses, and lifted up a dry portion of his shirt to wipe away the perspiration.

Pete figured that right now the team would be just about done with offense. He speculated who would be inheriting his place at guard. Pete's anger returned like the sun reemerging from behind a dense cloud.

As he approached the intersection of Emerald and River, he eyed an innocently-displayed stop sign; he wanted so bad to drive his fist into it.

This isn't fair! What did I do to deserve this?

All of Pete's dreams and ambitions were slipping away like sand through his fingers. The sweat in his eyes began to merge with his tears, and Pete was doubly-glad he had decided to wear sunglasses for his run.

Desperate for answers, and having no one else to turn to, Pete redirected his thoughts upward:

Why does this have to happen now? First, you leave me without a dad, and now you take away my dream. Why God? Why me? If you are real... if you really care about me... will you get me out of this mess? I can't live without football.

What was I supposed to do when I heard Julia scream? Just turn and walk away? Was I just supposed to let that low life have his way with Coach's daughter?

As Pete crossed Henry Street to enter the trailer park, he looked at his watch and noticed that he was going to easily break his personal record. With less than a quarter mile to go, he started down Strawberry Lane and readied himself for his final "kick".

Up ahead, three trailers past the intersection of Apple and Strawberry Lane, however, he identified two individuals. They were pointing at him which immediately made his blood boil. One was Adam Foster. The other was Josh Evans—Brian Taylor's friend. They were working on a Yamaha in front of one of the shabbiest, run-down trailers in Maple Village. Now Pete remembered why Josh looked so familiar; he must have seen him outside this trailer once or twice. Nevertheless, this was the scum bag that wanted a piece of him the other night.

Pete could feel the hate radiating from their eyes. If he made an abrupt left turn on Apple he could take a detour home, but he would feel extremely spineless. Although he had promised Coach Allen to avoid getting into any further trouble, it was against his nature to duck from his adversaries.

From what Pete could tell, it seemed like Josh was playing the role of junior mechanic; he had a towel in one hand, a socket wrench in the other. He was wearing a white tank top—was it to show the world he had no biceps?—and grease-covered jeans.

Obviously, he hadn't been granted permission to use the weight room while serving his time in prison.

Adam was wearing black shorts and a red and white Billington football shirt. As usual, his eyes were hidden behind greasy-brown bangs that drooped all the way down the bridge of his nose.

Pete hadn't a clue why Foster wasn't at practice.

Though Pete could have turned around and removed himself completely from potential conflict, he resolved to avoid eye contact with his two enemies. He stared straight ahead as continued along on his way to his trailer. When he was about 30 yards past them, he could hear their snickering. In a way, Pete was disappointed that they hadn't tried to start something.

About thirty seconds later, Pete reached his trailer, and he immediately checked his watch.

Thirty minutes and fifty-one seconds. A new record! Maybe I should go out for cross country. Yeah maybe if I could throw elbows at the other runners as I passed them.

Pete bent over his knees, forsaking the conventional wisdom—so often repeated by his coaches—that you will regain your normal breathing pattern more quickly if you stand up straight with your hands folded behind your head. After about 20 seconds, he stood up straight to check the time.

11:05 a.m. Defensive segment of practice—minus one dejected linebacker.

Pete located a patch of lawn behind his trailer where the brown grass was thick enough to do pushups. Before he could make any excuses, he dropped to the ground, sprawled out on his stomach, positioned his hands and feet underneath him, and cranked out 40 pushups. Next, he rolled over onto his back and did 50 bent-knee sit-ups.

Now his shirt was drenched with sweat and covered with pieces of dead grass and dirt. Pete walked over to the outdoor spigot and drank deeply from the badly worn end of a garden hose. When he could drink no more of the rubber-tasting water, he doused his head until his thoughts were interrupted by a thunderous roar of a motorcycle.

He quickly turned his head around and observed Josh and Adam strolling down the road. Pete met their glaring eyes with an icy stare of his own. Like a dog defending his home turf, his self-protection instincts were on high alert. As soon as they were directly in front of Pete's trailer, the motorcycle came to a halt.

Josh shut off the engine, released the kickstand, and hopped off his bike. Like a trained monkey, Adam followed.

Standing in the middle of the road, Josh stretched out his hands invitingly.

"Hey, Mr. Football Jock, want a piece of me now?"

Unable to resist, Pete stared into the eyes of his adversary as he felt his heartbeat quicken. He remembered how Coach Allen had specifically ordered him to stay away from any person that might lead him into further trouble. Yet what would his coach say about defending his home and defending his honor when trouble came knocking at his own front door?

"You hard of hearing, Jocko? What's the matter? You don't fight anyone unless they're too drunk to stand? He don't look so tough right now, does he Foster?" Turning his head around, he couldn't help but notice that his young friend Adam was beginning to backpedal away from the approaching trouble.

"Uh huh," agreed Adam, "but maybe we should come back later. This doesn't seem like a real good idea right now in broad daylight. I'd like to come back and hose down his front porch sometime, too—if you know what I mean." As he finished his last sentence, he lifted his leg as if to impersonate a dog urinating on a fire hydrant.

Fully aware now of the culprit who had urinated in his football locker, Pete's fists were clenched so tight his fingernails were beginning to penetrate the thick calloused skin of the palms of his hands. He was biting his lower lip so forcefully; he could taste his own blood. Confident that he could kick both of their asses with no trouble at all, he took a step toward them.

At the same moment, Josh reached into his back pocket and pulled out a switchblade.

A knife, huh? I guess that means that I'll have to take you down first, loser.

Crouching into a fighter's stance, Pete boldly approached his armed opponent.

All of a sudden, Pete heard a rattling sound coming from behind him. As he turned to look, he noticed the front door of his trailer beginning to open. He had completely forgotten about his mother.

Returning his attention back to Josh, he noticed that his challenger had already begun to retreat and was now hopping back onto his Yamaha, his friend Adam seated behind him, apparently having no desire to make acquaintances with Pete's mom.

"What's going on, Pete?" asked his mom, as the motorcycle made an abrupt 180 degree turn, burning rubber while leaving a thick, black cloud of exhaust.

229

"Just a couple of morons," reported Pete, intentionally shielding his mother from any knowledge that would cause her any further worry.

Cindy O'Connor observed an uneasiness in her son's eyes, but she didn't want to begin her day by cross-examining him. She looked at her watch and said, "Well, if we're going to have lunch before we meet with the lawyer, we better get moving."

"Give me five minutes to shower, and I'll be ready."

"Okay, Pete. That'll give me just enough time to water the geraniums. They're starting to take a beating from all this heat."

Coach Abraham looked at his watch for the umpteenth time, noticing that it was now 11:45—undoubtedly, Coach Allen and Oliver were wrapping up the end of the first practice he had ever missed in his illustrious 25 years of coaching. Keith was sitting in his recliner, and Carol and Julia were sitting on the couch facing him. The conversation had reached a standstill, and he was getting the impression that his wife was slowly but surely beginning to side with his youngest daughter.

"Keith, this is not a good time for Julia to be off on her own. She just went through a very traumatic experience. She needs to be around her family for support."

"I agree, honey. She does need our support, but she also needs a new environment. A fresh start away from all the negative influences…"

"Like Brian, for instance?" interrupted Julia.

"Yes, like Brian. I trust you are finished with him, aren't you?" inquired Keith, his eyes focused intently on his daughter.

"Of course, I am," answered Julia, her eyes staring down at her ankles. Then she added sarcastically, "Especially after all the damage he's done to *your* team."

"What's that supposed to mean?" asked Carol, coming to the defense of her husband.

"You know exactly what I mean, Mom, so don't pretend to be ignorant. You know the Juddville Jaguars have always been Dad's number one team. You and I and Sis, have always been second-string."

"I don't agree with you, Julia, and I don't think your sister Mary would either."

"Yeah, well I doubt that. Why do you think Mary moved all the way to New York City after she earned her degree? She couldn't wait to get free from Daddy's Football Kingdom."

230

Julia's words pierced the very center of Keith's heart. A direct hit.

"Oh Julia, you can't really mean that," responded Carol. "You know how much your dad loves us."

"Do I, Mom? Do I? Then why is he in such a big hurry for me to leave?" argued Julia.

"Honey, I don't know how much you remember from Saturday night, but Pete says that when he arrived at the scene, Brian was trying to rape you," said Carol.

Julia's face reddened, and she became quiet. Her memory of Saturday night was still clouded. She vaguely remembered screaming for help. The next recollection wasn't until she was at the police station; she would never be able to forget the look of shock on her parents' face. Of course, there was the physical reminder. On the left side of her face was some swelling and a slight bruise under her eye, and she was certain that Brian had been the one responsible, but as for the attempted rape allegations, Julia's mind was blank. Sure, there was a small amount of sand in her underwear, but that could have been from losing her balance when she was squatting down to pee or something stupid like that. The one thing Julia knew for certain was that she had drunk way too much alcohol that night. Furthermore, it hadn't been her first experience being intoxicated this summer either.

In spite of Pete's obvious association with her dad, Julia felt bad for him. She remembered seeing him earlier at the party. As far as she could tell, he was the only one out at the Pit who wasn't drinking. It seemed unfair that he should now be facing criminal charges for being the only one to respond to her cry for help. She only wished she could do something to get him off the hook.

Why did I have to get so wasted? If I only would have stuck with beer, I would have been fine! What was I thinking drinking Schnapps? I probably deserve this, but Pete?

Still stinging from the harsh words of his daughter, Coach Abraham got up from his chair, walked into the kitchen and poured himself a large glass of ice water. Then he retreated outside onto the deck where he could lick his wounds in private.

His mind kept replaying Julia's painfully-honest words, *"You and I and Sis have always been second-string."*

After practice Coach Allen and Coach Oliver met in the classroom. There was a message on the desk from the high school secretary. Jim picked up the note unsure of what to expect. It was a brief message from Coach Abraham stating that he would not be able to make the post-practice meeting. Family business. Keith would contact Jim later in the day.

Jim read the note twice and looked at Gary.

"Coach won't be able to meet with us. I'm sure he'll be back tomorrow, but let's prepare a Plan B, just in case," advised Jim.

"Sure, Coach."

"Tomorrow, we've got to prepare our kids to block the 6-2 defense and then the 5-3 on Wednesday. You'll want to spend the majority of group offense time reviewing blocking schemes versus the 6-2. But who knows what type of defenses we'll see in Friday's scrimmage. As much as we run the ball, we can expect to see 8 and possibly even 9 men in the box. Teams are going to try to jam the line of scrimmage with as many players as they can. If we had a stronger arm at quarterback, we could make them pay with a few deep play action passes. I just don't know if Riley has the arm, though.

"… Defensively, I don't know what we'll do if Coach Abraham isn't here. For group defense, I can take the inside linebackers for pass coverage while you take the outside linebackers with the defensive line. You can review all your stunts and work on tackling and pass rush. For team defense, I guess I'll diagram a few basic offense formations and plays that we might see on Friday for the scout team to run. While you run the scout offense, I can take the defense and run a few basic stunts and secondary coverages.

"I'd be shocked if Coach Abraham isn't here tomorrow, though. But in football, you always have to be prepared for the worst case scenario. That's why we train three centers to be able to snap the football isn't it? You never know who'll go down."

Coach Oliver had a look of panic in his eyes, "Coach Allen? Is Coach alright? I mean… this just doesn't seem like Coach Abraham to me. I've never heard of him missing a practice before."

Jim placed his hand firmly on Gary's shoulder, looked him straight in the eyes, and said, "Keith is going through a very difficult time at home right now, but he's strong. If there's one thing I'm sure of, his faith will get him through this crisis. God only knows how this will all turn out, but in my experience, when this type of adversity arises, it is usually the good guy who's still standing in the end. When it comes to 'Good Guys', they don't come any better than Coach Abraham. Keith and I have been through our fair share of challenges, and I'd like to believe that we've always come out wiser and stronger. I've got to believe that we are going to get through this in one piece, too. Sometimes, adversity comes around to test our mettle. And hey, aren't we fortunate to have you helping out right now? We would really be up a creek if you weren't here, Gary. And let me tell you, you are doing a great job with the line.

"In the meantime, we've got to stay positive. The kids have got to see that we've got things under control while Keith is gone."

"Sure, Coach. I just wish I could do more to help Coach Abraham. I'll be around my apartment most of the afternoon, and I'll be home tonight watching the preseason UFL game. Give me a call when you figure out the rest of tomorrow's practice plan."

"You bet, Gary. Hey, I bet you're getting excited for student teaching to begin. One semester, and then you'll be all set to start bringing in the big bucks."

"I'm going into teaching, Coach."

"Oh, yeah. Honestly, the money's not bad, and you won't get better insurance benefits any where, but you might want to marry someone who can bring home a paycheck, too."

"I'm not ready for that yet, Coach."

"I don't blame you. Might as well enjoy being a free agent as long as possible. Staying home at night and changing poopy-diapers will come soon enough. But I've got to admit, on days like this, I kind of appreciate having a family waiting for me when I get home."

"I think for now, I'll settle for my couch. I think I hear it calling right now."

"I think I hear my couch calling too, Gary. See you tomorrow."

Coach Allen sat back down at his desk and reviewed the practice schedule for the week. He made a list of things that had to be covered prior to Friday's scrimmage. He was absolutely panic-stricken over how productive his offense would be without their number one lineman to open up holes. Jim's brain was besieged by worries concerning personnel, the limited amount of offense put in thus far, and the availability of the head coach—not to mention the well-being of Pete and his mom.

Why was this happening to Pete? Why now? So unfair. His senior year.

The image of Cindy O'Connor's weather-beaten face lingered in Jim's mind. Though she was only a couple years older than him, she looked old enough to be his mother. Not that she was bad looking; it was just that her overall appearance exuded fatigue—like she was desperately in need of an extended vacation. Nevertheless, it was abundantly clear to Jim where Pete got his warrior mentality.

233

Every day must be a battle: a battle to provide, a battle to keep fighting, a battle to never surrender to the relentless tide of despair this world bequeathed upon her each morning.

Miraculously, she had single-handedly instilled optimism and self-discipline in Pete. The single joy in the life of the O'Connors was a game that took on gigantic proportions each autumn. A game requiring great passion, unselfishness, and extreme effort. Now this game was being stripped right from their hands. What was even more tragic was the impact it could have on Pete's promising future, of his goal of one day going to college and experiencing a much better life than the one his father had left for him.

There must be something I can do to help make things right for Pete, thought Jim. *Lord, help this young man who is in such great need of Your help.*

Suddenly an extraordinary idea occurred to Coach Allen: an idea which would compel him to venture out from his comfort zone into making a shot-in-the-dark phone call. It might not change Pete's legal circumstances, but it would surely brighten his day and show him that there were people who cared.

Chapter Twenty-three

Coach Abraham felt the touch of his wife's hand upon his shoulder as her soft voice beckoned gently into his ear.

"Keith, Keith. Wake up, honey. You've got a phone call from Roger Collins's mother," urged Carol, hating to have to awaken her husband who had been unable to get much sleep the last 36 hours.

His eyes slowly came into focus. He had fallen asleep in his favorite recliner in the basement. The television was still on, but the videotape he had been watching had long since concluded and had automatically rewound. The remote was still in his right hand. Carol was now kneeling in front of him, a reassuring smile upon her face.

"I must have dozed off. What time is it?"

"Almost four o'clock. I thought I'd better wake you. It sounded urgent."

"Oh... I better take it then. Mrs. Collins—no I think it's Perkins, isn't it—she's not the type of woman who is accustomed to waiting."

"Yeah, I got that impression, too."

"I'd better get this over with then."

Keith stumbled up the stairs, grabbed the phone off the counter, and walked out onto the deck to take the call.

"Hello, Mrs. Perkins?"

"Yes, I'm calling about my son Roger. He hasn't come home from practice yet. I hope there wasn't another problem at practice again… was there, Coach?"

"I don't really know, M'am. I wasn't at practice today. I had some important family business to attend to today. I haven't spoken with Coach Allen yet. Would you like me to call him for you?"

"Of course, I expect you to call him for me. I don't want to talk to that man, and my son was supposed to be under your supervision this morning. Since he hasn't come home I think it would be obvious that it is *your* responsibility to find out his whereabouts."

Oh boy, we've got a live one! Imagine… having the audacity to blame me for her son not coming straight home from practice. If I was Roger, I wouldn't be in a big hurry to come home either, thought Coach Abraham.

"I tell you what, Mrs. Perkins. I'll call Coach Allen and get back with you ASAP."

Click

Coach Abraham speed dialed Jim's phone number. Mary answered the phone.

"Hello."

"Hello, Mary. I hate to disturb you during dinner, but may I speak with Jim, please?"

"Hi, Keith. I'm sorry, but he's not home right now. I think he said he was going to stop for a quick visit with the O'Connors. Shall I have him call you as soon as he gets home?"

"Yes, I'm afraid it's urgent."

"Is everything all right?"

"I think so. It's just a parent whose son hasn't come home from practice yet. The mom just wants to know if Jim might know anything. That's all."

"I'll have him call you immediately when he gets home, Keith."

"Thanks, Mary."

At the conclusion of the phone call, Coach Abraham opened the sliding glass door entered the kitchen, and sat down at the kitchen table. He was beginning to worry about Roger; he was hoping that he hadn't got himself into any trouble or into an accident. In a way, it gave him momentary relief from his own problems.

Julia was over by the sink, cutting up a cucumber and some fresh tomatoes for dinner. He could hear Carol doing laundry in the next room. Although he genuinely appreciated moments when he and his daughter were home at the same time, he couldn't help but feel disappointed. This just wasn't the plan. She was supposed to be off at school, getting to know her roommate, experiencing all the bland meal choices of Tyler College's cafeteria. Instead, here she was preparing the salad for dinner. Keith wished she would just look up and at least acknowledge him with her eyes.

Maybe he should get up from his chair, walk over to her, put his arms around her, and somehow try to articulate how sorry he was that she had been subjected to such a terrifying ordeal. Perhaps he might then apologize to her for his failure as a father. Finally, he could convey to her how much he truly wished he could do something to help mend her broken heart.

Suddenly, the door bell rang.

"Honey, can you get that?" shouted Carol, over the din of the disorderly washing machine.

Keith walked through the kitchen and into his living room where he immediately noticed the WSLZ news van parked in his driveway.

What the heck is this all about?

Holding his breath, Coach Abraham opened his front door. On his porch was the one and only Gloria Jackson—infamous newshound—with her microphone in hand, pointed in his direction. Her wavy blonde hair and baby blue eyes were recognizable to just about any one who had lived in this corner of the state during the last decade. Positioned strategically behind her was a young male cameraman awaiting her command.

"Roll the tape, Kevin."

The cameraman followed her cue. The red light turned on.

"Coach Abraham?"

"Yes… what's this all about?"

"Can you tell us what you know about the assault that occurred out at Lakeside Park on Saturday night?"

"I'm sorry. I can not comment on that right now."

"Was the assault committed by one of your football players, Coach?"

"As I said before, I am not at liberty to discuss any of this right now."

"Is it true, Coach Abraham, that your teenage daughter was involved in this incident?"

Coach Abraham's eyes went hazy as he stared into the camera. He imagined how far the camera man might fly if pushed him off the porch.

"Would you care to comment, Coach Abraham?"

Keith suddenly realized that neither diplomacy nor violence would get him any where right now, so he opted to give Gloria one more, non-descript sound bite for tonight's broadcast.

"For a number of very good reasons, I can not comment right now on this matter. I am sorry."

Then Coach Abraham turned his back to the WSLZ camera and firmly shut the door behind him, locking it for good measure. In a state of near hysteria, Carol and Julia were seated next to one another on the coach in the living room. Keith closed the blinds and sat down in the adjacent love seat.

"We need to pray," suggested Carol.

"You couldn't be more right, honey," answered Keith, and he moved over to the couch on the other side of Julia, and they joined their hands together as Carol began to pray.

After the thirty minute meeting with the lawyer, Peter's spirits had sunk to an all-time low. Yes, the lawyer—Mr. Anthony Brown—thought they had a very good chance of beating the assault charge on the basis of self-defense and upon Pete's testimony that he had only been responding to someone's cry for help. There were a number of additional circumstances resting in Pete's favor: he had no prior juvenile record; he was perfectly sober at the time of the arrest, unlike the victim and the victim's "girlfriend"; the victim had a previous arrest and had allegedly been the one responsible for furnishing the alcohol at the party; furthermore, Pete had an exemplary academic and citizenship record at Juddville High School, with any number of teachers and coaches who would be willing to serve as potential character witnesses. On the unfortunate side, however, was the fact that Pete's pre-trial could not be scheduled any earlier than Monday of the next week—the week of their first official game.

Furthermore, there was one other significant problem working against Pete: the physical condition of Brian Taylor. Apparently, Brian had suffered a fractured jaw in addition to multiple facial contusions; as a result, he had incurred several hundreds of dollars of medical expenses. His face was almost entirely black and blue and was swollen to the size of a basketball.

The reality of Brian's physical condition and its potential impact on Pete's legal status was waiting for the O'Connors on the front step of their trailer. It was 3:30 p.m. when they returned home from their meeting with the attorney. After parking the truck, Cindy was one step behind Pete as he crouched down to look more closely at the front page of the Juddville Gazette.

Covering almost half of the front page was a gruesome photo of Brian Taylor's face. Cindy grabbed the paper from Pete and stared at it in disbelief. The headlines above the picture read, "Juddville Football Player Charged with Assault". Because Pete was only seventeen years old, there was no mention of his name, but he was referred to as a member of last year's state championship football team. The story contained very few details; there was no mention of Julia Abraham and no information about an illegal party where alcohol had been furnished to minors. The story concluded with a statement from the Superintendent of Juddville Public Schools, Dr. Paul Jones, who insisted that the student athlete being charged with assault would be suspended from all school activities until the investigation was completed.

Cindy handed the paper over to Pete and began a scavenger hunt through the trailer, desperately seeking a cigarette. In the meantime, her son retreated to his room where he would read the article three times. The impact of reading about his crime on the front page of the Juddville Gazette was too much to endure. The pain pulsating in his forehead made him want to scream. After closing the blinds on his window, he lay down on his bed and buried his head in his pillow.

Front page news... not for rescuing a damsel in distress though. That's not the way the paper sees it.

I should have stayed home on Saturday night.

I should have ignored her cry for help.

I shouldn't have fought back—no, I had to protect myself.

That punk deserved everything he got.

I don't deserve this. I worked too hard.

Pete rolled over on his back. He noticed the football on the floor next to his bed. He reached down and picked it up. The leather felt soothing to his fingertips. He tossed it upwards to the ceiling; as the ball began its descent, he formed a heart shape with his hands—thumbs together, index fingers touching each other. The ball landed softly into his hands, and he tossed the ball up again and again.

All alone in the confines of his room, his mind began to imagine what the fall would be like if he couldn't play football. It was nearly impossible for him to envision his team playing on Friday nights without him. He could hear the spirited chatter of the fans making their pregame predictions. He could feel the vibration of the drummers pounding an upbeat tempo in the end zone as the band prepared to make its entrance on the game field, leading the crowd in the school fight song. Then the band would form its tunnel, and the cheerleaders would stretch a banner for the Jaguars to sprint through as the fans howled in anticipation. The coaches and players were in the locker room, hearing the final charge of Coach Abraham.

Pete's heart began to pump excitedly. He felt the adrenaline surging in his veins. He felt the camaraderie of his teammates. They were in this battle together, dependent upon each other. As they grabbed hands for the team prayer, he could feel the energy from his teammate on his left flowing into his hand, up through his arm, shoulder and chest, and then down his right arm, his elbow, through his hand, his fingertips, and onto his teammate on his right. The love, the unity, the hope, the togetherness of being on a team…

The prospect of having all this stripped away brought Pete to tears. Ashamed at himself for crying, he buried his pillow in his mouth, trying to stifle the incessant sobs that refused to be restrained.

It's not fair. It's not fair. It's just not fair.

Coach Allen walked up the O'Connor doorsteps at approximately 4:00 p.m. His stomach was in knots, not a clue as to what to say.

Should I give Pete an official report on the team's progress? No, too depressing. Should I ask about how his meeting went with the attorney? Pete might not want to talk about that just yet. Should I try to add some humor? Or should I be solemn? Oh, God, I'm not good at this. Please help me.

Mrs. O'Connor opened the door, a lit cigarette in her right hand. Jim didn't recall her smoking during his first visit. Not a good sign. Her eyes were blood shot and swollen. She was dressed for the extreme August heat, wearing a tee-shirt and shorts, no shoes. Today's edition of the Juddville Gazette was lying upside down on the coffee table; Cindy had retrieved it from Pete's room over an hour ago so she could prove to herself that it wasn't just a bad dream.

"I hope you will forgive my appearance. It's been a pretty rough day," suddenly conscious of the cigarette smoldering in her right hand. "Do you mind if I smoke? It helps soften the edge…"

"Oh, that's fine, Cindy. It's your home after all isn't it? Now listen, if you think it would be better if I came back at another time, I won't be offended."

"No, Coach. I think it would be good for Pete to have a visitor. Have you seen the paper yet?" Holding it up for Jim to see, "Front page news."

"You have got to be kidding. There must not be much happening in the world today," trying not to allow his cynical view of the world to become too obvious. Jim quickly skimmed through the Juddville Gazette's latest example of sensationalism at its best.

"While you finish the article, I'll go get Pete. He's been alone in his room all afternoon. The meeting with the lawyer was a little discouraging. His pre-trial isn't until next Monday. He's going to go nuts not being able to play football all week."

Jim sat down in the recliner where he had sat the night before. The coffee table was cluttered with magazines, empty Diet Coke cans and an overflowing ash tray. He counted at least a dozen cigarette butts. It reminded him of his college roommate who smoked. What a disgusting habit. He chuckled when he was reminded of his own hypocrisy—or was it lunacy—when he would scold his roommate every time he had the audacity to put out a nasty cigarette in his *pristine* half-filled chewing tobacco spit cup. Nothing had been more revolting—at that time bizarre time in his life—than to pick up his cup to spit and have to take an unsavory whiff of a stale cigarette rather than his fermenting chew spit. Nicotine was one powerful drug. Jim had been addicted to chewing tobacco for seven years. Giving it up had been one of the most difficult feats he had accomplished in his entire life time. He must have tried twenty different times to quit. Every once in a while, Jim was tempted to give into the seduction of falling for just a little pinch between your cheek and gum. No, he could never take up chewing again, or he was quite certain the addiction would start up all over again.

Pete came out into the living room with an uncharacteristic frown on his face. Jim immediately got up and shook his hand and sat back down in the recliner.

"We sure missed you today, Pete. Want you to know, we're all behind you. When the team lined up for cals, they decided to proceed through the entire stretching routine without a captain up front since there is no one worthy to take your place. I was a little uneasy with this idea at first, but it worked out just fine, for the time being."

Pete's gaze was glued to the floor.

240

The silence broke a few moments later as he began to speak, "Coach, I guess I could be out for a while. The pretrial isn't until next Monday. And now everyone's going to think I'm a criminal. All I did was help Coach Abraham's daughter. She was getting raped. Why didn't the paper mention anything about that? Or that Brian was drunk and he'd bought alcohol for a bunch of minors? Doesn't anyone want to hear my side of the story?"

"Pete, you'll get your say. It might have to wait until your case gets to trial, but the truth will come out. And when it does a lot of people are going to owe you a huge apology. It used to be "innocent until proven guilty" in this country, but the media doesn't abide by this principle anymore. It's just a darn shame you have to be the one to suffer in the meantime. You and a bunch of pissed off teammates and coaches, I might add."

Keith Abraham wrapped his arms tightly around Carol and Julia as they concluded their time of prayer. The emotional weight of the last 48 hours was miraculously beginning to lessen. Though there was surely more pain to come, the Abrahams had renewed their hope; they had been reminded that their faith was not in people, not in the legal system, not in education, technology, or warm-fuzzy support groups. On the contrary, Keith and his family had affirmed together that their only hope was in God.

Carol excused herself to the kitchen while Keith and Julia remained on the couch.

Taking Julia's hand, Keith began to speak apologetically to his youngest child. "Julia, I don't want you to go to Tyler College if your heart isn't in it right now. We can put off college for a year or indefinitely if that's what you want. If you want, we can withdraw your registration tomorrow. It's up to you, honey. I am so sorry about how I've neglected you; if you give me a chance, I'd like to make it up to you. I'm sure we can still enroll you in a few courses at Lakeland Community College this semester, or we can wait until winter semester. Maybe, it's God's desire for us to stay together for a while longer."

His words came as a shock to Julia. For many years, she had yearned to hear him apologize for treating her like she was "second-string". Now she was dumbfounded, unable to mouth the right words to either accept his apology or condemn him for taking so long to get around to it.

Yet the words began to trickle out ever so slowly, "Daddy... I am sorry, too." Wrapping her arms around him, her voice muffled and barely distinguishable, "I know I've disappointed you and Mom... I..."

Coach Abraham embraced this moment, wishing he could hold his daughter like this for all eternity if it were possible. He had no practice to run to, no game film to watch, no phone call to make; it was just him and Julia—the home team—and he was hurting inside for having missed out on so much. For the next few hours, he sat with his daughter and beloved wife in the privacy of their living room, sheltered from the harsh, unsympathetic winds that were trying to wreak havoc upon his family.

A few minutes past 7:00 p.m., Roger Collins pulled into his driveway. His mother sprinted out the front door to meet him.

"Roger, where have you been? I've been worried to death. I even called that good-for-nothing coach of yours, and he, of course, had no idea where you were. I was just about to call the police."

"Mother, mother, just calm down, would you? What's the big deal? I wasn't gone that long."

"Did you ever think about leaving me a note or calling me at work to tell me where you were going?"

"Where's Bill?" asked Roger, attempting to change the subject.

"He's at a convention in Houston this week, remember?"

"No, but I should have guessed. Every time he goes away, you freak out like this."

"This isn't my fault, Roger. You're the one who acted irresponsibly. At least I know where Bill is. You, on the other hand, acting more and more like your father each day. Taking off whenever you please..."

When Roger's mom compared him to his father, his blood began to boil and his body would tighten.

"Just shut up, Mom. Maybe if you wouldn't have been such a bitch, Dad wouldn't have..."

Roger never got the chance to finish his sentence as his mom's open right hand hooked around, making full contact with the left side of his face.

Smack

His face stung, but his pride hurt more deeply. He pushed himself past his mother, and she began to wail like a wild coyote in the middle of the night.

The retired couple who lived next door—who had been weeding and pruning their flower beds—rose to their feet and entered the privacy of their garage.

Mrs. Perkins attempted to catch up to her son and grab a hold of his arm, but he was too strong.

"Roger, Roger... I didn't mean to hit you. You called me a..."

Her only child slammed the front door behind him. Running up the stairs, two steps at a time, he entered his bedroom and slammed that door shut, too, locking it securely behind him. Lying on his bed, he grabbed his old Wilson football—the one his dad had given him for his 10th birthday—and dreamed about when they used to play catch in the backyard.

Desperate for a diversion, Pete sat down in front of his television set at 8:00 p.m. This week's Monday Night UFL matchup featured the Los Angeles Bulldogs and the Miami Raptors. He didn't really like either team, but football was football—even if it was only a preseason game.

What Pete didn't expect to see was a preview for the 11:00 WSLZ News. At 8:30 p.m., Pete was contemplating a quick sprint to the kitchen to grab an apple or to make a quick peanut butter sandwich, but he opted to wait until half time. Immediately after Miami kicked their second field goal to increase their lead over the Bulldogs by the score of 6-0, the network went to a commercial break: a shocking promo for tonight's news. The background for the promo was a familiar one: the entrance to the home of the Juddville Jaguars.

"This is Gloria Jackson reporting to you from Raymond Sanders Stadium in Juddville. Here is what we're working on for tonight's newscast, airing immediately after tonight's UFL football game: the WSLZ investigation team has learned that a Juddville football player is facing possible criminal charges for an assault that occurred Saturday night at Lakeside Park. Tune into our broadcast following the game to hear an exclusive interview with the victim of the assault as well as a brief response from Juddville's head coach, Keith Abraham."

The video switched to a close-up photo of Brian Taylor, sitting on a couch, his face swollen and bruised to a point of non-recognition, his mother sitting next to him, arm on his shoulder, tenderness and deep sympathy in her eyes.

Pete stared at the TV; his first reaction was disbelief, followed by shock, and finally, outrage. Disbelief, that his hands had caused so much damage to another human being's face; shock, that a rapist was being portrayed as a victim; and outrage, that the entire viewing area was about to find out about Saturday night's incident.

What was most troubling, however, was how a 15 second clip could be so biased and misleading.

All alone in the confines of his living room—his mom was at work—Pete was in a state of panic.

Has the whole world turned against me?

Coach Allen was chewing on his first bite of pepperoni pizza when the WSLZ promo hit the air. He nearly gagged and had to quickly chase down his mouthful of pizza with a swallow of beer.

"You've got to be kidding," shouted Jim, to an empty kitchen. "Brian Taylor, a victim? A 21 year old, sitting on his couch next to mommy. That worthless piece of ...."

Jim slammed his down his glass of beer, a sip or two spilling over the edge on to the table. Jumping to his feet, he hurried across the kitchen to the phone and punched in the number of Coach Abraham. Unfortunately, he got a busy signal. After waiting 30 seconds, he tried again. Still busy. A minute later, two minutes, three minutes, then five minutes. Still busy. Fifteen minutes later? Twenty-five minutes? Same result.

Come on, Keith. I need to talk to you!

His heart was pounding as he sat back down in his recliner, and even though he had been sitting in front of the television for the last half hour, he was completely unaware that the second half of the game was about to begin and that Miami was ahead of Los Angeles by the score of 13 to 3. It had only been about two hours since he had last talked to Keith. He had heard all about Keith's abrupt interview with WSLZ, but who would have expected the story to be elevated to number one?

I pray to God that Pete isn't watching. But, of course, he is. He wouldn't miss a Monday Night UFL game.

Coach Allen lifted himself from his seat and began to pace back and forth across the room. He could feel beads of perspiration beginning to form on his forehead.

Suddenly, the phone rang. Jim picked it up before it had completed its first ring.

"Hello?"

"Jim, did you see the WSLZ promo?"

"Unbelievable. You talk about sensationalism, Coach. Unfortunately, most of this side of the state got a glimpse of it, too. Right smack in the middle of a UFL Monday Night game."

"I really thought they would wait until tomorrow to air the story. What do they possibly have to go on besides Brian Taylor's story? As far as I know, they haven't been in contact with Pete. I know he was advised by his attorney not to speak to anyone about the case. I spoke with a reporter from the Gazette this evening. He wants to interview me in the morning before practice. I'm afraid this is only going to get worse. What if WSLZ shows up at practice tomorrow? Do you know what kind of a distraction that would be to our football team?"

"Keith, you can't be worrying about the team right now. I assure you, we will survive. Did your daughter see any of the news clip?"

"Fortunately, she and Carol snuck out to buy a few groceries, hoping that most people would be home in front of their TV's. I told them I needed to stay at home, close to the phone."

"Are you still planning on practice tomorrow, Coach?"

"Yes, I'm not going to let WSLZ chase me away from my responsibility of coaching this football team. If their van shows up while we're on the field, I'll tell them they'll have to wait until after practice. And then I'll be giving them the same answer I gave them today: No comment."

"I'm a little worried about Pete. Do you think I should call him? I know for legal reasons, that you have to keep your distance, but he must be freaking out about right now."

"Jim, you do what you think is right. I know you've visited him once already today. I don't think we can do anything about the media. At least Pete's name has been kept out of the headlines, so far. Pete was the hero, not the villain. Tell him not to give up hope; he'll get his chance to defend his name, and there will be plenty of us standing with him."

"Alright, I'll think about it. I do think it's probably too late to call him tonight. I promised to stop in for a visit after practice again tomorrow. Well, I guess I don't have much choice now but to stay up and watch the news. I'm too irate to fall asleep anyways. I just can't believe WSLZ. They're going to be eating crow when all is said and done."

"You've got to remember, Jim. The news is as competitive a business as football. Profit is more important to them than integrity. *Whatever it takes* is their philosophy, as long as it draws in more viewers. So the viewer sees Brian's face, and they immediately begin to sympathize with him regardless that he tried to rape my daughter. I doubt the good people of Juddville will feel so bad, however, when they find out about Brian's character. In the meantime, please tell Pete I am forever indebted to him for coming to Julia's aid."

245

"I'll make sure to tell him, Keith. I think he understands why you can't be more involved in his defense right now. Anyway, it's getting late. I'll see you in the morning, Coach."

"Thank you, Jim, for everything. I don't know what I'd do if I couldn't depend on you to keep things in order while I'm temporarily out of commission."

After two hours of barricading himself from his mother's relentless pleas to open up his door and come down to the kitchen so they could talk, Roger finally conceded to the needs of his stomach and stealthily crept down the hallway, hoping that his mother might have retired to bed early—as was common when Bill was away on business.

He paused in front of her room; the door was ajar, and he could hear her gentle breathing from her bed. Her lamp was still turned on, which also was not unusual for his mom. He could see her now, book laying face down on her chest, mouth hanging open. Roger tiptoed past her room and down the stairs to the kitchen. He found some leftover pizza in the fridge, and he poured himself a large glass of milk while he waited for the microwave to heat up his dinner.

When the cheese began to sizzle, he pulled it out of the microwave and sat down at the kitchen counter. He turned on the television, keeping the volume low as to not awaken his mother. He checked the time on the kitchen clock above the pantry; it was 9:15. Roger clicked through a number of channels until he found the UFL Monday Night game. The Los Angeles Bulldogs were playing the Miami Raptors, and there was 1 minute and 18 seconds left on the clock until half time. The Raptors had just scored a touchdown; Los Angeles was receiving the ball. They returned the kickoff to the 33 yard line, and veteran quarterback Denny Maxwell was trotting onto the field.

Denny was notorious for his ability to run the two-minute offense. He called the play in the huddle—exuding poise in his every step and mannerism. As they broke from the huddle, he surveyed the defense of Miami. Seeing a mismatch over the middle, Denny audibilized to a quick slant across the middle to his favorite receiver Joey Swagger.

The veteran field general received the snap, dropped back three quick steps, and fired a perfect dart into Swagger's hands. Swagger eluded the first defender with a quick deek to the left and then plowed straight ahead for a gain of 16 yards. Ball on their own 49 yard line, the clock running, Denny Maxwell called the next play at the line of scrimmage. Again Maxwell dropped back three steps, pump faked to wide out Johnny Morris; the rookie corner bit on the fake. The ball arrived perfectly over Johnny's left shoulder, and he sprinted down the sideline before the safety pushed him out of bounds at the 20 yard line.

The clock automatically stopped, and Maxwell huddled his offense together and called the next play. Plenty of time left now—forty eight seconds—and the Bulldogs had two time outs left. This time the Bulldogs lined up with four wideouts, and Maxwell dropped back into shotgun, a single back lined up about 4 feet to his left. The ball sailed into Denny's hands, and he handed the ball to his running back, Albert Lewis. Lewis jab stepped to his left and then cut back to his right following the pulling guard. Lewis found an opening and was dragged down at the 12 yard line.

Maxwell called timeout and trotted off the field to confer with the head coach. Thirty-five seconds left, one time out remaining, second and two on the 12. About a half minute later, Denny was trotting back on the field with the next play. The announcers stated the obvious: the Bulldogs didn't want to score too early, leaving Miami with enough time to get a score of their own before half time.

The Bulldogs broke from their huddle into shot gun formation, this time with three receivers to the wide side and one lone receiver to the short side. Maxwell received the snap and rolled to his left—the overload side. Meanwhile, the running back blocked weak side and then slipped behind the rushing defensive end. Two offensive linemen released from their blocks and pulled out in front of Lewis. Maxwell dropped back three more steps, drawing four rushing linemen towards him. Then he dumped the ball just over the 6 foot 5 defensive end's finger tips. The ball sailed into Lewis's hands, he turned to run towards the goal line and found two offensive linemen directly in front of him. He followed the two blockers all the way into the end zone, leaving only 25 seconds on the clock.

Flag on the field. Offensive holding, Number 53, the center. The referee marched ten yards off from the spot of the foul. Second down and 11 yards to go from the 21 yard line. The Bulldogs broke from their huddle and lined up in their I pro formation. Maxwell received the snap under center, pivoted to his right, faked a hand off to Lewis, the halfback, and then bootlegged to his left. The tight end was dragging across the middle of the field with a linebacker chasing about a step and a half behind. Maxwell lofted a perfect pass to the tight end; he caught the ball out in front of him and turned upfield, running over the first defensive back to show before

247

getting dragged down by a linebacker and a safety pursuing to the ball.

The ball was spotted on the two yard line. There was 13 seconds left on the clock. Instead of calling their last time out, Maxwell lined up the offense immediately, single back with a tight end and wideout on both sides of the formation. The veteran signal caller began the cadence, the center snapped the ball, and Maxwell dropped back to pass. All of a sudden, Denny handed the ball off to the halfback. The draw—the perfect call—was wide open, and Lewis practically walked into the end zone, leaving only 4 ticks on the clock.

The camera zoomed in on the future Hall of Fame quarterback who was grinning at the pure joy of producing a touchdown—even if it was only an exhibition game.

Roger watched the entire series with complete reverence and admiration.

Incredible! He made it all look so easy. He was like a Four-Star General. Perfect execution and leaving only 4 seconds on the clock. I wish I could command that kind of respect. Maxwell's teammates would do anything for him. You can just see how much faith they have in him. That's the kind of leadership a quarterback needs. It's what Coach Allen is always harping on me about. That's why David's the quarterback and not me. But the true leader of our team is out of commission right now, and it's all because I...

Coverage of the UFL Monday Night football game broke for a commercial. Roger had just consumed his third and final slice of pizza, and had polished off his glass of milk. As he was about to turn off the TV and disappear to the basement to watch the second half on their big-screen television, he was startled by the image on the television screen.

WSLZ was broadcasting their second preview for tonight's post-game news. Roger slumped back down on his stool. It wasn't the condition of Brian Taylor's face that shocked him—as far as he was concerned, Brian deserved far worse. What chilled Roger to the bone were the outlandish accusations directed towards his teammate—the anonymous Juddville football player—the player whose identity was known by Roger, for he had been right by his side.

Until he ran.

Chapter Twenty-four

Coach Abraham's watch read exactly 6:25 a.m. when he parked his car in one of the many empty parking places in front of Martha's Cafe. Walking through the main entrance, he purposefully avoided eye-contact with every customer, praying no one would recognize him. He was not in the mood for small talk, nor did he want to answer any unwanted questions regardless of their good intentions.

Keith wanted this interview with Gazette reporter, Bruce Watson, to be over and done with so he could go on with the business of coaching his team. After missing yesterday's practice, he felt a strong magnetic pull to rejoin his team.

He sat down at a booth in the corner and ordered a cup of Martha's dark-brew coffee—no sugar, no cream, just pure unadulterated java. After a wait of less than five minutes, the reporter sat down in the booth across from him. The interview progressed smoothly for the first few minutes.

Questions about the charges against the unnamed player? Assault.

Questions about the school's athletic disciplinary policy? Automatic suspension unless the charges were dropped.

Questions about the player's history/character? No criminal record. Never a discipline problem in either football or in school. Blue-collar, honorable kid.

Then came the unwanted question, the one Coach Abraham had hoped might be avoided altogether:

"Coach, can you tell me anything about the relationship between the victim, Brian Taylor, and your daughter Julia?"

"I'm afraid I can't answer that question, Bruce."

"Come on, Keith. You know WSLZ is going to report on your daughter's connection, one way or another. Wouldn't it be better to get the facts out in print in your own words, rather than from some other unpredictable source? This is your chance to balance the story. You don't really want all the information coming from Brian Taylor or his mother, do you? Or what if there was another person at the party that came forward with information connecting your daughter to Brian? Here's an opportunity to set the record straight as far as your daughter's involvement is concerned."

"I'm sorry, Bruce, but I refuse to comment on any part of this incident having to do with Julia. Funny you should mention this party. Maybe you can tell me why I haven't heard about any investigation being conducted so far into who might have furnished alcohol to the dozens of minors at this party?"

"I'm not part of the law enforcement team, Keith. I'm just here to get the story on what happened to Brian Taylor on Saturday night. My job is to report the news, not create it."

"Yeah, I really wish you would listen to what you just said," responded Coach Abraham, taking a not-so-subtle glance at his watch. "If your aim is only to find out what happened to Brian, your missing the bulk of the story—if that matters to you at all.

"Well, I promised you 15 minutes, and my time is up. I've got a team to coach, so if you don't mind, I'll excuse myself. Here's a couple of bucks for the waitress for the coffee. If you don't mind paying the bill, I'm already running late."

"Sure thing, and thanks for your time, Coach. But I am going to be upfront with you. I'm going to have to do some more looking into your daughter's involvement in this story. My boss won't be very understanding if WSLZ comes up with an angle on this story that I've inadvertently missed. I've got a job to do too, you know."

"Go ahead and do your job, Bruce. But if I were you, I might do a little background check on Brian Taylor, or you might end up with a lot of egg on your face, and it won't smell as good as one of Martha's omelettes," pointing to the enticing egg dish the waitress was delivering to a hungry customer two booths away. "I happen to know the accused player, and I'd be willing to risk all of my reputation on his honor and integrity. And you can quote me on that."

"Would you risk all your reputation on your daughter's integrity too, Coach?"

Without thinking, Coach Abraham reached across the table, grabbing the reporter's collar with his right hand. Like a boa constrictor, he squeezed his shirt tight.

"Listen, you slimy-rotten filth. How dare you! Do you have any kids of your own? Do you have any idea what this has been like for my daughter? I'm going to warn you one last time: Leave my daughter out of this!"

Suddenly aware of the scene he was creating, Coach Abraham released his grip and hastily exited Martha's Café, hoping that there had only been Juddville Jaguar loyalists seated in the restaurant.

Coach Allen was sitting in his minivan in the school parking lot when Keith pulled in at 6:55 a.m. As they shook hands to greet one another, Jim could sense the fury still fuming from his typically calm, cool, and collected head coach.

"You okay, Keith?"

"I've been a heckuva a lot better. But I think I can ride this one out with God's help. I just wish there was more I could do right now for Julia and for Pete. I can't imagine having to deal with all this media exposure at their age. This story is being blown way out of proportion.

"Jim, I can't tell you how much I appreciate your going over to his house to support him. He's got no one else besides his mom, does he?"

Jim nodded, and chose not to acknowledge Keith's gratitude as he was only fulfilling his duty as a coach and friend. "I just don't get the police's angle on all this, Coach. I mean, are they trying to single out Pete just because he's a football player? If he was just a regular student, would the story be getting all this attention? It just isn't fair. They know Pete wasn't drinking and that he was on his way to work. What possible motive would he have to go off on Brian Taylor? Anybody who knows Pete would tell you he's not a bully. He doesn't go looking for trouble. It just doesn't make any sense."

"Yeah, the news doesn't have to make sense. All they need to do is flash Brian's pummeled face on the screen, and bingo, they've captured the viewer's attention. But I'm quite sure when the public—at least in the town of Juddville—finds out the rest of the story about the so-called victim, they're not going to feel a bit sorry for him. In fact, if I know this town at all, Brian and his mom might want to start putting their house on the market. Unfortunately, when the rest of the story comes out, my daughter's name is going to be right in the middle of it. I just wish I could do something to shield her from all these bloodthirsty news hounds."

"Is she going to talk to the media, Keith?"

"No, no, no. But I am afraid of what other witnesses might say about her, especially Brian. At this point, he hasn't mentioned her name. Julia's heart has already been shattered into a million pieces. Last night, she called up Brian to tell him their relationship was over. Carol was by her side, holding her hand the whole time. Normally, I'm sure, she would have chosen to break off the relationship in person, but under the circumstances that would have been out of the question. On top of all this, she still has to make a decision if she wants to attend Tyler College this fall."

"Has she been able to remember any more about Saturday night?"

"Unfortunately, her mind is a blank. She was pretty intoxicated, but I think it's pretty clear that her heart knows

251

something, though. According to Carol, she doesn't even have the remotest feeling left for Brian—which tells me there has got to be something to Pete's story. Why else would her feelings change 180 degrees? It sure wouldn't be for my sake, I can tell you that much. I'm just glad she has Carol to talk to about it. Part of me wants to kill Brian for what he tried to do, but a bigger part of me feels responsible for her ever being drawn into such a relationship. If only I had been closer to her… Anyway, enough about my problems, Jim. Let's go inside and go over today's plans."

"Sure. Oh, by the way, I forgot to fill you in on Adam Foster. Yesterday, I had to kick him off the field for taking another cheap shot. I told him if he wanted back on the team, he needed to meet with us this morning at 7:15, along with his mother. They should be here any minute, but to be honest with you, I don't think they'll show. If he does show, I think number one, he needs to make a formal apology to the whole team. Secondly, I suggest he be given extra conditioning after practice for the rest of the week."

"Well, I like your idea about apologizing to the team. And you're absolutely right; we can't have a player taking cheap shots at his teammates. One more time, and he's off the team. But I don't know about making him run after practice for the whole week though. I think we can get the message across after one practice. If he thinks he ran a lot the first time, he hasn't seen anything yet."

"I'd be surprised if we saw the Fosters, though. When I called the house yesterday, she wasn't home. Adam said he'd tell her the message, but he said she probably wouldn't be able to make it because of her job."

Keith put a hand on his assistant's shoulder and said, "Jim, I really appreciate all your support. It means so much to me to have someone I can count on, someone who is always backing me up. If Adam's mom is a no-show, I'll call her on the phone tonight to let know where things stand with her boy."

Pete's alarm clock sounded at 6:15 a.m. His eyes were already open. He had been tossing and turning since 5:00, trying in vain for the last hour to fall back asleep. It was hopeless. All he could think about was having to miss another practice. What he wouldn't do to be able to suit up with his teammates today.

He turned on his bedside lamp and grabbed the nearest pair of shorts, along with his Juddville State Champions tee-shirt, a pair of clean athletic socks, and then quietly dressed. He tiptoed to the kitchen and poured himself a glass of orange juice.

Before taking off, he wrote a short note to his mom. At the last minute, he remembered his wallet, then he was hastily out the front door. He unlocked his 10-speed, checking his tires to make sure the air pressure was still good.

What a relief, at least one problem was resolved.

The ride would take him 15 minutes if he pushed himself. He knew the Body Shoppe opened at 7:00, but he wasn't sure if that meant 7:00 a.m. on the dot or perhaps, a few minutes early. Pete had once heard that most bodybuilders loved their sleep, so he decided to save some energy for his workout and take his time pedaling to the gym. What was the hurry anyways? He had the whole morning to workout.

The temperature this morning was already beastly.

The boys will be really working up a good sweat today. Hope they all drank plenty of water before practice.

The breeze felt good on Pete's forehead. His thoughts turned from football to lifting weights. His plan was to go ultra-heavy on all three core lifts as there was very little chance he'd be practicing in the near future.

It's not like I have to worry about being sore for tomorrow's practice or anything. I'll start out with bench. A couple of light warmup sets and then 235 for 5. Maybe I'll go for 255 for 3.

Riding now at a moderate pace, Pete continued to rehearse his workout in his mind.

At exactly 8:00 a.m., Coach Abraham called the Juddville Varsity Football meeting to order. He began with a brief apology for missing practice the previous day, and then he officially informed them that he was unable to discuss in anyway the story that had transpired across the news the past 24 hours.

The podium was quickly turned over to Coach Allen who diagrammed the blocking schemes of their base plays versus a 6-2 defense.

"The key thing to remember when facing a 6-2 is that now we have eight men in the box to account for instead of just seven, so we don't have the luxury of a double team at the point of attack anymore. We need to area block instead. So if we are running the ball off tackle, the end blocks down to C gap—usually the defensive tackle or possibly a blitzing linebacker. The playside tackle blocks down to B gap—usually the linebacker or a "pinching" defensive tackle. The playside guard blocks the down guard who is head up on him unless the linebacker blitzes A gap. The center blocks backside A, and of course, the backside guard is pulling to the side of the play. The backside tackle has B gap, but we want him to try to reach all the way down to A gap to prevent any backside penetration.

"Although the 6-2 is stronger versus the run, they have one less man in the secondary. If we can sustain our blocks, there will be a lot more running room for the running back once he pops through the hole if the backside end gets to the funnel and the rest of the backfield carries out their fakes. I think it goes without saying that with one more man in the box, they have one less defensive back to defend against the pass. This should be great news for our quarterbacks and receivers."

Coach Allen continued his chalk talk, explaining the variations of blocking schemes for the inside trap, quarterback keep, play action pass, and the counter. Most of the team was alert—particularly the linemen—asking questions, and writing down notes in their playbooks. In the back row, however, one player's eyes were shut, his head being supported by his right arm. A spot of drool was beginning to emerge from lips. Adam Foster had showed up at the meeting with just three minutes to spare. Instead of stealing time away from the rest of the team, Coach Abraham had decided to postpone his heart-to-heart with Foster until the team meeting reached its conclusion.

At exactly 9:00, Coach Abraham dismissed the Jaguars to the practice field. Adam Foster—awake now—remained seated in the back. Having had his fill of the Billington transfer the day before, Coach Allen and Coach Oliver followed the rest of the team out onto the field. Meanwhile, Coach Abraham laid down the law for Foster: no more cheap shots after the whistle or any other discipline problems; his mother must call the head coach this evening or no practice tomorrow; and Adam would have to complete extra conditioning after practice, no exceptions. Foster expressed no formal objections to the ground rules, so he was out on the field only a couple minutes after his teammates.

Grabbing his clipboard and whistle before heading out onto the field, Coach Abraham breathed a sigh of relief as he observed no TV vans in the parking lot. On his walk out to the field, he offered up a silent prayer, pleading with God to protect him from the media until today's practice was over. Coach Allen was working with David Riley and Roger Collins on their throwing mechanics as they tossed the ball back and forth, warming up their arms. Coach Oliver was working with the long snappers, teaching them how to get a tight spiral using both hands.

At 9:15, Coach Abraham blew his whistle. The team promptly snapped up their chinstraps, and cruised around the field for their warmup lap. As they divided into their six lines for stretching, they automatically left the leaders' spots unoccupied. The coaching staff nodded their approval, and Riley and Daniels led the first exercise from their positions in the first row.

The coaches huddled behind the six lines of players, reviewing a few last minute practice details.

"Coach Oliver, we're going to start with defense today," announced Coach Abraham. "Take your defensive linemen and work on agility and tackling technique for the first 15 minutes. Then I'll bring the linebackers over to work on stunts.

"Jim, we'll go team defense from 10:00 to 10:25. Then after water break, we'll go offense as long as necessary—even if we have to go past 1:00."

The Jaguars completed their stretching and form running by 9:35.

A quick whistle, followed by Coach Abraham's brief command, "Get a quick water break and go immediately to your defensive position group."

Helmets came off as the team jogged over to the water trough, already dragging their cleats on the dry turf. The practice field was beginning to show wear and tear, particularly in the spots where they did form running and on the portion of the field where they did most of their scrimmaging.

Coach Abraham took his linebackers to the tackling sled. In the front of the line was a noticeable gap. Pete was always the first one in line for every drill.

"You're first, Wilcox. Right shoulder tackle. Hit, lift, and dump."

Rob Bast—number two in line and generally not one to make a lot of noise in practice—shouted out, "Come on, Steve, pop that dummy. Hit it for Pete. Hit it for Pete!"

The rest of the linebackers joined in on the chorus.

"Come on, Steve. Drive it into the turf just like Pete would if he was here right now," added Dan Hardings.

A smile appeared on Coach Abraham's face as he began the drill with a resounding, "Hit." It felt good. The camaraderie that was transpiring was one of those unique by-products of athletics. Moments like this were spontaneous—spawning naturally, without the need of any external intervention—almost as if the team was a single organism fighting for its own survival.

Steve exploded from his linebacker stance, crashing into the dummy, ripping his arms up, driving his hips, and slamming it into the ground—all to the thunderous applause of his comrades. He hopped to his feet, lifting the dummy sled to its standing position before retreating to the back of the line.

The atmosphere was euphoric; they were having a ball though they were supposed to be hard at work. Each of the linebackers had an opportunity to hit the sled three times with each shoulder before Coach Abraham brought them over to the parallel bags for agility. The bags were lined up with approximately three feet between them:

l   l   l   l   l   l   < Players

Coach

Again, there was an awkward moment of hesitation before the line formed in front of the first bag. This time Mike Simpson assumed Pete's customary spot in line.

"High knees, Mike. Both feet between each dummy," instructed Coach Abraham before blowing the whistle to commence the drill. Upon receiving his cue, Mike ran over the six dummies, lifting his knees chest-high.

"Pump those arms, Simpson," added Chad Williams, junior outside linebacker, waiting next in line for his turn to complete the drill.

The rest of the line began a rhythmic beat, clapping their hands together as one, hollering out encouragement as each teammate went through the bags. The second time through required a longer stride as they only stepped with one foot between each dummy. Next, they turned 90 degrees and went through the bags laterally.

"Keep your shoulders square to me, and watch the ball," commanded Coach Abraham, as he waved a football in front of him like a hypnotist. The degree of difficulty of this variation of the drill was much higher. One errant step, and a rendezvous with the ground was inevitable.

"Don't hit the dummies with your feet," yelled Coach Abraham.

Mike shuffled to his right, navigating over all six dummies without incident. On his way back, he tripped on the second dummy, and regained his balance just before Coach Abraham pitched the football towards him. Mike caught the ball while crossing the third dummy and tossed the ball back to Coach as he

256

passed over the fourth dummy. The last two dummies, he crossed over effortlessly, then turned and sprinted to the back of the line.

"Great hustle, Mike," shouted Steve from the back of the line.

Once the entire line had completed the drill, Coach Abraham moved every other dummy about three yards forward in the following arrangement:

Players

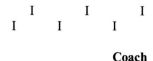

Coach

The players moved their line over, parallel to the first dummy. Coach Abraham blew his whistle.

"Quick feet now."

Mike sprinted diagonally between the first and second dummy, came to a screeching halt in front of the second dummy, backpedaled diagonally to a point behind the third dummy, sprinted in front of the fourth, backpedaled behind the fifth, and then dashed past the sixth and final dummy.

Once every player had completed the course, they formed a line facing the sixth dummy, so they could go through the dummies in reverse direction.

At 9:50, Coach Oliver brought over the TNTs—tackle, nose, and tackle—and Coach Abraham lined up a front seven with his two inside linebackers and two outside linebackers:

Outside LB	Tackle	Nose	Tackle	Outside LB
	Inside LB		Inside LB	

Then Coach Abraham asked each player to point to their gap responsibility in a 5-2 Normal. Next, he told them to set up in a 5-2 Eagle and point to their gaps. Finally, he reviewed stunts: Mike Right/Left; Inside Right/Left; Slam Right and Left; and Fire Right/Left and Double Fire. Much to Coach Abraham's dismay, there were an abundance of mistakes.

"Listen up, men," barked out Coach Abraham, "You've got to know your gap responsibilities on every signal call. It's really quite simple. In a Normal, the nose has both As; Inside backers, B; Tackles, C; Outside backers, D."

"Every position has a gap responsibility. All it takes is one person to fail, and our defense is compromised. If a tackle goes B instead of C, we've left open a humongous running lane between B and D gaps. You may get double teamed TNTs. When you feel pressure, you've got to drop to the turf and make a pile. We're depending on you. You probably won't make the tackle from that position, but you will prevent the running back from being able to run your gap. If they're doubling you, we should have one player freed up to make the tackle. This is called "Team Defense"; it only works as one unit, not as eleven individuals."

As Coach Abraham wrapped up his lecture on defense to the linemen and backers, Coach Allen and his defensive backs jogged over and took a knee behind their teammates who were listening intently to their head coach.

"If you take care of your gap, and your teammates take care of their gaps, we can stop any offensive attack. You've got to learn to depend on each other; you've got to learn to trust your teammates. That's the secret to football, men… and to life, as well. As you get older and wiser, you'll receive more and more responsibility. One day, you'll hopefully be fortunate enough to have a wife. And if you're really lucky… children. They will become your team, and they will depend on you so much. The success of your family will be a reflection of how well you have met your responsibility as a husband and a father. If you neglect your duty to the home team, they will surely suffer…"

Yeah, just look at me. Who am I to talk? I need to let one of my assistants give this speech next time. I am the worst of hypocrites. Just ask my daughter.

Coach Abraham turned silent.

Jim glanced at his watch. 10:00 a.m. The plan was to go to team defense—a desperate need at the moment. He had spent an hour preparing play cards for an offensive scout team. Jim waited another 15 seconds for Keith to introduce the next segment of practice.

An uncomfortable feeling hung in the air.

Come on, Keith. Team defense. Call it, Coach. Team defense. Uh oh… something's wrong. Oh, boy. This isn't good.

Coach Allen stepped forward and announced, "Water break, fellas. We're going to go to group offense next. You better hustle. We've got a lot more work to accomplish this morning."

The Juddville Jaguars slowly rose to their feet and jogged over to the water trough. Meanwhile, Jim cautiously approached his befuddled comrade who was now facing in the opposite direction of where the team had been huddled.

Keith was staring out into the distance. Sorrow painted all over his face.

"Hey… you all right?" asked Coach Allen.

Several seconds elapsed before Keith responded. His mind held captive by some distant force, "I… I was just thinking…"

"You want me and Coach Oliver to take it from here?"

Awkward silence. Jim had never seen his partner like this before.

"Hey… Keith?"

Suddenly, Coach Abraham snapped out of his trance, turned to Coach Oliver, who was standing back about 10 yards.

"Gary, let's start on the sled," turning from Coach Allen, he began to jog towards the 5-man sled.

Breathing a sigh of relief, Jim grabbed a couple of footballs from the equipment bag and trotted over to a patch of green grass that hadn't been torn up yet. He was going to have the first and second backfields review plays for the entire group offense session. Then they would have no excuse for screwing up their plays during team offense.

After 20 minutes of group offense, the team broke for another water break before coming together for team offense. The temperature was approaching 85 degrees, and a forceful wind blew across the field. Severe thunderstorms were predicted for late afternoon and early evening. The humidity was at least 90 percent. A good rain shower was needed. The underground sprinkling just couldn't supply enough water for this intense August heat.

Most of the players were now assembling around the football that was positioned on the 40 yard line. Coach Allen had dumped an armful of yellow scrimmage vests next to the ball.

"First offense, huddle up. Everyone else, get a yellow on. We're going to go against a 6-2 today. Defensive guards, tackles, and linebackers wear flippers for now."

Coach Oliver set up a 6-2 while Coach Abraham stood behind the offensive huddle where Coach Allen was giving a few final instructions.

"First play will be a 34 inside trap. When you get up to the line of scrimmage, I want you to take a knee so I can go over the blocking scheme one more time."

Jim backed out from the huddle as David Riley called the play. Once they broke from the huddle and jogged to the line, Coach Allen walked up to the football.

First, he made sure the defense was aligned correctly; then he quickly reviewed each offensive lineman's assignment.

"All right, now run the play."

As Jim turned to find a safe position to stand behind the offense, he couldn't help but notice the two rival news vans parked along the practice field. Evidently Coach Abraham hadn't seen them yet, but when he read the look of irritation on his assistant coach's face, he was compelled to turn and face the worst.

Without comment, Keith dismissed himself from the practice field, hoping to redirect the unwanted distraction away from his football team. Once he reached the edge of the practice field, he ushered the two crews in the direction of the meeting room where another surprise awaited him. Parked in his sparkling black Cadillac was Dr. Paul Jones, superintendent of Juddville Public Schools.

Meanwhile Coach Allen and Oliver carried on with the rest of the practice, doing their best to keep the team focused on football in spite of the unexpected media intrusion.

Chapter Twenty-five

Practice ended punctually at 12:00. Team offense went about as miserable as expected given the circumstances. At first, the majority of errors were made by the playside tackle and end. Instead of double-teaming the tackle—their scheme versus a 5-2—they were supposed to down block: end blocks C gap and tackle B gap. By the third repetition, the first team had finally caught on. The inside trap was a complete mess, however. The pulling guards weren't accustomed to the proximity of the defensive linemen they were now trapping—often running right by them, as a result. Then when the guards did get it right, the fullback failed to cut off their blocks, running right into traffic instead of taking the secure running lane right up the middle.

When the second offense got their opportunity, it was just about all the frustration Coach Allen could endure. This unit—Coach Allen was sure—still hadn't mastered blocking the 5-2. Years of experience had taught Jim the necessity of being ultra-patient with the second unit—many of the players were first year players or perhaps a little on the "slow" side mentally. The harsh reality, however, was that these players were just one play away from being in the ball game. If the starter in front of them goes down, guess who gets the call? The trick was to teach the second unit a few basic plays, and then bring them along slowly. By the end of the season, the second offense ought to be scoring touchdowns during the fourth quarter if the coaches have done any amount of coaching.

The last ten minutes had been spent reviewing kickoff coverage. Divided into two groups, each unit covered eight kicks in rapid-fire succession. By the end of the brief specialty session, the players were quite winded. Because of the Jaguars' extraordinary hustle and resiliency throughout practice, Coach Allen decided to reward their efforts.

"You did an outstanding job focusing on the task at hand today, men. It's not easy staying focused in the midst of all this heat. Coach Oliver and I have decided to let you off easy today, so there will be no gassers today."

The shouts of joy were almost as enthusiastic as last year's state championship post-game celebration.

"You earned it by your hustle during kickoff coverage at the end of practice. It would have been easy to dog it, and save yourselves for conditioning. But you didn't. That's the kind of spirit it takes to win big games. Every play, all-out effort, saving nothing for tomorrow. Speaking of tomorrow, we've got only two more days to prepare for Friday's scrimmage. We will spend the majority of our time on offense, blocking against the 6-2, but we are way behind defensively.

"I know you're all concerned about Pete and Coach Abraham. Believe me, we all are. The best thing we can do for them right now is to take care of our end: becoming a great football team. I truly believe that everything will turn out alright in the end. We've got to have faith. A lot of people are going to be asking you questions. I would suggest you tell them this: Don't believe everything you hear in the media. The truth will come out in the end, and it will sound a lot different from the story being reported right now.

"Bring it in, Jaguars."

The beleaguered-but-not-yet-beaten young men jumped to their feet, extending their sweaty, dirty hands into the hub of their team huddle.

"No matter what kind of adversity we face this season, we've got to be unified. We're a team. We stick together. No division. All for one. One for all. 'Team' on three. One... Two... Three..."

"TEAM," shouted twenty-eight players, minus their team captain and minus their head coach. As the team dispersed into groups of threes, fours, and fives, Adam Foster tried unsuccessfully to sneak off without being noticed.

"Foster, you've got exactly one minute to get a quick water and to meet me on the fifty yard line," barked Coach Allen, grateful that fate had allowed him to inherit the responsibility of administering extracurricular conditioning to one of his defensive backs who has been desperately crying out for more attention from the coaching staff. In about a minute, he was going to receive much, much more than he could possibly have imagined.

Adam dropped his helmet to the ground and trotted over to the water trough. His teammates were amused by the punishment that awaited him and quite relieved that he would be facing it solo.

After a quick drink, Foster reported back to Coach Allen and Oliver.

"How many players have we got on this team, Adam?"

No response.

"I asked you 'How many players on this team?' and I expect an answer, and I want an answer right now!" Jim's voice beginning to crack.

"Twenty-eight?"

"Wrong!"

"There were twenty-eight today," snapped Adam.

"You forgot someone. Someone who—unlike you—would do anything for this team. Since there are twenty-nine players on this team, you are going to start out by running a 50 yard sprint for each one of them. Every time you complete a 50 yard sprint, I want you to shout out the number. And if I don't hear the number clearly, it won't count. Do you understand me?"

Adam nodded reluctantly.

"Did you hear me?"

"Yes."

As Foster ran down the edge of the field, Coach Allen turned to Coach Oliver, "Gary, can you keep an eye on him. I'm going to go in and check on things inside a minute."

"Sure, Coach. I'll see you inside. But today, it's my turn to buy you a Coke."

"Thanks, Gary. I'm going to be needing one. But don't worry I'll be back out in a minute. I wouldn't want to miss Adam's workout for the world."

Roger's thoughts were in a tailspin. He was unable to focus on his next move, disabled by uncertainty, humiliated by his unheralded cowardice. The shame he was feeling about deserting Pete on Saturday night was beginning to overwhelm him. Now with all the media attention coming down on Coach Abraham, Roger felt about as low as he ever had in his entire life.

Sure, he could keep traveling down this current path: just keep quiet, and stay below the radar. Why tarnish his reputation by coming forward and admitting that he had also been at the scene. Only instead of choosing to fight, he opted for flight. Why would anyone expect him to put his own football season in jeopardy by sticking around?

Unfortunately, his conscience wasn't buying this self-protection ploy. Yet what good could he possibly accomplish by coming forward now? If he admitted to the cops that he had been at the scene and had been a witness to the attempted rape and the beginnings of a fight between Pete and Brian, wouldn't that raise further questions? For one, the authorities would invariably ask, "So why *did* you run, Roger?"

Oh, he could say always say that he was scared, but that would make him out to be a coward. Or he could tell them the truth. By admitting to being drunk, he would be volunteering information that would most likely lead to a two game suspension for violating team training rules. The upside, however, would be that Pete would be clear of all charges, and the media would back off from Coach Abraham, so he could get back to coaching the team again.

"Hey, Roger. Wait up."

Running up beside him was Steve Wilcox.

"What's the big hurry? Got a hot date or something?"

"No," unsure of how to answer, Roger responded fictitiously, "I just have to get out of the sun before I pass out. Aren't you glad we're getting done with practice right now instead of just getting started?"

As they reached the gate, they noticed the WSLZ and rival WORP vans parked in front of the meeting room.

"Can you believe all the attention?" noticed Steve. "We had less media hype last November when we were playing for the state championship. Who cares if Brian Taylor got his butt kicked? A lot of people would've loved to kick his ass. Do you think the media would be at our school right now if Pete had been a member of the soccer team or the chess club?"

A few moments of uncomfortable silence.

263

"Hey Roger, you were at that party too, weren't you? Did you see anything? I heard that Pete and Brian almost went at it earlier that evening."

"That must have been before I got there. Who told you I was at the party?" asked Roger defensively.

"Uh... I don't remember. Someone just let it slip in the locker room this morning, I guess."

Feigning ignorance, Roger remarked, "I wonder why Coach Abraham is receiving so much attention."

"Yeah, me too. You know, I've never seen him act the way he did at practice today. He was in another world..."

The two teammates walked side by side: Roger's head slung low, saddled by shame; and Steve's head looking back in the direction of the news vans, wondering when the Juddville Jaguars would be left alone to go about their business.

Steve resumed the conversation, "Did you see Brian's face on the news last night? Man, did Pete lay into him or what?"

A car horn beeped behind them. Roger turned to look and saw his mother; her head was sticking out the window, her hand beckoning him frantically.

His face turned crimson. Scanning full circle for any potential escape route, Roger had no choice but to acknowledge his lunatic mother.

What is she doing here?

"I've got to go, Steve. See you tomorrow."

"Yeah, you take care of yourself. We can't afford to lose anymore of our best players."

Fully embarrassed by the presence of his mother, Roger approached her car in fury. Walking around to the driver's side, he was poised to rip into her.

"What are you doing here?"

"How about I ask you a question instead? What are those news vans doing here, Roger?"

"What do you mean, Mom? Where have you been the last two days? You didn't hear that one of our players was arrested?"

"Are you serious? You'll have to fill me in over lunch. I told my boss I was having another migraine, so he let me have the afternoon off. I'd really like a chance to make up for last night."

"Oh Mom, can't we do this another time."

"No way, I took off from work for this. I refuse to accept 'No' for an answer. I'll follow you home, and then I'll give you 20 minutes to shower and get dressed. Then we're going where ever you'd like for lunch."

Being forced to submit once again to the authority of his mother did nothing to improve Roger's despair. The anticipation of a savory meal, however, did provide an opportunity for him to take his mind off his troubles for a brief period of time. Roger chose his favorite seafood restaurant, Fishermen's Wharf; unfortunately, it was located along the outskirts of Juddville, necessitating a most uncomfortable 15 minute ride alone with his mother.

For the duration of the drive, his mother fired off questions, and he tried to answer them, one by one, providing as little detail as possible while completely omitting his own involvement. The lunch crowd was just breaking up as they entered the restaurant, so they were seated immediately. Roger ordered the fried perch platter while his mother chose the salmon.

His mother hadn't watched any of the news the previous evening, having been preoccupied by the task of locating the whereabouts of her irresponsible son. As a result, she continued to question him while they waited for their food. Roger was relieved when the waiter finally set their meals before them.

The perch was superb, as usual. He emptied his plate in about seven minutes, requiring him to push his chair back to allow for the expansion of his stomach. For the next few minutes, he enjoyed a brief period of silence while his mother finished the rest of her meal. Once the waitress took away their plates though, she resumed her questioning.

"You weren't out at that party, were you, Roger?"

Roger stared out the window, watching a couple of seagulls circling around a little boy who was throwing leftover pieces of bread at them.

"I asked you a question, Roger. Were you at that party?"

Still staring out the window, Roger murmured, "I might have been."

"Well... you need to stay away from people like that, especially that Pete—what was his last name again?"

"O'Connor."

"So this guy he beat up is in pretty rough shape?"

"Yeah, he got it pretty good, but from what I hear, he deserved it."

"How can you say that, Roger? What could he have possibly done to deserve getting beaten up?"

"I don't know," lied Roger, trying to block from his memory the vision of Julia, attempting to pull up her pants while trying to recover from a vicious blow to the side of her face. "He's just a

265

big-time loser, Mom. Pete isn't the bad guy, regardless of what the news is saying."

"I think you're just siding with him because he's your teammate…"

How I wish that were true. I don't have the courage to be a real teammate.

His mom continued, "I would imagine he won't be your teammate for long though will he now? Has Coach Abraham kicked him off the team yet?"

"Kicked him off the team? He hasn't been proven guilty yet?"

"Well, you just said that he beat him up. Sounds pretty guilty to me. You can't just go around beating people up. No one has ever solved their problems by resorting to violence."

"Maybe he had good reason."

"Roger, in the real world, you just don't go and settle things with your fists. I don't know if it's good for you to be spending so much time around all this aggression. It's not healthy. If Coach doesn't do the right thing and remove this Pete kid from the team, I'll be taking up the matter with the superintendent. I'll take it to the school board if I have to."

"Mom—once again—you don't have a clue what you're talking about. Why can't you just keep your nose out of it?"

"I'm surprised at you, Roger. I would think you'd want me to do the right thing."

Before his mom could proceed to her next preaching point, Roger reached his breaking point.

"What in the heck do you know about doing the *right* thing? Did you do the *right* thing when you lied to your boss, telling him you had a migraine, skipping out of work for the rest of the day? Did you do the *right* thing Sunday when you told me to keep going when we drove by that accident? And did you do the *right* thing when you married Bill for his money, never stopping to consider what my feelings might be?"

"Anyone interested in dessert today?" asked the waitress, appearing out of nowhere.

"No thanks," snapped Mrs. Perkins, starting to feel a tidal wave of blood flowing to her brain. Once the waitress was out of hearing distance, she barked back at her son—her self-defense mechanism fully engaged.

"How dare you make those accusations? You have no idea what kind of hell I've been forced to live through ever since your father walked out on us. I've done my best to provide a decent home for you, and this is how you repay me? Just wait till you're

266

out in the real world, Roger. You think you're so smart. Don't you dare criticize Bill. He may not be what you think a *man* should be, but he is someone I can depend on. He'll never desert me like your worthless father."

"Dad walked out on me, too, you know," interrupted Roger, unable to suppress the tears pouring down his cheeks. "Football is the only thing I've ever had to take his place, Mom. You might not approve of Coach Abraham, but he's the closest thing to a father I've ever had. And my teammates... they're like the brothers I've always wanted... needed."

Without allowing his mother a chance for rebuttal, Roger pushed himself from his chair and exited the restaurant in a flurry. Once in the parking lot, he located their car, sat down on the front bumper, and desperately tried to regain mastery over his emotions. Meanwhile his mind was bombarded by a barrage of painful images: WSLZ and WORP vans... Two practices without Pete... Shadows... Blurred thinking... Fright... Flight!

Roger's thoughts were haunted by the brokenness in Coach Abraham's voice as he spoke about responsibility and family. Then the picture of Brian Taylor's face on the news kept flashing in and out of his mind—a pained expression far different from the arrogance he had displayed on Saturday night when he had cast a cold, hateful glare towards Pete all because he had had the audacity to come to the aid of a helpless victim.

But the piercing cries of Julia—echoing back and forth from one end of his brain to the other—were pushing Roger to the brink of madness; and he could not block out the panicked expression on her face, the blood merging with tears, her eyes like flashing red lights.

Roger tried to imagine the mental state of Pete right now. What kind of torment was he going through? Abandoned by a teammate. Arrested by the police. Ostracized by the media. Suspended from the team. Barred from the game he loved. And why? Because he had the courage to help someone in need?

Roger was unable to hold back his flow of tears.

All alone in the confines of his trailer, Pete was fraught by boredom and extreme anxiety. He could do nothing but worry that his situation would only get worse. After a long hot shower following his morning workout, he wolfed down two peanut butter sandwiches, a banana, and a large glass of milk. It was almost noon, and the trailer was heating up. He opened up the windows and turned on the fan in the living room, pointing it so the air would reach him on the couch. There wasn't anything worth watching on TV at this time of the day. He had already read his UFL *Sports News* Preseason Edition from cover to cover. Sprawled out on the couch, Pete began to ponder the future.

Will my lawyer be able to get me out of this mess? Will I ever get the chance to put on a football helmet again? Is this my destiny to join my father in prison? Is there no justice in this cold, cruel world? Was it my intention to hurt Brian so badly?

Slowly, Pete drifted off into a fitful slumber. Tossing back and forth on the couch, beads of perspiration forming upon his forehead, his mind reliving the shock of being fingerprinted at the police station. His mind fast-forwarded to a courtroom. His mother whimpering as the judge pronounced a verdict of "Guilty". Escorted out of the courtroom by two policemen, he tried in vain to look back towards his mother one last time. But he was helpless; hands secured behind him in handcuffs, fully-adorned in the compulsory, bright-orange, state-ordained uniform. His mom was alone. No coaches. No teammates. No friends.

"I'm sorry, Mom. I'm sorry," he yelled back to her, his head straining back for one last glimpse before the policemen muscled him through the exit.

A sudden bang on the screen door startled Pete from his sleep. He looked at the time on his watch.

2:30

He had been out for almost two hours. His hair was soaked with sweat; the temperature in the trailer felt like at least 90 degrees. What he would do for Mike's swimming pool right now.

He lifted himself up from the couch and walked toward the front door. It must have been the newspaper hitting the door that awakened him.

Here goes nothing.

Pete opened the door and looked down on his front step. The Juddville Gazette was laying front side up. He snatched up the paper and quickly stepped back inside where he could read in private. A 4" by 6" photo of Brian Taylor was staring him in the face. Above the picture, Tuesday's headline:

Player 'assaults' boyfriend of Coach's daughter

Brian Taylor, 21, of 148 N. Washington, was assaulted at 10:00 p.m., Saturday night at Lakeside Park. The alleged assailant's name is being withheld because he is 17 years old; he has been identified, however, as a member of the Juddville football team.

His name may be released to the press following the arraignment. The assailant may be tried as an adult due to the severity of the victim's injuries. Taylor suffered a concussion and fractured jaw.

In an ironic twist to the story, Taylor was also the 'boyfriend' of the daughter of Juddville's head football coach, Keith Abraham. According to Maggie Webster, mother of Brian Taylor, Brian had been dating Julia Abraham approximately a month. Both Coach Abraham and his daughter were unavailable for comment.

The unnamed football player has been placed under indefinite suspension until the outcome of his arraignment. Dr. Paul Jones, Superintendent of Juddville Schools, commented on the school's involvement, "Once all the facts are in, we will take additional disciplinary action. This type of violence will not be tolerated by any of our athletes or students."

Pete was about to snap. His situation was growing steadily worse, and it seemed that there was nothing he could do about it. He was completely powerless. All alone in the trailer, his mind began to accept the worst possible scenarios: jail sentence or possibly detention center; football career finished; reputation in ruins.

His blood began to boil. He was getting sick of sitting alone doing nothing. In effect, hadn't his sentence already begun? Sure, his lawyer promised to do everything possible to get the charges dismissed. At the moment, it seemed like an uphill battle with all the media attention Brian Taylor was receiving. It was just a matter of time now, and Pete's name would be spread through the entire community as the unnamed football player. Was it his destiny? Maybe it was time to just give in and embrace his natural calling.

Suddenly, he heard a rap on the screen door. With great apprehension, Pete walked slowly into the living room and peered through the dusty glass window. It was David Riley, holding a large paper bag under his right arm.

"Hey Pete," a slight nervousness in his voice.

"Come on in," said Pete, holding the door open for his teammate, ushering him into his living room.

Taking a seat on the couch, David noticed the front page of the Juddville Gazette on the couch next to him.

"How's it going, man?"

"Oh, I don't know. I feel like I'm on death row. Things are spinning out of control so fast. I'm scared to take my next breath. All I want to do is play football. I just wish…"

Silence.

David lifted up the newspaper. "I can't believe this trash. Guess the paper must be pretty desperate for a story right now. Brian Taylor, a victim? Give me a break. Three years ago when we were freshmen, he and two of his thugs threw me into a trash bin. I had a bump on my head the size of a golf ball. And the smell…"

"You know, David, I just wish I could rewind the tape and go back and replay the whole evening. How many guys on the team know what really happened?"

"Well, most of us remember Brian Taylor, and we figured he got was coming to him. No one's quite sure how it all got started, but we believe in you, Pete. In fact, I brought you something from the team."

David handed the brown paper bag to Pete who immediately reached in and pulled out a football.

Pete carefully examined the ball. In bold black marker just below the threads was written, "We miss you." The rest of the ball was smothered with signatures and corresponding jersey numbers of his teammates. Lifting the ball up to his nose, he inhaled the sweet aroma of genuine leather. A minute tear formed in the corner of his eye, and was quickly pushed away.

Crying out in anguish, "David, you can't possible imagine how much I want to be out there practicing with you guys. It's like someone cut out a big chunk of my heart. Sometimes I think if I fall asleep, when I wake up, this nightmare will somehow all be over."

"Pete, I don't know if this will make you feel better or not, but a lot of us are praying really hard for you right now."

The room became uncomfortably silent as Pete's eyes were fixed upon the floor. Finally, he lifted his head and looked David straight in the eye.

"You know, David, I'm not very religious, but right now I'll take all the help I can get."

David patted his teammate's bulky shoulder as he rose to his feet. "Hang in there, bud. We're all behind you. I've got to get going now, but if I don't see you at practice tomorrow, I'll stop by again… if it's alright."

"Sure, David. Sometimes I feel like I am about to go crazy, sitting here all by myself. And there is one more thing you can do for me: Tell the team 'Thanks'. I really appreciate the ball."

Chapter Twenty-six

Coach Abraham stared through his windshield at the barren football field. At 2:00 in the afternoon, the field was unoccupied—most of his players would be hanging out at the beach or hiding indoors somewhere from the relentless August heat. Keith was emotionally and physically wiped out. For nearly an hour, he had given the same response to just about every question fired at him:

"Can you describe the nature of your daughter's relationship with Brian Taylor?"

No comment.

"Did you ever kick Brian Taylor off your football team?"

No comment.

"What is your feeling about your daughter's relationship with Brian Taylor?"

No comment.

"Do you think jealousy could have been the motive for the assault against Brian Taylor?"

No comment.

"Does your daughter have a substance abuse problem?"

No comment.

"Will your daughter still be attending Tyler Bible College this fall?"

No comment.

And then the clincher:

"Was this assault the result of some kind of love triangle?"

"Damn you, you good-for-nothing media slime." The words were out of his mouth before he could reel them back in. Nevertheless, without offering an apology or even a feeble explanation, Coach Abraham stormed out of the meeting room, slamming the door in fury.

Out in the parking lot, he found his Honda Civic, and opened the door, hoping that the confines of his car might offer him momentary solitude as he slouched back in the seat as far back as possible, and waited... waited for the reporters to leave... waited to see if the superintendent of Juddville Public Schools might have the

271

decency to come out to offer a bare minimum amount of conciliatory support... and waited to see if he stayed in his car long enough, he might just wake up from this hellish nightmare.

When the reporters shuffled out of the meeting room fifteen minutes later, Keith looked away, praying that the back of his head would not be filmed for tonight's evening news. Once the vans had pulled out of the parking lot, he took a deep breath, and started up his car to leave.

Just as he was about to back out of his parking spot, the superintendent walked out, holding up his hand, signaling for him to stop. Keith rolled down the window.

"Got a minute, Keith?"

"Sure, I was just on my way home."

"Keith, I know you are going through a lot right now, and this must really be tough at home, with your daughter involved and all. You've put in a lot of years for this community; and we're all truly indebted to you. But right now I think the best thing for you to do is to take some time off. I think you need to be with your family right now. Take a long-deserved break from football until things settle down... until this legal affair gets resolved. I know you must be feeling..."

Keith wasted no more time before interrupting his superintendent's latest public relations speech, "No, Paul. I don't think you have a clue what I am feeling. Unlike you, I have more to be concerned with about here than just career and reputation. Obviously, you don't care about the student athlete who is being wrongfully charged for assault because he had the nerve to protect my daughter from the unwanted sexual advances of one of the most pathetic, depraved graduates of Juddville. Did you even bother to pull out the file on Brian Taylor? Of course not. Why don't you do a little homework before your next speech in front of the camera eye? As for my family, I'll be the one to make that decision. You have no idea what it's like to see your daughter's heart broken, and then to see her name dragged through the mud because her good-for-nothing boyfriend finally got what was coming to him. Meanwhile, the only person who acted with any degree of honor is being hung out to dry—without any due process—and is consequently, being denied the opportunity to live out his dream, to play the sport he has spent the last 10 months earnestly preparing for... and why? Because a handful of egotistical, glory-seeking adults are posturing for time in the spotlight to advance their pathetically-meaningless political aspirations.

272

"What ever happened to innocent until proven guilty, Paul? When I saw those two vans parked alongside our practice field, I was appalled that they would show no sensitivity to the rest of the kids on the team. I was hopeful, however, when I saw you. I figured you would do the right thing and send them on their way until a more appropriate time. After all, Dr. Jones has always been a trustworthy supporter of the Juddville Football Program. Last year when we were advancing through the playoffs on the way to a state championship, Dr. Jones was always quick to respond to any of our needs whether it was money for a Greyhound bus or money for a team meal on one of the many road trips. So it was truly a deserved privilege granted to Dr. Jones—and his grandson—to be included in the team photo down on the field as we hoisted the state championship trophy above our heads. Foolishly—I guess—I believed that our loyal superintendent would take care of things until we could at least have the opportunity to finish practice. After all, Dr. Jones is in the business of education; he would certainly realize how unfair it would be to disrupt the entire team's practice over a civil dispute that happened off school property at an event that was not in any way sanctioned by the school. What a shock when I discovered that my superintendent setup this informal press conference! Furthermore, it was his idea to schedule the meeting before practice was finished to allow the media to take film of the team and the coaches while they were busily preparing for their first competition. And do you want to know the worst part, Paul? You never bothered to mention any of it to me beforehand. Not even a "heads up" phone call, so I could at least know it was coming. No, Dr. Jones, you haven't a clue what I'm feeling. And now what am I to believe? Am I on trial, too?"

"Keith, don't you think you're overreacting a bit? I guess it's understandable under the circumstances; which is all the more reason why I think you should take a temporary leave of absence."

"Say what? You've got to be kidding me. Have you talked to the board about this yet?"

"Yes, of course, I have contacted Board President—Valerie Snow—and she assured me that the board only wants what is best for you and your family right now. I will set up a meeting with Coach Allen later this afternoon to inform him of our decision."

"Just like that... I have no say in the matter. I've served this town for 25 years and now..."

"It's only temporary, Keith. It's the right thing to do."

"The right thing? What do you know about right, Paul? Let me tell you something, Dr. Jones. When this whole fiasco is done

273

and over, and the truth gets heard, I think you'd better be prepared to make some sincere apologies. And you better hope that none of us are in the mood for a lawsuit of our own."

"Is that a threat, Keith?"

"No," looking squarely into Dr. Jones's eye, "that's a guarantee."

Keith rolled his window back up and shifted into reverse. As he backed up, he purposefully avoided further eye contact with his boss, and drove slowly across the parking lot to the entrance of Raymond Sanders Stadium. He stepped out of his car and walked out onto the game field. He kept walking in the direction of the home sidelines, and then sat down on the bench.

So this is what it feels like to be "benched".

For the first time in his twenty-five years of coaching, he had a sense of what life would be like without football. It would be absolutely impossible to compute the number of minutes he had devoted to the Juddville Football Program. Perhaps, it had all been in vain. Perhaps, he had given too much of his life away to the game of football. Perhaps, it was time for a change.

Jim's not going to take this very well. I'm sure this isn't the way he ever intended to get his first head coaching opportunity. He's certainly qualified, but he's loyal to a fault. He'll quit before he lets the school get away with this. But what about the players? They didn't deserve any of this. It's hard enough having to deal with all the pressure of following in the footsteps of last year's team. It would be devastating for them to lose their team captain and their entire coaching staff. No, I'll have to think of some way to convince Jim to finish out the season. There are 28 kids depending on it.

Unwilling to share the latest turn of events with Carol and Julia, Coach Abraham decided to return to his car and go for a ride. He drove aimlessly through town in search of a place to hide, a place free from the media, free from unrealistic parents, free from unpredictable players, free from the guilt he felt in the pit of his stomach every time he looked at his daughter.

He refused to pray. He refused to curse. The lining in his stomach felt like it was thinning by the minute. He reached into his pocket and removed two antacids, plopping them in his mouth, unable to chew and digest them fast enough. When he considered his behavior at the "press conference" he became nauseous. People would be quick to condemn. His reputation and honor were irreparably damaged.

Damn you, you good-for-nothing media slime.

What had come over him? He passed Ernie's Pub on the corner of Hayes and Fifth Street; secretly wishing he was a drinking man. Surely, he could at least find some refuge on a bar stool. Maybe he should call Pastor Jenkins. How could he face him, though, after cursing the media, shaming not only himself, but also his family and football team?

Coach Abraham, the worst of hypocrites. Gone is all the respect of every young man who has ever played for me. For the last 25 years, I've begun the season telling my players my priorities: God, first; family, second; and football and teaching, third.

Julia... Julia... I am so sorry. I failed you... You're right. I treated you like you were second string... You tried to get my attention. But I was too wrapped up in my coaching career to notice.

Keith pulled into Lakeside Park. The stage where an unfavorable fate had played itself out less than 72 hours ago. The parking lot was nearly full, but there was one vacant spot next to a navy blue minivan. He eased into the parking spot, leaving the engine running as he pondered his next move. All of a sudden he became paranoid that someone might see him parked so near to the scene of the crime, possibly arousing further suspicion. Now his mind was playing tricks on him. Sleep was a long lost friend.

As he relaxed in his air-conditioned car, from out of nowhere, the owner of the blue minivan appeared in his rearview mirror. A young father—probably in his late 20s—was dragging two beach chairs and a basket of beach toys. The mother trailed behind carrying an infant under her right arm, a diaper bag swinging back and forth from her left arm, while a pre-school aged girl and boy— all covered in sand—were trailing about 10 yards behind.

"Can we stop for ice cream, Daddy?" begged the little girl.

"No, Molly. I told you a hundred times. I've got tons of work to do at home. We stayed for an hour longer than I planned."

At this point, Keith wanted to pass on some friendly advice, but when he looked at his own image in the rearview mirror, he was painfully reminded of what little authority he had for sharing advice on fathering. Hoping to find solitude at the park, Keith realized that there were far too many people out enjoying one of the last Tuesdays of summer, so he shifted into reverse as he gave thought to his next destination.

As he pulled out of Lakeside Park, his desire to escape from his troubles intensified.

There's got to be somewhere I can go where I can be left alone... somewhere where I won't be bothered... somewhere where I can blow off some steam.

That's it! What I really need is some heavy-duty exercise.

Keith looked down and examined his attire. He was wearing a Juddville football tee-shirt and a loose fitting pair of grey coaching shorts. His coaching shoes were a bit cumbersome for distance running, but he could certainly get by wearing them at the gym. It had been a couple of years since he let his membership expire, but he could always get a day pass. Naturally, there was always the chance he might bump into a few familiar faces, but most of the lifters followed a code of silence until your workout was completely finished.

The thought of calling Carol entered his mind, but he could not imagine finding the composure to try to explain all that had happened at the "press conference", nor did he feel at all capable of discussing his pending leave of absence. He also accepted the fact that he was acting irresponsible by not contacting Coach Allen, but at the moment, he was fed up with the pressures of acting responsible. He had his own problems right now, and if he didn't do something about them soon, who knew what he might be capable of doing next? And the best way for him to reduce stress had always been to push his body to the limits by banging around a few barbells for an hour or so.

The comforts of home had never felt so good. As soon as the babysitter had left, Jim grabbed the Juddville Gazette and a cold Budweiser, opting to sit on his favorite chair on the deck where he could keep an eye on the kids playing on the jungle gym. He set the paper on his lap and tried to free his mind from football so he could concentrate enough to read or at least skim through the headlines.

Not even in his wildest imagination, could Coach Allen ever have envisioned a worse practice scenario than the one he just endured. Making matters worse, in less than 48 hours, the Juddville Jaguars were scheduled to scrimmage three very respectable football teams at Raymond Sanders Field, and unless some miraculous transformation occurred during the next two practices, the home team was surely to get their lunch handed to them.

There were way too many unanswered questions about the team right now. First and foremost, was the mental and emotional status of their fearless, normally rock-steady leader, Coach Abraham. Jim had no clue as to what had happened out on the practice field today. He had never seen his friend so rattled before;

Keith had started crumbling into pieces right in the presence of the team. The timing couldn't have been worse, right when they were about to break into their desperately-needed defensive session. When Jim tried to bail him out by abruptly shifting plans and going to offense, he couldn't help but notice the look of bewilderment and fear in the players' eyes.

Obviously, Keith had a lot on his platter right now.

Wow, there he was: Brian Taylor, his picture right smack on the front page of the newspaper. Right underneath the bold print headlines:

Player 'assaults' boyfriend of Coach's daughter

As Jim read deeper into the story, he was completely bewildered how the Gazette could so grossly distort the truth about Brian. By the time he had finished reading the article, he literally wanted to puke. Never in his life had he read anything so far-fetched.

It was not so difficult for Jim to imagine the scene: beach mostly deserted, majority of partygoers having scurried to their cars to begin their precarious voyage home, dark shadows covering the sand. No one to witness the act to which Brian so mistakenly felt entitled. No one to hear Julia's cry. Along comes some football jock unable to mind his own business. A battle ensues. Julia is momentarily off the hook. Brian underestimates the strength of his adversary and is too foolish to know when to wave the white flag.

Yet for some sickly-twisted reason, the Juddville Gazette has turned the plot inside out. The villain is transposed into a victim... the protagonist into a fiend.

Was there nothing that could be done for Pete? Due to the lack of evidence, couldn't the Gazette editor somehow retract the story? Didn't it basically come down to Brian's story versus Pete's? Just because Brian's face looks like raw hamburger, does this automatically presume innocence? How about a little background check on the "victim"? Was there anyone who might still come forward to defend Pete's honor before it was too late?

Nevertheless, the lone bright spot of this entire unfortunate situation was the team's reaction. Pete's absence had miraculously drawn the team closer together, prompting several unforeseen players to assume leadership responsibilities. However, exhibiting unlimited amounts of enthusiasm and hustle wasn't the same as executing a trap block with enough force to propel a defensive lineman onto his fanny—as only Pete could do.

Football? Why do I keep thinking about football at a time like this when my friend is in such dire straits? I should be with him right now. Cheering him up. Telling him things are going to be alright. How can I criticize Keith for losing focus during practice? He shouldn't have been out there in the first place. How would I react if Katie's name was dragged into the front pages news? And the one person who was truly there for Julia was now being depicted as a criminal?

What was the media trying to accomplish anyway? It seemed like the Gazette was trying to put Juddville Football on trial. Why drag Keith's name into the mud? And kudos to our spineless superintendent, Dr. Jones. Way to offer up support to your 25 years of service educator and coach, not to mention your 17 year old, "innocent until proven guilty" student athlete.

Pete must be terrified. The police are even considering trying him as an adult—meaning jail time, not to mention termination of his football dreams. This is ridiculous. Someone's got to do something. God, how can you let this happen? Pete is so young. He's a good kid. Help him out of this mess. Please?

The sound of the phone ringing pulled Jim out of his reverie. He opened the slider and grabbed the phone by the second ring. His heart began to accelerate as he feared what news awaited him this time. Assuming that the caller was Keith, Jim held his breath, hoping that by some miracle, the right words might come to him, words that somehow might offer him hope.

The voice on the other end of the phone, however, was the last voice he would have ever expected to hear.

Cindy O'Connor was struggling to keep it all together. Her mind was in mayhem. Her efforts to stay strong and optimistic were as futile as trying to fly a kite on a windless day. The disappointment and hopelessness mounting upon her son's face were breaking down the very last of her emotional defenses.

She couldn't think about groceries or meal planning, so she picked up some KFC. Normally, Pete would devour half a bucket of extra-crispy chicken in no time at all. Instead, he just nibbled on a drumstick, trying to express his gratitude for her thoughtfulness.

Normally at this point in the meal, Pete and his mom would be talking about Juddville football or some other topic revolving around sports. But at the moment, football was taboo. Furthermore, the mere mention of the Juddville Gazette or WSLZ was completely out of bounds. As a result, there was very little left to talk about.

"Honey, I hate to leave you all alone tonight, but I really have to go into work. I've got to earn enough money to keep us alive. It's killing me to see you being cheated like this. You don't know how badly I wish that there was something I could do to get us out of this mess. I'm sorry for the life I've given you. You deserve so much better."

"Stop it, Mom. This isn't your fault. You didn't have anything to do with it. I'll be okay. Stop worrying about me. We'll survive. What's the worst that could happen? The lawyer said at worst, probation. If I can't play football this season..."

Pete wanted to complete his sentence, but he felt a flood of tears on the horizon, so he choked them back down, and left his statement unfinished. Instead, he stared hopelessly at the mostly ignored bucket of chicken before him.

The flick of his mom's lighter broke the silence. She leaned back on her chair and inhaled deeply from her faithful friend. The ash tray on the table was overflowing with cigarette butts and dark grey ashes. Usually, Pete would have read her the riot act for displaying such a complete disregard for her health, but he felt responsible this time. He substituted anger for guilt as a result.

Slamming his fist on the table, knocking the ash tray a couple inches into the air, "It's just not fair, Mom. Doesn't anyone care about the truth? He was going to rape her!"

Cindy stared into her son's eyes. She believed him wholeheartedly; Pete had always been honest with her. Whenever Pete had done wrong—whether at home or at school—he had always owned up to the offense and accepted his punishment like a man. He never fidgeted, never tried to shift the blame. No, that just wasn't his nature.

Like most boys growing up, he had been in a few scraps—mostly back in middle school just after his father had been incarcerated. Once, back in the eighth grade, Pete had befriended a boy who had a stuttering problem. A trio of bullies would pick on him every day at lunch. They would purposefully sit at the same table as the helpless boy, and they would heap on the verbal abuse, ruthlessly mocking his impediment.

Once Pete got wind of what was going on, he warned the three bullies to cease and desist. When his warnings were ignored, Pete brought a quick end to their harassment with the use of his fists. One left jab to the nose of the most obnoxious bully, followed with a body shot to the ribs, caused the other two perpetrators to quickly scatter from the scene, hiding out in the bathroom until the conflict in the cafeteria had cleared out. What was most amazing was that there wasn't a single student or lunch lady who turned Pete's name into the office. The principal would never have even known about the fight had Pete not immediately turned himself in minutes later.

After hearing Pete's confession, Mr. Haynes was tempted to do nothing about it, but he opted to give Pete a reduced suspension of one day at home instead of the standard three day pass.

In the ninth grade, Pete told a belligerent noisemaker in his English class to shut his mouth so Mrs. Penne could teach. When the punk tried to jump him from behind in the hallway, Pete ducked, and his adversary went flying over him, smacking his head into the lockers. Then he pulled himself up off the floor and approached Pete wildly, swinging his arms like windmills.

Pete covered up initially. After blocking several weak shots to the head, he grabbed his attacker with both hands and drove him forcefully into the nearest locker. The eyes of his foe changed from boldness to fear. Pete pulled him towards him and then slammed him one more time into the locker for good measure. Then he released his grip and turned to go to his next class. The hall monitor, however, had other plans for Pete, escorting him directly to the principal's office.

After Pete told his story, he was about to receive a one day suspension. Mr. Haynes had picked up the phone and was about to make the call to Mrs. O'Connor when Pete's English teacher, Mrs. Penne, stepped into the principal's office. After hearing her story, Mr. Haynes reduced Pete's suspension to a lunch detention.

If Mrs. O'Connor's boy had one flaw, it was his inability to turn a deaf ear to the cries of the helpless—regardless of the personal consequences he might have to suffer.

Cindy grabbed hold of her boy's right hand tightly. Taking a deep breath, she spoke intently, infusing every available ounce of feeling into each word. "No matter what happens, Pete, I will always be at your side. I know you're telling the truth; sooner or later, everyone else will know, too. You've had to grow up way too fast. God knows I wish you could have had a dad these last few years… I've tried my best to make up for his absence."

Surrendering to another round of tears, she sobbed, "The world can be pretty unfair and downright cruel. What I want you to hear, right now, Pete, is that you have been such a help to me. You have given me the will to continue… to keep going… when there didn't seem to be any reason to keep living. I've always been amazed by your courage, by your stubborn determination. Most boys that have to grow up without a dad fall into drugs or a life of crime, and inevitably end up in prison. They grow resentful of their mothers and despise every person in authority. But you have always shown me respect. I don't think I could have handled the rejection of another O'Connor male. I don't give a rip what the paper and the TV are saying right now. They couldn't be more dead wrong. This much I know is true. I couldn't ever be more proud of you than I am right now. I may have lost your father to prison, but I refuse to lose you. You are innocent, Pete. If our lawyer can't convince the authorities of this, we'll find a new one and keep fighting."

Cindy rose from her chair, walked around the table, and hugged Pete with all her might. After a minute had elapsed, Pete let go of her and said, "Mom, you better get going or you're going to be late for work. Don't worry about me. I'll be okay, I promise."

Reluctantly, his mother kissed him gently on the forehead and said, "Always the responsible one, aren't you? Hopefully, I won't have to work overtime. Try to get some sleep, honey."

"I will, Mom. See you in the morning."

After his mother left, Pete put the leftover chicken in a Tupperware container and placed it on the bottom shelf of the refrigerator. There was enough left over chicken for another meal or a pretty hefty midnight snack.

Pete knew better than to turn on the television. The 5 o'clock news would be coming on soon, and he decided he couldn't stomach anymore "Sympathy for Brian Taylor" broadcasts.

Instead, he put on a baseball cap and sunglasses and went for a walk. Hopefully, he wouldn't be recognized. For some reason, he felt like he would suffocate if he didn't get out of this place. As he stepped out onto the porch, he remembered his confrontation earlier with Josh and Adam.

I can't hide away in this trailer, forever. If they want a piece of me, here I am.

Pete felt goosebumps up and down his arms as he imagined landing an uppercut under the chin of that slime ball Josh Evans.

After securing the door and double-checking that it was locked, Pete descended the steps and began his walk. By the time he had reached the end of his street, a Fed Ex truck had pulled up to the O'Connor trailer. Pete was too far away to notice a package being left on his porch. A package addressed to Pete O'Connor.

Chapter Twenty-seven

Kate Perkins sat in shock as she tried to comprehend the gravity of her son's predicament. Roger had just completed his voluntary interview with Officer Kane. She had never pictured herself sitting in the Juddville Police Station. A migraine threatened to split her head in two. How ironic that earlier today she had fabricated a migraine as an excuse to leave work early to have lunch with her son.

Now her mouth literally hung wide open as she listened to Roger explain his version of the altercation between Brian Taylor and the unnamed Juddville football player. She had remained quiet throughout the entire interview until Officer Kane had the audacity to ask her son if he had any ulterior motive for coming forward with his story now.

"I certainly hope you're not suggesting that someone put him up to this. Are you, Officer?" interrupted Kate Perkins, never missing an opportunity to go to bat for her son. It was only a few hours ago when she had literally pulled every trick from her purse to try to dissuade Roger from going to the police. But now her perspective had shifted 180 degrees.

"I would like to remind you that it took a lot of guts for Roger to come in today to help your department get your facts straight. You do realize—don't you—that he will face a suspension for admitting he had been drinking alcohol? I'm sure most boys his age would never even think about coming forward like this, so don't you even insinuate that Roger might be doing this for his football team."

"Mrs. Perkins, I'm not trying to insinuate…"

"Furthermore, Officer," cutting her way back in, "I am particularly troubled by the fact that neither you nor the press have made any mention of any investigation into who might have furnished alcohol to the dozens of teenagers at that party, including one whom happened to be my son. Certainly, you must be aware that this 'Brian Taylor' was the one who purchased the keg, aren't you?"

Officer Kane's face turned a bright shade of crimson as he attempted to respond to Mrs. Perkins's criticism. "I'm sorry, M'am, but that is a completely different case, one which I am not at liberty to discuss with you—or anyone else in the public sector—until all the facts are in."

"Excuse me," the volume of Kate's voice immediately rising to a monumental level, "but you obviously didn't wait until all the facts were in before you started leaking information out to the media on *this* case."

Standing up from her chair, fully aware that she had Officer Kane on his heels, Mrs. Perkins wagged her finger at him, "And what I find most troubling—as a woman—is that this so-called victim, Brian Taylor, was in the act of raping the Abraham girl. How screwed up can you be to make him out to be the victim? Have you ever been raped, Officer Kane?"

Officer Kane's eyes glanced over to the door, relieved that he had had the good sense to remember to close it before the interview.

Mrs. Perkins was still screaming, "It seems you're putting the wrong person on trial. Wait until the rest of this town gets word of this. You've got a lot of explaining to do. In fact, if I were you, I'd start putting together my resume."

Grabbing a hold of Roger's hand, she stood up to leave. Her son was in complete shock. He had never seen an adult get dissected so thoroughly by the sharp tongue of his mother.

She really should have been a lawyer, Roger thought to himself.

Once Mrs. Perkins and Roger had exited the office, Officer Kane closed the door and spent the next 15 minutes in solitude, contemplating what could be done to spare himself from further embarrassment and humiliation. When he finally emerged from his office, he went straight to the men's room where he splashed cool water on his face to help him get his bearings. Then he began the process of surreptitiously making phone calls to several people of significance in the Juddville Community.

On the drive home, Mrs. Perkins reviewed in her mind the unbelievable events of this day. What started out as a lunch date with her son had led to a most combative confrontation with the Juddville Police Department. At first she had chastised Roger for his foolish decision to come forward with information that would bring trouble upon himself. But Roger wouldn't listen to her selfish reasoning. When he said it was his duty to tell the truth, she had been shamefully silenced. Having no alternative, she agreed to accompany him to the police station. As a parent and as an adult who professed to be a responsible citizen, how could she possibly object to his resolve to tell the truth? Reluctantly, she stood by his side, cursing him in silence at first. Her silence did not last very long as she observed the incompetent handling of this case by Officer Kane. And as a self-proclaimed feminist, she had no choice but to become incensed at the police department's failure to take seriously the charge of rape.

283

Roger felt remarkably at peace with himself, and for once, he was actually proud of the actions of his mother. It's not every day that you have a front row ticket to view your mom thoroughly dismantle an officer of the law. Naturally, he felt nervous about the consequences awaiting him. Nevertheless, he felt about twenty pounds lighter having rid himself of the burdensome guilt he had been carrying around for the last 72 hours.

Coach Allen attempted a third time to dial Keith's number. Still no answer. Six o'clock and no one home? Given the circumstances, he couldn't blame him for not answering the phone. Regardless, it was urgent that Jim reach him. For the first time in what seemed like an eternity, there was cause for optimism. What was so ironic was that the most recent news had come to him from an unlikely source: Mrs. Kate Perkins. Jim just had to reach him.

As Keith finished his last set of abdominal crunches, he lifted his haggard body from the floor and staggered over to the drinking fountain for one last drink. It had been too long since he had enjoyed a workout like that, and for the first time in the last three days, he felt somewhat at ease. Though his situation had not altered one bit, he felt more at peace with himself and with God. He had done a lot of soul searching during his workout, and he had miraculously felt an undeniable assurance that God was still in control.

It wasn't until his last set of incline dumbbell presses that he came to realize a painful truth: it wasn't Julia's well-being that had been worrying him the most; no, it was the damage to his stellar reputation as the one and only Coach Abraham, proud pillar of the Juddville Community. The truth was that it had been his ego and selfish pride weighing so heavily upon him all this time. What troubled him the most was that the public was now in on his little charade: Coach Abraham was just an ordinary human being whose family had struggles just like everyone else.

When he returned the 45 pound dumbbells to the rack, the face staring back at him in the mirror wasn't the one he usually observed. No, this was a face of brokenness… of humility. And that was okay. There was a certain amount of relief in coming to grips with the fact that he was indeed human… that he was without a doubt imperfect… and that he would always be in need of God's grace and mercy.

Furthermore, Keith felt confident now of his next course of action. The move was bold. The move was radical. It was actually quite frightening just to think about, yet he knew it was the right path. Keith was quite sure that the move would cause quite a stir in the town of Juddville, but as a wise man once said, "This too shall pass."

Wiping off the sweat from his brow with a dry portion of his tee-shirt, Keith was ready to return to the home front and face whatever challenges awaited him. As he entered his car and began to pull out of the Body Shoppe parking lot, he noticed that it was already six o'clock.

Did I really work out a full hour and a half? Not bad for an old guy. What is Carol going to say when she finds out where I've been hiding the last couple hours?

What am I going to tell her? Should I tell her about how I blew up in front of the media? I am so embarrassed. How am I going to possibly break the news to her about my forced leave of absence? What will she think of me now?

Here I go again: Me... Me... Me...

Chapter Twenty-eight

Adam Foster gathered up his empty, grease-spotted French fries container, smushed his Big Mac wrapper into a wad, and grabbed his empty Coke cup, carrying them over to the garbage basket under the sink; then he walked inconspicuously into the living room where his mother was sitting on the couch, devouring her McDonald's supper while watching the six o'clock local news on TV. As usual, she made no notice of Adam's entry into the room.

Adam sat down on the reclining chair to the right of his mother on the couch. He lifted his left shoulder up as high as possible in an attempt to block from his view the distasteful sight of his mother ravenously chewing up her second Quarter Pounder with Cheese before moving on to her Biggie-sized fries. Adam aimed his focus instead on the WSLZ news. More wildfires in California. President Cooper hits the campaign trail promising to lower taxes. A car accident kills a young mother and two year old girl; the father is angered by the slow response of the medical response team. Coming up next, the feature story.

Anchorman Alan Pickens introduced the story from the WSLZ studio. "Gloria Jackson is out in Juddville with the most recent development in the Brian Taylor story. Gloria, can you fill us in with the latest development?"

"Sure, Alan. Today, in a press conference, Coach Abraham disclosed information revealing that he is even more closely involved in the story than previously believed. Not only was the alleged attacker of Brian Taylor a Juddville football player, but now it seems that Taylor also has a connection to the coach. Here is some exclusive footage from today's press conference":

"Coach Abraham, is it true that your daughter Julia is the girlfriend of Brian Taylor?"

A look of apprehension and regret, Keith responded, "I will answer your question with a 'Yes'. But I will have no further comment relating to my daughter's involvement in this case."

Gloria Jackson, with a follow up question, "Coach, can you tell us how long she has been dating Brian Taylor?"

"Again, I will not answer any more questions involving my daughter."

Undeterred, and seeming to enjoy the expression of exasperation on Coach Abraham's face, "Can you describe the current status of their relationship?"

The next video footage was of the back of Coach Abraham as he stormed out of the interview. The camera faded, and the broadcast returned back to the studio with Alan Pickens.

"Thank you, Gloria, for this exclusive from Juddville."

Next, a close up image of Brian Taylor's battered face.

"Police authorities reported earlier today that the alleged assailant of Brian Taylor—whose name at this point has not been released because he is 17 years old and considered a minor—is a senior captain of this year's Juddville Football Team.

"It is no surprise that the story has shaken the town of Juddville, especially since it comes out so close to the eve of the team's defense of their first state championship. Now, let's go back to Gloria Jackson who is with Dr. Paul Jones, superintendent of Juddville Public Schools. Gloria..."

"Thank you, Alan. Dr. Jones, can you tell us what course of action the school is planning to take in regards to the alleged assault by one of your school's football players?"

"Yes, I'd be happy to, Gloria. As you know, the student athlete is currently being held under indefinite suspension until his pretrial on Monday. The player's actions were unjustifiable, and the school will be waiting for the results of the legal proceedings before administering any further disciplinary measures. Also, because of Coach Abraham's relationship to both the victim and the accused, Coach Abraham has been placed on a temporary leave of absence until the outcome of this case has been decided."

"Was this Coach Abraham's idea or the Juddville Board of Education's?"

"Actually, it was my idea, but I have complete board-approval. I just want to add that Coach Abraham—being the dedicated coach that he is—was reluctant to take a leave at this critical juncture in the season. But I'm sure that under these unfortunate circumstances, the team and the community will realize that this decision is right for both his family and for the team."

"It looks like the Juddville Jaguars will have an even tougher challenge defending their state championship. This is Gloria Jackson, reporting to you from Juddville."

"Yee haw!" shouted Angel Foster in between bites of her second Quarter Pounder with Cheese. "I can't believe it. I'm sorry, honey, that this is happening to your new team, but my blood is still Billington Bulldog Red, and this is the best news I've heard out of Juddville since we upset them on their homecoming five years ago."

"I bet they're all whooping it up back home right now, aren't they, Momma?"

"No doubt about it, Adam. I'll have to give your Uncle Rich a call, just in case he hasn't heard the news yet. Do you know who the player was who gave that boy a licking?"

"Sure do, Momma. Last name's O'Connor. I can't remember his first name, though."

"Did you say O'Connor, boy?"

"Yes, M'am. And guess what. He used to live in Billington about seven years ago, too."

Angel sat pensively in her spot on the couch. She shoved her last quartet of French fries into her mouth, sipped from her extra large Coke and let out belch.

"You know who that boy's daddy is then, don't you? How come you never told me about this before, Adam? That boy's daddy run over your cousins. You mean to tell me you've been playing ball with that wino's boy all this time?"

"Momma, I've been getting some revenge. You should see what I've been doing to his locker."

"Locker? You call that revenge? I can't believe my ears, Adam. His daddy put your cousins into coffins, and you say you're getting revenge messing with his boy's locker?"

"What do you want me to do, Momma? He's built like a house. Didn't you see what he did to that Brian Taylor's face?"

"You're a coward, Adam Foster. You're Uncle Rich was exactly right about you." Angel grabbed a Kleenex from the coffee table. Beginning to cry, she said, "You know Alex and Andrew were nearly your age when they were taken from us. Do you remember when they died, Adam?"

"I remember the funeral, Momma. It's was the only time I ever saw Uncle Rich cry."

"You can't even imagine how much pain Uncle Rich and Aunt Martha went through. I'm glad this O'Connor boy is in a load of trouble, but it ain't anywhere close to the amount of trouble his daddy caused for us Fosters."

Adam was saddened by his mother's mention of his two cousins. He knew first hand how it had affected Uncle Rich. How could he forget the nightly workouts with his uncle the previous summer, and all the pressure he put on Adam during his jayvee season?

"Who's gonna be coaching the team now?"

"I imagine it'll be Coach Allen. But he's the biggest jerk I've ever played for. I'm thinking about quitting, Mom. Football just ain't the same as it is back in Billington. And I just don't think I will be able to endure the thrashing Billington's going to put on us when we play them the second game of the season."

"Don't you even think about quitting, young man. What would your Uncle Rich say if he were here right now? After all that time he put in with you last summer, how can you even think about quitting?"

"Uncle Rich ain't here, Momma, and to tell you the truth, I'm sick of football. It isn't fun no more."

Angel Foster reached down and picked up the remote from where it was wedged between her left thigh and the upholstered couch cushion. Turning off the set, she stared Adam in the eyes and said, "What are your talking about, 'sick of football'? Where are you getting these ideas from?"

"I don't need football. I want to get a job and earn enough money to buy a motorcycle."

"You most certainly will not…"

"What are you gonna do to stop me, Momma?" challenged Adam, rising to his feet.

Then for the first time in Adam's life, he turned his back on his mother, swaggered across the living room, yanked open the screen door, and stepped out of the front door of the trailer without another word.

"Get back here, Adam Foster. You hear me?"

Adam just kept walking. His back to his mother. No fear of her trying to run him down.

"Adam, where are you going?"

Without even bothering to turn around, he shouted, "To Josh's."

"Who's Josh?"

True to his word, David was standing in front of Steve Wilcox's house at exactly 6:30 p.m.

Jogging down the steps to greet him, "Hey, Dave. Anyone else coming?"

"Daniels, McDonald, and Osborn. They said they'd meet us at the clubhouse."

A look of apprehension in his eyes, "David, I don't know what I am going to say. If I start talking about football, Pete'll get all bummed out. If I say something about his altercation with Brian Taylor, he'll get even more upset."

"Don't worry about it, Steve. I'm sure he'll appreciate our just being there."

In silence, the two teammates walked down Henry Street about a half mile to the main entrance to Maple Village Trailer Park. In front of the clubhouse was a playground with a couple of swings and an old, rusty slide.

Looking down at his watch, David observed, "It's about quarter to seven. The other guys should be here any time now."

A couple of minutes later, Greg McDonald and Gary Osborn showed up. Gary had a bag of Doritos; Greg was carrying a 2 liter of Coke.

"Craig called at the last minute and said he couldn't make it. Some type of family obligation, I guess," said Gary, followed by a handful of chips stuffed into his mouth.

"Are those for Pete?" asked Steve.

"You kidding? They'll be history by the time we reach his place," vowed Gary, grabbing the Coke from Greg with his left paw and taking a big swig of pop.

"Thanks for coming with us, guys," said David. "I know Pete will appreciate this."

After storming out of his trailer, Adam was feeling pretty good about himself. He had never stood up to his mom before. He wasn't sure where this boldness had come from—perhaps, it was from his new friend Josh.

289

What he admired the most about Josh was that he did whatever he felt like and didn't give a rat's ass what other people thought about him. Sure, Josh had been in some trouble, but who hasn't? So what if he had spent a little time in prison? Right now, Adam didn't have a lot of options for friends. Furthermore, Josh had promised to help him pick out a motorcycle once he had earned enough money. Then they could go out riding together.

Adam walked one more block to Josh's trailer. Josh, as usual, was working outside on his Yamaha.

"Hey, dude. What's up?"

"Not much. Kind of bored, actually. What do you say we take another stroll by O'Connor's place? I saw Brian's face on the news again tonight. Can't let that moron get away with what he done, Adam."

Josh stopped working on his bike and stood up, a look of utmost seriousness on his face. "We got some unfinished business, Adam. If we don't hurry and settle up, he might be in jail or the juvie center before we get the chance."

His mother's condemnation still fresh in his memory, Adam nodded and added, "Count me in… I'm up for taking care of some business."

Josh hopped onto his bike and said, "Come on. What are we waiting for?" He scooted forward on the seat, making room for Adam.

As Adam made himself comfortable, the engine roared to life. He couldn't help but imagine one day soon when he'd have his very own motorcycle.

Ignoring the 10 mph speed limits posted throughout the park, Josh accelerated to 35 mph. They came to a screeching stop at the corner of Peach and Strawberry Lane. From about a block's distance, it looked like there was no one outside of Pete's trailer or any of the other nearby trailers. Some windows were open; a few voices could be heard in the vicinity—along with a few television sets—but most folks were inside taking refuge from the relentless heat.

"Let's leave the bike here and walk the rest of the way on foot," said Josh, parking his bike under a thick Maple tree.

Before setting out, Josh took a pack of Camel cigarettes out of his coat pocket, lighting one for himself and then offering one to Adam. Adam had never smoked before, but he refused to look like a wimp, so he accepted. He tried to pretend like he knew how to smoke, but after his second puff, he coughed fitfully like an old, rusted out Chevy.

They were standing about 150 feet from Pete's trailer. They stared at his place as they finished their smokes.

"Hey check it out. It looks like there's some type of package lying on his porch. Maybe it's his orange penitentiary uniform," joked Josh, all too familiar with the mandatory wardrobe of the incarcerated.

Adam broke the silence, unable to hold back his sudden brainstorm. "What do you say we go piss all over it?"

His new friend laughed hysterically at the suggestion. "That's a perfect idea. But we might want to have a look at the package first. There might be something valuable inside."

Finally, Josh gave his underling a command, "Hurry over to his porch and grab the package, Adam. We'll open it over here. If it's something worth keeping, you'll have to pee on something else."

Tossing his cigarette to the ground, Adam looked up and down Pete's street. The coast was clear. Slowly, he inched his way towards the porch. His heart was performing a heavy metal drum solo. He looked back over his shoulder to make sure that Josh hadn't split on him. He was still there, a grin of approval on his face.

The four Jaguar football players strolled down Strawberry Lane, following David's lead; no one else had ever been to Pete's trailer or the trailer park, for that matter. The park was relatively quiet. Most of its residents were either inside eating dinner or watching television. When they were about 200 feet from Pete's, David stopped dead in his tracks.

"Hold on a minute, guys. Isn't that Adam Foster up ahead?" observed David.

"Who is that older guy that he's with?" asked Greg McDonald.

"Whoever he is, he looks like trouble," responded Steve Wilcox, a sudden surge of adrenaline flowing through his veins.

It appeared that Adam had some type of package in his hand. Adam handed the package to his friend who was leaning against his motorcycle beneath a shady maple tree. The Jaguar teammates watched as he ripped open the brown package, pulling out a bright orange and royal blue New Jersey Dragon jersey. It was #54, a Keith Karchinski jersey, unmistakably intended for their teammate Pete O'Connor, without a doubt the biggest Karchinski fan in this area of the country.

"Look, they're stealing Pete's jersey," exclaimed David.

Like thoroughbreds charging out of the blocks, David and his three teammates sprinted in the direction of the two thieves.

"I want Adam Foster," declared Greg McDonald, a look of savage determination in his eyes. "I'm going to grind his nasty face into the ground."

Adam Foster had felt uneasy about stealing a package in broad daylight. His apprehension turned to trepidation when he saw four of his teammates advancing briskly upon them.

"Someone's coming, Josh," warned Adam, uncertain of how his new friend might respond.

"Aw, looks like a bunch of Juddville jugheads to the rescue. Hold this jersey a minute. I know exactly how to take care of these morons," boasted Josh, reaching into his back pocket for his switchblade.

Grabbing the jersey with both hands, Adam tried to hide it behind him, but he was too late. There was less than 10 yards distance before an inescapable mêlée would surely ensue.

The four Jaguars slowed their advance to a walk. They observed their teammate in his usual posture: eyes concealed behind greasy brown bangs, staring intently at the ground, as if waiting for something spectacular to magically burst out from the earth.

"What are you hiding behind your back, Foster?" asked Steve Wilcox.

Josh stepped forward, making sure that he would be the first one involved in any scuffle.

Waving his switchblade before him, Josh Evans asked, "Who are you, punk?" resting the blade down by his thigh, looking to his left then his right, checking to see if there were any witnesses in the area before continuing. "This ain't your neighborhood, fellas. I'll give you to the count of 10 to get out of here."

Ignoring the switchblade, David asked, "What do you think you're doing with Pete's jersey, Adam? You better hand it over right now."

"Sounds like your teammates aren't so bright, Adam. But I'm going to give them one more chance to split. One… Two…"

"Save yourself the trouble, loser. I doubt you can count to ten, anyways," taunted Steve Wilcox, who was becoming increasingly agitated. "If you don't hand over the jersey immediately, we are going to begin inflicting serious damage upon your face."

"Oooh, you think just because there's four of you and only two of us that you can threaten us. This knife will even the score, and believe me, this won't be the first time I've used it."

Adam uncharacteristically broke out of his silence, grabbing the left arm of Josh. "Let's get out of here before someone calls the cops."

He pushed Adam away. "You want to run? Go home to your mommy. I'm fighting, that's all there is to it."

"Hand over that jersey, Adam, and no one gets hurt," promised David.

Adam backed away as Josh moved forward, waving his knife in the direction of Steve.

Steve took one step forward, and proclaimed, "I'm not afraid of you, douche bag."

Slash went the knife in a 180 degree arc. Steve effortlessly sidestepped the weapon before abruptly lifting his Size 12 Reeboks into the testicles of Josh Evans.

Direct hit.

Josh bowled over in pain as Adam threw the jersey to the ground and ran off in the opposite direction.

The wounded combatant lay upon the ground, moaning like a woman in labor. Gary Osborn alertly pounced upon Josh's wrist, twisting it like a chicken bone until the knife fell loose. Greg picked it up and put it in his back pocket.

David went for the jersey.

"That's quite a foot you've got, Steve. Tomorrow, you're trying out for place kicker," joked Gary.

Just then a Juddville police car turned down Strawberry Lane; all of a sudden, its cherry red lights began flashing as it parked in front of the huddle of young men.

An officer immediately exited the squad car, followed by an unexpected occupant: Coach Abraham.

Josh Evans was still humped over gasping for breath, prompting the officer to check first on his condition before investigating the cause of his discomfort. The four teammates greeted Coach Abraham, and were feeling somewhat nervous about explaining what had happened.

"What's going on here, David?" asked Coach Abraham.

"Hold on, Coach, I think that would be my responsibility," ordered Officer Kane, who was still leaning over Josh Evans.

"I can explain everything, sir," offered David eagerly.

Officer Kane rose to his feet, and removed his notepad and pen from his pocket. "Okay, first, can I have your name?"

"Sure, my name is David Riley." Then David proceeded to recount one detail after another. As he progressed through his story, Officer Kane showed less and less concern for the physical well-being of the wounded young male. By the time David got to the end of his narrative, Josh was beginning to stir, and he looked like he was about to get up on his two feet.

"One moment, please," interrupted the officer. Then he stepped toward Josh Evans, helping him up to his feet, and then slapping a pair of handcuffs on him before escorting him to the backseat of his squad car.

When the officer returned to the group of Juddville football players, Steve Wilcox was holding out the jersey and Greg McDonald was cautiously holding out the switchblade, the latter anxious for the cop to take the weapon from his possession. Up until this point, Coach Abraham had been silent throughout the entire interview.

"Is Pete home, David?" asked Coach, taking the jersey from Officer Kane, admiring its authentic look and feel.

"We haven't had a chance to check yet, Coach. I'm assuming he's not because I think he would have discovered the package that was sitting out on his front step," responded David.

The conversation came to an awkward halt for several moments. Then Steve Wilcox, cleared his throat, and proceeded to ask the question that all four of them were anxious to have answered.

"Coach Abraham, what are you doing here, anyways?"

Officer Kane was quick to respond; "We're here to officially inform Pete that all charges against him have been dropped…"

The policeman's revelation was cut off midstream by a chorus of cheers and clapping.

After about a half minute celebration, Officer Kane interrupted, "A teammate of yours came forward with information that corroborated Pete's story. As a result, Pete has been exonerated of all charges. And Coach Abraham is here with me to tell Pete that he has been fully reinstated to the Juddville Football Team."

"Is he serious, Coach?" asked Gary.

"It's true," answered Coach Abraham, nodding his head in affirmation.

"That's the best news I've heard in a long time. I can't wait to tell Pete the news," said David Riley.

"Here he comes now, Coach," exclaimed Greg, jumping up and down with excitement. He pointed to the North to a beleaguered shape moving sluggishly in their direction down Strawberry Lane. Evidently, the presence of a police officer's car in front of his trailer had caused him to proceed at a snail's pace.

After locating the central office of JB's Tool and Die, Coach Allen parked his car in the closest available spot. He ran across the parking lot and opened the door without a single bit of apprehension. He quickly introduced himself to the shift supervisor who was sitting behind a desk, filling out paperwork. With the utmost politeness, Jim requested permission to speak with Cindy O'Connor; it was urgent.

The foreman turned on the microphone and said, "Cindy O'Connor to the central office, please."

About a minute later, Cindy appeared in the doorway, her safety goggles in her left hand, and her right hand on her hip. When she noticed Coach Allen's presence, she could not conceal her shock and worry.

"What's wrong? What's the matter? Is Pete in more trouble?" exclaimed Cindy.

She began to feel more at ease when she observed a humongous grin breaking out from Coach Allen's face.

"I was just on the phone with Coach Abraham about 15 minutes ago, and I wanted you to find out as quickly as possible. All charges against Pete have been dropped."

Cindy's hands lifted up to her face. Her knees began to bend, and her body swayed forward.

The shift foreman was clueless about what was transpiring, but he assisted Cindy over to a nearby chair, before exiting the room, offering his worker a much appreciated privacy to hear the rest of the news.

Jim sat in the vacant seat next to her.

"I don't understand," she responded, "yesterday, they were ready to lead him off to prison. Now you're telling me all charges are dropped?"

"Pete's been cleared. He can get his old life back. A teammate of his came forward and backed up his story."

Cindy leaned over and hugged Coach Allen, as a flood of tears poured out of her weary eyes. The foreman reentered the room, having no clue as to what was going on yet having the good sense to discern that his hardworking second shift employee was going to be needed elsewhere, so he gave Mrs. O'Connor some additional good news that she could have the rest of the night off if she desired.

"Well, what are we waiting for? Let's go find Pete and celebrate," suggested Jim.

On the drive over to Maple Village, Jim's mind was filled with wonder. How amazing to be a part of this moment. How inexplicable that God had chosen someone as imperfect as him to help out a family in crisis. In the past, Jim had always viewed his profession as an on-the-field occupation; he had always shunned personal involvement in the lives of his athletes, viewing it as an invasion into *his* private life, an intrusion into *his* free time. But in this case, he had been mystically called into coming along side Pete and his mother in a time of need. And he had been blessed, for he knew for a fact, that God could have used any number of persons infinitely more qualified for the job than him.

Coach Allen parked his minivan in front of the O'Connor residence; awaiting them was a sight to behold: the perfect medicine for a wounded heart. A party of mammoth proportion. The entire Juddville Jaguar team—minus one—was congregated in front of the O'Connor trailer. Pete was in the middle, receiving hugs and high fives with reckless abandon. Cindy was trying—unsuccessfully—to force her tears into submission.

Coach Abraham's car was parked right next to them, and the hood was covered with half-emptied boxes of Little Caesar's pizza. Coach Abraham and Coach Oliver were filling and refilling plastic cups with Mountain Dew and Pepsi. Pete's eyes were beaming with joy, and he looked downright *studly* in his #54 New Jersey Dragon Keith Karchinski jersey.

Coach Allen paused a moment before joining the fray.

Thank you, Jimmy Harrison, for being a man of your word. I had a feeling you'd come through. And thank you, too, Jimmy's ex-teammate, Keith Karchinski, for taking a moment out of your life in the fast lane to respond so quickly to an urgent request, a request that would bless the heart of one of your most fervent fans, one who will now surely do justice to your name and number. And God, what can I possibly say...

"Hey, Coach Allen, what are you waiting for? Get over here and have some pizza before it's all gone."

Jim cut through the mob of joyous teammates straight towards Pete. His mother—already looking ten years younger—was right by his side. Jim extended his arms wide open and gave Pete a big bear hug, lifting him right off the ground.

"Welcome back, Pete. Welcome back."

1751292

Made in the USA